CW00496338

Rabshakeh

Jill Francis Hudson

First published in 1992 by Lion Publishing, Oxford.

Reprinted 1997.

This edition published in 2014 by Glannoventa Publishing, Drigg, Cumbria.

Copyright © 1992 & 2014 Jill Francis Hudson

All rights reserved.

ISBN: 1502706202
ISBN-13: 978-1502706201

IN MEMORY OF SAUL

because there but for the grace of God go any of us.

Cover illustration: *David and Saul,* by Julius Kronberg, 1885

DAVID'S LAMENT FOR SAUL AND JONATHAN

(2 Samuel 1:19-27)

On the mountains of Israel her beauty lies vanquished,
Her mightiest warriors, once fearless, are dead.
Do not announce it in Gath or in Ashkelon,
Let not our shame be proclaimed in their streets,
Lest Philistia's daughters exult in our anguish,
Uncircumcised pagans rejoice in our pain.

May dew never fall on the hills of Gilboa,
Rainless and barren, let nothing there grow;
For the arms of the valiant are tarnished and broken -
The shield of King Saul, once anointed with oil;
His sword, ever baleful, invincible, merciless;
Jonathan's bow, which brought death to our foes.

For Saul and his son were beloved and lovely,
Together in life, now together in death;
Swifter than eagles that soar in the heavens,
Stronger than lions, proud kings on the earth.
Weep now for Saul, O you Daughters of Israel,
He clothed you in scarlet, adorned you with gold.

But the brave ones have perished, the battle is over;
Jonathan, slain on the mountains of home.
I feel my heart breaking, for you were my brother,
Your love burned so strong, that of women seemed pale.
How the mighty are fallen, the heroes defeated,
Their weapons abandoned, their beauty, no more.

ACKNOWLEDGMENTS

With special thanks to Keith (who for so many years has worked so hard and put up with so much, and whose first experience of driving abroad was through refugee camps on the West bank, looking for Gibeah), to Mandy (for tirelessly giving of her time, expertise and support), and to so many friends and family members who have encouraged and helped me along the way.

The City of David, Ziklag, Philistia.

To the reader, whether kinsman or stranger: the testimony of Eliphaz, son of Korah, Rabshakeh.

Here are inscribed the last words I shall ever write. Soon I shall be led away to die, alone and unmourned, far away from the tents of my fathers, condemned to death for killing the man I served, and loved more than my own flesh.

I know that they will not grant me many days to live, perhaps only hours. When David returns from his victory over my people, he will have no choice but to sentence me to execution. But I pray to Adonai that I will finish this task before my last moment comes. For although I am no poet or professional storyteller, I believe that I have witnessed events and learned mysteries which people in the future will say shaped the fates of millions. With my own eyes I have beheld the rise and fall of a man who was numbered among those they call the Shining Ones - the Few, who have truly communed with Adonai himself. And though my words may be disturbing, and my tale strange, hidden within it are joy and sorrow, wonder and wisdom, and knowledge of the Divine.

CHAPTER 1

It's hard to think about dying, when through the bars of my tiny cell I can look up into a cloudless blue sky, watch the spreading fronds of the date palms swaying gently in the breeze, and catch the scent of the spring flowers. It was on just such a day, some thirty years ago, that the course of my life was changed for ever.

The sun was shining, the desert a riot of colour, revived by the recent rains. I was barely eight summers old, a scrawny, wayward little boy with swarthy dust-caked skin and a tangle of crow-black hair. There were holes in my clothes, my feet were bare and I was permanently hungry. But these were facts of life, and I seldom let them worry me.

It had been a disappointing morning. To begin with, my elder brother Esau had gone out for the day without me. He had left the oasis at dawn, in search of new pastures for the flocks he minded. Not that any of these animals belonged to my immediate family; my father was the last in

1

line of six surviving brothers, and when his turn came, there had been neither sheep nor goats left for him. So he and Esau eked out a living for us all by minding those of our richer neighbours, and it was usually Esau who found the best grazing. As always, I had pestered and whined to be allowed to go with him; generally I could win him over quite easily. But today there had been no shifting him.

Disconsolate, I wormed my way back under the tent flaps, to find my mother crouching on the earthy floor, helping Timna unpick a mistake in her tapestry. I made a grab for her skirts, preparing to launch into a tirade against Esau for being so cruel, but she snapped at me and said I was in the way, that weaving was women's work and I was too old to tell tales. I wanted to protest, but there was a disquieting tremor in her voice which wasn't normally there; I stole a glance at Timna and saw she had been crying.

Timna was my twin sister, and she never cried. Nor was it her custom to stay at home weaving. She loved the outdoors as much as I did, and the stark awesome grandeur of the Negev; and I loved her as I loved myself. She and I were alike as two ripe olives. We had the same raven hair - though mine was unruly where hers was long and braided – and the same sharp black eyes and ready smile. My mother said we were like two sides of the same gold piece, and just as hard to prize apart.

Yet on this morning even Timna had no kind word for me. In fact, when I looked at her she wouldn't even meet my gaze. She fumbled with her yarns and hid her face behind a curtain of hair.

"Go outside, Eliphaz," my mother ordered me. "You're getting under foot. But stay near the tents, do you hear me? I don't want you wandering off where the Hill Folk might get you."

I pulled a face. The Hill Folk. It was always the Hill Folk who would be invoked when my mother wanted to threaten us. Apparently they lived in the mountains to the north, hence our way of referring to them. Their own name for themselves was the Sons of Israel. These people, I was told, posed a greater threat to us, the people of Amalek, than any of the wild desert creatures or even the bandits, for they sought to claim our territories for themselves, to build their cities and to plant their crops. I was too young to bear a sword, but I was taught to feel the hate.

"I'm not afraid of the Hill Folk," I boasted, wishing I had real grown-up weapons already, like Esau. "They won't catch me. I can run faster than any of the other boys. And I'd use my sling on them - like this!" I pulled the leather thong from a pouch in my ragged tunic and began whirling it furiously around my head. My mother reached out one arm and yanked it out of my grasp.

"How many times have I told you not to do that in here? Now do as you're told. Go outside, and don't you dare go out of sight of the tents. Are you listening?"

"Yes, Mother." Hanging my head, I stomped out again and flung myself churlishly into the sand, jaw set and teeth gritted. What had got into everyone today? It was so unlike my mother to nag at me, and still more unlike her to fret about my safety. All of us Amalekite children wore amulets around our necks, the sign of our gods' protection over us. Their power would be sufficient to ward off any evil I might come across. An amulet like mine could even keep away the demons that seek to make their dwelling in human souls.

And so there I sat, with nothing to look forward to but a dreary, empty eternity until sundown, when Esau and my father would come home, and we would sit down to our evening meal - maybe a stew, maybe my favourite, flour dumplings in hot goats' milk.

It was while I sat dreaming wistfully about food that I saw the traders approaching. A modest caravan of eight or nine camels, mere silhouettes at first against the haze of distance, wending its way slowly towards our encampment. Suddenly excited, I scrambled to my feet, because this meant there had to be a market today. Markets meant bustle, and noise, and spectacle: a ferment of pure, un-diluted pleasure. The travelling merchants would spread out their luxuries - gold and silver rings and brooches, little clay dolls and animals, aromatic spices and heady perfumes - and our women would haggle and argue, eager to get the best deals in exchange for their woven rugs and sheepskins. The younger girls would chatter with delight, there would be dogs barking, children shouting, babies gurgling happily as they were abandoned to grub about in the dirt... perhaps today would not be so bad, after all.

I wasn't the only one to have spotted the new-comers. Already women were emerging from their tents, calling greetings, carrying armfuls of their produce towards the irregular clearing near the pool-side which served as our market-place. The sleepy oasis erupted into life, the early-morning silence shattered by jabbering voices. I saw an aunt of mine struggling beneath a burden of brightly-coloured blankets, and impetuous as always, I muscled in to help her. Somehow my arms got tangled in the folds of fabric and I went sprawling in the sand, sharing the good-natured laughter of those around me. In the ensuing activity I almost forgot my self-pity, and the puzzling rebuffs I had suffered earlier. Then the traders arrived and set up their stalls, and as the morning wore on, the crowd grew, swelled by an influx of folk from neighbouring settlements.

So at first I didn't notice the thick-set, square-shouldered figure of my father moving among the multitudes of veils and headdresses and camelskin coats. It was only when I heard his voice, gabbling away to one of the strangers in a language I had never heard, that I realized for the first time that all was not well. He never came back to the settlement so early; he never had dealings with itinerant merchants - such things were always left to my mother. Without thinking, I walked anxiously over to where he was standing. He didn't so much as look at me, but he knew that I was there. I stood blinking in the sunshine while some silver pieces were idly shaken into his cupped hands.

I had never in my life seen so much money all at once. As I hung at his elbow, gaping and wide-eyed, someone grasped me roughly by the scruff of my neck. Before I had time to cry out, I was hoisted into the air and up on to the back of one of the traders' camels, where I found myself clutching the repulsively fat midriff of a middle-aged merchant, to prevent myself from falling.

I had plenty of time to cry after that, though. Through a film of tears I watched numbly as three more of the animals were detached from the rest of the train, saddled and made ready to travel. My father wheeled round and pushed his way through the crowds without speaking to anyone. Then I saw that my mother was there, weeping and keening as though someone were dead. Timna was with her, and Esau too, and both of them looked as pallid as corpses. Now at last the truth came home to me. I was to be taken away, and they had all known about it. Everyone had known, except for me, and none of them had lifted a finger to save me. Engulfed by a wave of misery and bitterness, I started kicking and screaming, lashing out at everyone until they bound me hand and foot, and I could only look on helplessly as my world fell apart.

I scarcely noticed when we left the desert behind, and entered a landscape increasingly lush and fertile. On the first days of our journey I had never seen such stretches of sand. Now I was taken aback by the abundance of green. When finally the journey ended, it was in a town surrounded by graceful terraces, fields that were cloaked with vines and creepers, olive trees and fig trees. The meadows were ablaze with flowers. Golden-yellow houses clustered sleepily beside the road, and beyond rose rocky hillsides draped with pine and cypress.

The town, small though it was, had a sturdy encircling wall which ran around its perimeter, rising and falling with the lie of the land. We entered through a plain but imposing gateway, and just inside it was an open market-place. Here I found myself standing, half-starved and caked in dust, my head throbbing, my hands bound together so tightly that my skin was rubbed raw. Alongside me was a straggle of other boys in much the same state. None of us spoke, for we were all past wanting to. The faces of the others looked empty and expressionless, and I wondered vaguely if mine looked the same.

Grouped around us now were various men of the township. Their appearance was strange to me - they wore neatly twisted turbans instead of the flowing head-scarves of the desert; their long sashed robes were fringed and finely worked, and many of them had curious ringlets of hair hanging down in front of their ears. They murmured and muttered amongst themselves, stroking their bearded chins, every so often coming closer to examine us more carefully. They pulled our mouths open and looked at our teeth, they poked and prodded our bodies and our limbs, as though they were buying donkeys or camels.

However, one of the men was different. He didn't poke or prod any of us. He didn't murmur or mutter to the others. He stood apart from them, and his demeanour was so striking that it caused me to give him a second look. He was appreciably taller than the rest. His clothing was of a richer hue and he carried himself with dignity. But, more important, his was the first kindly face I had seen since leaving Amalek.

Then I realized that he had noticed me, too. I couldn't think what had made him single me out from the others. Perhaps the anger I felt within me showed on the outside as spirit, for certainly I didn't feel quite so lethargic as most of the others looked. As I stood there watching him, dizzy with the heat, he quietly dropped some pieces of silver into the hand of one of my captors, and then he came over, untied me, and started to lead me away along the road.

The nearest hill appeared to be the highest, and set squarely astride its summit I could make out the stark profile of a stone-walled castle. Never in my life had I seen anything like it, and this was where we were apparently heading. As the track began to rise, zig-zagging up the slope between the houses, I found myself growing breathless.

I couldn't keep up. Patches in front of my eyes thickened and spread, and joined together. Noiselessly I sank into a crumpled heap on the dusty track, and the strange new world I had become a part of ceased to exist.

I awoke to find myself in a cool, shady courtyard, a damp piece of cloth spread over my brow, and a woman's face looking anxiously down into mine. I was given a bowl of thin, lukewarm broth and when I had finished, the woman made me lie down again and put the cloth back on my brow.

Food has always done wonders to restore my morale, and even that watery soup made me feel better. A short while later, the man who had brought me to this place arrived. He took my hands in his, and started to speak to me, very slowly at first. I was relieved to find that I could follow his meaning quite well, for many of the words were the same as those my own people used, though he spoke with a peculiar accent.

"You look a bit healthier now," he observed. "There's some colour in your cheeks, at least. So - what do they call you, where you come from?"

"Eliphaz," I answered, and was startled to hear that my voice sounded hoarse and cracked. "Eliphaz," I tried again, "Son of Korah of Amalek."

"Amalek!" the man drew breath sharply, and for a moment his steady gaze flickered, before the gloss of serenity returned. I opened my mouth to ask what was wrong, but the woman got in before me.

"Amalek?" she hissed. "You've brought an Amalekite here?"

"They said he was a Kenite! How was I to know? Anyway..." He tightened his grip on my hands, reassuring. "Would you rather he were a Philistine?"

The woman was silent, clasping and unclasping her hands. Her husband turned back to me. "Amalek. That's unfortunate. Still, it can't be helped now. But you'd do well to forget it."

Forget it? Forget Amalek? Inside I was bristling; I thought, wherever I am now, I shall *never* forget where I belong. But aloud I ventured, "Please - where is this place? Who are your people?"

"You're in the town of Gibeah, of the tribe of Benjamin. This is the land of Canaan. My people are the Sons of Israel."

It was my turn to be shocked. I shrank back instinctively and jerked my hands away from his. Wild notions ran amok inside my head, and my fear intensified. The Sons of Israel are wicked; this man must want me so he can torture me, or eat me, or sacrifice me to his gods.

"Don't be frightened," he said indulgently. "No one is going to harm you here. I am Kish, son of Abiel, of the clan Aphiah. This lady is Rachael, my wife, and this place is our home."

So many strange, foreign-sounding names. I began to feel very small.

"Are you the king?" I asked suspiciously.

"The king!" Kish threw back his head and laughed so loudly that I shrank back even further. "We have no king here. There is no king in Israel but Adonai."

Adonai? The name meant nothing to me, and I was

perplexed, for first he had said there was no king, then he had said there was Adonai.

"No, I am simply an elder in my clan, and chief overseer of Gibeah." Kish was continuing with his explanation. "There are a great many men in Israel more important than me."

"But what am I doing here? How long must I stay?" Already I felt trapped; as I looked around I could see that the courtyard was enclosed on all sides by walls or columns or buildings, and I deduced that I was inside the castle which I had seen from below. I wanted to run.

"Eliphaz of Amalek." Kish took hold of my hands again, tenderly but firmly, so that I couldn't pull away. "You are my slave. I bought you for ten pieces of silver. You must stay here until you grow old; you are to be a companion for my son."

All at once I felt furiously helpless and very far from home. I could feel my bottom lip quivering and my eyes were smarting. I will not cry, I thought, I will not; but the tears flowed despite myself.

"I want to go home," I wept. "I can't stay here. You aren't my people. I want my mother. I want Timna. I want..."

But there was now a fourth presence in the courtyard. Rubbing my eyes, and peering into the shadows that hung between the surrounding colonnades, I could dimly make out the silhouetted figure of a boy about my own age, and temporarily my spirits rose. He crouched motionless in the half-light, part hidden by one of the stone pillars, watching me in solemn silence. Clearly he hoped not to be noticed, but in this he was unlucky. Rachael turned towards him and looked at him in such a way as to leave him no choice but to break cover.

He walked towards us hesitantly, and I knew him at once for Kish's son, because in appearance the two of them were so alike. But if anything he was even more striking to look upon than his father. Although not much older than me, he must have been a full head taller. Slender and graceful as a girl, dressed in white, with bright gold chains encircling his neck and wrists, he had light-olive skin that made mine feel coarse and dark and dirty. Thick curling hair fell with affected carelessness around a perfect oval face, loose ringlets of darkest umber shot through with rich red tinges that glimmered like unwatered wine. Beneath the heavy fringe smouldered languid brown eyes, grave, intelligent, inscrutable, and even Timna would have envied him his lashes. His fine features wore a mask of studied indifference, then as he had chance to scrutinize me from closer quarters, I watched their expression harden into blatant disapproval. Something sank inside me, way down in the pit of my stomach.

"Come here, Saul." Kish extended one jewelled hand towards the boy and beckoned him nearer. "I want you to meet Eliphaz, your new companion."

For some while Saul didn't move. His eyes flicked from me, to Kish, to Rachael, and to me again. Then sweeping back his hair with exaggerated nonchalance, he turned round and walked out of the courtyard.

His mother sighed painfully and led me away to a large square room with low couches around three sides, and mattresses rolled up neatly and stacked by the wall. On the wall hung ancient weapons, and in one corner was a large wooden chest with heavy black hinges on the lid. This she opened, and took out a plain cream tunic of finely woven cloth, which she held up against me, nodding approvingly. She made me take off my torn and dusty clothes and my ruined sandals, and she rolled them into a bundle which she placed near the door. Presently an elderly servant appeared carrying a clay tub which he proceeded to fill from jugs of heated water. Rachael said, "Thank you, Boaz," and told him to take the forlorn little parcel to be burnt. Then she looked back at me and smiled. I felt awkward and ungainly, standing there naked before this woman I hardly knew, the familiar things being stripped from me one by one. Rachael made me stand in the tub while she poured water over my head and then methodically began to scrub my grimy skin with a coarse piece of rag. I stood transfixed, watching my flesh change colour and the water turn a muddy brown.

When she was satisfied with my cleanliness, Rachael rubbed a lightly scented oil all over my body, slipped the tunic over my head, and fastened it with a narrow leather belt around my waist. I was fascinated by the softness of the fabric, and ran my fingers over it, first to smooth it down, then again just because I liked the feel of it. In fact I was so enraptured that I scarcely noticed when Rachael deftly removed the amulet from around my neck.

"What is this?" she asked, examining it closely as she held it up towards the light.

"Give me that!" I shrieked, lunging forward to snatch it, but she raised it out of my reach. "It's my god! It protects me from danger. My mother says I must never take it off."

Rachael shook her head, tutting softly. "You have a

lot to learn, young Eliphaz. This is no more a god than you are. It's a piece of pottery, like that wine-jar over there in the corner. You won't be needing it here."

"You're a people without gods?" I hazarded in dismay.

"Quite the reverse," Rachael replied, but I didn't yet dare to enquire what she meant. She looped a plain but fine gold chain, like her son's, around my neck where the amulet had been. "That's better," she observed matter-of-factly. "Now, let's go and see if Saul has got over his shyness."

She took me back to the courtyard. I had more opportunity and inclination now to appreciate its appearance, for in itself it was an entrancing place. It was open to the sky so that you could see the sun and hear the birds singing, and it was festooned with brightly-coloured flowers: flowers in stone troughs, flowers in the cracks between the flagstones, flowers climbing up the walls and trailing from trellises. In the centre was a shallow pool upon which dappled sunlight played, and around its edge ran a low tiled wall.

On the wall the boy Saul was sitting. Beside him lay an open scroll, but he wasn't reading it. He was gazing distractedly into the water, and though he must have sensed our presence, he didn't look up.

"Saul," Rachael called, but still he took no notice. "Saul!" she repeated, louder. "Come and be introduced to Eliphaz."

This time Saul arose dutifully. He came and offered me his hand, but I didn't take it, for there was still no welcome in his eyes. "Saul has been lonely without brothers and sisters," Rachael said. "Well. No doubt you boys will get on better without an old woman under your feet. Saul, show Eliphaz the rest of the house. I'll come and fetch you when supper's ready."

She disappeared back into one of the rooms. Saul turned away without a word and went back to the pool-side. He made a show of picking up and reading the scroll, with his back towards me.

I had heard tell of people who could read, but I had never seen anyone doing it, and I was amazed that this boy could have acquired the skill so young. My curiosity got the better of me; I edged up towards him and stared at the black patterns on the papyrus. Finally I marshalled what remained of my courage and murmured, "I wish I could read."

"You'll never learn to read, Amalekite," Saul said, without looking up.

"Your father and mother - they're very kind."

"If you want to be treated like a baby." He paused, and when he spoke again, it was with calculated malice. "But I suppose that ought to suit a coward like you."

"I'm not a coward." I felt my hackles rising, and the colour rushing to my cheeks.

"Yes, you are. Crying like that, at your age. You ought to have more shame. You may be dressed like an Israelite, but you're still a son of Amalek. You're like all your people - a coward and a thief."

"My people are not cowards and thieves!" Now I was blazing.

"They are." At last he raised his eyes to meet mine, and his were brimful of hostility. "You're all the same, you're as bad as the Philistines. Raiders and robbers. You burn our cities and plunder our wealth because you have no proper lands of your own. I hate you." Saul shook back his hair again and spat scornfully on the ground near my foot; so near that I felt the spray from the spittle. Instinctively I clenched my fists. But then remembered that I was on enemy territory and, inwardly raging, I withdrew as far away from Saul as possible. At the opposite end of the courtyard I sat cross-legged on the ground, seething in silence and glowering like a caged lion.

The sky was beginning to be tinged with pink when Rachael reappeared to call us to supper. She saw us, still sitting apart and silent, but she didn't comment on it. She simply invited us to come and eat. Wordlessly Saul got up and followed her, and I did the same.

We went into the room with the couches, where the table had been laid with silver plates and goblets. At once I began to feel out of my depth. Kish was already seated, and he motioned me to do the same. The elderly servant came to wait on us, and it struck me as odd that I, supposedly a slave, should be served by another, and one who was so much older than I was. Clearly they didn't intend me to be a slave as others are.

Now the old man was bringing round a silver bowl of water, and a cloth, and I watched as each of them washed their hands and dried them, copying them scrupulously when it came to my turn. By this time the food had been laid out on the table: cakes of flat bread, and a huge earthen pot steaming with some kind of vegetable stew, which to my hungry eyes looked indescribably delicious, and its hot savoury smell made my mouth feel to be melting. But no one made any move to begin eating, and when I wrested my gaze from the treat set before me, I saw that they had all closed their eyes. This time I didn't copy, but sat mystified as Kish recited, as though to a god, "Blessed are you, Adonai, King of the Universe, who causes food to come forth from the earth."

I looked all around me in astonishment. I could see no god anywhere. And he had spoken that name again: Adonai. But there was just Kish, and Rachael, and Saul who sat with his head bowed, his curls fallen forward over his cheeks.

It had already been decided that Saul and I should take our lessons together. However, until now, Kish had tutored his son on his own, and our first attempt at a threesome was an unmitigated failure.

We sat in Kish's study, an open scroll spread before us on the table. I admired the reverent way in which Kish handled it, and he told me it was a copy of his people's holy writings. It contained the words of Moses, the father of their faith, who had given them their laws and their liberty. Kish explained that we should first of all examine the portion prescribed for that day, and in a low chanting monotone he began to recite it aloud. So far as I could see it appeared to consist of endless lists of bizarre rules and regulations, about what you could and couldn't eat, whom you could and couldn't marry, and my mind was already wandering when Kish asked Saul to take up the reading.

Saul muttered something and played with his hair.

"What's the matter?" Kish asked softly, prepared to be patient.

"I don't want to read."

"But why ever not? You read so well. Come along, show Eliphaz what you can do."

"What's the point?" Saul's sneer made him look almost ugly. "He doesn't understand any of it. Look at his face. He's confused already."

"Very well." Kish rolled up the scroll, and I wondered at his lack of perseverance. My own father would never have let me get away with such insolence. Presumably Kish wanted to avoid a scene in front of me. "Let's try some number work. It's about time you got to grips with these accounts."

He reached up and took a box of tablets from one of the shelves that ran along the wall. But Saul growled, "Accounts. It's always accounts. Who wants to be a farmer? I'd rather be a warrior. Or even a bard."

Again Kish showed no inclination to rise to the bait. He turned to me and said brightly, "Well, I'm sure Eliphaz can count. Don't look so anxious, my young friend. Let's hear what you can do."

Nervously I began to say my numbers out loud, but with Saul's eyes boring into me I got muddled, and ground to a halt. Saul leaned back with supercilious relish. "I told you he was stupid, as well as a coward. Send him back to Amalek, he's nothing but a savage."

His father regarded him steadily, until Saul was forced to avert his gaze. Finally, and not before time, Kish said, "I would hardly describe your behaviour this morning as very civilized."

I jumped as Saul sprang to his feet. He swept the tablets to one side, seized the scroll and threw it open. With dogged but bridled defiance he began reading out the passage which Kish had wanted him to read in the first place. When Saul had finished, he closed up the scroll and flounced out of the room.

Kish shook his head slowly, and I waited in numb silence. Then he said, "Not to worry, Eliphaz. We shan't go chasing after him. He'll come back when he's cooled down. I'll teach you some of your letters."

So I sat poring over a tablet while Kish formed the meaningless shapes and made me copy his examples underneath. Aleph, beth, gimel... but when he covered the originals to see if I'd remembered, my mind blanked out and I cringed. Perhaps Saul was right, and I was stupid after all.

Kish read my thoughts and gave me an unexpected hug. "Don't despair. It will come in time. Let's try again."

So we worked like that, side by side, with Kish's arm around my shoulder, and I thought little of it, until Saul reappeared.

He pushed the door open slowly, and walked towards us with his head down, both hands behind his back. Kish called him over.

"You're just in time, Saul. You can show Eliphaz how you write your alphabet."

Saul said, "I wanted to show *you* something."

"Well, go on then. What is it?"

"It doesn't matter."

"Of course it matters."

Kish's features mellowed into a smile. Saul hesitated a while longer, then brought his hands out from behind him. In his long fingers he was holding a delicate flute, with holes cut carefully down one side. He said, "I made it from a reed Mother gave me yesterday. Do you want to hear it?" Without waiting for a reply, he put it to his lips and blew gently across one end. An eerie, trailing melody wisped upwards like incense from an altar. I was stunned; it sounded so beautiful. He said, "I made up the tune too. Do you like it?"

I enthused, without thinking, "It was wonderful!" but Saul pretended that I hadn't spoken, which I rapidly decided was almost worse than being spat at. He repeated his question to Kish, who swallowed uneasily.

"Yes. It was lovely, Saul. Now, are you going to help Eliphaz?"

Saul failed to hide his disappointment. He said aggressively, "You didn't like it, did you? I can tell."

"Saul..." Kish held out his arms; if I'd been Saul I would have run to him. But Saul backed off still further, his face set hard like fired clay.

"It's all right. I don't care. You just pet your Amale-kite some more. I'll go away."

Now Kish was almost snorting with exasperation. "Saul, don't be so childish! You know very well that I admire your gift for music. I just wish you'd devote as much attention to the things that really matter, that's all. One day all my estates will be yours, and then you'll have no choice but to understand how these things work. Land man-agement, buying equipment, comparing yields, paying hired workers; I can't understand why you won't see..."

But Saul was gone. For the first time I felt sorry for him, and I knew he wasn't so sullen all the time just because he was jealous of me. After that, Kish dismissed me. I don't think he had the heart for any more studying that day.

The same night, I had bad dreams, the first of many. I was back home in Amalek, I had somehow found my family, but I was still wearing the plain cream tunic and no amulet, and no one seemed to know who I was. I grabbed hold of Timna and shook her until she screamed, but when I let her go, she slapped my face and ran away. The blow woke me up; I was sweating and gasping for breath. Across the room I could trace the outline of Saul's body curled up in bed, and I was glad I hadn't woken him. I didn't want him to see me all shaken up and scared. I wished they hadn't made me share his room.

The following day, we had no lessons. At first I thought that Kish had simply let Saul have his own way again, but gradually it dawned on me that today was something special. Rachael did no housework, and Kish didn't leave the fortress from dawn to dusk. Only the old slave Boaz went on pottering about as usual. There were extra prayers at the meals, and two candles burned on the dining table. However, I could make nothing of all this, and no one saw fit to explain. I waited for something out of the ordinary to happen, yet nothing did. The day after, everything just went back to normal.

But by degrees, patterns emerged, and my life fell into some kind of a routine. Each morning we had lessons, except for one day like this in each seven when nothing whatever was done. The lessons got worse rather than better. Saul derived his pleasure from looking down his nose at my mistakes, flying into tantrums on the rare occasions when he himself got something wrong. He never spoke to me at all after the day we were introduced. I was so miserable and homesick that I couldn't even think straight, and nothing that we studied stuck in my head at all.

I don't mean to say that I was learning nothing, but what I gleaned came from everyday life, not from our lessons, or it came from asking Kish afterwards when we were alone, away from the distraction of Saul's blatant derision. In this way I arrived at solutions to many of the mysteries I had encountered since arriving at Gibeah. But each one I solved seemed to give rise to twenty more. It was often my innocent blunders which caused me to stumble upon the truth. There was the day when I dropped a whole box of wax tablets I was carrying to the study for Kish, and I swore out loud by Moses, thinking how clever I was to use the name of an Israelite god in place of one of my own. Kish found this so amusing that he didn't even scold me for clumsiness - nor indeed for swearing.

"Moses is no god," he chuckled, bending down to help me gather the broken pieces.

I said, "But you read his words, in your holy writings."

"Moses was just a man like you or me. When our people had been slaves in Egypt for four hundred years, he led them back here to freedom in Canaan. His words became holy because he was a prophet, the greatest of the Shining Ones."

"Shining Ones?" I repeated, baffled.

"The Shining Ones are those who have met with our God," he explained. "They're also known as the Few, for there are few who've seen our God and lived."

"But sir..." I began, then faltered, suddenly feeling that my rashness was leading me into dangerous waters, as it so often did.

"Yes, Eliphaz? Don't be shy."

"But sir - it's just that, since I got here I've seen no gods at all. Rachael even took away the only god I knew. And yet before we eat, you say blessings - to someone. And now you say, people can meet with this god. I don't understand."

Kish smiled. "The ways of your people aren't our ways, Eliphaz. But it's like I said - there are not many of us who have met with the God. It is rare, and an honour beyond words."

I ventured, "Have you, sir?"

"Me? Oh no!" Kish laughed again, as though the very idea were unthinkable. "Only priests and prophets can meet with the Holy One. The rest of us worship him and sacrifice to him and seek to renounce all other gods - well, most of us do. But we could never meet him. Just the reflection of his glory can kill a man."

"You only worship one god?" I was awe-struck.

"That is what our most sacred prayer teaches," said Kish. "It's called the Shema, because it begins 'Shema Israel' - 'Hear O Israel, the Lord your God is One.' These are the first words which we speak into the ears of a newborn child, and the last which should be heard by someone dying."

"But - isn't that very dangerous? At home we had to be so careful, always to pay equal attention to them all."

"Eliphaz - there are no others."

"But... you mean... only Adonai is real?"

"I mean there's only one God. Even Adonai isn't his name. It just means 'The Lord'."

"There's only one god, and you can't even see him,

and he hasn't got a name?"

"Oh, he has a name. But it's so holy, only the Shining Ones know how to say it rightly. Only they have ever heard it spoken aloud. I can write the word down for you, if you like."

Still crouching on the floor, he wrote in the dust with his finger, YHWH, but he had to spell the letters out to me, because I still couldn't recognize the shapes. Feeling suddenly ignorant, I scraped up the rest of the tablets and fled.

In the afternoons, Kish would go off to inspect his domains or meet for discussions with his fellow elders, Saul would keep his own company, and after I'd polished off a few light chores I would be left alone to amuse myself. When I got too lonely I would go and talk to Rachael. She was usually busy in the kitchen, but was happy enough to chat to me whilst going about her work. We talked of home and family, and I think she felt sorry for me, but sometimes I felt sorry for her, too. With my customary lack of forethought, I asked her one day why she'd had no more children, if it bothered her so much that Saul was an only child.

"That wasn't what we intended, you can be sure of that." She smiled wistfully, and for a moment stopped grinding her corn. "I would have loved to have other children, I love babies more than anything. But I was very ill when Saul was born, and I've never managed to conceive since then. I suggested that Kish take another wife as well as me, but he wouldn't. I suppose I should be grateful for that."

I was old enough to realize my insensitivity. I

muttered, "I'm sorry," and began fiddling with the cooking utensils to hide my embarrassment.

"I couldn't even look after him myself," Rachael continued, seemingly unoffended. "We had a whole succession of wet-nurses, one after another, but none of them stayed. It was too quiet for them here, with no other women around except me, and I was scarcely good company. I never held Saul in my arms until he was two months old. He already felt like a stranger."

Unlike me, Saul never seemed to tire of his own company. He would spend hours composing poetry or music, and when he stroked his harp it rippled like a river dancing over stones. Music was what cheered him when his spirits were low - at times when I would have gone to find someone to talk to, he would play his flute, or more often the harp. He also did a great deal of reading. I couldn't imagine what a boy of our age could want with a holy book, but it seemed to fascinate him. Once, one evening when it was growing dark and chilly, I went into our room to get something warmer to wear, and came upon him unexpectedly, kneeling in the shadows with a lighted candle before him and his cloak drawn up over his head. He was mumbling to himself, and rocking back and forth on his haunches. A shiver went down my spine, and I ran out again, scared.

But Saul devoted more time to weapons than to anything else. He owned knives, a sword and spear. When he wasn't working on his technique, he was oiling or honing blades. Yet it was strange that he had no one to compete against or spar with. Kish would have nothing to do with this aspect of his son's upbringing, and made it quite clear that he didn't approve.

One afternoon Saul was sitting on the wall beside the pool in the courtyard, his dark head bent over the sword he was sharpening, when Kish appeared and asked him if he'd finished correcting some calculations he'd got wrong in our lesson that morning. Saul shrugged vaguely, and I watched Kish debating with himself, weighing whether to risk a showdown. Then he said, "Saul, give that sword to me. You can have it back when you've done as I asked you."

Kish walked forward and held out his palm, but Saul hugged the weapon against himself, flint-eyed and bristling.

"I'm not asking you, Saul. I'm telling you. You're too young to play with things like that, anyway."

Saul muttered, "I'm not playing. You don't know when I'll need to use it." And there was a peculiar expression on his face, that made my heart miss a beat. I guess now that he was referring to the Philistines, but at the time, my brain started doing cartwheels. I stared at the blade, its razor-sharp edge, I saw the heat in Saul's cheeks and sensed the odium inside him; and for months went in fear of my life.

CHAPTER 2

I had been in Gibeah for nearly a year when one morning, just as we were settling down to our lessons, the old servant entered the study and bowed briefly before Kish.

"Sir, your brother Ner is in the courtyard, and wishes to see you."

I looked up, surprised. I had never yet met or heard of any other members of this small family, and by now had begun to assume there were none.

"Show him in, Boaz."

The servant bowed again, disappeared, and presently returned, hotly pursued by a stout and swaggering stranger. I would never have taken him for any relative of Kish. He gave the impression of being as wide as he was tall, and wore his gown twisted up in his belt in the style of a peasant craftsman or a soldier. His face was wreathed in smiles and he held his arms out before him in a gesture of welcome, looking for all the world like the host rather than the guest. He strode over to his brother, who was still rising to his feet, embraced him enthusiastically and exclaimed, "Kish! How good to see you! How goes life in the ivory tower?"

"Well, we are honoured indeed," Kish remarked drily, when he had got his breath back. "For someone so delighted to see me, you don't exactly call in very often. To what do we owe this unexpected pleasure?"

"Oh, this and that," boomed Ner, with a wave of one huge hand. "This and that. For a start, I've got some good news for you. You know I always liked to be the bearer of glad tidings."

"And what might these tidings be?"

"The latest on our big brother Zeror up in the northlands. He sent me a letter back with that slave I lent to him. Apparently he's moved again, to Jabesh in Gilead. He's built himself a new house, because two of his sons are preparing to take wives. It seems there may soon be some weddings in our family."

My interest was aroused; so Kish had two brothers when I had credited him with none. I wondered which of the two here this Zeror resembled.

"You came over here especially to say that?" asked Kish suspiciously. "Come now, Ner. I'll wager that wasn't your real motive."

"See how well my brother knows me," drawled Ner, slapping his thigh and grinning broadly at Saul. "Kish, you are right as always. I really came to extend an invitation."

"An invitation? To what?"

"To accompany me and my companions on an errand of mercy."

Kish sighed and rolled up his scroll, resigned now to abandoning our studies. "This still doesn't sound much like the Ner we know and love. Tell me the whole story."

Without waiting to be invited, Ner sat down and ruffled Saul's hair affectionately. I was surprised to see that Saul didn't pull away. "Well, some shepherds east of Jebus have reported a young lion worrying their flocks. They have seen it but no one can catch it, and it has killed at least a dozen sheep. We are going to the aid of our fellow Israelites in distress! We mean to rid them of this menace. Are you with us, brother?"

Kish shook his head, chuckling. "I have business in town today, Ner. But I wish you success."

"Then suppose I take your son along?" Ner suggested brightly. "Saul looks like he could do with fresh colour putting in his cheeks. And it's time that spear and sword I gave him saw some proper action. What do you say?"

There was an awkward silence. I glanced at Saul and saw something flicker behind his customary scowl. It looked like eagerness, but also a little like fear. Kish's face looked like thunder.

"He's too young, Ner. You should know that as well as I do."

"Oh, come come!" objected Ner. "I'm taking our Abner. Saul can give him at least a year. I can't see why you're being so obstructive." Kish glowered, but Ner was not to be deterred. He said, "Why don't we let the boy speak for himself? Saul - what about it?"

Saul opened his mouth, but then looked sideways at Kish and no words came.

"See how tongue-tied you've got him," said Ner, but he was grinning again, evidently enjoying himself enormously. "You needn't worry, though - either of you. I'll be right there with him. He won't get into any bother. Well, young Saul. Have you made up your mind?"

"All right then. I want to come."

I waited for Kish to veto the plan, but it seemed he had suddenly had an idea. "You know I don't like this one little bit, Saul. But I'm prepared to let you go, on one condition."

"What's that."

"If you agree to let Eliphaz go with you."

Saul curled his lip. "But Father, he has no spear or sword. And even if he had, he wouldn't know how to use them."

"True enough," Kish agreed. "But he can watch perfectly well. And he can make sure that *you* keep well away from trouble."

Saul peered at me condescendingly through his fringe. Finally he mumbled, "All right. If I must."

A delicious surge of excitement swept through me. My heart was racing so fast I could hardly breathe, and I only came back to earth when Kish spoke my name. "Now then, Eliphaz. Don't let Saul out of your sight, do you hear? And Ner - I'm holding you responsible for his safety. You know I'm not at all happy about this."

"Yes, yes," said Ner impatiently, already getting up to leave. Saul appeared more animated than I had ever seen him. He scrambled for his weapons lest he give his father space to change his decision, and set off on the heels of Ner who was already making for the gateway.

Kish drew me to one side. "Take a sling and some stones, Eliphaz," he advised. "No doubt you learned how to use those among the sons of Amalek." I nodded and hastened to join my companions.

Outside, Ner had a noisy throng of dubious-looking roughnecks waiting. All the members of this motley crowd were wearing short or hitched-up tunics, and they were armed with whatever they had been able to lay their hands on: clubs and staves, mallets and bludgeons with spiked metal heads, bows, and here and there a few poorly fashioned swords and spears. Only Ner and Saul had decent-looking weapons, and the youngest member of the party, whom I figured must be Ner's son Abner. In his short, stocky build he was like his father, but his face had a certain look of Saul's about it. When his older cousin appeared, Abner gravitated to his side as flies do to a lamp when it is kindled at twilight. But Saul paid him little attention.

Accompanying the party were three donkeys, laden with wicker baskets holding fruit and full fat wine-skins. Evidently Ner's men intended making an occasion of the hunt. As we set off south in the direction of the city of Jebus, everyone was in high spirits: the youths in antici-pation of the chase, Saul and Abner proud to imagine them-selves men among men, I, because it just felt so good to be outside.

Our road took us through magnificent hill-country, all the more beautiful for me because I was seeing it through fresh eyes. The fields and the orchards and the pine trees beyond them entranced me, and I marvelled that the flocks could still find such lush grass to graze on when winter had long since flown. As I walked, I found plenty of smooth round stones for my sling, and slipped them into the folds of my tunic. We made good progress, and it wasn't long before we sighted the walls of Jebus, but we could go no closer to the city because it was still occupied by descendants of one of the tribes who had dwelt in the land of Canaan before the Israelites returned from their slavery in Egypt. Kish had spoken of these Canaanites in our lessons: they had once possessed many fine cities, with massive walls and majestic citadels, but time and prosperity had made them weak, and most of their strongholds had fallen to the armies of Joshua, Moses' successor, or simply sunk into decline. But some of their centres of dominion still remained, and no war-leader had yet arisen who could break their power and bring all of Canaan under Israel's control.

Once east of Jebus, the scenery began to alter dramatically. The terraced fields lay behind us now, the lush green faded to brown and then turned to red, the gently rolling hills gave way to soaring crags and deep gorges, and the track we were following fell away sharply, plunging into arid semi-desert. Ner clearly intended to comb this wild and barren terrain beyond the city systematically, beginning to the south and working gradually northwards, checking each cave and each rock outcrop for traces of a lion's den.

By midday, however, we'd had no success on any score. We had found dozens of caves, and searched acres of boulder-fields. We had seen lizards and snakes, snails and scorpions, ibexes and gazelles, but no lion. As we trudged along, some of our number had amused themselves by shooting at small game, and now we had the carcases of a couple of deer strapped to the donkeys' backs. One of them had been Saul's own catch; I watched agog as he dispatched it with a single well-aimed spear-throw. Ner clapped him on the back and he glowed with delight. Meanwhile little Abner had chased rabbits and rock-badgers and pestered Saul to help him catch one for lunch, but I heard Saul tell him crossly that they were unclean and forbidden as food.

When the heat had grown unbearable, we found a shady spot beneath some stunted broom trees and sat down to rest and await the coming of cooler air before pressing on down into the valley. Saul settled himself next to his uncle and shared his lunch, and although he barely spoke, he seemed calmer than he ever was at home. Ner nursed no lofty expectations, he passed no judgments; he just beamed at Saul and shared the banter of the youths who lounged about him. Ner's son had continued tailing his cousin doggedly and now sat at Saul's feet happily munching his way through a large bag of roasted grain.

I sat apart as usual, and played with my slingshots, watching everyone gorging themselves with all kinds of food and guzzling large quantities of wine. My mouth watered and I wished I had brought something to eat. After a while Ner, his mouth crammed with bread, looked me up and down critically and remarked, "Well, young Saul, don't you think it's time for some introductions? Let us all in on the secret - who's your new friend?"

"He's not my friend," Saul answered. "He's my slave. An Amalekite."

He put a calculated emphasis upon this last word, which elicited the desired response. Ner laughed heartily. "A little savage from Amalek, eh? Here, you young brigand. Have some food."

He tossed me a half-chewed hunk of meat, which hit

me on the leg, then landed in the dust. I was ravenous, but not enough to trade food for dignity. I left it on the ground where it fell.

"Not hungry?" Ner feigned surprise. "I thought you Amalekite raiders were well used to taking the food from other people's mouths. Perhaps you're thirsty then. Some wine for the Amalekite!"

Someone passed him a wine-skin. Before I had time to refuse, Ner bounded over and held it to my lips.

"Have a drink, lad! Surely you won't refuse good Israelite wine?"

I tried to pull away, but clearly I was to be given no choice this time. Ner seized me by the hair, tipped my head back, and poured the bitter red liquid down my throat until I almost choked. By the time he let go, my head was spinning. I was also shaking with anger and chagrin. The others had stopped eating, and everyone was gawking at me; Ner stood with his hands on his hips, roaring with laughter, and enjoying the general approbation. When the hilarity abated, he went back to his meal - as far as he was concerned, the joke was now over.

But he had reckoned without the callous brutality of youth. At first I think they just wanted some fun. The hunt had turned out to be boring; now here was a chance for some real entertainment. Ner's younger comrades linked arms in a drunken circle around me, jostling each other, sniggering and jeering, calling me scum, and cur, and leper, and guffawing at one another's pathetic attempts at humour. They pushed me and shoved me, jabbing me in the ribs, half-heartedly to begin with, then roughly, until I felt like a stuffed animal-skin which children will throw around at the roadside.

Someone forced my lips apart, and the contents of a second wine-skin was emptied into my mouth. Whoever had poured it was too fuddled to aim straight, and most of the wine splashed over my face and stung my eyes. I started howling and kicking and shouting but they thrust me down onto my stomach, and began to roll me over and over, shrieking with raucous laughter. With each revolution I saw the curtain of faces swing sickeningly above me, all red and bloated. Even little Abner was laughing with the rest. Then amongst them I glimpsed Saul; not laughing, but staring, with cold, narrowed eyes.

It was at that moment that one of them yelled out, "Death to the sons of Amalek! Death to the scourge of Adonai's people!" and in a single instant the mood had changed. The laughter died, and the chanting began. In rhythm with their taunting they were punching me and kicking me, again and again, until the pain was so intense that I couldn't even scream. Then I heard Ner's voice cut through the uproar.

"Come on now, lads, that's enough. Break it up."

At first this had no impact; it was said with little conviction. I don't suppose for a moment he really cared a fig for my wellbeing; I just think he didn't relish the prospect of answering to Kish. But when I stopped struggling and lay still, with my eyelids squeezed shut, the blows got less frequent and less vicious. Ner's voice came again.

"Leave him be, I said. Can't you see he's dead to the world? You won't get any more fun out of him now."

Gradually I sensed them fall back. I lay there winded

and bruised all over, clutching my stomach, pretending to be unconscious until I was sure they had lost interest. The pain eased off, and though I was quivering with shock, I decided I wasn't as damaged as I might have been. Eventually I tried to stand up, but my head reeled, I was seeing double and I felt dizzy and sick. Somehow I managed to crawl back into the shade; and then I really did pass out.

When I came to, there was total silence all around me. I sat up trying to recollect where on earth I was and how I had come to be there. Then I decided they must all have gone off home and left me for dead. I rubbed my eyes but I still couldn't see straight, and my head felt as if it had been stuffed with fleece. The sun was well past its zenith but it was still very hot. I was slimy with sweat, my skin was caked in filth and dried blood. Finally I realized that I wasn't alone after all. Ner's men and boys lay sprawled all around me, most of them snoring. I was about to lie down again, when it struck me that Saul and Abner were nowhere in sight. Puzzled, I crouched there blinking and squinting, but it was true: there was no sign of them.

I held my head and tried to collect my thoughts. I couldn't imagine where the two cousins might have gone, nor why they would have wandered away from the others. I wondered vaguely whether bandits might have kidnapped them, though it seemed unlikely, with our party being so big.

That was when I started panicking. For all of a sudden, I remembered: I'm supposed not to let Saul out of my sight. Now something terrible has no doubt happened to him, and the whole thing will be seen as my fault. In fact it *is* my fault, for being too pig-headed to pick up that piece of meat Ner threw at me. I noticed a high rocky knoll nearby, and slowly - for I was having difficulty balancing - I picked my way over to it. I climbed up to the top, and shading my eyes from the still dazzling sun, I peered across the desolate valley to the cliffs beyond. They looked to be broken by caves. Was it possible that Saul could have grown tired of waiting, and decided to pursue the hunt? I had no other clue to follow, so taking my sling and the pebbles I'd collected, I clambered carefully down the hillside towards the rocky escarpments below. The ground was overlaid with loose scree, and my feet sent flurries of dusty stones clattering downwards.

I hadn't gone far, when some distance below I saw young Abner climbing steadily up towards me; but he was alone. When we met I grabbed him by the shoulders, demanding, "Where is Saul?" and hearing my voice throaty and fearful.

"He told me to go back," said Abner, disgruntled. "He made me. He said he would hit me."

"But where is he? Where has he gone?"

Abner turned and pointed towards the cliff face. I swallowed hard and told him to carry on back up to the others, giving him a push to reinforce my meaning. Again I floundered on alone. Frequently I tripped and stumbled, for the ground was uneven and punctured by hidden crevices. By the time I drew level with the first of the caves, my ankles were cut and bleeding, and the fine tunic Rachael had given me looked like a pedlar's rags.

Methodically I began to search the musty caverns. The first two only extended backwards a few spearlengths, and were empty except for branches and twigs and the ashes of old campfires. But the third appeared black and fathomless, and a tremor of dread ran up my spine as I felt my way into its inky depths. I could see no evidence of Saul's having been there, and was on the point of turning round, when something inside me said no. Then as the darkness closed in around me, I heard an ominous snarling, and at the same instant, the plaintive cry of a child.

"Saul? Saul!" I shrieked without thinking, then shrank back in terror as I realized what a foolish thing I had done. I heard his voice answer from the bowels of the cave, but it was faint and muffled. Perhaps he was badly wounded and I was already too late. Momentarily I stood rooted to the ground, my eyes still adjusting to the dim light which filtered back from the entrance. Now I could sense the louring bulk of the beast lumbering towards me, and it gave another growl, louder this time.

Instinctively I seized my sling and fired a stone in the direction the noise had come from, then I jumped to one side - and just in time, for the creature sprang into view. At least now I could see my target, and for a moment was taken aback, for it was a young lioness, and not a lion at all. Then I gathered my wits and fired again, landing the animal a blow straight between the eyes. She reared up, roaring in frenzy, filling the cave with thundering echoes that made my flesh creep. I had succeeded in drawing her away from where Saul must be - but what could I do now? I doubted that I had the strength to kill her with slingshot, no matter how well aimed.

Then I saw something gleaming on the earthy floor just beyond my reach. Saul's spear! He must have thrown it, missed, and been unable to retrieve it. Quickly I flung another stone at the lioness to distract her, then made a dive for the weapon. Spinning round, I threw it, with little skill, but all my might - and planted it right in the creature's throat. Blood spurted and gushed onto the ground, splashing me as I fell to my knees, in blank amazement at what I'd achieved. A moment later, and the lioness had keeled over and lay twitching in the dirt. Another moment, and she was still.

Drawing a deep breath I tottered to my feet, and shouted Saul's name again, but this time there was no reply. Stretching out my hands on either side of me, I felt my way further into the cave. Thankfully Saul was not far back, slumped fainting against the wall. I took hold of him by the shoulders, and managed to haul him most of the way to the entrance, before my foot struck against something soft and warm. I gasped in alarm and took an involuntary pace backwards, feeling the sweat break cold on my brow. Then swallowing my fear, I ventured forward once more, and saw what I had touched. It was the carcase of a lion, a young male, with Saul's sword driven deep into its flesh. For a moment I stood transfixed. Then I got a grip on myself, and dragged the languishing Saul out into the daylight.

He was indeed wounded. There were jagged lacerations all down his legs and a deep gash in one arm which was still bleeding profusely. Unhesitating I tore a strip from my tunic and bandaged the wound, realizing too late that I could have used my sling. Saul's face was as white as a dead man's - clearly he had lost a lot of blood - and there was a big raw swelling on his forehead which perhaps explained why he was dazed and seemed unable to speak. He was not quite unconscious - his eyes were open, and although they kept wandering, he was clearly trying to look at me.

"Can you walk?" I demanded. "I can't carry you across all those rocks. Come on." Holding his arm across the back of my neck with one hand, and with the other grasping him awkwardly round the waist, I part walked him, part carried him, back across the rough valley bottom and up to the others.

It was a subdued party which returned to the fortress of Gibeah that evening. Ner walked along muttering under his breath about how on earth he was going to explain Saul's injuries to Kish, and bemoaning the fact that we hadn't even destroyed the monster that caused them. I was no happier myself, for by now I was convinced that I would end up bearing the blame for the whole incident because I had let Saul go off without me. I would be stripped and beaten to within a hair's-breadth of my life. Or I would be left in the desert as prey for hyaenas and vultures. But I was past caring. Perhaps Saul was going to die; I wondered if I cared about that.

When we arrived at the fortress, I didn't wait to hear the explanations. I slipped through into the courtyard and sat by the pool-side, my head in my hands, gazing down into the water, watching the last rays of sunset fade from its darkly dappled surface. The same thoughts kept churning round in my brain. I had been brought here to make Saul happy. Instead I had let him die. I was a failure, a murderer. If only there were some way to escape, to put an end to the misery and the pain. Dimly I wondered what it felt like to plunge your head under water, and leave it there until you drowned.

It was long after nightfall when I heard Kish's footsteps approaching.

"Saul?" I whispered. "Is he all right?"

His father lowered himself slowly onto the pool-side wall beside me. "He will be, thank God. He's asleep now; Rachael's with him. He'll recover."

I nodded faintly, gazing back into the water. My spirits lifted a little, but I was spent.

"Eliphaz - he told me what happened. I came to say thank you."

Everyone else must have been in bed for hours by the time my mind had stopped racing enough to let me sleep. Painfully I dragged myself indoors to our bedroom. By the soft light of the little lamp burning in one corner, I could see Saul stretched out on his mattress, alone now, a bandage wrapped around his head, his hair still dishevelled and matted with blood. He was sleeping, but fitfully, his breath coming shallow and irregular. As quietly as I could, I unrolled my pallet and stepped out of what remained of my filthy tunic, stopping to examine the grazes on my legs, and to feel my bruised ribs.

I lay down, but didn't sleep. My insides felt too strange, and my chafed skin too tender. After a while, I got up again, and went over to see if Saul was any better.

He was still asleep, his long lashes twitching over cheeks that were a little too flushed to be healthy. He looked so innocent, so pure without the sneer that twisted his features when he was awake. For some reason I hovered there, musing, wondering what images coloured his dreams. His breathing was less troubled now, and he didn't stir in all the time I was standing there. So when I turned to go back to bed, I was shocked for more than one reason when he called out my name.

He didn't say anything else; there was no need. Besides, I don't think he could have thanked me or asked my forgiveness even if he'd wanted to. He wouldn't have had the slightest idea where to start. But I saw that he was smiling.

When I eventually crawled back to my mattress, I was asleep before I could even take in what had happened. No dozing, no nightmares, no tossing and turning. Somehow I wasn't even missing Timna any more. I hadn't slept so soundly since leaving Amalek.

CHAPTER 3

I wasn't so young or so foolish as to suppose that all would be sweetness and light between Saul and me from that moment on. He'd never had a friend in his life, nor did he know how to be one. Things changed so slowly, I could have torn out my hair. But little by little a shy sideways grin, a shared barley cake from Rachael's kitchen, some small gift left under my mattress, told me he wanted to start out afresh. We may not have talked much to begin with, yet now I knew he was on my side, and that made all the difference. In our lessons, I picked things up quickly. Our free time we started to spend together.

Often we would stand side by side on the walkway which ran around the battlements of the fortress, gazing at the blue of the hills on the horizon, or watching the Gibeah children larking about in the streets below.

"Why do we never join in?" I asked him once, seeing a curious distance mirrored in his eyes.

"With them?" He looked down his nose, suddenly

defensive. "They're common and stupid and they fight over nothing."

But I was starting to see through his arrogant words, and the haughty tilt of his chin. I knew when he was scared.

"Anyhow," he went on petulantly. "My parents wouldn't allow it. They think if I go outside I'll melt or something."

I said, "They let us go hunting with Uncle Ner."

"And look what happened then. They went on about it for weeks. I tell you, they think I'm made of Egyptian glass."

"It's only because they love you. You're all they've got."

"Huh. They've never loved me. I'm not the son they wanted. Nothing I ever do can be good enough for them."

But I'd already had my fill of his gloomy intro-spection. He was still so moody and melancholy much of the time, and I often couldn't fathom it. So all at once I shouted, "Hide and seek - you're on!" and slapping him on the shoulder I dived off down the steps into the courtyard before he had time to object. He hadn't the faintest idea what I meant. I left him gawking there clueless as a halfwit, while I darted back and forth between the pillars of the colonnade, calling up, "You have to catch me! It's only a game."

I watched him debating with himself what to do. Then he hitched up his clothes and came after me. At once I stopped shouting; I ran into the store rooms and crouched in a ball behind a great pitcher full of olives. Stifling my giggles, I heard his echoing footsteps cross and recross the yard, then his shadow darkened the doorway. I knew he would find me in no time now, so I took to throwing olives straight in his face. When he promptly tracked me down, he thrust his hand into the pitcher and stuffed a fistful of the sticky fruit down my neck. He was laughing; it was the first time.

To distract me from always wanting to venture outside, Saul decided it was time I learnt to handle proper weapons. We began with the spear, and he would spend hours with me, showing me how to stand, working on my grip, positioning my arm and shoulder. We progressed to the sword, and the use of a shield; Saul was patient but particular, and it was clear he wasn't self-taught. Now and again I glimpsed Kish watching us from a doorway, but he didn't interfere.

One day in autumn Ner came again to the fortress. He hadn't dared show his face since the occasion of the hunt; now I think he was minded to set things right. He didn't choose a wise method of going about it. He told Kish he was planning some games in honour of their late brother Nathan; there were to be weaponry contests for the boys from the town, and how about Saul and Eliphaz taking part?

I couldn't imagine why Kish reacted so savagely. I hadn't suspected he had it in him. But I really thought he was going to floor Ner on the spot. I'd never even heard of this Nathan, and I doubted that Saul had. Still, Kish needn't have worried. Saul said, "No thank you, Uncle. I'm afraid I'm not interested," and Ner went away.

Afterwards I said, "You idiot, Saul ben Kish! I bet you're the best swordsman in Gibeah under military age. And I've never seen the boys in the streets throw a spear as well as you. You'd walk away with every prize in the book."

"No I wouldn't. My father's right. I'm no good at anything. I wouldn't win."

I thought, surely he can't really mean that? I said, "Well you wouldn't come last, and that's a certainty. You definitely wouldn't show yourself up."

"But what's the use of bothering, if I'm not the best? There isn't any point. It's a waste of time."

I was set to argue further, but he gave a great shudder, as though a rope was wound round his chest and he couldn't shake it free. And there was a look on his face that warned me off, so I held my peace and thought that despite the care he took to seem always so patient and reasonable in the way he treated his complicated son, Kish had much to answer for.

We did leave the fortress again, after a time. Kish gave his permission, so long as we stayed on his estates. But gradually these weren't enough for us; we grew tired of the orchards and vineyards, and wandered the hills and forests beyond, sharing our secrets.

One winter morning we rose early, and left before dawn, so that we could smuggle out bows and arrows and go hunting. It soon became obvious Saul had done this more than once before, and I was no match for him. He was light on his feet, quiet as a panther; I was rash and impetuous, too keyed up to aim straight. He brought down a young deer, and I leapt forward to finish it, but he called me back before I could touch it.

"If we're going to have this to eat – well, if *I* am - we need to do the job properly," he said, and drew a knife from the folds of his tunic. I looked on, impressed, as he slit the

45

creature's throat with one clean stroke, tipping its head so the blood drained out in a stream. It was a merciful way of killing; unconsciousness was instant. But I knew that this wasn't why Saul insisted on its use. I already knew what he meant when he used the word "properly."

He let me help him skin it, and carve it up for cooking. We built ourselves a campfire and feasted like victorious soldiers in the field. With my mouth full of meat, and fat dripping down my chin, I asked, "Where on earth did you learn to do that?"

"Learn to do what?"

"Slit an animal's throat like that. You didn't even retch. All that blood... you've done that before."

He grinned. "Ner used to bring me all the time. Then Mother found out. I made her swear not to tell *him*. But I had to promise not to do it again."

I tutted, ready to say what I thought, but he hushed me. "Just enjoy your meal, Eliphaz."

And so the months flew by; spring came again to Gibeah, and along with it Passover, the most important festival in Israel's calendar. This was the only family event in which Saul had taken any interest, in the year before we were friends. I had supposed it must be the bustle and bedlam of all the spring cleaning that he enjoyed, or perhaps the huge quantities of special food, most of which he'd made sure I missed out on.

"The meal isn't the main thing, though," he explained, as we loitered in the kitchen hoping for some tasty scraps to whet our appetites. "It's the history that really matters. Celebrating when Moses led us out of Egypt to our freedom."

"Oh, I know what it's about," I said, not relishing the prospect of a lecture just now. Besides, I had always loved the story myself, knowing first-hand what it meant to be a slave. I knew just how the Hebrew captives had felt as they toiled beneath the merciless Egyptian sun, because I had stood by Gibeah's gates with bound wrists, the flies buzzing around my head, my tongue swollen and my mouth parched with dust. I could imagine the excitement they must have felt as they passed on Moses' secret instructions: tonight is the night we make our escape. Don't put yeast in your bread, there's no time to let it rise. Sacrifice your Passover lambs and paint their blood on your doors, so the Angel of Death will see it and pass over your houses when he kills the firstborn sons of your oppressors... No, I certainly didn't need lecturing.

Rachael guessed what we were waiting for, and gave us a piece of piping hot matza each, with a dollop of Passover chutney smeared on the top. I said, "Let's go and get some fresh air - race you!" and we darted from the stuffy kitchen laughing and elbowing and pinching one another, up onto the battlements where a delicious cool breeze took the sting out of the midday heat.

Down below, Gibeah's streets were empty; anyone with sense was snatching a siesta - at least, those who could spare the time away from the cooking and the cleaning. A solitary stranger riding side-saddle on a heavily laden donkey was making slow progress up the hill towards the fortress.

"Who's that?" I asked idly, unintentionally spitting crumbs in Saul's face.

"Pig!" he retorted; then, "How d'you expect me to

47

know?"

"Whoever he is, he's coming here," I said. "Quick, let's get out there before Boaz."

We clattered back down the steps into the courtyard, and dragged the gates open. The stranger dismounted, a swarthy-faced, middle-aged man wearing long striped robes and a rakishly twisted turban. He bowed ostentatiously and asked to see our father.

"*Our* father is out on his estate," answered Saul, giggling, and I laughed too, wondering if he really had taken us for brothers. Then dancing forward excitedly, Saul threw back the cover protecting the stranger's baggage from the elements, and on finding a small wooden harp announced in delight, "A bard!"

"That is certainly one of the titles I have been given." The stranger smiled, an irregular, toothy smile. "There are others, not all so complimentary."

"Come inside," Saul insisted. "We haven't had any musicians pass this way for ages. I'll tell my father to let you stay" - and when the man hesitated - "What I mean is, I'll *ask* him. But you must come in for now. You look tired."

"Well, a little," the stranger admitted. "I've ridden a long way since this morning."

"D'you want something to eat? Mother's baking for Passover."

"Not just now, thank you, not just now. But a cool drink? I could murder a mug of wine."

So the stranger was brought inside, and sat sipping wine by the pool-side, while Boaz tethered the donkey and unpacked its panniers, and Saul and I plied our new friend with questions. He said that his name was Nahum - at least, it was when he was in Israel. In Phoenicia he was known as Naram, and in Greece Nestor; in his line of work, flexibility was essential. We laughed; he told us some jokes he'd collected on his travels, agreed to let Saul try out his harp, and by the time Kish returned at sunset, there could be no question of the bard's not staying the night.

The conversation around the dinner table that evening was naturally a good deal more animated than usual. Nahum had recently come down from the north, where he had sung for the chieftains of Asher and Naphtali, the farthest flung of the Israelite tribes.

"And what about the Philistines?" Saul enquired. "Did you play your harp and sing for them, too?"

"Well, I have done in my time, I do confess it." Nahum grinned, and stroked his beard. "Sometimes one cannot afford to be fussy." He took another draught of Kish's best wine. "Not lately, though. It would give too much offence hereabouts. So many people have lost their land."

"On the coast, you mean?" asked Kish, leaning forward.

"And further inland, up north at least. Plenty of refugees on the roads."

Kish sat back again, frowning distractedly. Rachael said, "Let's have some music, Nahum. There shouldn't be gloomy talk at Passover."

Saul looked disappointed; I think he would have liked to hear more about the Philistines. But he soon cheered up when Nahum began singing, for he alternated his serious ballads with funny ones, so that heroes and jesters seemed to dance side by side. When he had finished, all four of us applauded, and Nahum was invited to stay for the Festival.

"Well, a few days perhaps," he accepted graciously. "But I shall leave before the night of the feast, if you do not mind. It is a family affair. I would not want to intrude."

"Where will you go?" I asked him. "Where's your home?"

"Oh, I am not one for settling down," he smiled. "I shall carry on south, perhaps down to Beer Sheva. I have some long-standing friends down there."

"That's in the desert," I said, suddenly thrilled. "Have you ever been further south still? Have you ever been as far as Amalek?"

Momentarily Nahum's smile wavered. Then he said, "Yes, of course. Many times. I once played my harp for the king down there."

"Maybe I'll pack my bags and come with you next time you go." I winked at Saul, but he had gone unexpectedly quiet and was staring at the floor. I shrugged, and asked Nahum to sing another song.

Noting my interest, he sang of the desert: a weird, haunting melody accompanied by softly stroked chords on the harp that riffled like the wind across the wadis. It was so long since I'd been homesick that I could feel the tears pricking behind my eyes.

Nahum turned out to be a friendly sort; a life on the road had made him easy with strangers. He would chat away nineteen to the dozen with Kish and Rachael about corn prices or the current political climate. But he seemed at his happiest with Saul and me, and when I said so, he agreed: children were his favourites.

"Their minds are not closed to the things of the spirit," he explained, sitting cross-legged on the ground between us, in the welcome shade of the colonnade. "The mysteries of life, its joys and its sorrows; after all, that is the stuff of which the best songs are made."

"The things of the spirit..." Saul mulled the words over, then suddenly bold, he touched the bard's hand. "Is that why you play, to get closer to God? Can you feel his presence? Are you a prophet? A Shining One?"

Nahum ruffled Saul's hair and smiled. "Do I really look like one of those wild-eyed types to you? No, no, young man. I am not so favoured. The Shining Ones really do shine, you know."

"What d'you mean?" Saul pressed him eagerly. "Their faces glow? Like clouds when the sun goes down?"

"In a manner of speaking." Nahum took up his harp and began strumming it absently. "I once met Samuel, the holy man from Shiloh. But he had more in common with a thunderstorm than a sunset."

Saul was staring at him, awe-struck, so I butted in, "You've met someone who knows God, *and* the King of Amalek? You must've been to so many fascinating places! I'd love to spend my days travelling about like that."

"It is a tough existence, unless you were born to it."

"Nahum, how far is it from here to Amalek? How many days would it take you to get there?"

"Amalek again," said Nahum thoughtfully. "You seem to have a rare interest in Amalek. Might I enquire if there is some special reason?"

I could feel myself blushing. "Yes," I confessed. "I was born there. It's where I used to live."

"I thought as much," the bard observed with satisfaction. "I thought you were rather too dark for a Hebrew."

"I'm an Israelite now, though," I corrected him quickly, noticing that Saul's face had fallen again. "I've lived here for two years. I haven't seen Amalek since I was eight."

Nahum smiled again. "That does not make you an Israelite. The Sons of Amalek stay nomads for life. It is in your blood. You cannot change nature."

For some reason these words disturbed me profoundly, though at the time I just shrugged, and we talked of something else. But when darkness fell and Saul was ready for sleep, I said, "You go to bed. I'll be along in a moment," and I went to speak with Nahum alone.

He was in Kish's study, perusing a scroll by soft yellow lamplight, and barely glanced up when I knocked on the open door and walked towards him. He didn't seem at all surprised to see me; it was almost as though he'd expected me to come.

"Nahum," I said. "Can I ask you a question?"

"Of course, young man. Ask away."

"What did you mean, when you said I'm not an Israelite? When you said I'll always be a Son of Amalek?"

Still examining the scroll he said, "You should be proud of your birthright, little friend, deep in your heart. It's no use pretending to yourself to be something you are not."

"But everyone hates Amalekites here," I protested. "And this is where I have to live. I want people to think of me as an Israelite."

At last he looked up. He studied me intently and said, "What you want, and what they will do, are two entirely different things. It is all bound up with their religion, you know. If you are not part of that, then you are not part of them."

"Them?" I repeated. "You mean *you* aren't an Israelite?"

"Just think about it. Have they ever involved you in any of their festivals? Do they insist on your keeping the Sabbath? Stop you eating unclean food? Make you pray three times every day?"

"No, they wouldn't do anything like that," I answered defensively. "They - they respect me. They'd never force me."

"I'm not talking about force," said Nahum gently. "I am talking about invitation. And I should wager your own gods do not mean very much to you any more, so there is not much danger of your being offended. I do not see you wearing your amulet." My hand shot to my neck, and I could feel the colour rising in my cheeks again. When I said nothing, he went on, "Take Passover for example. Did you get to take part in that last year, the service itself, and the meal, I mean?"

"Well - there was a lot of work to do. I'm supposed to be a slave after all. I had to help with the serving."

"It would have made no difference if you were free. Are you invited this year?"

"Well I suppose... I mean, I'm not sure."

"There you are, then. You see, Passover is a big thing with these Hebrews. The great annual affirmation of their unity as a nation. If you are not circumcised, well..."

"Circumcised? What's that?"

"They haven't even told you that?" Nahum chuckled softly into his beard. "Put it this way, that is the reason why

I cannot stay for the Feast."

"You aren't an Israelite?" I asked again.

"My real name is Nahath, my friend. I am an Amalekite too, for my sins. A member of the doomed race. That is why I keep my birth a secret, proud of it as I am. Round here it is better to be a Philistine."

I had to sit down. I perched on the edge of Kish's chair, my mind in ferment. Of course, I should have known he was no Israelite. The way he looked, the whole way he spoke, his too-precise Hebrew. But I'd been too pre-occupied with my own origins to draw any conclusions about his. Eventually I managed to croak, "Doomed race? I don't understand."

"No. I did not expect you would. They are hardly likely to have told you - especially if you do not even know what circumcision is. But every last one of us is destined to die. Adonai has sworn to wipe out our entire people."

I didn't wait to hear any more. I clasped my hands to my ears and ran out into the courtyard. The sky was clear; a myriad stars danced and swirled overhead, and their re-flections in the pool swung dizzily before my eyes. I sat on the wall, desperate to talk to Saul, but sure he would be asleep by now. Besides, he had been so quiet and withdrawn all evening, and I didn't know why. Perhaps he had known all along what the bard was going to tell me. He must have been hiding the truth from me deliberately, and I had been a fool ever to trust him, to trust any of them. My parents had warned me about the Hill Folk all my life, and I had let myself be taken in. They would use me, and when they had no further need of me, they would kill me.

When at last I crept into our bedroom, it must have

been midnight. But the moment I entered, Saul's voice said, "Eliphaz, is that you? Where have you been all this time?"

I said, "I thought you'd be asleep."

"I can't. Have you been talking to Nahum?"

"Yes. Why shouldn't I?"

But Saul didn't reply, and I was still too distressed to pursue the matter. I lay tossing and turning, with Nahum's - Nahath's - words going round and round in my brain.

When I got up next morning Nahum was gone. He had left at dawn, when no one but Boaz was about, and I wondered why. When we had our lesson, things went almost as badly as they used to do when I first came. Saul was sullen and remote, and I couldn't think straight. I don't think I would have paid any attention at all, if we hadn't chanced to be reading a portion of Moses' law concerning the manumission of slaves. It said that after a slave had served his master for seven years, he was to be set free.

I demanded, "Is that still true? Does it still happen?"

Saul said icily, "It only applies to *Israelite* slaves."

I was too agitated to question why he said it. All that struck me was that again it was being stressed to me that I wasn't an Israelite. When Kish chided Saul for being so tactless, he stormed out, slamming the door behind him, and I blurted at Kish, "Why didn't you tell me the truth about the Amalekites?"

"The truth?" Kish seemed genuinely baffled. "What are you talking about?"

"That we're all going to die. Adonai has sworn to destroy us."

Kish opened his eyes very wide. Then he said, "In God's name, Eliphaz, where did you get that from?"

"What does it matter where I got it from? I just want to know if it's true!"

"Eliphaz..."

As soon as Kish held out his arms to embrace me, I knew the answer. Devastated, I let him hold me close, while reluctantly he told me how the liberated Hebrew slaves, on the run from Pharaoh's men, had become lost in the Sinai wilderness, and wandered in circles. How they had made a camp at a place called Rephidim, and then been treacherously and viciously attacked and robbed by rampaging hordes of desert-dwellers. How thousands of Adonai's Chosen People had been left lying dead and wounded, at the mercy of the jackals and the ever-encroaching sand. How Moses had been commanded to wreak vengeance on the raiders; how Joshua had defeated them, but not succeeded in obliterating them. How, many years later, Gideon too had dealt them a bitter blow, but not bitter enough to crush their power for ever. How Adonai had sworn that some day, somehow, Amalek would be utterly annihilated.

I mumbled through my tears, "But it was all so long ago. Why can't it all just be forgotten?"

"Your people still raid our lands, Eliphaz - the lands that Adonai himself promised to us. They still plunder our crops, and graze our pastures to barrenness. They create desert wherever they go."

"No," I objected feebly. "That isn't true. *Your* people steal *our* lands, to build your ugly cities that turn people into prisoners..."

Kish held one finger gently against my lips. "You see, it's true, Eliphaz. We're fighting already. There can be no peace between Hebrew and Amalekite, between settler and nomad, between the Sons of Israel and the Sons of the Desert."

I muttered, "You should have told me before. Why didn't you tell me."

"What good could it have done? We'd bought you from the slave-dealers; it was too late to take you back. We hoped you would never need to know."

"But you ought to have killed me! It says so in your Torah. All of us must die. How could you have disobeyed Adonai's law?"

"Because you were so small, and so afraid, and so homesick." Kish squeezed me closer against himself. "And because Rachael lost her heart to you, and so much wanted another child. And now... Now you're part of our family, Eliphaz. You have helped Saul so much. He loves you like a brother ."

I sniffed bitterly. "I wish you were right."

"About Saul loving you? I'm in no doubt. Or - do you mean about being part of our family?"

"I don't know." Suddenly I felt so confused, so lost. "I did want to be one of you. But now... well, there's no point, is there? It just isn't possible."

"I didn't say that."

"Yes you did. There can never be peace between us. Those were your exact words."

"Eliphaz - I've never said this to you before; it didn't seem right. You were so young and impressionable... but you *can* become one of us. You can eat the Passover with us this week as a Son of Israel."

I pressed my fingers to my temples. "I don't understand. Adonai's law..."

Kish said, "That's not his only law, Eliphaz. There's also the law that we must be kind to the foreigners who live amongst us. And the law that we must accept as one of us whoever turns to our God, as Ruth of Moab did."

"But how?" I whispered. "How can I change what I am?"

"You don't need to change what you are. But you can become part of our covenant, the contract that makes us the people of Adonai. Our b'rit milah."

"B'rit milah..?" So many strange words and thoughts were jangling round my head that I could no longer think at all.

"B'rit milah is the mark of Adonai," said Kish. "The covenant of circumcision. It's the sign by which Abraham was marked out as God's Chosen One, the ancestor of all the Chosen People of the Lord. Amalek, the father of your people, was Abraham's great-great-grandson. If your ancestors hadn't turned away to other gods, you would be circumcised already."

I said without hesitating, "Then I want it. I want it done now."

"You ought not to plunge into this too rashly, Eliphaz. You would have to accept all the teachings of the Torah. It won't be easy. And the making of the mark on your flesh - that will be painful."

"I don't care. I want it. I want to belong."

I suppose I had assumed while I was talking to Kish that Saul would be sulking where he usually did, by the pool-side. But he must have been listening at the door all the time. He threw it open and came at us like a whirlwind.

He grabbed my arms and tried to drag me from Kish's embrace, screaming, "Father, no! You mustn't let him do it! I won't let you!"

"Saul!" Kish managed to seize his son's wrists and pull him away from me. "What is this? What has got into you today? Whatever is wrong?" But Saul's chest was heaving, he was choking on his own breath, and he wasn't listening to a word his father said. I'd had enough; without thinking I turned round and slapped him as hard as I could across the face.

Saul walked backwards into a chair, and sat there staring at me, one hand on his cheek, the other on the chair-arm, white-knuckled and juddering. Kish took his silence for acquiescence, and rising to his feet, said, "Well, Eliphaz, if your mind is made up, I suggest we don't waste any more time. Otherwise fear of the pain might get the better of you."

And so it was done. I will spare you the details of the ritual - though the prayers are beautiful, and Kish was as gentle as only he could be - for the operation is unpleasant, and the agony excruciating. I'm sure it's true when they say it's much worse for a boy than for an eight-day old baby, which is when they make Adonai's mark on their own kind. Afterwards I was too wretched to do anything but go to bed, and lay there hurting and moaning, with Rachael holding my hand and dabbing my forehead with water, as she had been doing when I first laid eyes on her. Saul didn't come near, but to begin with I was in no fit state to care, or even to notice.

If everything had gone as it should, they said I would have been almost myself by the next day. But my skin went red and inflamed round the wound, my body was burning and freezing by turns, and I had to stay in bed four more days. Kish and Rachael were worried, I could tell, and I suppose Kish must have questioned whether he had done the right thing for me. But by the end of the fourth day, the only thing that worried *me* was why Saul hadn't been to see me. He hadn't even come into our room to sleep; he must have taken a mattress up onto the battlements and slept under the stars. Finally, when Rachael stroked the damp greasy hair back from my brow and said, "I wish there was something more I could do," I said, "There is. Please make Saul come in here."

He trailed into the room and sat with his back to me, hanging his head. Without moving - it hurt too much - I said, "I thought it was me who was supposed to need comforting. What's the matter?"

At first he didn't speak. I sighed, knowing I hadn't got the energy to prize it out of him. But eventually he said morosely, "You're going away. I shall be all alone again. I thought I'd start getting used to it now."

"I'm not going anywhere. What on earth is all this about?"

"Don't pretend you don't know. I'm not stupid. You and Nahum hatched this whole thing together. He'll come back for you when you're fifteen and take you home."

"Why when I'm fifteen?"

"Oh Eliphaz, don't play games with me! That's why you wanted to be circumcised. So you could be an *Israelite* slave and be set free after seven years. You don't want to be one of us. You want to leave."

At last I understood. I started laughing - I couldn't

help it, though it made the pain worse; I was just so relieved. "Is that really what you thought?"

"Eliphaz, don't laugh at me. I need you. You're my friend."

Still giggling, I began, "Saul, I'm not laughing *at* you, it's just... well, sometimes I'd like to forget I'm a slave, and not your brother."

I hadn't planned my last four words. They were born on my lips, and I almost gasped at the sound of them, because I didn't know how Saul would react. He regarded me steadily, then he said, "Do you really mean that?"

"Well – of course I mean it."

"Then let's do it, Eliphaz. Let's be brothers."

A chill ran up my spine. I asked, "What do you mean?" but in my heart I already knew. Saul continued to scrutinize my face, and his own was so solemn and grave that I almost wanted to laugh again. Then he took out the knife which he kept inside his tunic, the one he'd used to finish the deer. It was the most exquisite thing you could imagine: bronze, with a blade as bright as a star, and a hilt inlaid with jewels, like the ancient swords of his ancestors, which hung on the dining-room wall. They had been passed down as far as Kish's father; no one used them now.

He said, "If we do this, we'll be brothers for ever. What d'you say?"

His eyes glittered, twin flames in the half-light, and as he looked at me they seemed to penetrate right into the core of my being. I didn't know what to say. Back home in Amalek I knew there were boys who had cut themselves and shared blood like this, but usually they'd been drunk and laughing. Saul still looked so serious I felt awkward. I hesitated, and his voice, dismal and shaky, broke the silence.

"You don't want to, do you." He drew back a little. "Perhaps we should wait till you're better. Perhaps you've seen enough of your own blood."

He looked so dejected then, I could have cursed myself. Without speaking, I thrust my wrist out towards him, my eyes screwed shut, waiting for the pain. Again his voice broke in on my thoughts.

"You have to promise first."

"Promise? Promise what?" I swallowed hard, but my mouth was dry and there was no saliva to swallow with. I wished he would stop dallying and do the deed quickly.

"That you'll always stand up for me, and never see me hurt, and you'll never lie to me, or keep secrets from me, or betray me, as long as you live."

"Oh shut up, Saul," I interrupted him, stifling the giggle of embarrassment I felt rising in my throat. "Of course I promise."

"And I promise the same to you."

Then I did feel the cold metal against my flesh, but the cut was small and neat and it barely hurt. Then he pressed his own pierced flesh against mine, and I felt the throb of his pulse, strong but too fast. The people of Israel believe that the life force of a creature is in its blood, and they are right, for I'm convinced that in the moment when ours mingled, our fates became one. I no longer wanted to laugh.

"Now we really are brothers," Saul announced with satisfaction. "You're not Eliphaz the Amalekite any more. You're not even going to be Eliphaz, not to me. I'm going to call you Eli. It'll be our secret name for you."

"Eli?"

"Eliphaz sounds so foreign. But Eli is a true Israelite name. It's the name of the priest at the sanctuary at Shiloh, the holiest place among my - our - people. The place where Samuel the Shining One serves the Lord, and the place of Adonai's presence." Then his eyes flicked down to the little jewelled knife, which he was still clutching between his bloodstained fingers. Slowly he held it out towards me. He said, "And I want you to have this. It was my grandfather's. Go on, take it. It's yours."

I shook my head vehemently. "Don't be stupid, Saul. It belongs in your family. It must be worth a fortune."

"No, I mean it. I want you to have it. You *are* family now." And when I still didn't move, he leaned forward and pressed it into my hand, curling my fingers around it.

I sank back onto my pillows, staring at the treasure I was holding, thinking it was just about the only thing in the world I could rightly say was mine. Absorbed in my own thoughts, I barely heard what Saul was saying to me.

"... And you mustn't tell anyone what we've done, Eli. My parents especially. It's not something which people like them would ever do, and no one would understand. It's our secret, like your new name. Will you keep it?"

My eyes wandered, from the little knife to the thin red slit in my flesh, then up into Saul's earnest face. "Of course I will."

"Then we'll be together for ever, Eli. You'll see."

CHAPTER 4

I was so insanely happy that night, I found myself unable to believe how Saul couldn't think that all this was enough. After what I'd been through, to be loved, to be accepted, to belong to a people chosen by the living God, seemed to me to be all that anyone could ever need or want. Yet it became increasingly clear to me that Saul craved more. He spent as much time as ever moping and brooding when left to his own devices. It started to niggle me that the answers I had found were merely the roots of questions to him. But although I longed to talk it through, whenever he got that look on his face there was a distance around him that set him apart and made me scared to intrude.

By now it was approaching the hottest part of the year. The fields had turned yellow, and our herdsmen were beginning to have trouble finding enough pasture for the flocks. Sometimes Saul and I would ease their burden by taking some of the sheep off their hands and heading into the hill-country for the day, having to range further and further afield as the season wore on.

I remember there was one particular day that summer which was hotter even than the rest. It was still and silent and sultry. The sun hung heavy and torrid in a thick blue sky, the full-grown corn stood motionless, even the rattling whisper of the silver olive leaves was peculiarly hushed. Saul and I had taken two score of the younger ewes and this year's lambs, and gone up through the forested hills to the south, and beyond, where there was little but rocks and patches of prickly grass. We had walked a long way, and by the time we reached a place with enough green for grazing, the sun was almost at its peak, and we were sticky with sweat. The trees had petered out and we found what shade we could amongst the boulders. Here we took turns guarding the sheep and dozing. I watched first while Saul closed his eyes and was asleep almost at once, his dark curly head drooping on his chest. But the fierce brightness of the sun, the shimmering heat, and the low hum of insects soon had me drowsy. Twice I caught myself drifting off, and nipped myself awake when I saw that Saul still slept. But the third time I was too far gone to rouse myself, and it must have been a good while later when I blinked, panicked and sat bolt upright. I looked round urgently to see where the sheep had got to, and found myself instinctively counting heads. But all of them were there, nibbling away contentedly, and Saul was carving his name on one of the boulders.

He must have been awake for some time - and I must have been pretty well dead to the world - because he had reached the 'n' in Saul ben Kish. His hammer was a rock, but the chisel he carried around with him inside his tunic, along with a new dagger and a handful of spare arrowheads. He was crouching bare-headed in the full heat of noon; it was a miracle he hadn't passed out with sunstroke. But he was utterly engrossed, lost to his surroundings, and it didn't even register when I knelt down right beside him. I examined the letters, each so accurate and regular; you would have thought he was carving a tombstone for a king, not idling away his time while he waited for me to wake.

I said, "I'm sorry, Saul. I must've gone to sleep. I didn't mean to," but he took no notice, just went on working, biting his tongue between his teeth in fierce concentration. I heaved a long-suffering sigh, and leaned back against my boulder, deciding I had better keep my eyes on the sheep.

But he didn't leave off when he reached the 'sh'. He went on to add his clan, and the name of his tribe, and I was quietly going frantic whilst the sun progressed inexorably across the sky, and some of the lambs began to stray so I had to keep retrieving them. Eventually I said, "Saul? Don't you think it's boiling out here? Isn't your head splitting? Mine's on fire! Let's go home."

"You can go. I want to finish this first."

"Saul, you are impossible sometimes! You must've carved your name on a hundred boulders and trees already. Leave it, and let's get moving."

"But I've nearly done it. Besides..." - he rocked back on his haunches and surveyed his handiwork appraisingly - "I've never done it as well as this before. Look how neat it is."

"Yes," I said drily, "It's lovely. Anyone would think

you wanted it to last for ever."

"But I do," Saul insisted. "That's the whole point. I want to be able to come and see it still here when I'm an old man. I want my children and their children to be able to come and see it. Then they'll be able to remember who I was."

"Saul," I announced, "You're crazy."

"No I'm not. I'm not at all." He put the finishing touch to the second 'n' of 'Benjamin' and blew the dust out of the grooves. "Don't you want to leave something behind you when you've gone?"

I shrugged. "I don't suppose I'll mind. I mean, when I'm dead I won't care much about it, will I?"

"But doesn't that bother you? All the years you've lived, everything you've done... and it will all be gone for ever, just like that? All your precious memories and the things you spent years learning? Just think - you could die tomorrow, and you'd probably be forgotten by this time next year."

"Oh, thanks!" I retorted. "You mean, you wouldn't even come and put some flowers on my grave? You wouldn't light a candle for me or say the Kaddish?"

Saul dismissed my indignation with a careless wave. "Well, *I* might, yes. But suppose I died too? *And* my mother and father? Suppose we all died of something together?"

"Saul, this is getting really morbid. Can we go home now?"

"No, it's not getting morbid." Saul cleaned off his chisel and put it away. "It's just getting interesting. And you're always saying you want me to talk to you more, about things that matter. I mean - my father's the most important man in Gibeah, right? He's the richest man in the town, and its overseer, and an elder in the tribe, but when he dies it won't be fifty years before they forget him - it'll be as though he never lived at all. Well, I don't want to be forgotten. I want to do something great, so everyone remembers me."

"Look who's talking," I snorted. "The spoilsport who wouldn't even go in for Ner's competition and win himself a name for one day."

"Eli, sometimes you don't even try to understand." Saul sat down sulkily, his knees drawn up to his chest, his jaw set in vexation. "I mean - I wonder what you'd have to do, to *really* gain a reputation for yourself? I suppose you'd have to win some great battle, like Joshua at Jericho, or rescue a whole nation from captivity, like Moses. *I'd* like to rescue Israel from the Philistines. We could make a vow to give our lives in the service of our country, Eli."

I sniggered. "What's the point? If you gave your life, you wouldn't be around to see if you got a great reputation or not."

Saul's eyes spat fire at me. "Can't you take *anything* seriously? All you ever do is make fun of what I say. Anyhow..." - and he arched his brows in a look of withering contempt - "you can't *prove* I won't be around to know. Maybe our souls live on when we die. I've heard that some prophets have said so before now. If they're right, then it wouldn't be as bad somehow. Things wouldn't seem so stupid and meaningless, if we could go on living for ever with God. Maybe we could look down out of the clouds and watch what's happening."

"Or up from Sheol," I pointed out. "I never heard

anyone say we go up to the sky when we die. I thought we all just wafted around like ghosts, under the earth."

"That's what annoys me, though, Eli. That's what I can't accept."

"What? What's what you can't accept?"

"The way we don't know *anything* for certain. I mean - there's nothing about these things in Moses' teachings. I've looked. He doesn't tell us what happens when we die, like if we all go to the same place, however good or bad we've been."

"How could he tell us? He wouldn't have known himself."

"But he talked to *God*, Eli! Moses was a Shining One. Don't you think he asked God about that sort of thing? Because I would. If I met God, that would be the first thing I'd ask him."

"I wouldn't. I'd ask him for a thousand gold pieces."

"Well that just shows how childish you are." Saul hunched his shoulders gloomily, then noticed my grin, and grudgingly returned it. But almost at once he was frowning again. "Don't you ever think about *anything* that's really important, Eli? Don't you ever stop to think there must be - more?"

"More what? If you mean more gold pieces..."

"Will you stop blabbing about gold pieces? I mean more to *life*, you idiot, more to God. More than just learning stories and believing what your parents tell you."

"Well - I don't know," I said vaguely, and I thought, I can scarcely even *remember* what my parents told me. And I have learnt so much lately, if there *is* any 'more', well I don't think I could cope with it. Saul was studying my face from beneath his still furrowed brow, then his eyes drifted past me and I decided he had given me up as a lost cause. But all at once he seemed to change his mind again, and goaded by some surge of inspiration he leapt to his feet and grabbed me by the cloak-pins.

"Just think for one *second*, Eli. If Adonai lives, why can't we see him? Why can't we all talk to him, like Moses did? Why shouldn't we *know* him, *feel* him? The Earth Folk, for example; *they* feel *their* gods, I know they do. We should have *more* than them, not less."

"The Earth Folk? Whatever are you going on about now?"

"The Canaanites, of course." Saul flung back his hair and shook my shoulders impulsively. "The people who came to dwell in our place, and worked the land while our ancestors were in Egypt. They feel something. I know they do, although they do evil and their gods are idols. Uncle Ner has told me. He's seen their rites, he's even taken part, though Adonai's law forbids it. They go into trances and the spirits enter them. But if Adonai is alive, we *must* be able to reach him. He acted in the past. Why not now?"

I was beginning to catch his meaning, and the germ of his excitement. I ventured, "But have you really made an effort to - well, to get through to him? Have you any idea how to set about doing it?"

"That's just it, Eli." He ground his teeth in frustration. "I reckon I've tried everything. I've prayed and prayed till my knees were raw, I've played my harp and waited, I've made every kind of offering, but still I don't hear anything. And I know in my heart that sacrifice means nothing to him, it's not what he really desires. He wants obedience."

"But you do obey him. You follow all his laws, I've watched you. Shouldn't that make you happy enough?"

"No, Eli, it doesn't!" He seized my hand and hauled me to my feet, pointing at the sleepy grey-gold hills and valleys spread before us, dipping away into the smudged blue distance. "Don't you wonder what all this is for? What life is, what death is, why we struggle for survival day after day, only to return to the dust that we came from? Don't you want to know what it means, to feel the power of the One who made it?"

I didn't reply; there didn't seem to be much I could say. Then suddenly he squeezed my hand tighter, and said, "Come with me, Eli. I want to show you something. Then you'll see what I'm saying."

I began to protest, but he was already dragging me after him, back along the track the way we had come. He seemed to have forgotten about the sheep, and indeed about everything except what was making him so excited. I was almost running to keep up with him, as we headed back towards the woods we had passed through to get here. Only now Saul had abandoned the familiar road and was forging upwards on a narrow, overgrown path bordered first by stunted shrubs, then by oaks and cypresses. By the time we drew near to the summit of the hill, the woodland had turned to forest. The trees grew closer and the undergrowth sparser; it was dark, and despite the weather I began to feel cold and uneasy. The great trunks towered higher and closed in over our heads. Again I demanded to know where we were going, but Saul said nothing, plunging heedlessly onward though I was short-winded and cursing. Then all at once the path levelled out; the trees thinned and I held my breath.

In the clearing before us stood the collapsed, weed-choked remains of some kind of sanctuary. It was on the very peak of the hill, though there was no view because of the trees crowding all around, and the place must have been entirely invisible from everywhere below. We were standing on the grassy edge of an ancient courtyard, its pavement now uneven and fingered with crevices, spiny brambles growing up between its sunken flagstones. On the far side was what must once have been the shrine, but its roof had fallen, and grey tinder-dry bushes grew spikily from its walls. A great standing-stone reared up in its shadow, and across its threshold lay a tumbled wooden pole, the shattered foot of which still stood stubbornly upright in the ground. In front of this was the massive stone altar, worn and cracked, with the dark red stain of centuries' blood ingrained down its side. The eroded sherds of cups and libation-bowls lay strewn around its base, and behind it, leaning drunkenly, sat the blackened, timeworn figure of some age-old god or goddess, its harsh lines softened by the years, its features eaten away, but still staring balefully with its eyeless sockets. The whole place smelt dank and fetid and full of ghosts. Although the day itself was unusually soundless, the silence here was deeper, uncanny, and it made my skin crawl.

I whispered hoarsely, "Saul, I don't like it here. Let's go."

"There," he said with satisfaction. "You can feel it, can't you. The Old Religion. It's very strong here."

"I can feel evil," I said. "And I don't like it. Please -

let's go back to the sheep. Your father will kill us if we lose any of them."

"Don't make excuses, Eli. You wanted to understand."

I watched in horror as Saul began to walk across the lichen-blotched flagstones towards the shrine. He couldn't resist flaunting his fearlessness, but I couldn't bring myself to follow. I shuddered again as he ran his fingers around the belly of the standing stone, and I panicked inexplicably as he slipped out of sight behind it, then reappeared pert, brazen and smiling. I wanted to grab him and run, for I knew he was taunting me now, and that made me angry. But I noticed that he wouldn't go into the shrine. Finally he came walking back towards me grinning rakishly, and took my arm.

"Do you know what this place is?"

I shook my head, not knowing, and caring less.

"It's a temple of the Dark Gods of the Earth Folk; one of their High Places. They say Joshua destroyed it when our forefathers returned from Egypt. Uncle Ner brought me here once; there aren't many people now who know where to find it. But some still come. They still worship the Mother, and her lover who dies and is reborn each year to make the crops grow. And they still pour blood on the altar. You can smell it."

I stared. "Who? Who comes here?"

"Oh, the Earth Folk who remain. Who knows how many are left? And traitors to Adonai."

"What? Some of your - of our own people?"

"There will always be rebels," he said. "Some of our people still think of Adonai as the god who led us out of

73

Egypt, and then gave up on us: that here in Canaan the Earth Gods still reign. But can't you sense it? The silence, the prayers, the shades of the victims? It's all still here."

I nodded feebly. Yes, the place was full of gods; their eyes were everywhere. Saul scanned my face again, trying to read my thoughts. Then he said softly, "They come here because they need it, Eli. We all need it. We all need to feel the divine in us. Don't you see? It will only be when we experience Adonai like this that these evil places will disappear. The idols, the human sacrifices, the magicians and mediums - they poison our land. But you can't destroy them and put nothing in their place."

"No." I looked around at the dreary secret world where no tree rustled and no bird sang, feeling the hairs on the back of my neck prickling and a heaviness pressing down on me, like the weight of a great stone on my head. For the first time I wondered if I should have got circumcised at all. But Saul was in no hurry to leave.

"It's like the widow-woman they say lives in the wood outside Gibeah," he said, and he still kept hold of my arm. I think he was aware that I was itching to run. "She tells the future by consulting the spirits of the dead. She ought to be stoned, by the laws of Adonai, but they don't do it, and it's not out of pity. It's because they need her magic as much as she needs their money. They can't hear Adonai, so they listen to her."

I said tetchily, "But some people do still hear Adonai. What about Samuel, the holy man from Shiloh. Nahum seemed to think *he* knows God. What can a man like him have got, that we haven't?"

Saul pouted. "I wish I knew. I did ask my father,

once."

"And what did he say?"

"He says Samuel's someone really important, the most influential man in Israel. He acts as adviser to the leaders of the tribes, and whatever he says, goes. But Father doesn't seem to know how he came to be in that position. He seems to think Adonai called Samuel in person, when he was only a boy, maybe not even as old as us."

"And that's what you hope he'll do one day for you?"

"I don't know, Eli." Saul's brash sauciness had vanished; he looked suddenly as dismal as the forest that surrounded us. I tried again to coax him to come back with me down into the valley, but he had gone all distant and disconsolate and dreamy. He sat down among the thistles at the edge of the pavement, his head between his knees, his arms wrapped around them. "Sometimes that's what I think I want. But other times it scares me out of my wits. There are some days when - and for God's sake don't laugh, Eli - there are some days when I can honestly see myself as Adonai's champion, rooting out idolaters, brandishing a great sword and driving the Philistines howling back into their boats. Then there are other days - I could just crawl into a hole and die. Everything seems so futile, and I feel so small inside."

He looked up, then, and his eyes were almost moist. "Maybe one day it'll all work out," he said. "Perhaps one day everyone *will* be able to know Adonai if they want to. Some of the prophets have foretold it. But when will it happen? How long can we stand this suspense?" He threw back his head, sucked in a huge breath as though he could absorb the numinous through his lungs. "Don't you see? I want this, I need it. The atmosphere here, the way you can just wallow in the otherness of it all... But I want it from Adonai, the God of my people. I want to feel him in my veins, in my blood! Can't you see what I mean yet?"

"I can see, Saul."

I could see - but I could bear it no longer. The sickening tide of foreboding welled up inside me once more, and when I looked at Saul, with his eyes closed and face tilted up towards the sky, he seemed more of a stranger than ever. Without waiting for him, and no longer much caring whether he followed me or not, I spun round and made off headlong down the hill, crashing wildly through the trees and the tangled undergrowth, running like one possessed, not noticing when I tripped over roots, not stopping to brush away the creepers that caught around my face. I hugged myself miserably as I lurched on, and wished I had my winter cloak, for absurdly I was shivering and my sweat was cold. I don't know how I didn't get lost, for the forest was dense and mocking on every side and I was too scared to look where I was going. The hollow staring eye-holes of the hideous idol haunted me, and Saul's rapt face, drinking in the mystery I feared.

Somehow I made it back to the rocky outcrop where we had sat resting, and I flung myself panting on the ground, dimly aware that the sheep weren't where we'd left them.

When at last I lifted my head, Saul was standing beside me, smiling faintly as he admired the inscription he had cut into the rock, and Kish's sheep grazed on unconcerned at his feet.

CHAPTER 5

When Saul and I were thirteen years old, our childhood ended. It died in a single week, and four years of peace, growth and innocence passed with it.

Summer was gone, the first rains came, and the world hardened itself for winter. It was Sabbath Eve; dusk had fallen, and Rachael had lit the candles to welcome the day of rest. But they gave little cheer in the thickening darkness, and their fragile flames flickered and guttered as the chill murmur of the wind soughed at the doorway, and breathed damp draughts around our necks. Saul and I sat gloomy, having been kept indoors all day by the weather, but we were impatient to eat, for the cold had sharpened our hunger. Boaz had already brought an earthenware pot of stew to the table, where it stood sizzling and steaming and making our mouths water. But Kish hadn't come home, and Rachael looked fretful.

"I'm starving! Where's he got to?" Saul complained irritably.

Rachael scraped a stray lock of hair from her brow. "I haven't seen him since early this morning. He went off with your uncle Ner and some of his heavyweights from town. They said there was some trouble, but no one seemed to know what or where."

"Probably nomads raiding the fields again," Saul said airily, with a wink in my direction. He knew that such remarks no longer unsettled me.

"Or some hired men claiming that you didn't work out their wages right," I teased back. But I could see that our light-hearted banter was getting on Rachael's frayed nerves, and she snapped at us.

"He's never late back, not when it's Shabbat. Something is very wrong. I know it is."

Saul and I exchanged suitably cowed glances, then we all jumped, and smiled as we heard the familiar creak of the fortress gates opening, and then banging shut with the force of their own weight. Rachael gave a relieved sigh, but then caught her breath again, for the heavy oaken bar was being drawn across them; and finally the bronze bolts were dropped into place. In all the time I'd been at Gibeah, I had never known the bolts to be fastened. Then we heard Kish's footsteps crossing the courtyard.

He came in looking as weary as a man twice his age. Without even shedding his rain-sodden cloak he eased himself down onto a couch as though every bone ached, and his face was lined and haggard.

"Adonai have mercy," said Rachael. "What has happened? Is someone dead?"

"No one is dead, my dear. Everything is fine."

This was so obviously untrue that none of us

bothered to contradict him. Then Rachael said, "Saul, Eliphaz, go to your room please."

Saul began to protest, saying it wasn't fair, we hadn't done anything, and if something was wrong we needed to know, but Rachael turned imploringly towards her husband, and he barked, "Saul, you heard your mother. Do as you're told."

Saul still didn't look much like obeying, so I took hold of his hand and propelled him out of the dining-room. With Kish and Rachael so ill at ease, the last thing I wanted was an ugly scene. But as soon as we were outside in the colonnade he twisted out of my grasp and flattened himself against the door post to listen. When I made as if to leave him to it, he seized my wrist and pulled me back into the shadows beside him. I could smell his anger.

"The Philistines have reached Gibeah," Kish was saying.

"What - their whole army? Just like that, without any warning?"

"No, of course not their whole army, Rachael. Do think before you speak. A small detachment, maybe a couple of hundred or so. They're building some kind of camp up on the hill just outside town. We've been observing them all day."

"Are you sure they were Philistines? Might they not have been bandits, or Earth Folk, an independent group of some kind?"

"Ner knows a Philistine when he sees one, even if he doesn't know much else. But if this is just an advance-party, the rest can't be far behind. We're in big trouble, Rachael. There's no doubt about that."

"But what can we do?" The pitch of Rachael's voice was rising, and her agitation was sorely trying Kish's patience. "Is there time to get away? We could take the boys and go up north to your brother Zeror in Jabesh. We're bound to be safe from them there."

"Don't be foolish, woman. The Philistines have been causing trouble in the north for months. In any case a man in my position can't just turn tail and run. Gibeah's people will expect a lead from me - and rightly so."

"But you can't bear a burden like that on your own shoulders! Surely direction should come from the council of tribe-leaders? There should be a co-ordinated plan, each town ought not to have to fend for itself like this. No wonder the Philistines have managed to pick off so many of our settlements one by one."

"Exactly." I heard Kish's fist thump down on the table. "But since when has the Tribal Council ever decided *anything* worth while? Not even Samuel can get them to forget their petty rivalries. If he can't unite Israel's factions, with *his* charisma, who can? In any case - the temperature's getting pretty hot out there among Gibeah's menfolk. They won't be content to wait for bureaucracy."

"What do you mean?" Rachael's voice had shrunk to little more than a whimper. "Surely none of them would risk going out there and attacking this - this camp, without authorization? Surely they would never do a thing like that unless it were under your auspices?"

"Rachael, they know perfectly well that I have no intention of leading anyone into battle. But they may not wait for me, either. There is always Ner for them to turn to, and he'll make the most of his opportunity, believe me. He's already talking about organizing resistance, though he must know it's futile. The Sea Peoples have horses and chariots and iron weapons. No one in Israel knows the art of taming horses; and few men in Gibeah possess even a bronze sword, let alone an iron one."

Momentarily they fell silent, which was when I realized that Saul was still seething with ineptly smothered rage. I glared at him, with one finger to my lips, but his passion was beginning to boil over. "It's *not* fair!" he hissed at me. "Why do they try to keep us in the dark like this? Do they think we're still babies? They want to cocoon us in this place like they cocoon themselves... Why won't he stand up and fight like a man?"

But there were voices coming from inside the room again; I clamped my hand over Saul's mouth and temporarily he gave way to me. "What do we tell Saul?" Rachael was whining. "And Eliphaz too, for that matter? They're bound to realize something is going on, and start asking awkward questions."

"We mustn't allow them out of the fortress for the time being, that's for sure. It's far too dangerous. We could tell them an infection has broken out in the town, and we must stay inside to avoid contact with it."

Of course, this pushed Saul right over the edge. I cringed as he threw the door open and burst back into the room. "You mean, you're going to lie to us! You're going to hide the truth from your own son!" he was shrieking. "Well I've had enough, do you hear me? I won't be treated like a child any more!"

He was met by a stunned silence; not surprisingly. I slid my way around the doorpost, hoping no one would notice me, and indeed they didn't. Rachael was staring at Saul as though he were a total stranger, but I was alarmed to see that Kish was on his feet, shaking with fury.

"Saul, I told you to go to your room! How dare you disobey me! Get out, before I throw you out."

"No, I won't get out! Just how long is this going to go on? Are you going to keep sending me to my room until my hair is grey? Because soon I won't have a room to go to! The Philistines will march into Gibeah and take this fortress, and *you* won't lift a finger to defend it! You're an old woman, Kish ben Abiel, that's what you are. An old woman!"

"How dare you talk to your father like that! You insolent brat, how dare you!" Kish thundered, his face turning crimson and his veins bulging.

"Because I'm ashamed of you, that's how I dare! Sometimes I can't even believe that you *are* my father. You're a coward, and a disgrace to Adonai."

"Oh yes? And you think that making vows before Adonai and then trampling all over them is somehow more honourable? You think that would increase my standing in his sight? You are an expert on all matters of religion now, are you? You'd do well to learn the fifth commandment!"

"Vow? What vow? I don't even know what you're talking about!"

For an eternity Kish didn't reply. At first I thought he had calmed down; the colour had ebbed from his face and he was no longer shaking. Then I realized he was now as white as a leper, and the leper's cloud of despair had settled over him. He knew he had said what he had never wanted to say, and now it was too late to take it back.

Rachael said, "You don't have to tell him, Kish," but he gave no sign of having heard her. He just looked ill. A gust of wind made the candles sputter, and one of them went out. Kish stared at the place where the flame had been, and when he spoke, his voice seemed to come from another world.

"I made a vow to Adonai when I was younger than you are. I was ten years old, my brother Nathan was seven. Your grandfather had taken us out hunting. My spear was well-aimed but Nathan ran in its path. One moment he was laughing. The next..."

Of course, there was no need for him to carry on. Everything at once became so clear that the intensity of it stung the backs of my eyes. Saul repeated mechanically, several times, "You should have told me. You should have told me. Why have you never told me?" Then he screamed with all the breath in his lungs, "In God's name why didn't you tell me!" - and fled.

The first half of the following week was hell. The five of us remained cooped up inside the fortress, hiding from one another as much as from the threat lurking outside. Saul and I spent most of our time up on the battlements watching for developments, but there was nothing to see. We barely spoke. I knew that Saul should apologize, and he knew what I thought, but he was too distressed to do it. Kish had withdrawn into a silent shell, and I found I was seeing shades of Saul in him which I'd never suspected were there.

On the fifth day of our self-imposed siege, Ner arrived at the fortress with a deputation of six Gibeah householders, demanding to know what our illustrious overseer proposed to do about the Philistine presence. Apparently the camp had been completed and fortified, with a solid stone wall and wooden stockade, and a second batch of troops had turned up to occupy it. They weren't all soldiers, though. There were women and children among them, and even a few sheep and goats. We learned these things by pestering Ner, while Rachael went to fetch Kish; Ner explained to us how all this must mean that the Philistines were intending to plant a permanent domestic settlement here, rather than simply a military base.

"What will that mean?" I asked. "Is it better or worse?"

"Well, it explains why they haven't moved to attack us," Ner replied. "But confrontation must take place sooner or later. They will need land to grow crops, and pasture to graze their animals - that's if they have enough livestock already, without purloining some of ours. They'll have to support themselves somehow or other."

At this point Rachael reappeared. She said that Kish was sick, and was not prepared to see anyone.

"Typical," snorted Ner. "That's just typical. And what does he expect *us* to do, meanwhile? Languish on our backs and wait to be enslaved, like *he* obviously intends to do?"

Rachael said, "I'm sorry, Ner. He's not himself. You should do whatever you think is right."

For a moment Ner appeared taken aback, then he squared his great shoulders, saying, "I shall do just that," and the seven of them left.

I whispered to Saul, "What *will* he do?"

"Train up the men and youths for battle. Post spies

to watch what the Philistines are up to. That's what I'd do, anyway. If I was ever allowed to do *anything*."

For a moment I said nothing. I was too busy thinking. Then I asked, "But what *will* you do? What will *we* do?"

Saul peered at me curiously. Then he saw what I meant. Kish was in no shape at present to make our decisions for us. We were thirteen years old, the age when they say you become a Son of the Torah, and for the first time in our lives we were confronted with the freedom that turns boys into men: the freedom to choose our own course of action. And there was so little now to stop us unbolting the gates and just walking right out into Gibeah's streets with our spears and our shields, and our swords in our hands.

So that was what we did, though not until next morning. It took us that much time to pluck up courage, to quell our scruples, and to come to terms with the tacet shift in our status. We put on our finest tunics - mine was scarlet, Saul's pure white - and Rachael made no attempt to stall us when we collected our equipment. We each had our own weapons now, for Saul had passed down his child's set to Abner, Ner's son, and Ner had seen to it that when he got his nephew new ones, I got some too. We buckled our swords to our belts, and our shields to our backs, held the smooth, sleek shafts of our spears in our hands, and embraced, high on the thrill of nervous exhilaration. I felt inside my tunic, checking for the little jewelled knife Saul had given me, though I knew already that it was there. As we marched out of the fortress and down the hill through the town, our bronze spear-heads glinting in the pale morning sunshine, we must have looked like callow boys, but we felt like warriors.

Ner's house lay on the far side of town, built into its walls. It was a relatively substantial residence, with several rooms arranged about a central courtyard, and here we found Ner himself surrounded, as he so often was, by a good portion of the manhood of Gibeah. Many of the youths were no older than Saul and me, and a couple were younger, Abner being one of them. He grinned when he saw us, and beckoned us over. He was as stocky and sturdy as ever, but a good deal taller now - taller than me, in fact, though Saul could still give him almost half a span. He greeted us warmly, with his father's ebullience, and Saul smiled briefly, then lounged against the yard wall watching the action. Each man or boy had a weapon, whatever he could find, from bows and arrows, spears and swords to slings and makeshift wooden clubs. Everyone was practising for all he was worth - sparring, dodging, slicing, throwing; and it felt so much better to be here among those with a purpose, than fretting away at home.

At this point, Ner himself spotted us and came over.

"Saul, Eliphaz - good. We need every fighter we can get. I see you have your spears; there are targets over there. Practise your aim until you hit every time. We can't afford to waste precious weapons on lax shots."

It was sobering yet reassuring to see Ner so grave. At once we set to rehearsing and polishing our technique - casting and fetching, casting and fetching, until our arms ached with the strain of it. My own skill was easily a match for anyone else already present, and I was quietly glad of the hours Saul had spent showing me the ropes, for the approving looks I sensed at my back felt good, and I basked in them without shame.

But Saul was unrivalled. Standing poised for the throw, with his white tunic twisted up into his belt, his long legs apart and firm-rooted, his back straight, spear-arm flexed and the other stretched out in perfect balance, he looked like a Cretan prince on a trader's pot. And as he pitched forward, tossing his curls from his eyes, his spear would sing as it flew, as though it took joy from being handled by a master. Each time he threw, he would step back an extra pace from the target, and each time his aim was flawless. I couldn't help smiling when I recalled his groundless fears about taking part in Ner's contest. And I couldn't help overhearing the hushed murmurs as men turned to watch, the voices whispering, some of them asking who the boy's father was, and exclaiming in astonishment when they were told. Once I looked up, to see one of Abner's sisters ogling at Saul from an open lattice window. When she caught my eye her face went pink, but she didn't stop staring. I wondered if Saul would ever have acquired such skill and composure if he hadn't had to get them in defiance of Kish.

There was sword-work too - Ner had some weapons with blunted blades for practice, but even they can do damage, and one or two men went home branded with their own blood before we so much as laid eyes on a Philistine. I got a shallow gash in my arm, nothing to bother about; Saul remained unscathed. All day we trained - our limbs were sore and our bellies grumbled - but only when the daylight failed did the men start to disperse. I collected my things and prepared to leave, but Saul put his hand on my arm.

"No, Eli. Wait. If we go home tonight, we won't get out again so easily tomorrow. Mother will be quicker off the mark once she realizes what we've been doing. Why don't we stay the night with Uncle Ner?"

"You're welcome to stay," Ner shouted across. "But I'm taking over the watch later on, outside the enemy camp. So if you want to be with me, I'm afraid you'll be sleeping rough."

"Saul," I hissed, "That's going *too* far. Suppose something goes wrong? It's not fair on your parents, they'll be beside themselves. Anyhow " - and I lowered my voice further - "I still think..."

"... I need to apologize to my father."

"It would help him, Saul. I'm sure it would."

He must have reached the same conclusion himself, however reluctantly, during the course of the day, because he didn't take much persuading. But walking home through the dusk-shrouded streets, we caught wind of a disturbance coming from the direction of the market-place. It was the screams we heard first: female screams, so that to begin with we supposed that some poor woman had been set upon by robbers. Then the shouting: some male voices, but women's and children's too. Saul and I exchanged glances, then the temptation to go and see what the trouble was overpowered all of our noble intentions.

They had her bound to a post in the middle of the square, near enough to the very spot where I had once stood bound myself. For that reason alone my heart would have gone out to her. But in addition, she was clearly in the most acute physical agony. Splintered stones lay scattered around her feet, which were stained dark brown with dust and blood. Her face and arms were bruised raw, here and there the flesh was punctured, and tears of gore dribbled through the grime. Her hair hung loose and torn, and someone had yanked at the neck of her dress so that it fell about her waist, and there was blood on her breasts. By the time I had taken in what was happening, she was no longer screaming.

I was shocked to the root of my being, and shaking inside like grass in the wind. When Saul whispered, "It's her, Eli, it's her!" I neither knew nor cared who he meant. The stones were still flying, though they were plainly super-fluous, and the crowd was still howling, "Death to the sorceress!" "Scourge of Israel!" "Your blood be on your own head, your witchcraft has brought the heathen to our doors!" Then I realized that I did know who the woman was, for Saul had spoken of her on the day when he had taken me to the heathen High Place. But I could no longer look at her; I felt to be intruding on her nakedness and degradation. So I looked at Saul, but that was worse, for mixed up with the horror inscribed across his features was awe, and something hideously close to approval. Then instinctively I caught hold of his wrist, for bearing down on us from the opposite side of the square was Rachael.

I don't know to this day whether she had known what was going on, or if she was out looking for us. But as soon as Saul saw her, and the fear-honed resolve on her face, he abandoned all thought of going back home. I'm in no doubt that she saw us, fleeing for refuge in the warren of darkening alley-ways; she must have known that we were running from her, and exactly where we were going. I'm also sure that she didn't try to follow us. We arrived back at

Ner's breathless and trembling: Saul with excitement and the joy of rebellion, me with the trauma of what we had witnessed. But there was no time to talk it through now, for everything was suddenly happening at once. Ner said, "Come along, it's time for our watch," and before we'd even got inside the house, we found ourselves on the road out of Gibeah.

It was too late now to question what we'd let ourselves in for. My mind could no more keep pace with my body - I was numb from the nose up, and the rest of me felt ill. Ner strode along with an air of grim determination; Saul was floating on a cloud of eager expectancy; Abner was running to catch up, bringing each of us warm cloaks and food. We passed through the town gates and out into the fields; it was drizzling again slightly, and there were few stars to see by. With a single hooded torch to guide our steps, we picked our way over rising ground until we could make out the shape of the wooden stockade drawn in silhouette against the twilight sky. We didn't stop walking until we could hear the babel voices of the heathen inside - not only the guttural tones of the men, but the calling of women, the cries of infants, even the barking of a dog. Somehow it had never occurred to me that monsters like the Philistines could possibly have families, or feelings.

Then Ner was ducking down behind some stunted bushes that grew between a cluster of occupied sheepfolds. Motioning for silence, he pulled the three of us down into the undergrowth beside him. Razor-sharp prickles were scratching my ankles, and a vicious thorn jabbed into my thigh.

For several hours we crouched there, watching the

faint orange glow on the horizon getting feebler, the rain clouds dispersing, the pale moon rising, and stars beginning to gleam frostily overhead. Terrified and drowsy by turns, I had to keep blinking the sleep from my eyes, but Ner remained vigilant, every muscle and sinew taut and alert. I tried desperately to copy, but the stress of the day had taken its toll and I knew I was slipping. Abner was already sound asleep, his limbs curled for security round his cousin's hunched body. Despite his earlier enthusiasm, Saul too had surrendered to the lure of slumber.

Then unexpectedly I sensed Ner bristle and jolt forward. He gripped me by the elbow, clasped a hand over my mouth, and pointed into the darkness. I couldn't see a thing. But gradually, once my eyes had focussed, I fancied I could make out what Ner had spotted. A group of shadow-figures was moving silently downhill from the direction of the camp towards the outskirts of the town. Ner gestured at Saul and Abner, and I understood that I was to wake them. Pressing my hands to their mouths as Ner had done to mine, I shook each of them urgently, and seconds later, all our drowsiness had evaporated. We were ready and watchful, and I was no longer frightened - I think I had used up all the fear that was in me.

"Come on," hissed Ner, and we started to creep on all fours through the scrub, fixing our eyes on the advancing spectres. There were about half a dozen discernible figures now, and they were almost level with the first of the cottages and shepherds' huts that straggled out beyond the walls of the town. Then without warning they split off into pairs, and two of them were heading in our direction. We couldn't tell if they had seen us, nor what they were intending to do. We froze in our tracks, as they drew almost close enough for us to see their eye-whites. Then they veered away from us, heading for the very place where we'd been hiding, and instantly the situation became clear. They were making for the sheep-pens, to abduct our livestock.

Before we had chance to assimilate this revelation and respond, the sinister pair had gone into action. One of them edged up, silent as a ghost, behind the herdsman who was dozing in the doorway of the nearest enclosure. Bringing down both fists swiftly on his victim's head, he savoured the satisfaction of seeing the wretch crumple unconscious onto the ground. His partner began driving the sheep from the fold, rounding them up with well-practised dexterity. But although they were armed, I don't think they'd seriously expected opposition, because they weren't ready for Ner. Snarling like something wild, he hurled his spear at the first of the rustlers, and helplessly transfixed I watched him keel over, mingled surprise and horror stamped on his face, forging him a gruesome death-mask. This time yesterday I had never seen a human being die. Now I had seen two. But while I stood gaping like a fool, Saul threw too; and there we were, with two Philistines dead at our feet, gazing at one another awe-struck as the significance of the thing began to penetrate. Blood had been shed. Israelite had killed Philistine. And Saul had killed his first man. Who could tell what we had started.

We were catapulted back to reality by shouts and screams coming from across the field, searing the night-time tranquillity like the screeching of vultures. Clearly the shepherd on guard over there had been more awake than his fellow when he was attacked. As we raced to his aid, we became aware of others running with us. The commotion had roused the community, and here and there, then all among the outlying cottages, lighted torches appeared and began to converge on the sheepfolds. More figures poured out from the Philistine camp, blades flashed in the moon-light, and all at once men were running everywhere, stumbling over the bleating sheep which had scattered amok in panic, lurching among prone bodies as the battle was joined and its first victims fell. In the dim light of the moon, you couldn't tell which were Israelite and which Philistine; chaos and confusion engulfed us, and we found ourselves in the thick of the fighting. There was no time now for fumbling or faltering. I had my spear and sword, I knew how to use them, and I did so. I started cutting and slashing at whoever came at me, seeing the agony scored on their faces, hearing the strangulated howls of those dying around me. I still wasn't frightened; I knew only the urgency brought on by the nearness of death, and the blood pumping fierce and vital in my veins.

Then at once, as quickly as they had come, the Philistines were gone. Perhaps they took us for more than we were, perhaps they thought it wasn't worth dying for the sake of a few stolen sheep. We couldn't tell; all we knew was that one moment we were surrounded by desperate men, and a heart-beat later there was calm. Instinctively my eyes searched for my companions. Here was Saul, still clutching his sword, his white tunic spattered with blood, his eyes sparkling with a feral elation; there were Ner and Abner, quietly stripping Philistine corpses for weapons and gold. None of the four of us was hurt beyond the odd cut and graze, but Israelite blood had flowed, and some of the maimed and dead were men I recognized. I tried to look away from the lifeless bodies, from the faces with their ruptured eyes fixed sightless on the night sky, but I had to keep looking back, to be sure it was all real.

I think it was as well that I got my first taste of battle in the dark. The blood didn't seem so thick and vivid, the twisted corpses so ghastly, the moans of those whom death had fingered, so chilling. The grisly moonlit battlefield looked like something from a dream. I felt distant from it, cushioned, drifting. But all the same, a wave of nausea swept over me. I ran behind one of the sheepfolds and was violently sick between my cupped hands and all down my ruined red tunic. I hoped no one had seen me.

CHAPTER 6

The next day, a blanket of shock and sorrow settled over Gibeah like a fall of silent snow. We buried and mourned our dead with quiet resolution, and I guess the enemy did the same. After that, neither side was keen to force another encounter, and Israelite and Philistine crouched licking raw wounds and watching one another suspiciously from a safe distance, while we strengthened our defences, and they gradually increased the area which they controlled.

As for Saul and me, we went back home - to show his parents that we were still in one piece, as much as anything. There were no recriminations (what would have been the point?) and I think Saul paid his debt of apologies, though all that hardly seemed relevant any more. For a while he fostered a fixation on warfare, deploying armies of pebbles in the courtyard and trying to get me to play complex games of strategy, but I had no head for that kind of thinking, and left him to pursue it alone. What I wanted to do was talk about the stoning, but as far as Saul was concerned, there was nothing to talk about. The woman had been an infidel, a witch, and had got nothing worse than she deserved; the only injustice was that she had been allowed to live on borrowed time for so long.

We soon began to hear of further Philistine expansion, into other Israelite territories as well as our own. Not long after our modest skirmish, we learned that they had taken Beth Shan, a major Hebrew city well inland, a long way up north in the Vale of Jezreel. This seemed to shake people's complacency radically, and we kept hearing folk questioning in hushed tones why Adonai didn't raise up another Joshua, Gideon or Samson to smite these uncircumcised impostors for good. Kish, when obliged to give his opinion, said we must wait, and trust in God's providence. Others lost hope and bowed to their idols at the secret places in the mountains.

And so fierce argument raged among our neighbours regarding who was to blame when Shiloh fell.

It happened perhaps two years after that first incident at Gibeah. As the reports began to filter through, they were greeted first by disbelief, then by terror. Shiloh was the central sanctuary of Adonai, the holiest place in Israel. Here the old priest, my namesake Eli, served the Lord, assisted by Samuel the Shining One, prophet and priest, judge and confidant to the twelve tribal chieftains. And here the Ark of the Covenant was kept, the symbol of the presence of Adonai himself, an object of such power it was said to strike dead any who dared look within it. It had travelled with the Israelites from the desert days, when Moses had met with Adonai and placed inside it the tablets of stone on which were written the holy laws of the newborn nation. The Ark had been carried into battle for generations and had frequently wrought havoc among the enemy as the Israelites sought to drive out the Canaanites and repossess their Promised Land.

But now Shiloh was no more - and the Ark had been taken. It hadn't been surrendered without a fight; the tribe-leaders had accumulated an impressive army, which Ner and some of the more seasoned warriors from Gibeah had gone to join, but the Ark had been seized from the battlefield and taken in triumph back to Ashdod, one of the five great Philistine cities on the coastal plain. Ner was one of the few Israelite soldiers who returned. In the fighting, the two sons of Eli had lost their lives, and Eli himself was now dead of grief. For there could be no doubt - Adonai had abandoned his people.

I cannot begin to describe the hopelessness, the despair which struck at the very core of the life of our people. Our sanctuary, our priest and our God were gone. Like all the women, Rachael tore her clothing and wept and wrung her hands. Like all the men, Kish sat for hours in stunned silence, asking himself over and over what this could mean; what sin our people could have committed, or whether even Adonai himself was powerless in the face of the foreign aggressors and their gods.

Only Saul seemed curiously unaffected. Perhaps it was because he had faced all these questions before, as he sat in meditation by the pool-side or out with the flocks. "A God like Adonai can't just be captured like a man," he told me. "If he's anything, then he's more than a box made of wood. He's supposed to be the One who made the heavens and the earth. Either he's that, or else he's nothing."

And indeed, Saul turned out to be right. Within the space of seven full moons, the Ark was back among its own, and it was the Philistines themselves who returned it. It had brought such evil luck to their cities that they grew frightened of it and restored it to Israel, along with barrowloads of gold to make amends for their impiety. It was said that plague had broken out among them, and the statues of their gods had toppled from their pedestals and smashed into thousands of pieces. So they carried the Ark on a cart to the town of Beth Shemesh - the first Israelite settlement they came to - where the people welcomed it with incredulous joy. However, their jubilation was short-lived: some of their citizens dared to look inside it, and we heard that they had fallen dead on the spot, just as the legends predicted. I was awe-struck, and took to wondering once more what kind of God Adonai must be. The people of Beth Shemesh must have wondered more than I, for they were too fearful to have the Ark among them any longer, and it wound up in Kiriath Jearim, where it remains to this day. All Israel heaved a sigh of relief - we didn't anticipate any further aggravation from the Philistines now for many years to come. The office of chief priest to Adonai passed from Eli to Samuel, but Shiloh was never to be rebuilt. Someone told me that Samuel had gone back to his birthplace of Ramah in the hill-country and that he made his sacrifices at a holy place high above the town.

So life in Gibeah went on much as before. I have noticed that this is always the way of things: kings and armies come and go, power changes hands, noble houses rise and fall, but the fields have still to be ploughed, sown and harvested, the vines and olives still ripen, the sheep and goats graze on, the rains come and the sun shines. The things that truly change lives are of a different order, and for Saul and me, life was about to change as it had never changed before.

We were fifteen years old, healthy, bronzed and athletic, with puberty behind us, and the wind of youth in our sails. I'd been Saul's servant for over seven years, and now I'd had my earlobe pierced as a sign that I was willing to serve him until I died. Summer's end was approaching and Saul and I were preparing to go out into the olive-groves to assist in harvesting the crop, when Kish came out into the courtyard and called us back.

"Oh, thank God you haven't already left," he said. "Two of our donkeys have gone missing, the two best. I need you to go out and find them. Boaz swears that he tied them up yesterday, but his memory isn't what it was, you know. I've got enough workers to manage in the orchards on their own for today."

We agreed readily enough. It gave us an excuse for a walk in the hills rather than a day's hot and back-breaking work; and donkeys are valuable creatures in a hill-farming community.

"They could have gone a fair distance by now if they escaped last night," Saul pointed out.

"That's if no one has taken a fancy to them himself," I added grimly. "Such as our Philistine friends up there."

Rachael emerged from the kitchen carrying some crusty loaves still warm from the oven, and some fruit wrapped up in pieces of cloth. She began fussing around us, stuffing the food inside our tunics. These days her motherliness made me smile, for both Saul and I now towered over her short ageing figure. She had begun to look old before her time, but we thought nothing of it.

We took our swords and our spears and began our search, scouring the town itself first, but we saw no sign of them, nor could anyone we met say for certain whether they had seen them. We widened the horizons of our hunt, spending most of the morning making a circuit to the south, almost as far as Jebus, but still found no clue. Eventually we chanced upon a herdsman who had been out on watch all night near the Jebus road and had definitely seen no trace of any stray animals. So we thanked him and turned to go north.

By now the sun was high in the sky; we were hot and thirsty and our feet were starting to ache. We returned through Gibeah, passed near the Philistine camp without misadventure and had got beyond the next little town, Adasa, before we sat down beneath a cypress tree to rest and to eat.

"This is hopeless," Saul sighed. "They could be anywhere after all this time. My guess is that some poor farmer found them and took them for a gift from Adonai. They'll be munching away in his stable by now."

So we sat for a while, doing our own munching, and soaking up the rugged beauty of the mountain scenery that was opening up before us: the rise and fall of the dappled green slopes that drew our eyes into the shimmering haze of the distance, the last parched survivors of the season's flowers, ruffled by the hot breeze, accompanied by the honeyed scent of scorched vegetation and the rasping of the crickets in the branches overhead. Then reluctantly we brushed the crumbs from our clothes and took up our search once more. Towards sunset we fetched up not far from Ramah, and again had to stop and rest.

"I think we shall have to go back home, Eli," said Saul. "You know how anxious my father gets these days. If we stay out much longer he'll stop worrying about the donkeys and start fretting about us."

Then I had an idea. "The holy man, Samuel," I said. "Isn't this where he lives now? In Amalek if something precious was lost, we used to go and consult a seer. Isn't that done here?"

Saul arched his brows. "Go and ask Samuel himself? We couldn't trouble him with a small thing like this. As if he hasn't got more pressing problems to worry about."

"It isn't a small thing to your father," I said.

"No." Saul sighed audibly. "But what could we give him? We've no gold or jewels with us. We've even eaten all the food."

"I've got a small piece of silver in my purse," I ventured, and Saul chuckled a little, but agreed to try out my suggestion. After all, we had no other alternative but to go home empty-handed. And from the glint that grew in his eyes, I knew that, as with me, there was more anticipation in Saul's mind now than that of recovering his father's lost property. So we headed off towards the little town, nestling quietly on its stony hillside in the soft evening sunshine, its tangle of flat-roofed houses huddled together as though in fear of tumbling into the valley below.

As we approached the first group of dwellings there were four figures coming along the road towards us. Drawing closer, we saw that they were young girls carrying tall earthenware jars on their heads, for it was early evening now, the time of day for fetching water from the well. They bore the heavy pots with effortless ease, holding themselves like princesses as they walked along and chattered lightly of women's things as they went. I nudged Saul.

"Let's ask them which is Samuel's house," I whispered. "It isn't every day that we get to talk to girls." In fact this was something of an understatement. I hadn't spoken to one since leaving Amalek, except for Abner's little sisters. I doubted Saul had even done that. Most Israelite fathers guard their daughters far too well. It occurred to me that these maidens of Ramah, no doubt being modestly raised, might walk straight past us without even answering, but I was wrong. Something fluttered in my stomach as it dawned on me that already they were stopping, even though we hadn't yet spoken to them. Three of them were scarcely more than children, with breasts just forming under their flimsy bodices, but the fourth was tall and buxom and womanly, and I had to make myself look away.

It was then that I realized that they, too, were not staring at us in a generally curious kind of way because we were strangers. When they looked at us, they saw men; and the three younger ones had begun to blush and giggle and be embarrassed. But the eldest was looking directly at Saul, and their eyes met, and held. In that instant I became aware of the thing which had struck me when I caught my first glimpse of Kish's son in the courtyard all those years ago, but which had scarcely occurred to me since. Saul was uncommonly beautiful.

I say beautiful, rather than handsome, because he was still young enough for there to be a feminine quality about his comeliness. His skin was still clear and smooth, his hair a mass of shining, red-tinged curls, his figure lissome and willowy, his movements lithe, but strong, like a leopard's. His features were still the even, regular features of a boy - the wide, sensual mouth, the arrow-straight nose, the high cheek-bones, and those grave, languid eyes that swallowed you like an ocean when you looked into them - but now his cheeks were flushed, and his eyelids trembled.

I looked back at the girl his eyes had chosen. Above her veil all I could see was her own eyes, dark, sultry, smiling, and shaped like almonds. A ringlet of jet-black hair had escaped from its fastenings and curled over her cheek, and she too was blushing, though whether from modesty or shyness or something else, I couldn't tell. Growing impatient, I cleared my throat and heard my voice asking, as though it belonged to someone else, "Excuse me. We're looking for Samuel, the seer. Could you tell us where to find him?"

"Of course." It was one of the younger ones who answered me. "He's on his way to the sanctuary - he'll probably come past here. It's the easiest way up. There's going to be a sacrifice to Adonai at sunset, at the holy place. If you're lucky you'll catch him before he sets off up the hill."

I touched Saul gently on the arm. "Come on. We're just in time."

But Saul didn't respond. He didn't even seem to hear me, or see me, or feel the tug on his sleeve. He was still staring at the girl as though bewitched, and she had raised her eyes while I was speaking, and looked back at him. They said no words to one another, but the air was full of their talking.

"Saul!" I tried again. "Come on! Have you forgotten what we came for?"

This time he heard me, but still could find no voice. He nodded vaguely, and allowed me to lead him away up the track, between the first clusters of cottages that straggled out to meet us. The girls picked up their water jars and walked on, but still Saul didn't speak.

"What is the matter with you?" I asked, and was startled because my tone sounded much sharper than I'd intended. "Your father will be furious if we don't hurry. The sun is starting to set already."

"I've got to have her," Saul said.

"Have her? What? What are you talking about?" I demanded. I couldn't understand why I was being so irritable. I didn't mean to be.

"I want her for myself, Eli. Something has happened to me, inside." Unexpectedly he turned and gripped me by the shoulders and looked right into my eyes. I swallowed and looked away. Yes, something had happened right enough, but I lacked the words to talk about it, and was strangely disinclined to. Dimly I realized that Saul was still speaking, but I hadn't heard the half of what he said.

"... I will talk to my father when we get home. I will ask him to get her for me. We will send Boaz to find out who she is, and approach her parents. Then I shall marry her."

"*Marry* her? But you're far too young to marry," I protested, realizing at once that he was not. He was nearly sixteen years old, wealthy and of good family; though no doubt Kish and Rachael would have said he wasn't ready. I began to be morbidly depressed, and now it was my turn to walk along in silence, while Saul prattled on broodily.

"... I just hope it won't count against me, being from the tribe of Benjamin, and from Gibeah too. Her family are bound to know of our shame, where women are concerned. Don't you think so, Eli?" - and when I made no reply - "Don't you think they'll know?"

"Know what," I said between gritted teeth.

"About Benjamin, of course. About how our tribe was nearly wiped out by the rest of Israel because of the shameful atrocity committed by the men of Gibeah two generations ago."

I knew nothing of any shameful atrocity, but I hoped passionately that it was shameful enough to make her family shun his for ever. And I wished he would stop talking, because I was starting to feel like hitting him. But he didn't.

"... Some men of Gibeah raped and murdered a girl who belonged to a guest of the town. The rest of Benjamin stood by us but the man hacked her body in pieces and despatched them all over Israel, to summon the tribes to avenge the crime. Gibeah was razed to the ground. The fortress and everything had to be rebuilt. I never thought it mattered before; it was all so long ago. What do you think, Eli? Do you think it will matter?"

Still I strode on without speaking, then was vexed to hear Saul laughing out loud as he ran to catch up with me. He reached out his hand and grasped me by the shoulder again, swinging me round to face him.

"By heaven, Eli, you're jealous!" he jeered, "Well, don't you worry. I will spend half of each night with her, and then after we've made love a hundred times, I'll send her away and spend the other half with you. After all, you know, the men of Gibeah only raped that girl because they couldn't get their hands on her handsome boyfriend."

I was speechless. It was a full seven years since I had known Saul deliberately try to humiliate me, and I couldn't credit what I was hearing. Perhaps it was spending all day out in the pitiless heat that was making him so insensitive and me so irritable. But I was livid. I tore myself away from him and marched off up the hill into the middle of the town, his words echoing over and over in my head.

I was so wrapped up in my own rage that it was some time before I realized there was something unusual about Ramah, and what it was. The place was deserted. Apart from the four girls fetching water, we had seen nobody, although the sky was already dyed crimson with late sunset, and the evening air was now fresh and cool. Perhaps everyone was at the sacrifice; but it gave the town an air of veiled mystery which started to make me feel the way I had felt up at the high place, and I didn't like it. I was about to suggest returning home after all, when a sudden movement up ahead made me start. Coming around the next corner was another group of four figures: men this time, bare-headed, dressed alike and strangely in faded brown cloaks, short tunics and thonged sandals, and they were heading rapidly in our direction. Involuntarily I stopped, though I didn't quite understand why I was doing so, but the four figures continued to bear down upon us and I felt my hand, of itself, move to my sword-hilt. As the men drew nearer I saw that three of them were young, with long, loose-flowing black hair and untrimmed beards, but the fourth was much older, and as soon as I saw him I knew who he must be.

He was considerably taller than the others, in fact I think he was one of the tallest men I have ever seen, Saul included. He was also the most unnerving. His build was lean and spare, his bearded face gaunt and deeply etched, and he had a shock of wiry white hair which blew about unrestrained in the fitful breeze. His brows were shaggy and met above the bridge of his nose as though in a fixed frown, and his small, deep-set eyes were quite blue – something I had never seen before - and restlessly probing. His cloak was ragged and threadbare, and he carried a long staff, which he stabbed down decisively as he walked, although he didn't appear to need a stick any more than I did.

Saul had stopped making fun of me by now, though there was still a barbed atmosphere between us, and a yawning gulf which neither of us was yet ready to cross. So I stood and looked on while Saul stepped forward and asked hesitantly where Samuel the seer was to be found, though to me the answer seemed inescapably clear already.

For a moment it looked as if the four of them were going to sweep past us without even acknowledging our presence, but then without warning the old man stopped dead in his tracks, and his three companions halted behind him like a triple shadow. He began to peer at Saul so intently that Saul visibly shrank under his gaze. He had turned pale and stood staring at the stranger as if unable to help himself, until finally the man spoke, and his voice was unexpectedly normal and vigorous. "Don't look any further, young Saul. You've found him."

Although I had already known it, my stomach still heaved. Samuel the Shining One was standing not a spear-length away from me - and he knew Saul's name. I looked up into the seer's piercing eyes, and froze, as they suddenly shifted from Saul to me, and now it was I who couldn't look away. There was something unnatural about their brightness, their unearthly blue, something that made me shrivel inside, and know that I could hide nothing. I felt that he was reading my life by just looking at me, though to look at him, he seemed in all but this like any other man. But somewhere deep inside him, discernible though invisible, there was the rushing of a wild wind and a core of pure power. Then his eyes flicked away from me again to rest on Saul, and briefly I relaxed.

"You two must come with me," he said. "The sacrifice can wait. Both of you will eat with me and my guests, and you can stay the night. I shall answer your questions tomorrow." Then he looked at me again and said, "Don't worry about the donkeys. They've been found." My head swam: could he truly read my mind? "It's you they are searching for now - and I don't just mean Kish and Rachael," Samuel continued. Me? Who was searching for me? I started, but when my eyes focussed once more on the seer I saw that again he was addressing Saul. "You and your father's family."

"What?" Saul backed away, but he was still staring at Samuel, physically unable to tear his eyes away, yet looking inexplicably desperate to do so. In fact he seemed utterly terrified, as though panic ate at his very soul. There was no clear reason for us to be afraid, and yet we were, and Saul especially so. I had seldom seen him so overwrought. He opened his mouth to reply, but when the words came, they seemed to spill out of their own accord, without his controlling them. "I belong to the tribe of Benjamin, the smallest and most despised tribe in Israel," he faltered, and then when Samuel made no response, his words gathered their own momentum and he babbled, "My clan is the least important in the tribe. No one can be searching for me. I don't know what you mean. Why are you talking to me like this? Leave me alone!"

For a brief moment I feared he was going to turn and run, but the seer's uncanny allure still ensnared him. Samuel said nothing, but narrowing his eyes he wheeled about and struck out once more along the track, with his three shadows falling in obediently behind - and Saul and me following. I moved as though in a trance. Everything seemed distant and unreal, and I felt to be floating, not walking. We had passed beyond the town now, and were climbing gradually up the hillside above it; stunted, wind-driven pine trees jutted from the outcropping limestone and sharp stones dug into the soles of my sandals, for we were moving at speed and I couldn't look fast enough where I was putting my feet. Risking an upward glance, I was startled to see that directly in front of us, perched among rocks as if it were carved from living stone, was a solitary house. The other dwellings of the town had fallen away far below us, and this one stood apart and aloof, its blind black windows defying all comers. Its shape was irregular, for it clung to bedrock wherever it could find footing, but it was unexpectedly large and imposing. An air of neglect hung about it - the brickwork was crumbling, thorny weeds grew from the cracks in the walls, and sections of the roof balustrade were missing. As we approached it, Samuel cast a backward glance over his shoulder, and beckoned us to follow him inside.

We found ourselves in a spacious reception room, and I swallowed, for it was full of people. Reclining on the couches ranged about the walls, chatting informally, were Samuel's guests. There must have been about thirty of them, all men of middle age or older, and all attired richly yet with out ostentation, as befits those who are nobly born. In the centre of the room were a number of low tables groaning with food of every imaginable variety, and it seemed that the meal had already begun, for some of the men were eating and drinking as they talked, and stewards moved among them, dressed in plain brown cloaks like Samuel and his companions.

But as soon as we entered the room, all conversation ceased abruptly. The stewards stepped backwards and stood against the far wall, as smartly as if Samuel had clapped his hands at them. There was a heavy silence, and thirty pairs of eyes fixed us like daggers. Samuel walked forward, nodding his head at each man he passed, but it was not principally him that they were looking at; he knew it full well, and approved.

Then I saw that next to the host's seat, in which Samuel was now sitting, were two empty places, and two of the brown-cloaked attendants were steering Saul and me gently but firmly towards them. Wordlessly we sank down onto the cushions. Samuel motioned to one of the stewards, who had taken up their positions behind us. "Bring the portion of meat I showed you," he said. "The one I told you to set aside."

Another attendant came forward with a bowl of water for us to wash our hands; another washed our feet. Then almost at once a steaming plate of food appeared before Saul. Arranged upon it was the largest leg of lamb I had ever seen, coated with a rich sauce and surrounded by so many beans and lentils I thought that three men couldn't have eaten them. A more modest dish was placed in front of me, but I turned away, unable to face even looking at it. Neither did Saul make any move to eat. He sat staring at the food as though at a corpse.

Then a sudden wicked thought goaded me - perhaps Saul knew what was going on? I was at a loss to know how he could do, but his expression was like that of a child who has awoken from a nightmare only to watch it come true before his very eyes. Samuel was studying him appraisingly.

"You must eat it," he said. "It has been reserved for you. You are to eat it now, in front of the guests I have invited."

I watched dumbly as Saul began mechanically to chew the food and to force himself to swallow it. I couldn't think why he felt he had to obey. The eyes of every guest were upon him, but once he had begun to eat, they seemed satisfied, and one by one they turned away and went back to their own meals. Somehow Saul ate every last morsel, but when the servants came to take away our plates, mine remained untouched. Yet although everyone had seemed so insistent upon Saul's eating, my own lack of appetite didn't seem to bother anyone.

When the meal was finished, I half expected some kind of explanation to be given, some speech to be made, but it wasn't. The guests simply bowed and drifted away, whispering among themselves until Saul and I were left alone, with Samuel. Again I hoped for an explanation, but again I was disappointed. The seer had continued to watch us closely all evening with his steady frown, but now it relaxed slightly and he said, "Come, it's time for you boys to sleep."

In the corner of the room, a flight of steps led to the flat roof. Lifting a small oil lamp from its bracket, Samuel took us up, and showed us to two mattresses already spread there, side by side. It was quite dark now; the moon had risen, the stars sparkled, the mountain air was crisp and bracing. I took a lungful of it and felt better, then thankfully we lay down on our mattresses, and Samuel was gone.

CHAPTER 7

For some time we lay in silence. Our quarrel still hung between us, but now there were other things too, and normal speech felt out of place somehow. I lay on my back gazing up at the night sky, but despite how tired I felt, sleep wouldn't come. For six years I'd been closer to Saul than a brother. We had learnt to share everything, even our deepest thoughts, our darkest secrets - or so I had believed. Now suddenly, inexplicably, I found myself wondering if I had ever known him at all. But finally I had to say something to break the tension.

I whispered, "Saul? Are you awake?"

"Of course."

"Saul - please tell me what's going on. I don't think I can take much more of this. I want to go home."

For a moment Saul didn't reply. Then he said, "We can never go home."

"What?" My mind felt foggy; I wondered if I'd heard right. "What are you talking about? What about your parents? And the donkeys..."

"Oh, we can go back to Gibeah," he reassured me, yet his voice sounded remote, and different. "But we can't go home. Not back to where we were. Something has changed, Eli."

"What? What has changed?" I was fully awake now, and I could feel my temper rising again. I fought to quell it.

"This is it, Eli. My destiny, I know it. I can't escape it now."

"Saul, what on earth are you talking about? For God's sake..."

But when he answered, his voice was weary, like that of someone who must face his sworn enemy, and face him alone. "Go to sleep. It's not yet time."

"Time for what? Saul, why are you talking in riddles to me? Look, if I was being childish before, when we met those girls - well, I'm sorry."

But this time he didn't reply at all. He turned over and pulled his cloak around his shoulders. So I tried to sleep. I lay this way and that, tried to get comfortable, and after a time dozed fitfully, but the slightest noises constantly awakened me. A murmur of breeze, the distant hooting of an owl, the rustle of a pine tree. Finally I blinked my eyes open and saw that Saul was no longer lying next to me. I sat up, and traced his slender silhouette opaque against the starlit sky. He was standing motionless by the low parapet of the roof.

"Saul? Are you all right?" I called in a loud whisper, but again he didn't answer. I got up and went to stand beside him, but he didn't even notice me. Then I saw that his eyes were closed and his lips were moving, and I realized that he was praying.

But I had never seen anyone pray like this, not even in Israel. He was absorbed, lost, apart. The world didn't exist for him. The space around him had become holy ground. In silence I backed away and lay down again. This time, despite myself, I slept.

When I awoke, it was full daylight. The birds were already singing and the air thrummed with the rasp of crickets. Saul lay sprawled on his mattress in deep sleep, and I wondered how many hours he had stood in prayer. I was reluctant to go down into the house alone, so I sat on my own mattress hugging my knees for comfort, waiting for Saul to wake up, but he didn't. I desperately wanted to patch up our quarrel and to try to make sense of yesterday, but still Saul didn't stir. I longed to shake him, but something held me back. I sat gazing down at the familiar face, the tangled hair, the lithe body abandoned in sleep. He had been my friend; now he was different - and it is rude to shake a stranger.

The sun had climbed above the hills of the horizon and the bright heat of late summer was burning my face when he eventually murmured and opened his eyes. And at that very moment, Samuel's voice called up from below. I cursed under my breath.

"Saul? Eliphaz?" (So he knew my name, too). "Come and eat breakfast. It's time for you to be moving."

Without a word, Saul stretched, got up and went downstairs. I waited a few moments, then slipped off my sandals and crept noiselessly down the first half dozen steps. Samuel was already talking to Saul, in hushed tones. I paused, and listened.

"Saul, it is most important that I speak to you alone before we part. The three of us will walk together as far as the other edge of town. Then you are to send your servant on ahead. No one must hear what we say. Do you understand?"

Saul nodded, at first hesitantly, then decisively, and just as decisively, I determined that I *would* hear. I replaced my sandals and came down into the room. Samuel stopped talking at once but I pretended not to notice, and the three of us sat in silence and ate a breakfast of bread, fresh olives and sour milk. Then Samuel gave us some food for our journey and we set off back towards the town, to the point where our track branched off back to Gibeah.

"Eli, you go on ahead," said Saul. "I'll catch you up. There's something I need to do."

Without comment I shrugged my shoulders and headed off along our road. Luckily for me it wound quite sharply downhill and plunged its way very soon among rocks, so it was easy for me to slip between them and hide, without the others knowing whether I was still on the way or not. Crouching there I could see the two of them quite clearly, and hear every word that passed between them.

From the folds of his tattered cloak Samuel drew a small alabaster oil-jar. Saul looked at it, then slowly he dropped to his knees, right there on the track, closed his eyes and bowed his head before the seer, so that his loosened curls tumbled over his face and I couldn't see it. But he no longer seemed frightened or confused. He knelt calm and still as Samuel took the lid from the jar and began to pour its contents over his bent head. The oil gleamed in his hair and ran down his cheeks and neck but he didn't flinch or wipe it away. He swayed slightly, but that was all. Then Samuel placed his hands on Saul's head, and when he started to speak, his voice was melodic, lilting, chant-like, and it seemed to stem from some source other than himself. Then I saw that his hands were shaking as he intoned the words.

"Saul, son of Kish, take courage and don't be afraid. You are chosen by Adonai. He has anointed you to rule his people and protect them from their enemies. You will know it, because you will see signs, this very day, and you will become changed. Saul - before the sun sets tonight you will realize your dream. You will know Adonai. You will become a Shining One. Stand up, my son - our God is with you."

For some moments Saul appeared unable to obey. He was swaying again, and I wondered whether he would even manage to remain upright on his knees, much less stand up. Then somehow, slowly, he got to his feet, pushed back his hair, and his eyes fluttered open. He and Samuel regarded one another searchingly, then suddenly Samuel's frown was gone. He grasped Saul by the shoulders and kissed him tenderly, as a father might have done, and for an instant he looked almost human. Then the moment passed, the frown returned.

"Listen carefully," he continued. "These are the signs you will see as evidence that what I am telling you is true. When you leave here, you must make your way back to Gibeah by the normal route. When you come to the tomb of Jacob's wife at Zelzah, you will meet two men. They will tell you that the donkeys have been found, and that your father is now worrying about you. Then go on until you

117

come to the Sacred Tree at Tabor, and there you will meet three men, on their way to offer a sacrifice at Bethel. They will have with them three goats, three loaves of bread, and a full wine-skin. They will greet you and offer you two of the loaves, and you must accept them. Then just outside Gibeah, where the Philistine camp is, you will meet a band of prophets coming down from the old holy place on the hill there. They will be dancing and playing flutes and drums, and the spirit of Adonai will be strong among them. That is when he will come upon you. His spirit will take control of you and you will join in the dancing, and you will prophesy. And Saul - from that moment you will receive a new nature, Adonai's nature. When this happens, you must do everything he tells you, because you will be able to hear what he is saying to you, in your heart. Do you understand?"

Saul nodded, and his face was flushed and burning with emotion. I had never before seen his features so betray what was inside him. Then suddenly Samuel threw his arms around Saul's back, holding him close, ruffling his oiled hair as though he were a small child. And Saul seemed to melt into his embrace, as he had never done with Kish or Rachael. Something within me seethed again, and irrationally I wanted to hate Samuel, to wipe the joy from his face, to suspect his affection for Saul of springing from the worst of possible motives. For what felt like an age they stood locked together, as though something of Adonai had already forged a bond between them. "I knew it the moment I saw you," Samuel was saying. "Adonai had told me, more clearly than he has ever told me anything, that you were the One. It wasn't what I wanted, but it has to be."

Saul pulled back a little, scanning the seer's blue blue eyes. "It wasn't what you wanted?"

"Those men you saw at the meal," Samuel went on, "They were the leaders of the twelve tribes of Israel, and their counsellors. They came four days ago to ask me to grant them a king. I was unwilling. Israel has had no king but Adonai, for a thousand years. I fought it. I fought with Adonai for three days and nights. But times have changed. The Philistines threaten, and Israel is weak. A loose association of our tribes is no longer enough. Adonai showed me I was wrong, and then when I saw you, I knew... oh, Saul, my son!" The seer's voice thickened, choked with unwept tears. "You are honoured and blessed beyond belief. If you listen to Adonai, you will be greater than Joshua, or Gideon, or Samson. You will be like Moses. You will have something no one else alive possesses, a relationship with the Creator closer than even I have known. But you must listen. Always. You must learn to hear his voice within your heart. And you must listen to me, for I am his prophet, his mouthpiece. Will you do it?"

Saul put his head on Samuel's neck, making me squirm. "I will do it."

"Now - go." The seer squeezed Saul's shoulders briefly, then without looking at him again, he pivoted on his staff and began to stride away down the road, dust skirling at his heels.

Saul stood, alone and apart, watching him go. The Chosen One. Suddenly he looked very young, very vulnerable. The breeze flicked at his red-tinged curls, and a trickle of oil ran down his neck and glistened against his collar-bone. I thought, oh God, you are still Saul, you are still my friend, whatever has happened. I had to break cover.

Slowly I walked towards him. He looked round and saw me, but didn't speak. I said, "I'm sorry, Saul. I heard everything."

For a horrible interval he just went on looking at me, and I waited for his anger. Then his eyes closed and I saw the relief spread over his face. He put out his arms to embrace me, but I was on my knees on the track in front of him. I don't know why; it was through no conscious decision of my own. I had wanted to make some joke so that life would seem normal again, or clap my hand on his shoulder and tell him to forget all this, that Samuel was just a crazy hermit who didn't even know what he was talking about. Instead, I was saying nothing, with my lips. But my body was saying: you are the King of Israel, and I swear never to disobey you again.

In the event it was Saul who sought to deflate the tension. He said, "Stand up, will you? You're making me nervous."

I stared at him, questioning, and then I grinned, for he was smiling. Our quarrel was forgotten, and he really was glad I had heard.

I said, "We'd better get back. Your father will be out of his mind."

We set out arm in arm, friends again, but with questions still hanging in the air between us which as yet could not be answered. Saul quickly lapsed back into his own thoughts, despite his efforts to escape them, and my mind was so full that I didn't at first grasp what it meant when near the tomb of Jacob's wife we came upon two of

Ner's youths from Gibeah, hailing us and waving their arms. They ran up to us, breathless and beaming; one of them clapped us both on the back and exclaimed, "Thank God you're safe. Kish is beside himself."

"The donkeys have turned up," added the other. "Someone brought them back last night."

The news was unimportant now, but it was the first sign. The youths went on their way, cautioning us to return home quickly. Saul and I exchanged glances and walked on.

This omen had taken me by surprise, but the next one didn't. The Sacred Tree of Tabor is a well-known landmark, standing gaunt and gnarled against the sky, and you can see it on the horizon from every side long before you are close enough to throw a stone at it. It is no wonder that the simple folk used to come here to offer their sacrifices; there are still amulets and fetishes hanging from its branches. The three men stood in its shade, waiting for us, and I was glad enough when Saul accepted their two loaves, for my appetite had suddenly returned, with double its customary vigour. We sat down to eat, then walked on, until we were among the first of Gibeah's pasturelands, dotted with rough stone sheepfolds, and we could see the Philistine camp perched on its hilltop close to the town. And I knew the third sign must come.

We heard them before we saw them. The steady thumping of the drums, the high-pitched wailing of the flutes, that made the nape of my neck tingle and my blood run thin. When they came into view over the crest of the ridge, I panicked and made a grab for Saul's arm, for the music grew suddenly louder and hurt my ears, echoing and bouncing from the rocks and hills so that it came at us from all sides.

I'd seen groups like this before, from a distance, going up to a high place, or walking together in the town, but I'd never been confronted with the strangeness of these people at such close quarters, nor had I come across them at worship. And never had I seen a band as large as this. I suppose there were about fifty of them, though it felt like thousands, all chanting, all bareheaded, all dressed in the brown cloaks I now knew for the mark of the sons of the prophets. Only some of their cloaks had come unpinned at the neck, leaving their chests exposed, and their long hair streamed behind them as they sang, danced, beat their tabors or shrilled their pipes, and their eyes were glazed, seeing nothing but the spectres of their own wild imaginings. Some of them shouted, and some shrieked, but their words meant nothing - they spoke a tongue or tongues I didn't know.

Despite being so close to us, they didn't see us, and I pulled Saul out of the way lest we be trampled. Louder and louder the drums thudded, and a fierce wind seemed to have sprung up from nowhere. Clouds had gathered and now loured over us - soon it would be time for the first rains of autumn, but surely not yet? The driving rhythm of the music began to pulse in my head until it felt to be on fire, and I clasped my hands to my ears, but I couldn't shut it out. My eyes ached and flashed and I had to close them against the pain. The wind blew stronger, so that I could scarcely stand. Yet Saul stood unflinching beside me, expectant, aroused.

And all at once, I knew there was another presence there - separate from the prophets, separate from Saul, separate from me, and yet above all of us and present in everything. I felt that the sky was falling and pressing on my head, which throbbed ready to burst. My arms and legs turned weak, then went rigid and I think I was screaming, though I couldn't hear myself against the thunder of the worship. Suddenly the earth seemed to shake beneath me and I was thrown violently to the ground. In that instant I knew with awesome certainty that Adonai lived, and that he was here, and I knew why Rachael had taken my amulet and laughed at my gods.

Then gradually it dawned on me that Saul was no longer standing beside me. The spirit which had shaken me and convulsed me and thrown me to the ground was inside him. With my eyes half open, I watched in horror as his body began to move with the rhythm, his eyes clouded, he flung back his head and drank in the ecstasy. Now he was among them, he was one of them; he twisted and leapt and whirled like a wild creature, he shouted and howled and the words which poured from him made no sense. And his face! Instantaneously I knew at last what it meant to be a Shining One, in a way I had never understood it before, and have seldom seen it since. Saul was radiant; radiant so that I couldn't tear my eyes from him. I was in anguish, but he soared, ecstatic, transfigured, oblivious of all around him, caught up in a rapture of elation. Grovelling there in the dust, I was sure this pain would kill me, yet in the presence of the same spirit, Saul and the prophets stood erect - and not only stood, but danced, and sang, and prophesied, and exulted, their heads tilted up to heaven, and their faces ablaze.

I have no idea how long I lay there pinned to the

ground. I was conscious - in fact acutely so - of everything that was going on around me, yet somehow I knew I couldn't move, and I didn't try. It wasn't until I sensed the music beginning to die back into the distance, the wind subsiding with it, that I felt able to stand up. With relief I saw that the mantic band had passed me by, but now it had drawn nearer to the outlying houses of Gibeah, and people were coming out through the gates to see what was happening. There was no sign of Saul; I presumed he must still be with the prophets. Groggily I tottered to my feet, having vaguely conceived the idea of returning home to reassure Kish and Rachael that we were safe, though thinking back on it now, I cannot imagine why I should have considered Saul to be so.

As I staggered towards the town, I found myself engulfed in the crowds which had gathered to witness the spectacle. All around me people were whispering, "The prophets! The prophets are here at Gibeah! What can it mean?" "Adonai has come among us. We shall all die!" "Who are these people? How come no one knows where they are from, who their parents are?" But none of them took any notice of me. I stumbled on, brushing against shoulders, prodded by elbows, once or twice falling then picking myself up again and blundering onward. I heard someone say, "Have you seen who is with them? It's Saul, Kish's son. Chanting and dancing like the rest of them," then another voice respond, "No, not Saul. He's so quiet and serious. It must be somebody else."

Just then someone yanked me by the shoulder and shook me. Wresting myself free, I saw it was Ner. "Where have you been?" he hissed at me, "Where is Saul? Kish is demented with worry."

"Er - looking for the donkeys," I stammered. "We couldn't find them. We went to see Samuel."

"Samuel?" Ner shook me harder, making my aching head pound all over again, and peered at me suspiciously. "What did he say to you?" he demanded.

"He said - they'd been found," I answered, and tore myself away from him before he could ask me again where Saul was. Eventually, somehow, I reached the fortress, and propping myself against the gate, I mustered all the strength I had left, and hammered until I heard the bar drawn back and Rachael's voice asking who was there. When I said it was me, she pulled the gate right open and dragged me inside.

I had already gone to bed when Saul came back. The sun had barely set, and I saw his long shadow fall across the doorway as he lurched, reaching out his arms in search of support, and steadied himself exhausted against a pillar. He was all but naked - his tunic was gone and his loincloth was torn. His dishevelled hair hung about his head in matted strands, still lank with oil. But his face was on fire and his eyes sparkled, and he was smiling. Shakily he walked over and sat down on the edge of my bed.

"It has happened, Eli," he said. "What I've waited for - it's happened. I am filled with the spirit of Adonai, just like Samuel said. I *know* him. I *feel* him. He's in every sinew of my body. Eli - I'm alive! For the first time. It's real."

I forced myself to smile, to keep calm, to ask what it was he felt.

"I'm not sure. Power. Strength. I really feel like I could rule Israel. I feel like I could rule the universe! I just want to shout, to dance, even here, on my own with just you. I'm reborn."

But I shook my head sadly. I couldn't help it. Saul had moved on without me.

"Eli - you can be reborn too. I know you can."

Again I shook my head. "No, Saul. This time it truly is something for you alone."

"Eli, no! Just give yourself to him, like I did! Let his spirit flow into you. Listen to your heart. He can speak to you too, I'm sure of it."

"No. He doesn't speak in my heart," I said softly. "He throws me to the ground and he makes my head ache. It's you who must listen to him. That's what Samuel said."

For a moment I thought he was going to plead with me again, but he didn't. I think he had decided that for once I might be right.

CHAPTER 8

When I awoke the next day Saul was already up, his mattress neatly folded and stacked against the wall. I found him sitting in the courtyard by the pool, shoulders hunched, head bent, fingers trailing absently in the cool water. At first I hung back, thinking he might be praying again, but he must have heard me fidgeting, because he called my name. I went to sit beside him, but he said nothing. Eventually I asked what was the matter.

"I wish I knew." He sighed and hugged his knees under his chin. "It's just - when I woke up this morning, everything seemed so normal. The birds singing, Mother getting breakfast, Father organizing the farmhands' work for the day. Did it all really happen? Did I really prophesy? Did I really have Adonai's spirit in me?"

I couldn't stop myself grinning. "Oh, you did, right enough. I never saw anything like it."

He looked relieved, and the tension in his shoulders relaxed a little, but he didn't smile, and presently lapsed again into a petulant silence.

"Don't you feel him in you today?" I prompted gently.

He shrugged. "I don't know what I feel. I'm confused. I don't think I want to be king of Israel. I can't see how it's going to happen, I don't know what I'm supposed to do."

I grinned again. "It's you who wanted to do something big. Make your mark, be remembered. It looks like Adonai's answered your prayers. I can't think of anything bigger than this."

"But what does Samuel expect me to do? Amass an army, and seize power? Or does he want me to go on living here as though nothing had happened?"

I pulled a face. "How should I know? He didn't even want me to know anything about it."

Saul bristled. "Eli, this is serious. Who will listen to me, a Benjaminite, and from Gibeah? I'm so young, too. And I'm not a leader of men. You know me, Eli. You know I would have less fear of the Philistines' swords than of addressing my own subjects."

I opened my mouth to object, but closed it again, because of course he was right. For a while neither of us spoke; Saul stared disconsolately into the water, and I studied his face, reading his self-doubt. Then a fresh thought occurred to me.

"If Adonai has chosen you, he must be going to give you the power," I pointed out. "Samuel says you're the Lord's anointed. Didn't the signs come true?"

"Perhaps," Saul admitted, but he looked no happier. For a while I sat with him in silence, then I thought, maybe he needs to be alone, so I slipped away. But I was worried. While I walked through the courtyard trying to make sense of it all, I ran into Kish. He was standing near the gates, frowning, and holding a clay tablet which a messenger had brought in. The youth still stood in the doorway, and he was wearing a faded brown cloak.

Kish fixed me with suspicious eyes. "Perhaps you can shed some light on this, Eliphaz," he said, and his tone put me on my guard.

I asked dubiously, "What is it?"

"It's a letter from Samuel, the priest at Ramah. He says there is to be a gathering of all the tribes of Adonai at Mizpah, on the second Sabbath from today, and that this message is going out to the head of every clan in Israel. But he also says it is particularly important for me to attend, along with my son. And I have never met the man in my life."

I said nothing but I could feel the colour rising to my cheeks. I bowed my head and tried to hide behind my fringe, which was foolish, for my redness probably felt worse than it looked.

"You do know something about this, Eliphaz, don't you?" Kish handed the tablet back to the messenger, and dismissed him. "I don't think Saul has told me the whole story of the last few days. I believe the time has come for the three of us to have a little talk."

Without waiting for my consent he led me by the arm back to the pool-side where Saul still sat fretting, swinging his legs and staring. I made up my mind to say nothing about Samuel unless Saul did, for what had happened was his business in a way that it wasn't mine.

But he said nothing - about Samuel, or about any-thing else. He simply sat gazing into the middle distance and acted as if Kish were not there at all. Kish questioned and probed, quietly and gently at first, then insistently, but by degrees his proverbial patience was failing. I hung at his shoulder, willing Saul to say something, anything, to show his father some respect, but he didn't.

Finally Kish could take no more. He grabbed Saul by the neck, and shook him violently until he cried out. I was appalled, and for one awful moment thought he was going to slap his son in the face, but at the last instant he remembered himself, swallowed, and let go. When he walked away, his eyes were dismal and worsted, but I'd never seen Saul nearer to tears. For so long he had made no effort to talk to his father; now when he really had wanted to, he'd found himself utterly incapable of doing it.

When the morning of the second Sabbath came, I awoke with an ache of dread griping at my belly. Saul wouldn't get up at all. He said he was ill, and indeed he did look deathly pale. I pleaded with him, told him he had no choice, that Samuel had spoken and he would be sure to know if Saul were not there, but as I bent down to help him up, he shook his head vehemently and gripped my hand so hard that his nails bit into my flesh.

"Eli, for God's sake tell Father I'm sick. I can't go. I can't go through with this."

"Go through with what?" I said. " It's only a Sabbath gathering."

"They are going to proclaim me king, in front of all Israel, at Mizpah. I know it. Eli - I'm going to run away. Come with me."

The raw terror in his eyes made my blood freeze, and I almost agreed. But then something fell into place in my mind.

"Saul, how do you know? How can you be so sure they will make you king today?"

He loosened his grip a little and closed his eyes. "I don't know."

"*I* do," I said, "And so do you. Adonai has told you. I cannot think how, but somehow he has spoken to you. Hasn't he."

Saul nodded lamely.

"Then you *must* go through with it," I concluded. "It's like you said: you can't run away from your fate, Saul. And if he's still speaking to you, then he's still with you. Whatever you feel like."

The whole way to Mizpah Saul lagged behind and kept stopping to rest and ask for water. I began to think that perhaps he might be ill, after all. When we eventually reached our journey's end, much later than we should have done, the hillside was already crowded with people. It took us quite some time to search out the other men of our tribe and to find our place among them. As well as men, there were tents and wagons and pack-animals, for some people had had to travel for many days and cover considerably more distance than we had. The autumn sun still had enough heat in it to be harsh and unforgiving at midday, and Saul looked so sick that we sat down behind one of the wagons, because they were the only source of shade to be found. Saul sat with his cloaked head between his knees, his arms wrapped round his body, rocking himself backwards and forwards in silence. I couldn't tell if he was fainting, praying, weeping, or just quietly going to pieces, and I didn't feel much better myself. Kish kept peering at me askance but I just shrugged my shoulders and forced myself to watch the swarms of men still arriving, gathering from every direction and sitting themselves down to wait. It was an impressive sight. There were thousands upon thousands of them, and the air hummed with expectancy. At the very bottom of the hillside, a clearing had been made among the people, and it was here that the gaunt, cloaked figure of Samuel had appeared, distant and small as an ant. But I would have known him anywhere, from no matter how far away. For some time he didn't speak, for people were still arriving in their hundreds, but at last the seemingly endless stream of men dried up; the last stragglers found places to sit, and a hush fell upon the assembly as the seer raised his staff above his head and began his address.

"Men of Israel!" he shouted, and his voice rang out deep and powerful across the valley, thrown back and forth between the hills so that it came echoing from every side at once. "This is the word of Adonai, the God of our people! I brought you up out of Egypt, and delivered you from every power which has sought to oppress you. But you have rejected me as king. Your leaders have asked for a human king, like the nations around you. So now you must present yourselves before me and await my choice."

An audible gasp arose from every part of the audience. I looked at Saul but he hadn't moved. Kish was staring down at Samuel, unblinking. The seer had begun to walk up and down, up and down, scrutinizing each tribal group in turn, whilst behind him his three brown-cloaked attendants had appeared, one carrying the ephod containing the Sacred Stones, Urim and Thummim, the lots which reveal the will of Adonai; the next bringing a heavy scroll; the last bearing on a cushion a circlet of gold, etched and faceted so that it flashed in the bright sunlight. We were too far away to watch the stones being cast, but there was no escaping the conclusion when Samuel lifted his staff and pointed directly towards our tribe, the men of Benjamin. All eyes had turned on us, some in surprise, many in guarded anger, but no one dared speak against the Sacred Lots. I watched the other Benjaminites shuffling, glancing round, anxiously wondering where the choice of Adonai would fall. There could have been many candidates. There were wise and faithful old men who had lived three score years without bowing the knee to the Baals. There were success-ful businessmen, prosperous farmers, proven warriors in the prime of life. Samuel ordered each clan to come forward, one by one, and for each in turn he cast the lots, but shook his head and the clan was dismissed. When our turn came I touched Saul gently on the shoulder, but still he sat with his head on his knees and didn't stir. Kish had already stepped forward to join the others who were slowly threading their way down through the ranks of the other clans towards Samuel.

"Saul!" I hissed. "Get up. It's Aphiah. Our clan."

But still he didn't respond. Then someone seized me by the arm and pulled me forward, and I found myself propelled involuntarily down the hillside. Samuel had finished casting the lots, and the man with the ephod had retired. But the old seer was still striding up and down, and he had begun to look angry. Then his eye fell on me. I stood rooted to the ground, and returned his gaze as steadily as I could.

"Where is he," Samuel said, and his tone sounded more like that of a threat than a question. I opened my mouth to reply, but no sound came out.

"Where is he?" Samuel repeated. "Where is the Chosen One? Let him come forward!"

I glanced round in dismay, but there was still no sign of Saul. Behind me, the men had started chattering nervously, asking one another who could have dared to defy the summons to Mizpah.

"Saul, the son of Kish!" thundered Samuel. "Find Saul! He is here. I can feel the presence of the Lord's Anointed. Bring him to me."

I wheeled around, and as a cacophony of voices broke out, echoing Saul's name and asking if anyone knew where he was, I began to fight my way back up the hill. If I didn't fetch him, someone else would, and I doubted he would even make it to the front without me. Someone was already shouting that he was here, behind the supply-wagons. As I broke through the last cluster of men, gasping for breath, I expected to find him still huddled there insensible.

Thankfully, however, I was wrong. He was on his feet, gazing around at the boundless sea of heads. There was still no colour in his cheeks, and he looked shaky and bewildered, like someone awoken in the middle of a nightmare. But as he stood there struggling with his doubts, it seemed that he drew strength rather than fear from the awesome scene unscrolled before him. You could almost watch him growing. As he began to walk down through the multitude towards Samuel, he didn't even recognize me.

When he passed between the ranks, every man shrank back from his path, so that a wave of movement rippled away from him each way across the hillside, as though a stone had been dropped into the human ocean. With each step, his shoulders got squarer, his back straighter, his head higher. And as he came to understand what was going on inside him, the radiance returned. His pale face shone, his eyes blazed like burnished copper. If Adonai's spirit had filled him when he was with the sons of the prophets, then it filled him doubly now. You would have sworn that every vein in his body pulsed with royal blood.

I studied the faces of the men sitting closest, as they nodded their respect and watched him go past. Many of them were our own townsfolk, but they stared as though they had never laid eyes on Saul before that moment. Some seemed entranced by his beauty and his bearing; some raised their brows as they attempted to equate the solemn, solitary youth they knew, with the noble stranger who moved through their midst like the king he must become. But I couldn't fail to hear the low, angry mutters of those who sat further away.

Now Saul had drawn level with Samuel; the seer's wrath dropped visibly from him and something like paternal pride took root in its place. Saul knelt before him once more, as he had in the dust of the lonely road at Ramah, but this time every man in Israel saw him do it. Though for Saul and Samuel, gazing now into one another's eyes, it seemed to me that the bond linking their spirits made them again the only two people present. The silence enveloping them was profound and total and pregnant with awe. Gently the seer lifted the folds of Saul's cloak away from his head so that his hair fell shining over his neck, and taking the golden circlet from the attendant who bore it, he placed it, unhesitating, among the tumbling curls. And he barely had to raise his voice, to be heard by every man at Mizpah.

"This is the One. This is the king whom your Lord has chosen. There is none like him in the whole of Israel." He laid his hands once more on Saul's head, tenderly, reverently, with love. Then he looked up at the hushed assembly and shouted, "Hail your king! Hail Saul, King of Israel!"

At first no one responded. I could only hear my own heart, pounding painfully in my chest, and I saw a shadow pass across Saul's face. Then from somewhere close to me, a man's voice called into the stillness, "Hail King Saul!" And another took up the cry, "Hail King Saul! Hail King Saul!" Then another, and another, and two more, and ten more, and a hundred more, and then a deafening tumult which erupted like an earthquake from every side.

The cheering seemed as though it might go on for ever. I couldn't wrest my eyes from Saul, who was now on his feet again, elated, breathless and high on his own glory, the virgin royal circlet gleaming in his hair. So I hadn't noticed the third attendant step forward and begin to inscribe a record on the great scroll while Samuel started to explain to the people the role of king - what their master could expect from his subjects and what they in turn could expect from him. But I scarcely heard, because something the seer had said much earlier had just dropped into place in my mind. *You have rejected me as king.* Those had been the words of Adonai. And I thought, they have raised Saul to the place where their God should be. Surely that cannot be good.

My attention revived as the seer's speech was drawing to its close.

"... Men of Israel, Saul your king has already sworn to listen to the voice of Adonai and follow him in all his ways," Samuel was saying. "So now you must swear to follow Saul."

This time there was no hesitancy. From every quarter the cry went up like a battle-chant. "We swear! We swear! We swear!" until no man dared reveal any reticence, and finally Samuel had to bid them all be silent, so that he could bless them and dismiss them to their homes, and the assembly was ended.

For a while I stood without moving, while the other Benjaminites broke ranks and whispered among themselves. I went no nearer to Saul. Again the space around him seemed holy ground. Neither did anyone come and speak to me. I watched the men start to gather their belongings and drift off to begin their journeys home. Their faces told a dozen different stories - some excited, some thoughtful, but some with furrowed brows and hardened eyes.

When almost everyone had started to head off, it became apparent that here and there a few were not moving. They sat or stood in ones and twos across the hillside, and a cluster of five where the clansmen of Aphiah had been gathered. Once the crowds had cleared out of the way, they began walking down, exchanging wary glances as they came, to converge in a circle of twenty around king and seer, who still stood together, Samuel's arm resting lightly across Saul's shoulders. All the men were young, some hardly more than boys, and all carried swords.

Momentarily I panicked, and my hand went to my own scabbard. Then I realized that the group of five were lads from Gibeah, and one of them was Abner. Just as I recognized him, he stepped forward from the circle. His throat tightened visibly before he spoke, but when he found his voice, it was steady and clear, though in striving to be formal, his words sounded stilted.

"If the king is willing, I should like to serve among his personal bodyguard," he said to Samuel. "My name is Abner, son of Ner. I am Saul's cousin. I believe these friends of mine from Gibeah share the same desire."

One by one the others introduced themselves, each in turn echoing Abner's intentions. I was too dazed to remember their names, except for that of one youth whom I hadn't seen before. For some reason he stood out to me from the rest - perhaps it was the combination of his boyish appearance and his military record that impressed me. He was tall and attractive, with straight black hair and a fresh, open face, and he wasn't much older than Saul and me, but he already had five battles to his credit, and said he'd fought against the Philistines at Shiloh. His name was Eliab, son of Jesse from Bethlehem.

"And *is* the king willing?" Samuel asked, turning to Saul.

Saul started; it seemed to surprise him that his opinion should be relevant. He scanned the arc of faces, fastening his eyes on each one. Then with a sideways glance at the seer, he nodded. I don't think he trusted himself to speak.

"That is good," Samuel observed. "A man in authority always has enemies. True friends are worth more than all the treasure he could amass in a lifetime."

Saul remained silent, but he smiled faintly at Abner. His cousin's face lit up, the way it used to when they were children. Abner had idolized Saul all his life; perhaps he was thinking that today his dogged devotion had been vindicated.

"But come now." Samuel motioned the twenty closer. "You men must take a special oath. You must swear that from this moment on, you will give your own lives before you see any harm come to your king. And you must give up all thought of returning to your own homes. You will have to come with Saul and myself to Ramah. If you can't do these things, then you must leave now."

He waited for some while, but none of them moved. So one at a time the old seer made them come forward, lay their swords at Saul's feet, and repeat the oath. Then Saul embraced each of them, and though he did so with due dignity, I caught the joy in his eyes, because already men had followed him.

It was only when Samuel seemed about to lead Saul and the Twenty away, that I remembered myself, and began to feel the rejection. I suppose at the back of my mind I'd already questioned why Samuel hadn't made *me* take the oath; some arrogance had told me he had seen the scars on our wrists. But now I realized it was my pierced earlobe that counted for more in the prophet's eyes.

Then as I lingered behind, desolate, Saul turned from Samuel's side and started back towards me. I was about to sink to my knees again before him, for I sensed Samuel's critical gaze trained upon us and it made me feel awkward, but Saul seized me by the arms and held me on my feet. With a quirky grin, he said in mock solemnity,

"Stand up, Eliphaz Rabshakeh."

Rabshakeh? I said nothing, but no doubt my eyes asked the question.

"Eliphaz, Cupbearer to the King," he translated – from Assyrian, for his own language had never before had need of such a word. "They say no one is closer to a king than his cupbearer." Then he turned and ran back to join the others, a spring in his step and a lightness in his spirit as he allowed himself to accept what fate had bestowed on him. He wound one arm around Samuel and one around Abner; I walked along behind, trying to look happy for him, but my heart was heavy.

CHAPTER 9

We didn't return to Gibeah that night, nor indeed for many weeks. Samuel took us back to his home at Ramah - Saul, the twenty men who would serve him, and me. For days on end crowds of people flocked to the seer's house from all over Canaan, to extend their felicitations to the boy become king, and to shower him with gifts. The rich merchants and farmers brought their finest jewels, chests laden with gold pieces, silks, furs, fine pottery from the West, spices and perfumes from the East, the poor brought jars of olive oil or a single lamb or dove; but in a matter of days Saul had become not only king but also the wealthiest man in Israel.

The leaders of the Twelve Tribes came and swore their own solemn oath of allegiance, and brought Saul a magnificent mace, a heavy chain of office and a matching gold wristband which they'd had engraved with the sacred symbols of each tribe. Yet I couldn't help but notice that there were some distinguished noblemen who were conspicuous by their absence.

I'm not sure exactly how long we spent there, but it was long enough for the winter to come, with its lashing rains, its hailstones as big as fists, and even falls of snow up in the mountains; and then for it to pass again and the warmth of springtime to return. Slowly I got used to the strange new life, to the twenty youths who shared it with us and whom I gradually came to know well. Besides Abner and Eliab, there were Joachim, Simeon, Er and Ahimaaz from the town of Gibeah itself; Jacob and his four brothers who lived just outside the walls; Eliab's younger brother Abinadab; Barak, Nathan, Joseph and Joab from the hill-country around Jebus; and Jannai, Amos, Lamech and Harim who came from somewhere way up north.

I even grew used to living constantly under Samuel's eye, but there was still something about the old seer that made me uneasy, and though I tried to hide it, I was sure that he knew. Saul never seemed to feel it; he appeared to see in Samuel the kind of father he had always wanted, and Samuel apparently doted on him like a son.

For there were so many things which Saul had to learn, and only Samuel could teach him. The seer was already an old man, and he must have known that he was not long for this life. In a hundred ways he had been almost king himself. He had toured the country judging disputes; he had called the assemblies when matters of state needed to be discussed and decided; he had rallied the Israelites against their enemies; and he had sacrificed for the nation to Adonai and relayed his words to the people. It was Samuel's resolve and his prayers which had stifled the power of the Dark Religion and driven the Baal worshippers underground, and which had more or less kept the Philistines at bay until now. So now there was an air of urgency in the seer's eagerness to pass on his wisdom to Saul.

As Saul's cupbearer I was in the young king's presence almost every moment of those strange days and nights at Ramah, but scarcely ever was I alone with him. Always Samuel was there, talking, teaching, chiding, encouraging. The bond between them grew stronger, whilst I grew more alone and my suspicion of Samuel intensified.

I don't suppose I was the only one to feel the bite of jealousy. There were Samuel's sons also. It had never once crossed my mind that the old man might have anything so normal as a wife and children; yet it turned out that though his wife was dead, she had borne him sons who still lived. But while Samuel's blood undoubtedly ran in the veins of the two youths who carried his name, their souls seemed to have a different father. I only ever saw them once. They arrived together at the house one day, asking for money, but two of Samuel's brown-cloaked disciples sent them away before ever they got near him, for it was rumoured that they had already squandered their inheritance on feasting, wine and women. It was scarcely surprising that the leaders of the tribes had feared a future without Samuel, where his power might devolve into the hands of his wastrel offspring. Nor was it surprising that Samuel's eyes would cloud with disappointment whenever his sons and their ways were brought to his mind. It was only when he looked at Saul that the light of hope was kindled on his face, and Saul would smile, and know.

As our days hummed with activity, so the nights rang with worship. Most evenings Saul would take his harp or his flute, and join Samuel and his disciples as they gathered to commune with Adonai. I never dared go near - I had no desire to wind up in agony flat on the ground again - so I never found out quite what they did, except that I heard the frenzied singing and the ecstatic voices shouting prayers and prophecies in a language not of this world, and I saw Saul's face, awash with bliss, when many hours later they would at last emerge. If he went in tired, he came out refreshed, if he went in gloomy, he came out glad, if he went in sickly, he came out well. Excluded and isolated, I was eaten up inside, but my fear was stronger than my jealousy, and whenever Saul suggested I come with him, I would shake my head violently and slip away before he could make me change my mind. I had been circumcised a follower of Adonai, but more and more I was seeing him as Saul's God, not mine.

And so I watched, as the weeks went by and Samuel began to involve Saul in every detail of his life and responsibility, and Saul sought to absorb into himself the ancient knowledge and wisdom of which the old seer was guardian. Samuel took Saul with him when he went on his circuits of the country listening to disputes and giving his verdicts, and gradually it was Saul who heard the cases and gave the judgments. Samuel arranged meetings between Saul and the leaders of the tribes to discuss the governing of the land, and the forging of the old, haphazard confederacy into a single, unified kingdom. He taught Saul the secrets of the leading of men and the strategies of war, and made him train for combat each day with the Twenty Companions. He instructed him in the Law of Herem, the Holy Ban - the war with the Philistines which was inevitably coming was a Holy War, and its spoils must belong to Adonai. The pagan cities must be burned, every man must be put to the sword, along with his livestock, and any treasure was to be placed in the central sanctuary of Israel's God.

In addition, Samuel taught Saul the manner in which he was to be king. There was to be no extravagant palace for the ruler of Israel, no harem of women, no worship of the monarch. Saul was never to be king in the way that the Egyptians had kings - more gods than men, living in shameless luxury surrounded by grovelling courtiers and the plunder from their victories. He was to be a man, as other men are, performing the tasks other men perform, and above all he must learn to remain humble and to listen for the voice of Adonai within him.

I was surprised to see that this still didn't come easily to Saul. Often he struggled, unsure what sprang from the fountain of the Divine, and what was the product of his own fruitful imagination. Gradually he learned, gradually he gained the discernment, yet it came slowly and sometimes made him anxious.

But there was one task which Saul was never allowed to perform. Samuel never permitted him to offer the sacrifices, and I found this hard to comprehend, though I pondered it frequently. It was as if the seer were saying - you may be judge, you may be prophet and war-leader, yes, you may even be king - but you shall not be priest. Perhaps this also was because he feared for Saul's humility before Adonai; he wanted him to remain in healthy awe of the sacred mysteries. But I wondered.

As the time for Passover drew near, I noticed a

change in Saul, a restlessness such as I hadn't seen in him since our coming to Ramah. His mind wandered when Samuel was giving him instruction, and when the local people came for his advice and rulings he often had to ask them to repeat their requests. More than once his spear missed its target during training, and I saw Abner's eyebrows go up. Whenever he could, he would shake off those who clung around him, and go up on the rooftop alone, scanning the tangle of houses and streets in the town down below as though he searched for something or someone, but what, I didn't know. Finally Samuel must have decided it was time to intervene, and one morning at breakfast asked him outright what was on his mind.

"It's nothing," said Saul. "It will pass."

"It may pass, but not without consequence," Samuel chided, and the edge to his voice was like a sword-blade. "Come - you have been troubled these two Sabbaths past, and it is interfering with your education and your duties as king. I think it is time for you to tell me."

Saul looked round, then exhaled slowly. "Very well then," he began with deliberate smoothness. "I will tell you. It is the Feast of Passover in less than one week from now. Never in my life have I missed celebrating it with my family. But this year it seems I must remain here, as you have said nothing which leads me to believe otherwise. I'm unhappy, Samuel. I miss my parents."

I thought, and you parted from them with bad blood between you; for I could see the guilt behind his eyes. But the seer just nodded pensively, turning Saul's words over in his mind. I wasn't surprised that he had difficulty coping with the concept that family ties actually meant something to some folk.

At length Samuel conceded, "Yes, my son. You have reason to be disturbed. Yet some things are necessary, and must be endured when you are king."

"Do you think I don't know that?" Although Saul kept his voice down, I smelt the conflict rising. I dreaded to think what would happen if Saul's clash of wills with his father were re-enacted here. "But I am needed there too," he persisted. "I know I am, and it's making me depressed. I'm not sleeping, Samuel. Something is wrong at Gibeah. I just need to go home."

Samuel scratched at his beard. "Your place is here at Ramah, my son. This is where you keep court and where the sacrifices must be performed. Ramah has been the focus of our people's hope ever since Shiloh fell. This is your home now."

But Saul was not through. "With respect, sir," he said, "I would prefer to keep court at Gibeah."

I swallowed my breath. The two of them were studying each other in a way they never had - with suspicion. Each was on his guard, each weighing up the strength of the other's resolve, considering his next move. The tension in the air was almost tangible, and I was sure that I was not alone in wondering who was truly king in Israel. When Samuel showed no intention of breaking the deadlock, Saul continued, but more nervously, "The Ark of Adonai is not kept at Ramah, is it? By rights our court should be at Kiriath Jearim, not here at all. But Gibeah is my home, Samuel. I want to go back. Today."

"Very well." Samuel waved one hand dismissively, but his tone threw out the challenge. "You are king. You must do as you think fit. But you know what I told you on the day I anointed you. You must listen to Adonai, and you must listen to me, for I am his prophet."

Saul lowered his gaze and regarded the untouched plate of food before him. Then without looking up again, he shoved it angrily away, sprang to his feet and strode out of the room.

For the rest of the day, they didn't speak. Samuel presently left the house and went up to the sanctuary, where he remained until nightfall. Saul stormed about fuming silently, and resolutely packing his possessions into a large gilded chest some clan chief had brought him as a gift. But he didn't leave. He could have walked right out of the door at any moment he chose, yet he didn't. Nor would he speak to me.

Then at the dead of night, his shadow appeared above me in the flickering lamplight.

"Eli! Eli, get up," he hissed in my ear. "We're going."

"What - now?" I mumbled, sitting up and rubbing my eyes. The night air was cold about my shoulders and I shivered compulsively.

"Yes, now. We're needed at Gibeah. I know it, and I can't sleep for thinking about it. Come on."

"But it's pitch black outside," I protested rather fatuously.

"So much the better," he said, furtively glancing round and handing me my cloak. He was fully dressed and had his own cloak wrapped around his head, so that his face was hidden. "I don't want Samuel to know we're gone until dawn."

"What about the others?" I persisted. "They'll all be

asleep, except whoever's on guard duty. And what do we tell him?"

"It's Abner's watch. We'll take him with us. Eliab and the rest will have to use their initiative in the morning. Now get moving."

So I scrambled out of bed, slung on my cloak and my weapons, and stole out after Saul. He carried nothing but his spear and sword; clearly he had abandoned all thought of taking the chest with him. I didn't think it prudent to ask why we were escaping in darkness like prisoners when we could have walked out freely in broad daylight and seen our road clear before us. Perhaps Saul did feel to be a prisoner, and leaving like one seemed fitting.

In the dimly slanting moonlight we could just make out the broad figure of Abner crouched by the doorway, his drawn sword resting lightly across his lap. Saul crept up on him from behind and clapped his hand over his cousin's mouth before he could exclaim in surprise. "We must return to Gibeah," Saul whispered, "And you're coming with us." He released Abner from his grip - being better drilled than me, Ner's son asked no questions - and the three of us slipped outside into the night.

The sky was cloudy and the moonlight patchy; at times we could hardly see the road a fathom in front of us. We had no lamp with us and no means of lighting a torch, so the journey was a fearful one. Every unexpected sound made me start, every cracking twig or rustling branch put me in mind of lions, or bears, or Philistines. I sensed that Abner too was tense and apprehensive but Saul forged ahead regardless.

"It's not far," he kept insisting. "We'll make Gibeah

easily before dawn. Then there will be my mother's bread to settle our stomachs, and soft mattresses for us to catch up on our sleep. And I shall be free."

"Free?" I repeated stupidly, then cursed as I tripped on a straggling olive-root. "What do you mean? You can't run away from the kingship now."

"I don't intend to," Saul replied from between gritted teeth. "I intend to be king for the first time. I have been ruled by Samuel long enough. Adonai has chosen his man, remember."

Be careful, Saul, I thought, but didn't dare say it.

We were still on the road when dawn began to show in the eastern sky.

"I only hope we shan't be too late," Saul was muttering.

"Too late for what? Passover isn't for five days yet," Abner pointed out breathlessly. But Saul didn't answer.

By the time the first houses of Gibeah came into view, there was a distinct red glow on the horizon and the sky was starting to be darkly blue instead of black. But there was no one about yet except the odd shepherd by his fold, silhouetted against the rapidly brightening heavens. Those houses which had shutters still had them closed and everywhere was silent. The sentries at the city gates raised their eyebrows but nevertheless bowed and let us past without a word when they saw who we were. We climbed the hill, panting and flagging, and I heaved a sigh of relief as we reached the fortress; Abner and I flung ourselves thankfully on the ground to get our breath back while Saul hammered on the closed gates.

"Mother! Father! It's me, Saul!" he shouted, and his

voice rang out brazen against the early morning stillness. No one replied, and he called again, "Kish! Rachael! We're home! Open up!" But still there was no response, except that here and there lights appeared at the windows of nearby houses. Puzzled, he began pounding again with his fists, until the very gates shook in their sockets, but to no avail. His puzzled expression had set into anxiety.

"Where can they be?" he demanded irritably. "They must have heard."

"They could be sleeping on the roof," I suggested. "They might not hear us from up there."

This time all three of us began banging on the gates and yelling until our throats hurt; but still nothing. Saul was swearing under his breath - something I'd never heard him do - and there were beads of sweat glistening on his brow.

"I knew we should have come earlier," he growled distractedly. "I just knew it. Samuel was right: I should have listened. We are too late. We are too late." He stood clenching and unclenching his fists, staring at the barred gates in helpless frustration. Abner, exhausted, simply sat on the ground and watched him.

Finally I said, with an effort at lightness, "Let's not get worked up about this. I'll climb in."

"Climb in?" Saul exclaimed. "The walls are twenty cubits high. The place is built specifically so you *can't* climb in."

"But it is built to be defended," I said patiently. "If there's no one here to fight us off, climbing in will be an easier matter."

I was right: hours spent shinning up palm trees pilfering dates as a child paid off, and the walls turned out to be no insurmountable barrier. They were of crude local design and construction, made of large irregularly dressed stone blocks with jutting edges, and there were many places where the mortar was missing and I could win a firm hold for my fingers. Eventually I hoisted myself safely over the teeth of the battlements and dropped onto the walkway. Then it was a simple matter to run down the steps to the courtyard below, and draw back the bars of the gates to let Saul and Abner inside.

Now the three of us stood side by side in the yard, feeling the familiarity and the strangeness. There was no sign of anyone, and the place still lay in deep shadow. Instinctively we drew our swords as we crept into the living-quarters, unsure of what to expect, and not daring to voice our conjectures. My mind raced, beset by images of sickness and death, by the echo of Saul's voice saying we were too late, too late. The silence around us prickled and the darkness stung our eyes. In the unlit room we could barely pick out the shapes of the mattresses, rolled up and stacked against the wall - no one had slept there that night. Clearly something here was very far from right. There could be no harmless explanation for Kish and Rachael being away from home with the sun not yet up. Besides, with the gates barred, I failed to see how they could have got out. I couldn't escape the conclusion that they must be somewhere in the fortress, and that they must be in trouble.

We could no doubt have hastened our search by separating, but none of us wanted to suggest it. Together we went from room to room with drawn swords, but found nothing. In the kitchen everything was scoured and scrubbed and in its place, and there was no smell of food lingering. The storerooms still contained jars full of olives, baskets of corn and fruit, bales of hay, and farm implements, but no sign of life. Kish's study was scrupulously tidy, the scrolls and tablets piled neatly on their shelves, the table top bare, which was disturbing, for he was always engaged on some study or agricultural calculation. Soon we had checked every cubit of the fortress, fetching up back in the courtyard again, and the message was abundantly clear: Kish and Rachael were gone, and they had been gone for some days at least.

Then we heard a faint muffled sound in the shadows behind us. We froze, every nerve in our bodies straining; in the ensuing silence I began to wonder if fear was playing tricks on our ears; but then it came again. Someone or something was tailing us. My heart skipped a beat, my mind ran through all the natural possibilities: Philistines, bandits, some wild creature which had taken possession of what humans had abandoned. Supernatural explanations were too awful to contemplate. The third time it came, there was no mistaking it; Abner and I were so edgy that we jumped simultaneously and backed up against the wall. But Saul spun round impulsively, and with all his strength flung his spear into the gloom. There was no howl of agony, no beast's roar, just the twang of the spear as it implanted in a wooden lintel. But when the vibration ebbed, the sound followed it, and this time we knew it for what it was - a muted human voice.

"Saul! Master! It *is* you! Oh, Adonai be praised."

Boaz! Our relief was almost as overwhelming as our fear had been. The old servant shambled towards us with some difficulty, for in the months we had been away he had aged ten years and shrunk until he looked as frail and brittle as a dried reed. His hands and arms shook as he embraced Saul, then Abner and me.

"Boaz, where are they?" Saul pleaded. "Where are my parents? What has happened here? Why didn't you answer us when we were shouting and banging on the gate? My spear... I could have killed you."

Boaz shook his grey head regretfully. "I fear my ears are not what they were, master - Your Majesty. In truth I didn't hear you until you were inside, and then I thought it must be robbers. I didn't expect you before daylight! But we knew you'd come. That's why I stayed here, to give you the message."

"Message?"

"They have gone away, Your Majesty. They left two Sabbaths ago. Your father entrusted me with this letter, to give you on your return." From the folds of his cloak he drew a small scroll stamped with his father's seal. Saul's fingers fumbled as he tore it open and got it unrolled. Day was slowly invading the courtyard; soon the sun would be up, and already there was enough light to make out the words.

To my Lord the King of Israel, being my dearest son Saul ben Kish: the testament of Kish ben Abiel your father. May Adonai grant you his blessing.

I cannot begin to find words to express how your mother and I have missed you in the months since you have been gone. The house is silent and empty and not a day passes but that we wonder what good or evil fortune has brought you, and whether you have time occasionally to think of us. We hear reports of your judgments and your wisdom, and we can hardly yet believe our own son is ruler of all Israel. Every man who has seen you speaks well of you, and we want you to know we are so proud. I only wish you had felt able to tell me what had taken place at Ramah that day... but I should have trusted you. I am so sorry.

It grieves me to bring you sad news, but I have to tell you that your mother is sick. It is not your fault - you must have noticed that all was not right with her even before you left. That is partly what has persuaded us to leave too. The Philistines still control the hill outside Gibeah, and have taken more territory since you went. Some of our townsfolk are now landless, and uncircumcised men grow their corn on fields which have belonged to Benjamin for generations. We are powerless to defend ourselves - our bronze spears are useless against their iron, and you know I would not fight even if I could. Your mother has been too frightened and weak to leave the fortress all winter, and her only comfort is that you are not here to see what she has become.

I have written all this because I want you to understand why we have shut up the house and left Gibeah, and why we shall never return while things remain as they are. Besides, the place holds too many memories and we could not face the thought of Passover there without you.

So we have gone north to stay with your uncle Zeror in Jabesh Gilead. We shall safer from the Philistines there, and Zeror's wife will take care of Rachael. Your uncle Ner and his family are with us, just until Passover ends - they miss Abner too.

I have entrusted the house to Boaz until you should arrive. Please keep him on as your servant - he is too old to make the journey up to Jabesh. The livestock and the estate I have left in the care of our neighbour Yezanel, whom I would trust with my life. He has the use of them and the rights to the produce of the land until you return, so you must make arrangements with him when you do so.

Please kiss Eliphaz for us, and tell Abner that his family are safe and well. Do not come up to Jabesh - your duty lies where the Philistines threaten most urgently. We look forward to the day when you defeat them and liberate our land, then we can all be reunited. We pray for you constantly, and wish you the joy of Adonai.

I don't know how I expected Saul to react. But he merely rolled up the scroll, slipped it inside his tunic, and walked over to the pool, where he sank onto the low wall he had so often sat upon, a lifetime ago. He pushed the folds of his cloak off his head, his brow still damp with perspiration, and ran his fingers slowly through his loosened hair, the gold circlet catching in the first rays of sunshine and looking oddly out of place. While I was labouring to find words, he whispered, "Why didn't I listen."

"To Samuel?" I prompted gently.

"To myself; to Adonai! I had known for two weeks we should come home. If we'd come then, we'd have been on time. Now I shall never see them again."

Without thinking I put my arm around him, but it felt so strange. Once I would have done it easily - now all that seemed so long ago. "Of course you will," I reassured him. "The Philistines are only men. If Adonai has determined to use you to defeat them, he'll do it. Then your parents will come back." I wished I believed it, and wondered why Saul didn't. Did all those who knew Adonai have the inner sight, like Samuel?

"If only I'd realized how much they loved me, how much I loved them," he was moaning, pounding the palm of one hand with his fist, drowning in the gulf somewhere between grief and anger. "I wounded my own father as mortally as if I'd stabbed him. And I didn't even see that my own mother was sick. Did *you* know?

"No," I said, but even as I spoke, I remembered once thinking that she was ageing before her time. Yes, I had seen the signs, yet made nothing of them.

Then he whispered, "Why didn't Samuel want to let me come home?"

"I don't know, Saul." Again for his sake I was loath to voice my doubts about the seer, but then decided that my reticence was helping neither of us. So I asked, "Do you think he might be jealous?"

"Jealous?" Saul seemed genuinely shocked. "Jealous of what?"

"That you are king and he isn't. That you have a family worthy of the name, and he hasn't. And jealous of your relationship with Adonai."

"What relationship," said Saul bitterly.

"Oh, come on, Saul. He told you to come home, didn't he?"

For a long time Saul made no reply. When he did give an answer, it wasn't the one I was expecting. He said, "I don't know, Eli. Perhaps he did. Or perhaps it was just me."

Then he lowered his circleted head and held it in his hands.

CHAPTER 10

For the rest of that day the three of us did little but eat, drink and sleep. But the next morning Saul rose with the dawn. I found him seated at the table in Kish's study, surrounded by an ocean of open scrolls and clay tablets and thoughtfully playing with the lid of a small silver casket which stood squarely in the midst of the clutter. He shook back his hair with studied nonchalance, and smiled a greeting.

"Come here, Eli, we've got work to do," he said cheerfully. "Today I must get these accounts balanced - worse luck - and see Yezanel to redeem my property. Then we need to check that the estate is in good repair, make sure that the hired men have been paid, and get ready for the Passover."

I was startled to hear him mention Passover without any apparent chagrin. He read my surprise and his smile broadened.

"Oh, we shan't be eating it alone," he said. "I'm

afraid you must go on another journey for me this morning. I want you to invite Samuel and the rest of my Companions to share in our celebrations."

"What? You mean to invite twenty men to eat the Passover with us?"

"I mean to invite twenty men to *live* with us, Eli," answered Saul, and it was obvious he was in the sort of mood to enjoy making my eyes start out of my head. "They are my family now. I'm going to set up my court here at Gibeah, as I told Samuel. If he has any real concern for me or for Israel, he'll come. So! Will you go and convey our generous invitation?"

"Well - yes," I agreed hesitantly, "Though I can't imagine how he will take it. He must be boiling with rage by now."

"I don't think so," Saul demurred. "He's wise as well as obstinate. It is as much in his interests to make up our quarrel as it is in mine."

"Very well." I turned and prepared to leave, but he called me back.

"Wait, Eli. There's someone else I want you to visit in Ramah."

"I'm sorry?"

"You can't have forgotten already!" He feigned disappointment, then laughed, and coloured. "I want you to find out the name of the girl I'm going to marry. Go to her house and ask her father for his consent. I don't care who they are or what clan they are from, or anything. Just find her."

I had opened my mouth to reply, but no sound came out, and in any case, I had no idea what I meant to say.

"Don't you realize, Eli?" Saul brought his fist down on the table, and his eyes flared. "We must have lived in Ramah for half a year and I never saw her once! We don't even know one end of Ramah from the other. What an idiot I've been! But not any more. Take this silver casket to her father as a betrothal gift. Tell him to name his bride-price, and whatever it is, say that I'll pay it."

All I can remember of the two weeks that followed is a blur of frantic activity. The fortress heaved and struggled for breath beneath surging throngs of people decked out in all their finery - first Samuel and the Twenty for the Passover, along with the army of women we had to hire and the extra slaves we bought to cope with the special cleaning and the cooking; then the wedding guests in their hundreds - chieftains and noblemen and their families from the farthest reaches of Canaan, as well as familiar faces from Gibeah and soon-to-be familiar ones from Ramah. It isn't uncommon for wedding festivities to last a week among the Israelite people, and when the groom is a king, a banquet in heaven might pale by comparison.

The bulk of the organization devolved onto me, for Boaz was too old to come to terms so quickly with how the grounds of his life had all of a sudden shifted under his feet. Tables groaned like tortured souls in protest at the burdens they had to suffer, as we servants staggered in and out bearing plateful after plateful of every kind of food. Wine flowed like the Jordan, into bellies which like the Salt Sea drank but were seemingly never satisfied.

A magical glimmer of anticipation had settled over Gibeah, and on the night of the wedding itself it was fanned into flame. The sun had barely begun to set when Saul, aglow with impatient excitement, appeared at the gates of the fortress to lead the procession to Ramah to claim his bride. He was dressed in white, from his trailing headdress to his silken slippers, with the glint of gold around his neck, wrists and ankles and gleaming from the royal circlet, with which his headdress was caught into place. He wore his burnished sword belted at his hip, and the cloak pinned at his shoulders swirled to his ankles like plunging water. With Samuel at his left and me on his right, he marched through the crowded streets cheered on by the hordes who lined the roadsides waving branches torn live from the palm trees, and throwing garlands of spring flowers which Saul caught and twisted laughing into his own hair. He swam in a sea of adoring glances; his bride, Ahinoam, the dark-eyed maiden from Ramah, deceptively demure in deep blue gown, embroidered veil and the family jewels, stood radiant in the twilight between her tearful parents.

For an interval hush descended, as Samuel himself bestowed the wedding blessing upon the two bowed heads, then the tumult erupted again, and the landscape caught fire as torchlight ran amok, passed hand to hand among the people; every man, woman and child now held a blazing brand aloft and waved it exuberantly as we passed. The air echoed with their chanting and singing; psalms to Adonai and to Saul mingled and became confused, but we were all too elated to notice or to care. Saul was in paradise. His eyes reflected the fire of the torches; he revelled in the attention and the adulation, his customary fear of crowds dispelled by the wine and the ardour of young love.

The procession wound its way back through Gibeah

and entered the fortress in triumph. I moved among the smiling guests, pouring wine, collecting plates, directing the other servants, tapping my feet to the driving music of the dance. A snaking chain of men, arms linked, faces alight, dipped and twisted among the tables; a band of young girls with flutes and tambourines goaded the dancers to frenzy as they relentlessly wound up the volume and the rhythm, and I watched them eyeing Saul and vying with one another for his glances. Then one of them turned, winked, and blew me a kiss, and I almost dropped my tray of food. The music and the dancing stretched far into the night, until long after Saul and Ahinoam had slipped away to seal their union, and for the rest of the week, I don't think Saul's feet touched the ground.

Even after the feasting was ended and the guests had reluctantly gone their separate ways, the fortress still hummed with activity, for Saul had drafted in skilled craftsmen to build on a second storey to house his Twenty Companions and our extra slaves, and to furnish a chamber for Ahinoam, which he had others line with colourful tapestries and carpet with woollen rugs. He had women choose fabrics from the traders for fashioning his bride's royal gowns and cushioning her couches, and I was sent to buy a slave-girl to be her personal handmaid. For himself, he had a state room fitted out, with a great chair where he could sit to receive delegations and to administer judgments, and with fine couches around the walls for when he sat in council with the leaders of the tribes. The fortress's defences were strengthened, and a lookout tower added at one corner, which the Twenty took turns to man. When everything was completed, no doubt the Pharaoh or even a

Philistine king would still have turned up his nose at the uncultured simplicity of it all, but to us this was magnificence and luxury such as we had never seen, and I don't doubt there were those who begrudged it.

Saul seemed suddenly sure about everything - his ability to rule; his power to drive the Philistines howling from our shores when the time was ripe; his intimacy with Adonai. It didn't even unsettle me when Samuel announced that he was returning to Ramah, for he embraced Saul as he left, and I sensed no atmosphere.

Striking as it did amid such buoyant optimism, the crisis we had to face barely a month after the wedding assailed us with double force. I was lounging in the courtyard drowsily supervising the closing stages of our building programme. It was late afternoon, and work had recommenced after the noontime siesta, but I was still groggy with sleep, for I had been working hard all morning and had barely awoken from my well-earned rest. There was no real need for me to assist physically with the building - the yard swarmed with hired men and slaves breaking rocks, carrying mud bricks, sawing timber, crooning and whistling bawdy songs as they toiled - but not having been a king's cupbearer for long, I wasn't used to watching others work while I stood on my dignity. Accordingly, I was as sweaty and grimy as the rest of them, stripped to the waist, with my dust-caked tunic twisted up between my legs. I was resigning myself to the fact that it was time I put my shoulder to the wheel once more, when I felt an urgent tug at my elbow and found the old servant Boaz hovering anxiously behind me.

"Master Eliphaz, there are some ambassadors here

from Jabesh Gilead, to see my lord the king," he whispered. "I don't think it's good news."

I grimaced. I hadn't seen Saul for hours, and was hardly attired for receiving official delegations myself. I ordered Boaz to show the ambassadors into the courtyard, while I went to look for Saul. The state-room was empty, but Abner was squatting in the doorway, idly polishing his sword.

"Abner, where's Saul?" At home, between us, he was still Saul, never His Majesty.

Abner shrugged. "I think he went out to the fields to see Yezanel."

Cursing, I ran back into the courtyard. Boaz had already brought the envoys inside. There were six of them, all men of middle age and sober appearance, presumably the elders of their city. Each of them wore an ankle-length robe of soft wool, and an elegantly wrapped turban, but the fabric of their cloaks had been torn in token of mourning. Their faces wore masks of studied gravity, but the veneer was thin. Their eyes betrayed what lay beneath. Unalloyed fear.

"The King is out on his estates," I apologized, acutely conscious of my dishevelled appearance as I had to tell them I was Eliphaz Rabshakeh, Saul's personal attendant. "Can I be of any help to you? Or would you care to wait in the reception-room while I fetch him?"

One of the six, apparently elected as their spokesman, ran his eyes along the line of his comrades, then stepped forward and bowed solemnly. If I'd been less apprehensive, I might have found the thing amusing: this distinguished, sumptuously-dressed elder doing obeisance to a dirty, half-naked youth of sixteen who was still technically a slave. "My name is Simeon ben Remaliah, my lord," he said, with faultless courtesy of tone, but the flicker of dubious concern in his eyes didn't escape me. "With respect, our mission is urgent, and I think the king may prefer to hear what we have to say when he is alone rather than here among his - courtiers. With your permission, we will accompany you."

"Very well," I agreed, my lips dry now with foreboding, and with the six august strangers following me, I set out from the fortress, taking the road which snaked down the hill and then led through the eastern gate of the town out into the fields of Saul's estate, where the ripe corn swayed rich and golden in the shimmering heat.

Thankfully I had no difficulty locating Saul. He was standing some distance away, thigh-deep in his crop of solid sunshine, chewing on a corn-stalk and deep in conversation with Yezanel, whom we now employed to manage the farm. The harvest had already begun; teams of oxen were hauling away creaking carts laden with sheaves, whilst the red-faced labourers were loading the next ones. It was against one of these wagons that Saul was leaning, his eyes scanning his flourishing domain with relaxed approval as he talked. He wore nothing but a plain linen tunic, a short sword slung carelessly at his hip; his tanned arms and legs were bare, and only the heavy wristband and the circlet glinting among his riffled curls marked him out for who he was. To our visitors he probably looked little more like a king than I looked like his chamberlain. As we approached he turned and grinned at me. But the moment his eyes flicked from me to the members of my entourage, he picked up the atmosphere; he stood up straight, letting the stem of corn drop from his fingers.

I bowed my head with formal correctness, but kept my eyes fixed on his. I said, "My lord, these men are from Jabesh Gilead. I think - they have bad news."

Saul's eyes narrowed. The ambassadors' spokesman repeated his introduction and added, "Part of our message you may wish to hear in private - Your Majesty."

The other envoys had already retreated to a respectful distance. Without speaking, Saul waved Yezanel away, but motioned me to come closer.

Despite the alleged urgency of his mission, the noble Simeon ben Remaliah didn't begin his speech at once. He must have known already that the new king was young, yet he seemed ill-prepared to deal with a fresh-faced adolescent who hadn't seen seventeen summers. When finally he spoke, it was with the steady, deliberate voice of a man who has rehearsed his words so many times that the heart has gone out of them.

"Your Majesty, all Israel fears the might of the Philistines. But many have allowed themselves to forget that on our eastern borders we have a much more ancient enemy. No one seems to heed it except those of us who are forced to live on its doorstep. But now I regret that we have no choice but to recognize it, though our attention may have come too late."

"What?" Saul responded tetchily. "What are you talking about? Will you come to the point?" He was still too young and too inexperienced to have learnt to hide his frustrations behind protocol.

"My lord, the Ammonites who live to the east of the

Jordan under King Nahash have attacked our city. Many of the inhabitants are already dead. Now they have us under siege and if we do not get help within seven days we shall have no alternative but to surrender to them. They will accept our capitulation on one condition only. They intend to gouge out the right eye of every man, woman and child in Jabesh as a witness before all our enemies to the weakness and disgrace of Israel - and of her king."

"The Ammonites," Saul repeated, and he spoke softly, but his fingers were curling and his eyes still smouldering. "They haven't dared attack our territories for generations."

"I know, my lord." Simeon's voice was less steady now, the veneer less polished. He was clearly at pains to maintain appropriate decorum, but his despair was becoming visible despite himself as it came home to him that the only standard his people had left on which to pin their flags of hope had turned out to be little more than a child. "But we are in desperate straits. Our people are paralysed with fear, and as their leaders we are powerless to defend them. Only an army gathered from all Israel will be strong enough to defeat Ammon. You must grant us permission to convene a council of tribe leaders so we can persuade them to come to our aid. If we fail - my lord, the security of the whole of Israel will be at risk."

I can't imagine that there was anything Simeon could have said which would have excited Saul's simmering anger more rapidly than that. "A council of tribe leaders?" he retorted, the smoke in his eyes bursting into flame, his cheeks turning crimson. "Is that what you're asking for? Do you imagine that Israel has a king merely for the sake of appearances? If I decide to summon the tribes to fight, they will fight."

Simeon's eyebrows had gone up, as he was forced to revise his estimation of the slender youth standing before him, quaking with rage and slighted pride. The other envoys were exchanging nervous glances, and the air hanging between us all sparked with foreboding. Simeon said, "Your pardon, my lord, but that isn't all."

"What isn't all? Speak your mind and stop talking in riddles." Saul's voice came rough and threatening and instinctively I took a step backwards. I had seen him like this enough times now to know when to move out of his way. Simeon was less prepared than I was, and showed it. Predictably, this pushed Saul past his limit. I froze. He had drawn his sword and held it levelled directly at the worthy ambassador's throat.

"Are they living or dead," Saul demanded, grinding his teeth, and no one needed to ask who he meant. Simeon retreated a pace but made no reply.

"Speak!" Saul was shrieking, "Or I swear, you won't live to speak again!" His cheeks had passed through crimson to ashen, his eyes were like blazing coals thrown into the snow of his face. Every nerve in his body was locked rigid with fervour, and I knew then that something more than human rage possessed him. Something from outside himself was feeding on his anger and transforming it. Simeon ben Remaliah, elder of Jabesh Gilead, cowered pathetically, and only when the chill of Saul's blade touched his flesh did he manage to stammer, "My lord, they are dead."

No one spoke. My eyes filled up - the figures of Saul

and Simeon blurred and swam, and all I could see was the two faces I would never set eyes on again. I forced myself to blink away the tears. Still quaking with passion, Saul had torn his tunic, and with trembling fingers was clawing up the dust from the ground and pouring it on his head, while with his other hand he still held his weapon, wavering dangerously now, under the wretch's chin. Then without shifting his gaze, he said, "Eliphaz. Summon my Companions."

"My lord?" I was so shaken, I wasn't hearing or thinking straight.

"I said, summon my Companions!" Saul screamed, and his blade shook so alarmingly that his victim closed his eyes, ready for the end. "Is everyone here deaf, or bewitched? Move!"

Dimly I became aware that a crowd had begun to gather around us, and I had to fight for my way as I stumbled back up to the fortress. I can't recall anything of what I said to Abner and the others - perhaps my stricken face spoke for me. They seized their arms and came running; and found their king transfixed and trembling with silent fury, holding his sword at some miserable stranger's throat.

"How," he was saying. "I want to know how."

"Your father died honourably in the fighting, my lord. He fell with his sword in his hand."

"Liar!" thundered Saul, "Tell me the truth, or you'll pay for your sins here and now, I swear it."

But it was one of the other envoys who told him.

"Your Majesty, your mother was very sick. Your father was - not himself. They took their own lives."

Saul made no response. He lowered his sword, then stood motionless with bowed head, and I thought, now he surely is weeping. I moved closer to comfort him, but he shouldered me aside and his eyes were still dry. He said, "This is it. Israel has grovelled too long at the feet of uncircumcised barbarians. It is time to show them that we are the people of Adonai."

No one dared speak or move. Saul had become a terrifying fulcrum of latent power. Simeon sagged against one of his comrades. The Twenty Companions formed up in an arc around Saul, their weapons unsheathed, Abner at his cousin's elbow.

Saul raised his head and cleared his throat to choke back the passion that threatened to stifle his voice. With forced evenness, he said, "You Twenty, I want heralds sent to every city, town and village in Israel. I want every man between the ages of fifteen and forty assembled at Bezek as soon as they can get there, with whatever weapons they can lay their hands on. Abner - you will organize them into fighting squadrons. Where's Eliab?"

Eliab stepped forward and bowed hurriedly.

"I want Samuel brought from Ramah, with everything he needs to perform the sacrificial offerings for battle. Then in three days' time we shall break the power of Ammon for ever. After that, we shall deal with Philistia. This is why I was chosen."

Still no one moved.

"What are you fools waiting for?" Saul demanded, and the steadiness in his tone was crumbling again. "Get moving! We don't have much time."

I watched the Companions exchanging doomladen

glances. The first real challenge was upon us; they felt the heaviness of it keenly.

"With respect, my lord," began Abner patiently, "It is the grain harvest. The men may not exactly be willing to come."

"Willing?" Saul bellowed, "Willing? They do not have a choice, Abner. This is a royal edict. What do you expect me to do? Waste crucial time gathering their leaders from the four corners of Canaan, then arguing politics while our brothers and sisters in Jabesh are half blinded? Those days are over."

"Your Majesty," said Eliab, "Even the great judge Deborah couldn't persuade every one of the tribes to fight. Reuben, Dan, Asher..."

He never finished his sentence. Saul had turned whiter than death. His eyes were rolling and unfocussed. He had taken his sword with both hands and was swinging it wildly above his head like someone crazed, until the blade sang and wailed like the keening of a thousand mourners. I didn't know what demon goaded him - revenge, guilt, despair, or the spirit of Adonai himself. All of us threw ourselves by instinct to the ground, as he whirled and slashed his weapon through the air what seemed like a finger's breadth above us.

Then I retched, as with one clean, curving stroke he severed the heads of the two oxen harnessed to the cart beside him. Their decapitated bodies lurched sickeningly, hung and twisted from the yoke which had become their gibbet; blood gushed and spread over the earth beneath us. A wave of nausea surged to my throat, and my stomach heaved, but Saul wasn't through. As we staggered to our

171

feet, he was methodically chopping at the felled bodies until they lay in a hundred pieces, and his sword-blade was scarlet and draped with lacerated flesh. Then he stooped, and with his bare hands he flung the chunks of raw meat one by one at the feet of his Companions. His fingers were red with gore, and the garments of all those around him were spattered vermillion. When he spoke, his voice wasn't his own. But I knew now that it was no demon that possessed him.

"You may tell the gallant warriors of Israel that these are the tokens of their king's wrath. Last time they were used to call for the destruction of Gibeah. This time we fight the heathen. Proclaim that whoever does not follow Saul and Samuel into battle will have this done to his oxen; and their chieftains will have it done to their own flesh. Then we'll see who is king in this land."

At once the arc widened, collapsed, dispersed. The Twenty couldn't get moving fast enough. The crowd of watching farmers melted away; the envoys from Jabesh bowed themselves out of Saul's presence, and fled. Saul and I stood alone in the ruined cornfield. Saul was trembling from head to foot.

I said, "For God's sake let's go home. You need to lie down."

But he shook his head distractedly, still not in full possession of his wits. Then he said, "No, Eli. This is no time for lying down. We have too much to do."

"We're not leaving for Bezek straight away?" I exclaimed, hoping passionately for his sake that we weren't. He put his arm around my shoulder; whether to reassure me, or to keep himself on his feet, I wasn't sure. He shook his head again.

"No. We leave tomorrow at dawn. Tonight we pray."

Slowly we began to make our way back towards the fortress. As we passed through the fields and the streets, I could feel the staring faces at our backs, the air gravid above us. The very sky itself seemed leaden with horror. I felt crushed, shattered, in need of time to come to terms with my grief, and with the crisis we now faced. But Saul seemed pent up, poised to meet the challenge that would confirm or condemn him as king. He said nothing about his parents.

So while the Companions scattered to deliver their gruesome gifts, and while the farmers of Israel grimly laid aside their scythes and sickles and headed north with whatever weapons they could find, Saul and I went inside, into the room where we had slept as boys, and closed the door. Saul gave orders that we were not to be disturbed, and only Ahinoam dared disobey. She must have heard the rumours and been anxious for Saul's well-being; she crept in bringing a tray of food and a flagon of wine, but Saul waved it aside and she took it away. He always fasted when he meant to commune with Adonai. Spreading a mattress on the floor, he kindled a lamp to tame the darkness, then he dropped to his knees and knelt a while, saying nothing, staring absently at the lamp which he still held flickering in his hands. A silence grew between us; I felt awkward again, like I shouldn't be there. Besides, it was so long since I'd been with him alone. Finally I muttered, "I'm sorry, Saul. Your parents. I don't know what to say."

"Then don't say anything." He didn't look at me as he spoke; his eyes were open but I knew they saw nothing.

"The time for empty words is over."

I mumbled, "Don't blame yourself, Saul."

"I don't. Not any more." He set the lamp on the floor in front of him, his gaze held in its flame.

"Any more?"

Still he didn't look up. "I knew I would never see them again. I told you when we got back from Ramah."

"You should grieve," I chided him gently. "There is healing in weeping." I think I was angry inside because my own grief was gnawing at me, and he who should have felt it more deeply seemed fixated on something else.

He ran his fingers through his hair. "I've cried all my tears. This is the testing, Eli. It had to come. Adonai doesn't bestow his spirit for no purpose. I will avenge their blood. I will set Israel free. Come - we need to pray."

He drew his cloak up over his head and closed his eyes. His palms lay upturned in his lap, ready, receptive. I sighed, and laboured to offer my own feeble petition to Adonai. But I felt to be shouting into a void, my prayers just glancing off the ceiling. Frustrated, I looked up, but already Saul was far away, lost to me and to everything around him. So I tried again, but the grief inside me was welling up now, and though desperate for his sake not to give way to it, before long my face was streaming.

Saul's hands were so gentle that I scarcely noticed as he laid them on my head. But I felt the heat, the tingling, spreading downwards through my body like warm rain inside. A heat that reached the very tips of my toes and fingers; a strange, surging tide of intoxication that made me feel almost faint with its tender power. Suddenly I could think of nothing but the high place, and the prophets, feel nothing but fear... and I pulled away. His eyes came open, and they were moist with disappointment. He knew what it was I had felt, and he so much wanted it for me. "I'm sorry, Saul," I murmured. "I'm not ready for all that." I got up and felt my way to the door. "You pray. I'll go and get my things sorted out for tomorrow."

"Eli? Eli - please stay with me," he called hoarsely from the shadows. "Please. Even if you can't... I mean... Eli, please. I need you here."

I sighed, hovered, faltered, then walked slowly back, but already the spirit was on him. He swayed gently like a reed in the wind; his lips moved wordlessly. He was lost, open, vulnerable. It crossed my mind that he would hardly know if I stayed or went, yet I didn't go. I watched him, so devout, so bizarrely tranquil; it was hard to believe that such a short time ago he had been consumed by a divine rage stronger than that of any demon. I suppose it should have occurred to me even then, that if he had the capacity for such wrath, it might not only be the forces of good which could harness it. But I already had enough on my mind.

The scene at Bezek took my breath away. The hillsides were black with men, standing dense as pinewoods, spreading in all directions as far as the eye could see. Above the mass of heads bristled the forest of weapons - bows and arrows, clubs and sticks, spike-headed bludgeons, here and there the glint of a polished spear. As we drew nearer, the horde became ranks, the outlined heads grew faces, turned, watched us, grim and silent. In the centre of this forest was a clearing, and there Samuel stood unmoving, the fire on the altar beside him already smoking, sending a thin black spiral wisping up snake-like towards the waiting heavens. Grouped about him were the six ambassadors from Jabesh, expectant now, their dignity restored; then the arc of the Twenty, with Abner and Eliab in the centre, their tasks completed, each holding a tethered ram by its horns.

When Saul and I came out over the crest of the ridge the silence thickened; even the rams stood mute and made no struggle. Every eye was locked on Saul, and I had to admit he looked incredible. Resplendent in bronze, white and leather, it was difficult to imagine how he could have created a more stirring impression. As on the day of his marriage, all of his garments were white. The sunlight breathed fire onto his breastplate and helmet, upon which the crest nodded and rippled in the light summer breeze. His belt, greaves and armbands were of studded leather, and he carried one of his grandfather's swords, with its jewel-encrusted hilt and its depictions of ancient battles. Every eye saw him, but only I heard the heavy sigh whistle through his teeth, and saw the momentary flicker of uncertainty shadow his brow, then vanish.

He glanced at me sideways; I smiled, and watched his confidence swell as he began to make his way down to the clearing where the seer was waiting for him. It was like Mizpah re-lived, only now Saul came as king, and it was Samuel who bowed to him. He motioned the seer to get on with the sacrifices; the blade flashed, the blood flowed on the altar, the air grew thick and acrid with the stench of burning flesh. Samuel dipped his hands in the blood and touched Saul's brow, but as their eyes met, both faces wore masks.

Saul turned to the envoys and spoke calmly into the

silence. "Go back to Jabesh. Tell your people that by noon tomorrow they will be free. Tell King Nahash of Ammon that if we do not cut him to pieces and display his head on the walls of your city, he will be welcome to do with us all as he wishes."

At dawn the next morning, the attack was launched. The host which yesterday had gathered in sombre quietness, today erupted into frenzy; pouring from the hills, swarming across the Jordan, chanting and yelling for Saul and for Adonai, our army hurled itself like a tidal wave upon the enemy in their camp before they could rub the sleep from their eyes.

The fighting was fierce, the slaughter unspeakable. The skirmish we had fought at Gibeah paled to insignificance, drained of all meaning beside what I saw now. Here the tumult and the turmoil, the killing and the maiming, the agony and the horror were multiplied a thousandfold. Terror and panic stalked the trampled earth; men shrieked and moaned like exorcized devils. Blood ran in the cracks of the parched soil, the land groaned with corpses hacked, torn and mutilated.

Saul, conspicuous by his height, his tossing helmet and his spattered white raiment, fought like a wild thing at the head of his host, cutting, slashing, boiling with the passion of Adonai. He was inflamed, possessed, his nostrils breathing fire into each son of Israel, and fear into every Ammonite soul.

Fighting by his side, uplifted by his ardour, I myself did battle like a hero, and though I earned a slash in my arm which made me howl with pain, I must have killed thirty men with my own sword that day. Saul himself ran Nahash through with the point of his spear, and sliced off the wretched monarch's head, swinging it aloft to spur our troops on to victory. By noon every Ammonite had fled, or lay bloodless on the battlefield. In contrast, our casualties were as nothing.

Then the gates of Jabesh were thrown open and the people spilled out like flood-waters, scrabbling to touch Saul's hands, to kiss his garments, to carpet his path with branches of palm. He struggled out of his helmet and breastplate and gave them to Eliab to carry; Abner, delirious with success, swung his cousin up onto his broad shoulders and swaggered with him through the gates of the city, our cheering warriors thronging in his wake, amid shouts of delight and squeals of acclaim from the townsfolk.

Eliab and I walked behind basking in the reflected glory; beside us marched Samuel, cool and impassive. Saul, pale, dazed, bloodied, smiled and waved and drained the cups of wine that his grateful subjects pushed at him, and struggled to keep going now that the battle-fire had left him. When Abner finally lifted him down from his shoulders, he leaned on mine, and with our arms linked we floated through the streets like men dreaming. A cacophony of ecstatic voices chorused, "Hail King Saul! Hail King Saul!" louder than at Mizpah, and here there were no scowling faces to take the edge off our exhilaration. Eliab and three of the other Companions dragged a gaggle of squirming soldiers before Samuel and denounced them as men who had opposed Saul's coronation. They wanted permission to have them flogged and executed as an example to the rest, but Saul, in love with power and with life itself, held his fingers against the seer's lips, declaring that no one else should be put to death today, for today Adonai had granted us victory and set his people free.

That night we were feasted until we could eat no more. As a friend of the king and hero of the battle, I found myself honoured and waited on with the best of them. The Twenty Companions drank and sang lewd and extravagant songs in Saul's honour, Abner and Eliab drank until they danced on the tables, and Saul drank until he wilted and slept with his garlanded head on my knees. Samuel drank more than anyone - and sat sober and watchful and withdrawn. Out in the streets our men still chanted. Drunken choruses swelled and ebbed, surged and faded into the night. My eyelids grew heavy; gently I lifted Saul's head from my lap and laid him on a couch, and with my own head resting on my folded arms, I let myself doze. Then Samuel said, "Come, my brothers. It is time to go."

Hazily I asked myself whether I could have heard him aright. All of us were exhausted, most were drunk, and some were wounded. None of us was good for anything but sleep. The crisis was past and there seemed no reason on earth to deny ourselves a hard-earned rest or to hurry anywhere. But the seer was restless and preoccupied, and there was a hardness in his blue blue eyes that should have made warning signals ring in my head, but I was too fuddled to recognize them.

"Go?" I repeated muzzily. "Go where?"

"We must go to the holy place at Gilgal," Samuel replied, already rising to his feet and gazing thoughtfully at Saul, sprawled insensible beside me. "Saul must be hailed as the instrument of Adonai, and confirmed as king while this victory is still fresh in Israel's mind. This time there will be no opposition."

"Now?" I baulked. "Can't it wait until the morning?"

"Tomorrow is another day." He set down his goblet on the table, walked over to where Saul lay prone, and laid one hand on his head until he sat up, groggy and confused.

"Come, my son. It is time we were leaving." He spoke softly and without innuendo, but gave Saul no opportunity to resist him, for already he was helping him to his feet and steering him towards the door. A vague whisper of unease chilled me now. Samuel had again seized the reins, for Saul was burnt out and malleable.

All night we marched without respite. The sun rose, hugely red and smouldering, and still we tramped onwards. There was no shouting now, just the solid presence of the thousands who pressed on behind, resolute and uncomplaining. But as the world awoke and saw us coming, women, children and the aged poured out from their homes and joined the procession, and the chanting soared afresh as the news of our victory swept before us like a flashflood in the desert. Our world filled up with laughter and tears, hysterical women darting and running amongst the ranks; wives found their husbands, mothers their sons, and all Israel exploded into celebration.

By the time we reached Gilgal, having taken no rest along the route, it was almost sunset again, and Saul could hardly stand. I strove to keep him upright, as through half-closed eyes he stared at the mass of waving arms and streaming faces. He held his hands to his ears, for the raucous psalms of praise threatened to shatter the very rocks with their piercing shrillness.

Again the altar-fires were kindled and Samuel meticulously slit the throats of the beasts that the grateful people brought to him. The pungent smoke from the sacrifices clogged our nostrils and almost choked us, and through the uproar the seer's voice rang out high-pitched and close to manic: "Long live King Saul! Hail the tool of Adonai! Our God has saved his people! Hail Adonai!" Then he seized Saul's wrist and raised his arm in the air, dragging him away from me to stand beside the blood-steeped altar. Saul blinked and tottered and tried to smile. With his free arm, Samuel thrust his staff above his head and signed for silence. Gradually the chanting waned and died, tears were dried, order vanquished chaos.

"Men of Israel," the seer commenced, in a voice at once sweet as honey and hard as iron. "You have seen now with your own eyes that Saul is the king appointed by Adonai. The victory over Ammon was not wrought by human hands; your God has not abandoned you, though your sins are like the reek of death in his nostrils. If you listen to your king and he listens to his God, there will be no end to your conquests; the curse will be lifted and your land will be free. But be assured that if you turn away from Adonai, if you bow before false gods, and if your king begins to listen to his own pride and not to the God within him, Adonai himself will become your enemy. And he will not rest until Israel lies ravaged and broken and her king is snuffed out as a candle is extinguished with the coming of dawn."

CHAPTER 11

The vanquishing of Ammon heralded a honeymoon of peace and prosperity such as Israel had not seen since the days of Joshua. Philistia cowered, and gathered her children within the walls of her coastal cities, like a startled dove fearful of giving us any cause to harass her. All Amalekite raids in the south halted abruptly as the men of the desert abandoned their spoils and fled into the wilderness. A mantle of tranquillity extended the length and breadth of Saul's realm. Wherever Saul walked, the land blossomed and the people flourished; not even the oldest folk could recall a time when they had slept more soundly in their beds at night nor enjoyed such freedom from anxiety by day. The worship of Adonai thrived; the devotees of Baal melted into oblivion, the dealers in witchcraft and necromancy were hounded and banished, and righteousness bloomed like a desert rose. It appeared that the world was in love with Saul, and he with the world. Nothing seemed to shake him, troubles didn't touch him.

He grew more handsome with each month that passed; Ahinoam was the envy of every woman in Israel, and she knew it. Saul loved her with an intensity I had never known any man feel for a woman, and they spent endless hours together, walking in the fields, exploring the hills, drinking in the beauty of their Promised Land. And in the dark evenings they would hold hands and talk about nothing, studying each other's faces, catching each other's laughter and smiles, or Saul would stroke his harp whilst Ahinoam sang in her low sweet voice the ancient songs of her father's clan.

The first rains of winter had barely softened the ground when the news broke that Ahinoam was carrying Saul's child. A wave of joyous anticipation engulfed the fortress and rippled out across the kingdom, to the mountains in the north and the deserts of the south. Saul was ecstatic. He would suddenly grip me by the shoulders as I went about my duties, shaking me until my eyes rattled, and repeating, "I'm going to have a son, Eli! A son!" over and over again. When I got my breath back I would try to impress upon him that the baby might just as likely be a girl, but he would have none of it, and when in due course the tiny infant arrived he was proved to be right.

They named him Jonathan, gift of the Lord, and from the day he was born Saul was besotted. He was overcome by the miracle of birth, of growth, of the handing on of life, and spent hours holding the child, rocking it, soothing it, tickling it, laughing in delight at the first smile, the first tooth, the first word. He would talk and talk to the poor mite, not caring in the slightest that the little black-haired creature understood not a jot of what he was saying.

"You are the prince of Israel, heir to the throne of Adonai's people," he whispered as he sat by the pool in the courtyard, holding Jonathan aloft to see the golden-flecked ripples and the matching golden fish he'd had me acquire, flicking about serenely in the water. "Grow up strong and brave and clever, for one day you will be king after me." Ahinoam would stand and look on, her face awash with delight, until it was time for her to take the child away and feed him.

The days flew so fast, it seemed that in the blinking of an eye Saul's son was walking and talking and charming everyone he met, for he had his mother's jet-black hair and his father's faultless features, and the sweetest nature of any child I have ever known. The weeks became months, the months years, and as he grew and flourished, Saul taught him to read, to write, to use a sword and a spear, and to say his prayers to Adonai, so that it almost made me weep again for Kish and Rachael, and for my own lost childhood. Jonathan learned quickly - like his father had been as a boy, he was sharp, intelligent, audacious, but without Saul's melancholy brooding.

Ahinoam was strong and healthy and more children followed - two more sons, Ishbosheth and Abinadab (who was named for Eliab's brother, as they shared a birthday), and two daughters, Merab and Michal - all of them sturdy and attractive and as alike as grapes on a vine. The fortress echoed with childish laughter, though Saul and I felt scarcely more than boys ourselves. Yet there was still work to be done, business to be attended to, and often when Saul sat long in council or was away from home making a circuit of his kingdom, I would wind up amusing the older children while Ahinoam and her maidservant nursed the babies. I told Jonathan the stories I had loved when I was little - Joshua capturing Jericho, Gideon defeating the Midianites; especially Moses leading the slaves to freedom. Later I helped Ishbosheth and Abinadab to take their first steps, and taught them to say their names, though Ishbosheth could only manage "Ishvi" and it stuck.

When Saul returned from his expeditions we would relax and drink together, and he would tell me about the places he had visited, the meetings he had presided over, the disputes he had solved. He was gaining experience daily; administration was starting to come easy to him.

"Sometimes I even forget to consult Adonai," he confessed to me once. "It's strange, you know. I'm sure the pressure of being the Lord's Anointed is hardest when things are going well. It's so easy to turn round and realize you haven't really prayed for days."

But when Ahinoam was carrying their sixth child, nature began to take a different course. During her other pregnancies she had hardly stayed a day in her bed until the time for her final confinement came. This time she could scarcely venture out of it. She was constantly sick, and her face grew pale and wasted. Saul hired physicians and midwives to sit in constant attendance on her, and many times in the dead of night we were all dragged up out of our beds, for they thought she was going into premature labour and would lose the baby. It was late one evening when the real contractions began. Pain tortured Ahinoam's sunken face, and with every spasm Saul too was racked with agony. Finally, somehow, the midwives and I got him out of the room into the fresh air. It was raining. Someone sent for

Abner, and with our arms twisted around Saul's elbows to restrain him, the two of us sat by the pool-side with the drizzle seeping down our necks and the wind biting our faces. If we relaxed our grip for a second, Saul, insane with dread, would heave upwards and try to wrest himself free and run back inside.

Mercifully it wasn't long before the chief midwife came out to us through the dripping shadows, clutching a tiny parcel to her breast.

"My lord, you have a son," she said. "He lives. He is perfect."

Saul held the warm bundle with trembling arms, his eyes searching the woman's face for a clue to what he really wanted to know. I saw the pity written on her features and my heart sank.

She said gently, "Your wife is dead."

Saul didn't respond. At first I thought he hadn't grasped what she was saying; that his ears had shut out what they didn't want to hear. He stared blankly into the darkness; but then it seemed to me that the life was ebbing from him along with the raindrops that dripped from his hair and clothes. Then, still clutching the pathetic parcel in his arms he hung his head and sobbed, choking and heaving and straining. Abner looked at me in consternation and slipped away. I said nothing, for there was nothing to be said, but quietly eased the new baby from Saul's grasp before he smothered it, and gave it back into the arms of the midwife. With shaking fingers Saul began tearing at his garments until the cloth hung in tatters; clawing at the dust become mud, he smeared it in his hair and over his streaming face. I thought bitterly, if this is the fruit of love, I would rather live my whole life alone, for I don't know how a man can bear it. Then Saul said in a broken voice, "Eli - pray for me."

"What?" I looked up, blinked, panicked. "What do you mean? Now? Out loud? I don't know how."

"Oh God, Eli, you don't need to know how. Just do it, I beg of you! I need to know he still loves me. But - I have no words."

I held my head, grief and terror battling inside me and pounding on my temples. I was only thankful it was dark and he couldn't see that my cheeks burned scarlet with embarrassment and confusion. I closed my eyes, took a deep breath and began, slowly, hesitantly, feeling my way, calling on Adonai over and over again to lift Saul from his agony. I don't know what I said, and I soon ran out of ideas, finishing lamely, "I'm sorry, Saul. I don't know what else to say."

"Amen," said Saul softly.

"What?"

I opened my eyes to look at him, but already he wasn't seeing me. His own eyes were closed, his lips parted, his head thrown back so that the cool of the rain washed the hot tears from his cheeks. Incredulous, I watched my prayer being answered. I hovered, uncertain whether to stay with him or back away from the sacredness around him, but in the end I stayed, until the rain relented, the clouds rolled back, and dawn began to show with the promise of new life. I was half asleep when Saul's voice, calm and normal, roused me.

"Adonai has given and Adonai has taken away," he said, and while I sat and fought to understand, he went inside and ate the first proper meal he had eaten for weeks.

It took me many months to accept that Saul could have taken the death of his beloved Ahinoam in his stride. Of course he grieved, as any man would grieve, yet somehow his faith kept him afloat. For a time he seemed to lose interest in his public duties and engagements, but he still had the children to bind him to reality, all of whom he adored, and maybe spoiled, and all of whom had something of Ahinoam in their looks and natures.

But as Saul's marriage ended, so did the honeymoon of Israel's peace. We began to hear it rumoured that the sleeping tiger on our coast was rousing from its slumber and sharpening its claws once more. Perhaps the death of the queen had been reported in the Philistine cities, perhaps they saw the period of the king's mourning as the opportunity they were waiting for.

At first we heard merely of local raiding parties harassing the Israelite settlements nearest to the coastal plain, but gradually the names that cropped up in the reports belonged to places further and further inland, and alarm grew, for Kiriath Jearim where the Ark now resided lay not so much further east. Philistine garrisons returned to the outposts they had deserted, and once more voices of men and beasts were heard in the camp outside Gibeah. New posts sprang up too - first one at Geba, then more at Michmash, Bethel, Anathoth... some were further inland than Gibeah itself. Clearly the time was coming when Israel would have to show her teeth once more, but I was loath to say anything to Saul until I had to.

And so it fell to Abner to shake Saul from his lethargy and make him face up to what had to be done.

Nature had granted Ner's son little more sensitivity than looks, but he was solid, dependable, patient, and still as devoted to his cousin as he had been as a child. Little by little he coaxed Saul back into combat-training, taking him hunting, praising his courage and prowess, and he talked to him ceaselessly about the Philistines. I had never thought of Abner as someone who gave much thought to the things of the spirit - he had always cared more for action than for words - but he knew the things to say to make Saul listen.

"Don't you remember? It's why you were chosen!" he would exhort him earnestly, seizing his cousin's hands and squeezing them between his short strong fingers. "Adonai chose you out of all the warriors in Israel because he knew only you could drive the Philistines from the land, and liberate his people. Now is the time, Saul. Now!"

And at mealtimes when we ate with the other Companions, Abner would continually steer the conversation round to the latest enemy expansion or atrocity, until Saul could no longer look him, or Eliab, or any of the Twenty in the eye without seeing the word 'Philistia' inscribed across their expectant faces. When Saul and I were together, we talked gradually less of Ahinoam, and more of the challenge that lay ahead, and then one day Saul emerged from his evening prayers, drew his cloak back from his head and said, "Eli, it is time."

Once again the farmers answered the summons to leave their fields, the craftsmen their workshops, again Samuel came from Ramah to offer the sacrifices and invoke the blessing of Adonai. Saul himself became eager and alert, his misted eyes brightened, and the spark of life ignited in them once more. His enthusiasm fed on itself and became infectious - all Israel seemed buoyant with optimism, confident that the Day of the Lord was coming and that soon our nation would rise and shake itself free from pagan fetters. There was no need this time to send out gruesome tokens of warning. Even old men with white hair and gawky lads of barely fourteen years were volunteering to fight.

Young Jonathan seethed with frustration at being left at home with the children and servants, for by now he was highly skilled with the sword, and I had seldom seen a finer archer. It amused me to see him and Saul acting out the old scenes I had witnessed as a boy, with the one who had been the son now cast in the father's role. But Saul wouldn't hear of him going anywhere near Beth Shemesh, where the Israelite camp was established, let alone the battlefield, though by now he was no younger than some of the smooth-cheeked youths who turned up eager to see some action.

But what everyone had expected and hoped would be a swift, decisive assault turned into a protracted and frustrating campaign. The five Philistine cities were too strongly built and well-defended for us to besiege, and the officers of their army doggedly refused to be lured into any kind of direct confrontation. Still they held the monopoly on two seemingly invincible weapons - they had iron, and they had chariots, and with these they maintained control of vast areas of what had once been Israelite territory. Yet despite their strength, their military expertise and superior organization, we kept them at bay, beating them back wherever they pushed forward, redeeming villages and towns they had seized, and seeing many of their warriors fall dead at our feet.

However, time was wearing on, and Saul knew full well that we couldn't maintain an army of farmers in the field indefinitely. Our men had crops back home to be harvested. They had wives and families and parents who missed them. Unless we notched up a victory on a large scale soon, the ardour and commitment would start to fade and we would find ourselves facing serious problems. For far too long our scouts had sat gazing down upon the five cities, five abominations in the land which Adonai had promised us.

Then at first light one morning one of our lookouts reported a sizeable Philistine force of infantrymen and chariots making its way up towards the hill-country, in the direction of Kiriath. Saul and I were still in our tent taking breakfast together and weren't even dressed, let alone armed, and many of our men were still sleeping, when the herald came with the news. Saul got up and began pacing the floor and running his fingers through his hair.

"They wouldn't risk taking the Ark again, not after what happened last time," I said, incredulous.

"Don't be too sure," Saul cautioned, and I detected the hint of a tremor in his voice. "Perhaps they have different plans this time for how to dispose of it. It's a powerful symbol, Eli. They know very well how much it means to our people, and what it would do to Israelite morale if they could deprive us of it permanently. They know what it would mean for me too."

"For you?" I pushed away my plate of bread and fruit, which suddenly I had lost all appetite for.

"Don't be naive, Eli. How can the Presence of

Adonai be taken from his people if their king is God's Anointed? Samuel would be roaming the country with his jar of olive-oil, and you'd be building my tomb."

I swallowed hard. "So what do we do?"

"You go and fetch Abner. When you get back I'll be ready." As I turned to obey, he threw off his robe and began searching distractedly for a fresh white tunic.

Abner's tent was pitched adjacent to our own. When I lifted the flap I saw that he was already dressed, armed and awaiting orders, though snatching a last-minute breakfast: clearly he had a stronger stomach than me in the face of battle. By now the herald's message was all round the camp; the trumpets were blaring, everywhere men were spilling out of their tents, and the air thrummed with nervous anticipation.

"What's the strategy then?" Abner asked with his mouth full, grabbing his gear and making for the doorway.

I shrugged and motioned him to follow me. When we ducked back under the flap of the royal tent I started, and hovered uncertainly on the threshold, for aside from his loincloth Saul was stark naked, and kneeling on the ground with bowed head and upturned palms. Ready? I thought, and stepped back awkwardly, blushing at our intrusion, but Abner, standing formally to attention, coughed gruffly so that Saul's eyes swam open. However, he appeared neither angry nor anxious. He stood up, pushed back his hair and said, "I have the battle-plan worked out, Abner." Then I knew what he'd meant by being ready, and that he was.

"Yes, my lord." Abner bowed and waited. He always observed strict protocol when we were in the field.

"The enemy will almost certainly take the valley route towards Kiriath - it's the only way they'll be able to get their chariots and horses through. But they must under no circumstances come within range of the town. I want you to divide our forces into three. The main force will meet the Philistines head on in the valley, with our archers in the vanguard, who must aim at the horses so the chariots will be crippled and cause maximum confusion. The other two forces will conceal themselves on the high ground either side of the valley, and once battle has been joined they will sweep down and the enemy will be trapped."

Abner nodded and smiled briefly, with measured approval. "And the commanders?" he enquired.

"You will command one of the hill-forces and it will be your responsibility to decide the moment to descend. Eliab will take the other, and he must head down as soon as he sees you move. I shall command the main force myself."

So while the day was still fresh and the sky shimmered with haze, Saul and I set out in advance of the main detachment. In Saul's shadow marched Eliab's brother Abinadab, with Joachim and Simeon at his shoulders, each carrying a sword, a slender javelin and a leather shield. Behind them streamed our squadron, line upon line of men, chanting and jeering, armed with clubs, mallets, slings and staves, but still pitifully few spears and swords, and headed up by the archers with their makeshift bows and bronze-tipped arrows. By the time we reached the valley road and put Kiriath Jearim at our backs, we could already see the enemy rolling relentlessly towards us: an iron-clad military machine borne on the wings of its eagle-swift chariots. My heart wavered - as always, I feared for Saul, conspicuous and vulnerable, his white cloak billowing, and crested helmet gleaming, marching at the head of his troops; though I knew he wouldn't have wanted to be anywhere else.

As soon as we came within range, he gave the order and the sky turned black as our archers let fly. Arrows rained down on the ranks of chariots; horses snorted, panicked and reared, and a roar went up behind us as we watched the enemy formation thrown into chaos before even the two armies converged. Chariots collided and became entangled, horses plunged and fell, and behind them the infantry, goaded onwards by their officers, stumbled and were trampled, unable to force a way through. Now we were within spear-range, and Saul with a blood-chilling shriek brandished his weapon above his head and hurled it into the enemy ranks as a signal to our other spear-men to do the same. By the time the two armies clashed and the hand-to-hand combat began, we had gained a clear advantage.

No matter how many battles you have fought, how many seasons of war you have weathered, that moment of contact always knocks the breath out of you and shatters your braced nerves. It breaks upon you like a storm, with the suddenness of lightning, the intensity of a thunderbolt, and you always taste your own blood in your mouth when you see the whites of your enemy's eyes. Now I was in the thick of the fray, fighting for survival, my own life-force pulsing and roaring inside my brain.

Then Saul fell. I only glimpsed him from the corner of my eye, for I was locked in my own desperate struggle with a huge Philistine swordsman who was skilful and fast on his feet, and I knew I couldn't afford to look away for a second. Even so, I was thrown off my guard, and would doubtless have perished myself, had not my antagonist at that moment crumpled to the ground in front of me, pierced by the ill-aimed javelin of one of his own comrades in the ranks behind him. Paralysed with horror I saw Saul sprawled in a spreading pool of his own blood, his body twisted out of shape, his face contorted with agony. It only remained for his assailant to thrust a sword into his belly while he was down, and end everything.

But while I hung there, frozen and staring stupidly, I became aware, dimly at first, then keenly, that Saul's adversary was already fighting with someone else. A slight, lizard-quick figure in a huge bronze helmet, with a bow and quiver slung over his back, had materialized from nowhere and was cutting and thrusting and dodging for all he was worth. His great sword dwarfed him, yet he handled it with dexterity; his faded leather breastplate was much too large for him, yet it didn't cramp his style. For what seemed an age I could do nothing but watch awe-struck as the dynamic form leapt forward to strike, then recoiled out of reach; then somehow I gathered my wits enough to see to Saul.

He had managed to sit up, but his face was bloodless and he was clutching his thigh, in which the severed tip of a spear was embedded. Our front line had gained ground and the battle-action had shifted on beyond us, so I had time to bend down and get my fingers around the spearhead without serious risk of further injury to either of us. Eventually I worked it free, and rending strips of cloth from my tunic, I stuffed some into the wound and wrapped the rest tightly around his leg.

He was still fully conscious, but I wasn't sure that this was such a good thing, because he was demented with pain and howled in agony when I tried to haul him to his feet. I began casting around for someone to help, but except for other fallen men everyone had moved on. A searing wind had got up and my shouts for assistance were lost on the current. There was no sign now of the stripling who had saved Saul's life, so that I began to wonder if he had been of humankind at all. Again and again I tried to lift Saul up off the ground, beads of sweat breaking out on my brow, and my heart pounding with exertion, but my own strength had been sapped by the fighting and I was flagging. Saul's fingers pawed at my clothing, his teeth were clenched, his eyes black and too bright against his warped features. His struggling threw me off balance: I staggered sideways, then felt a strong arm coil around my back and draw me gently out of the way.

Abinadab! I managed a grateful smile and leaned panting on his shoulder. Joachim and Simeon were with him and had already got Saul upright; they must have seen him fall, and come running as soon as they could tear themselves from the fighting. With one of Saul's arms held across each of their shoulders, they dragged him from the field. Abinadab splashed water in my face; I wiped my arm across my perspiring forehead and felt better. When Joachim and Simeon tired, Abinadab and I took over, and somehow between us we managed to get Saul back into his tent.

I stripped off his armour and got him as comfortable as I could, on a pile of rugs and mattresses. Then I tried to make him rest, while someone sent for a physician. But he wouldn't lie still - even while the physician laboured to wash the wound and put on ointment and fresh dressings, he kept heaving himself up onto his elbows, grunting against the pain, and muttering that he needed to get back to the fighting. Each time someone entered the tent - and many began to come, anxiously enquiring how the king fared - he would groan, as much with frustration as discomfort, and demand to know how the battle was going, whether we were still on the offensive, whether Abner and Eliab had made their attack. And when the physician had gone, and we were on our own, he clawed at my arm and grilled me over and over again: "Eli, who was it? Who saved my life?" But I could do nothing but shake my head, shrug my shoulders, and ease him back onto his pillows.

It wasn't yet noon when the message filtered through that the enemy was routed and Kiriath saved. Abner and Eliab had swept down simultaneously into the valley, and what Philistines there were who survived the onslaught had scattered in confusion. Not long after, we heard the swelling crescendo as our jubilant army returned to camp, chanting in unison the familiar refrain, "Hail King Saul! Hail King Saul! Hail King Saul!" and through his pain a wan smile softened the lines on their hero's haggard face. Only then did he lie back and stop straining; he closed his eyes and drifted into a light feverish sleep.

At first I tried to dam the tide of admirers who came to congratulate the king on his victory. I suppose they must all have known by now that he was wounded, but none seemed able to believe that their idol could be badly injured. Abner and Eliab swaggered in, arm in arm, drunk with pride in their own accomplishments, but they sobered up quickly when they saw Saul's condition. Abner slipped from Eliab's embrace to his cousin's side and shot me a fearful glance, but I said that I was sure Saul would pull through. Abinadab and Joachim returned to check that all was well. Then Simeon came in weeping, and said that Er and Ahimaaz the other two Companions from Gibeah were dead.

It was very much later, when the sun had begun to sink, and the physicians, messengers and well-wishers were gone, that the shadow of a lone, slight figure blotted out the gentle evening light slanting in beneath the half-open tent flap. It wore a huge bronze helmet, a bow and quiver, and a faded leather breastplate; and it said in a small and nervous voice, "Eliphaz - how is my father?"

I was holding a bowl of water in my hand, which I had been dabbing on Saul's brow. As I dropped it, it smashed in a cascade of droplets and skittering fragments, but Saul didn't stir. I murmured, "Adonai have mercy."

He came towards me hesitantly, pulling off the helmet so that Ahinoam's raven black hair fell free, and the face that could have been Saul's looked at me with large, anxious eyes. Knowing him, I think he would have liked to stroll in smiling, but for once fate hadn't granted him the opportunity to indulge his vanity.

"Eliphaz - oh God, he isn't...?"

"No, Jonathan." I sighed wearily, and when I put my arm around his shoulder, it was as much to reassure myself as to comfort him. "He's sleeping now. He'll get well."

I felt him relax against me. He passed his hand across his brow as the fatigue started to claim him. "Will he send me back to Gibeah?" he whispered, his eyes searching beyond me and settling on his father's pallid face. "Eliphaz - please tell him to let me stay."

I shook my head half-smiling, wanting to explain to him that it wasn't my place to tell the king do anything. But I heard myself saying, "I think you've already shown where your rightful place is, Jonathan ben Saul." I mussed his hair - it seemed only yesterday he had been a little boy - then held him at arms' length and looked him up and down. He was dirty and dishevelled, his tunic was torn and bloody, he looked pale and shaken and little more than a child, but it was only too obvious that he saw himself as a warrior. And it was true that he was no younger than Saul and I had been when we fought our first battle.

I said, "I think you'd better get some rest."

For a moment he didn't move. He gazed at his father with a strange expression on his face, then gratefully he began unbuckling his breast-plate, and I helped him unstrap the bow and quiver from his shoulder. Wrapping a blanket around himself, he lay down on the mattress, which was still damp and stained with his father's blood, and stretched out with his head on Saul's chest. He had fought like a man, but he slept the peaceful sleep of a baby, and there was nothing more I could do tonight for either of them.

CHAPTER 12

It wasn't many days before Saul was back on his feet. At first he stalked up and down, up and down in the tent, his jaw set, fiercely determined to work suppleness back into his stiffened joints. Later he ventured outside, making daily circuits of the camp to show himself recovered and thus keep the troops' morale high. Not that it could have soared much higher - our army felt itself immortal, invincible, primed to deliver Philistia her death blow and drive her pollution from our land before the year was out.

Jonathan wasn't sent home. Saul, forced at last to face the truth that his son was of age, kept him at his side and took him wherever he went, resolved to make of him the warrior he felt himself to be. Every man whose path Jonathan crossed fell under his spell; the army doted on him. Charm exuded from his pores, and leadership came as naturally as breathing to him; men and boys fell over themselves to please him, and did what he asked without question. He never doubted his abilities for a moment -

he'd had Saul for a father, not Kish. If this self-confident adolescent had been anyone other than his own son, I'm sure Saul would have burned with jealousy, but he was Jonathan, and he could do no wrong.

So it came as no surprise to me that before many months had passed, it was Jonathan who despite his youth wound up in charge of men - first half a dozen, then a dozen, then fifty, then hundreds. Er and Ahimaaz were dead, but Jonathan more than made up for both of them. Abner, as Saul's lieutenant, gradually entrusted the king's son with more and more responsibility, as he demonstrated his aptitude for command. Saul and Abner led us to victory after victory, and each time Jonathan fought a hero's battle. Now we were back on the offensive - again Philistia cowered while we picked off her outposts one by one - Anathoth, Bethel, Michmash; Gibeah.

Nor did our other hostile neighbours escape the pitiless bronze of Saul's sword. Ammon already lay vanquished; now he smashed Moab, and Edom, and Zobah. Carried away on the crest of his own zeal, he even turned on the people of Gibeon, a small group of Amorites living within our borders, with whom Joshua himself had been tricked into making a treaty of friendship. Saul had the greater part of their population put to death, and razed their city to the ground.

Soon all the ancestral enemies of Israel lay crushed and broken and crying for mercy, with but one exception: Amalek. As the others fell, so Amalek stood brazen as the Tower of Babel amid the rubble of the nations. Saul and I never spoke of this, but sometimes when the victory songs were sung in the long dark evenings, the hero-tales related in the firelight, I caught his eye, and the thing hung over us like a dagger suspended on an invisible thread.

Again, I was little surprised when it was Jonathan who finally triggered the all-out war with Philistia which Israel had both wanted and dreaded for so long. With one thousand men he marched north and launched an attack on the Philistine outpost at Geba, and with his own hands butchered the commander of the garrison. The Philistines must have known then that they could no longer afford to leave the gangrene of Israel to fester and grow, and suddenly the tables were turned on us once more. The largest Philistine army which had yet been seen in Canaan began to muster, up at Michmash, and the knowledge of this wrought devastation among our troops.

Warriors who only yesterday had extolled Saul's virtue to the stars, today went weak at the knees; heroes who had sworn to follow him to earth's ends, quivered in their boots and their nerves turned to jelly. Overnight morale plummeted, faith died, and terror gained a foothold in every heart. When our camp at Beth Shemesh was dismantled and the painstaking transfer of men, weapons and supplies northward to Gilgal began, there were those who angled to go home, and some who did, deluding themselves into believing that if they turned their backs on the awful truth, the threat would miraculously vanish.

It was as though the wind had changed, and now blew cold and savage from a new and ill-omened direction. Saul sensed it too, and was troubled. As we watched the tents being folded away, the ox-carts being loaded, the first clans and tribes beginning to wend their way reluctantly north, his breathing came heavy and his face showed strain.

"You shouldn't be anxious," I said, with an effort at brightness. "This is what you've waited for. You say it's Adonai's will that the Philistines are destroyed. We're sure to gain the victory if he is with us."

"I know, I know." Saul sighed, then shuddered as though squirming for the first time in years beneath the burden of his kingship. "But this isn't the way I would have chosen. It's too soon, Eli. Perhaps I've allowed Jonathan too free a rein; I've expected too much of him. He is young - perhaps this time he's been foolish."

"It's possible it had to be this way," I reassured him. "Maybe the time would never have seemed right."

"I have a bad feeling about this, that's all." His eyes still followed the operations, but I knew he wasn't seeing them. "All these years, I've prayed, I've asked Adonai to show me the right time to make our attack. And now it has come to this. I don't like it."

"Perhaps this is his answer," I suggested, clutching at a ray of hope.

But he shook his head. "Adonai doesn't deal in signs with me, Eli. He speaks to me. But this... he hasn't said anything about anything like this."

I exhaled heavily, sensing the trap which ensnared us, and knowing what it was his eyes saw. For a while we stood silent, sharing the burden but feeling it no lighter. Then he gripped my shoulders and said urgently, "Eli, you must go to Ramah for me again. Bring Samuel with you to Gilgal so he can offer the sacrifices. We shall need Adonai's power and blessing as we have never needed them before - and this time I'm not sure we shall have them."

I glanced down at his fingers as they grasped the

fabric of my tunic. The knuckles stood white against his olive skin, and they shook a little, though whether from fear or fervour I couldn't tell. I nodded my agreement.

"I will meet you at Gilgal, Eli. Good luck."

As I set out, black clouds gathered and loured oppressively from the heavens, the air hung thick and threatening; the ground crawled, every cubit watched by avid Philistine eyes. Spurred on by the keenness of my own dread I moved fast and low across country to the seer's place. But when I reached Ramah, Samuel's house was silent and deserted, the door flung wide and banging in the storm-wind, the threshold spattered with huge droplets of rain which had started to fall, singly and heavily. I pulled my cloak tighter, and with my head down against the wind I struggled up the hillside towards the sanctuary. If he wasn't there, then I didn't know where to look.

The path was rough and stony, the newly-wet ground slippery under foot. As I neared the crest of the ridge, the wind blew stronger and it took me all my time to make headway against it. At the summit I found him, on his knees and motionless, though I could scarcely stand upright in the gale that raged about him. Thunder growled in the distance; the rain came on stronger, and I shivered, partly at the wet trickles down my back, partly at something else. I hung back, suddenly afraid to approach. The seer knelt facing towards me, but gave no sign of recognizing me or even acknowledging my presence. His arms were raised to heaven, his tattered cloak swelled from its fastenings; a fork of lightning split the sky and flashed moon-bright across his tranquil features. It fell also upon a group of his companions, who sat huddled cross-legged in a circle some way off; and one of them saw me.

I walked towards them uncertainly.

"Eliphaz Rabshakeh," the black-bearded man said, without expression.

"I need to see the seer." My voice sounded hoarse and nervous. I cleared my throat and waited.

"Yes. We knew you would come." He uncrossed his legs and stood up; I followed him at a distance. He touched the prophet lightly on the shoulder, and when his blue eyes opened they rested on me at once, as though he knew exactly where I was without looking. With his white hair streaming across frigid eyes he said:

"So. He has sent you for me again, Eliphaz of Amalek."

"Sir - we are in desperate trouble," I blurted out, shouting against the noise of the wind. "The Philistines are assembling an army tens of thousands strong. We need you to come to Gilgal and make the sacrifices."

"The king's son is rash," Samuel remarked, and I shivered again, for clearly he shared Saul's unease. "Nevertheless, I shall come. Tell Saul I will meet him at Gilgal in seven days. He must not move against the Philistines until I arrive."

I hesitated, taken aback. "With respect, sir - my orders are to bring you with me."

There was a fearful pause. Even the wind held its breath. I backed away from the seer's gaze, for his face had become like the storm, black, implacable. Then he said, "You may have your orders, Eliphaz. But understand this. I take orders from no one but Adonai. Return to Saul and tell him what I have told you."

"But sir..."

"I have spoken," Samuel said, and as he turned his head away from me a clap of thunder pounded my ears and seemed to shake the very mountain to its roots.

Crestfallen, I began to retreat slowly back down the hillside, my heart heavy with foreboding.

I knew there was no way I could make it to Gilgal that day. It was already late, and suddenly I was tired; my destination lay as far from Ramah as Ramah was from Beth Shemesh, and I was unsure of the way. I spent the night dozing fitfully in a cave, shivering with the damp, cold and hunger, my teeth chattering, wondering vaguely if this was what Sheol was like.

The next morning, with the drizzle still seeping, I plodded onwards, weary and confused by the shapes of the hills, which all looked the same to a stranger's eyes. I had seldom been so far north, and I was disorientated and famished. Eventually I came upon a tiny hamlet clinging to a wet green hillside, and forced to trust that its inhabitants were friendly, I asked the way. But I must have looked in bad shape, for the villager I accosted insisted on my eating and staying the night with his family. I was torn - acutely anxious to get back to Saul, but knowing I should never make it without food and sleep. So I accepted, and slept the sleep of the dead in my host's cramped smoky room, with his children curled up around me and his sheep and evil-smelling goats scratching in the straw.

Next day I lost my way all over again; and after that I lost count of the days too. By the time I reached the new camp, I could well have been on the road more than seven.

It was late evening when my nightmare ended, but

Saul wasn't asleep. As I ducked exhausted into the tent, he leapt from his mattress, and grabbed my cloak-pins.

"Eli, thank God! I thought you were dead! Where is Samuel?"

I tried to pull free so I could sit down, but he shook me earnestly.

"He - isn't here yet?" I mumbled, almost asleep in his arms. "I lost my way. I thought he would have got here before me."

"You didn't bring him with you?" Saul demanded, his relief swallowed in dismay.

"He wouldn't come," I explained, blinking hard to keep my eyes open, and striving to focus them on Saul's face. It was drawn and grey; dimly I wondered if he hadn't been eating. "I think he had business to do with Adonai. He told me to tell you to wait until he arrives."

"But when?" Saul rasped, shaking me again and making my head hurt. "When is he coming?"

"He said seven days, but I don't know how many… I mean, I got lost and…" I couldn't go on; everything swam in front of my eyes and as Saul let go of my arms I drooped shattered onto my mattress.

"For crying out loud!" Saul shouted, raking his hands through his hair, as he'd grown accustomed to do when he got agitated.

"It wasn't my fault!" I heard my voice whining like a slighted child's and I was too tired to master myself. "I tried, believe me. He was praying at the sanctuary. He would hardly talk to me at all." I threw myself back onto the mattress, struggling with the realization that my journey had been for nothing. Saul let me alone, but I could hear him muttering under his breath, oh my God, oh my God, oh my God, over and over again until I could stand it no longer and sat bolt upright yelling, "Saul, will you stop it? What is the matter, for pity's sake!"

He sank down beside me and sat with his head on his knees.

"Our scouts say there must be thirty thousand Philistine chariots over there at Michmash, and six thousand horsemen - and no one can begin to imagine how many foot-soldiers. Some of our men have been here three days already, and they're petrified. I've had more complaints than I can stand, Eli. If we don't attack soon, we shall be destroyed by our own terror before the enemy even get near us."

"Then why don't you just attack them?" I retorted angrily. "Forget Samuel. Forget the sacrifices. You know Adonai is with you. You're *his* Anointed. I don't think Samuel even cares."

He tossed his head violently. "We will not fight without Samuel's sacrifices. We must not. We'll be massacred. He will come tomorrow."

But he didn't.

Nor did he come on the day after that, nor on the next, nor the next. With every hour that passed, the pressure intensified, and I wound up firmly convinced that Saul was going under. Whether or not he'd been eating before, he certainly wasn't now. And once my anger against the seer had been brought out into the open, its power over me increased, and all my feelings of concern for Saul got channelled into it. Yes, I thought bitterly, I see it all now. Samuel chose Saul on *purpose*, because not only did he know he couldn't cope, but that's precisely what he wanted all along. He didn't simply pick someone he could mould into his own puppet; that's not the reason he went for someone so young and vulnerable, from a tribe everyone despised. He actually *needed* him to fail. He needed to be able to turn round to the leaders of Israel's tribes who had asked for a human king, and say, I told you what would happen. I told you that you were making a tragic mistake. But now, he is afraid that his plan has been thwarted. Saul has not only survived; he has succeeded. Progressively, undeniably, spectacularly even. So now Samuel has set out to sabotage everything. No doubt he was sure that Saul's lack of confidence would bring about his own downfall soon enough. He didn't bank on Saul actually relying on Adonai.

The whole thing seemed so obvious to me; I never paused to question whether I might be wrong.

At noon on the following day, the Philistines launched an assault. Our men fought desperately to defend themselves, but it was hopeless. By the time the sun set, half our army was gone. Many lay dead, their mangled bodies left for the vultures and the hyaenas on the ravaged battlefield, two of the Companions Joab and Jannai among them. Many more were wounded. Simeon lay in his tent with his arm severed below the elbow - he had lost a deal of blood and would be lucky to live. Others had fled for refuge wherever they could find it - caves, wells, pits, fissures among the rocks. Some had even crossed the Jordan and disappeared into the wilds of Gad and Gilead. Another two Companions, Lamech and Harim, whose homes were up here among the northern hills, hadn't been seen since morning.

Saul was beside himself, and the troops who remained were paralysed with dread. Jonathan simply could not credit it that his father was still not prepared to mount a counter-attack unless Samuel came and the sacrifices were made. Abner and Eliab, predictably, were also in favour of attacking immediately. As the five of us sat in council in the royal tent that night, Saul agonized, and took out his resentment on us. I sucked in my breath, watching his temper flare as of old.

"This is Adonai's war, Adonai's!" he thundered, banging his fist against his other palm, his afflicted eyes glittering mephitic in the candle-light. "If we fight without his blessing we shall be torn to pieces."

"For God's sake, Saul, can't you see?" Abner demanded, formality abandoned. "If we don't attack soon, we shall have no army to attack with."

"For God's sake, for God's sake," Saul repeated, blazing. "You say the words, but you don't understand, do you?"

Abner scowled. "What are you talking about?"

"This whole campaign *is* for God's sake. That is why there can be no prisoners, no looting. We are fighting a holy war!"

Eliab leaned forward gravely. "My lord - some of my men have already made plans to desert back to their wives and families," he whispered, forcing himself to stay calm. "What am I to tell them? Stay here, and wait to be butchered?"

"Tell them to be gone, if that is all the loyalty they have," Saul snapped at him. "Is it any wonder that our land is overrun by uncircumcised heathen? None of you cares, no one honours Adonai any more. He brought us from slavery to freedom, he has promised us this beautiful country as our inheritance for ever; but you mindless soldiers imagine that these victories have been all your own doing, and now the odds seem to be against us, you want to throw in the towel. You know the Sacred History. You heard the stories of Moses and Joshua in your cradles. But you understand nothing."

No one dared speak. Saul's face was ablaze and he struggled for breath, his nostrils flaring and both fists clenched. Then Jonathan's eyes caught mine. I looked at him steadily; slowly he got up and went to stand behind the royal couch. Swallowing, he wrapped his arms gently about Saul's neck. His father's eyes closed.

"Perhaps you need to remind *all* our men of this," he suggested. "They are just ordinary farmers. They know little of your - I mean, of our God. Perhaps you need to make them see."

At first Saul ruminated in silence. His eyes were still closed; he scratched his temples distractedly and the muscles in his neck tightened. The rest of us regarded one another with unease. Then he said, "Very well. Abner, Eliab - and you, Jonathan - go and assemble the men in their tribes. I will speak to them at once."

The three warleaders bowed themselves out and left us alone. Saul sat vacantly inspecting a discarded wine-cup on the floor. His anger had trickled away, and when at last he looked up at me only despair was left. He said faintly, "We have heard no view from you, Eli. What do you think?"

I didn't know what to say. I certainly didn't plan the

words that came gushing out of me. "I think I wish Adonai had never chosen you. I wish we could have grown up quietly and farmed your father's land. I wish... oh, why did he have to pick on you, Saul? Why you? If he is all-knowing, he should have known that the burden was beyond your bearing. Why didn't he choose Abner, or Eliab? Even Jonathan? Someone who enjoys responsibility? Someone confident and carefree and unthinking and insensitive and..."

"Shut up, Eli."

"What?"

"I don't think you understand any more than they do." He dropped his head onto his folded arms, and spoke so quietly I could barely make out what he said. "He had to choose me. He couldn't choose someone capable of leading in his own strength. Why can't you see it? Why can none of you see? This is Adonai's war, and everyone has to know that it's his power which has won it. Without Adonai I couldn't rule this nation for a single day. I haven't got what it takes, you know that! But I wanted Adonai. *That's* why he chose me. And *with* him... with him I can do anything, Eli, anything! Never let yourself believe it's just me. I am nothing."

"Yes, Saul." I sighed, knowing there was no point in saying more. Suddenly I couldn't bear to look at him a moment longer. I knew I didn't understand. Adonai and his ways seemed more and more of an enigma to me. I got to my feet and walked slowly out of the tent and up to the field where those of the men who still remained were already flocking to assemble. I could see Abner and Eliab and Jonathan moving about among them, seating them in ranks, settling them ready to listen. Not feeling much like speaking to anyone, I sat apart somewhere at the back. I didn't expect Saul to appear for some time; doubtless he would want to spend time praying, meditating on what he was going to say.

But immediately a ripple of anticipation stirred the crowd, and looking up I saw Saul already walking to take his place at the head of his troops. An expectant hush had descended, but I couldn't hear him speaking. In fact I don't know to this day whether he said anything at all; all I can remember is gasping in astonishment as they dragged towards him a fully grown bull, which was snorting and bucking and pawing the ground so that it took half a dozen strong men with ropes to control it. Then I noticed that directly before Saul, a makeshift field-altar had been hastily constructed of rough stone blocks, and that its flame was already burning.

My God, I thought, he is going to perform the sacrifice himself.

I have no idea why I was so appalled, so totally certain he was doing the wrong thing. Perhaps it was simply that never before had Samuel allowed him to perform any sacrifice in all the years he had been king, though I still didn't know why this should be.

Saul, with Jonathan at his side, raised his sword high above his head, then with one decisive stroke brought it down and slit the great creature's throat so that it collapsed lifeless to the ground. Unconsciousness was instant. Its lifeblood spilled into a deep bronze bowl which Jonathan held out to catch it; Saul took the bowl from him and held it high, his head tipped back, his eyes raised to heaven, before throwing its contents against each of the four sides of the altar. Now he was slicing through the bull's flesh; the flames sizzled and leapt as he piled the portions onto the fire.

A shadow fell across my field of vision, and the seer stood not two paces from me. His blue blue eyes were riveted on Saul; he was muttering under his breath and his face was a nebula of turmoil. I couldn't move, and I was aware of nothing, except Samuel's muted voice hypnotically repeating, "I knew it. I knew it would come to this. I knew. I knew."

Before I could shake myself out of my stupor, he had begun to push his way forward through the assembly towards Saul, but once he had passed me, the spell was broken and I knew I could skulk here no longer. My place was with Saul, even if he was in the wrong. I scrambled to my feet and jostled my way through the crowds after Samuel, but though he didn't appear at any point to hurry, I kept tripping over legs and weapons in my efforts to keep up. Somehow I made it through and took my place at Saul's side.

The prophet's body was quaking. I expected anger; I heard grief.

"Saul, my son." He stumbled forward, his arms spread wide, embracing nothing. "What have you done?"

"You didn't come." Saul's tone was cool, stiffly controlled, but laced with unexpected venom. "I needed you, and you didn't come!" He spoke louder now; his composure was crumbling already. "My men were deserting. How could I attack without Adonai's blessing? I had to do it! You left me no choice."

"And you suppose he will bless you now? Saul - you have been a fool, a stupid fool. And now it is too late."

"Too late?" Saul retorted, "Too late for what? What else could I have done? Gone into battle in my own strength? We would all have been dead meat! You know that better than anyone."

Samuel didn't reply. For a while king and prophet stood in silence, confronting one another like a pair of lions poised for combat. In front of us the men sat appalled, some sunken into shock, some labouring to make sense of the scene being played out before them. Then at length Samuel spoke, his voice thin and sharp as a dagger-blade.

"You could have done what I told you to do, and what Adonai was telling you to do. Or have you still not learned the most important lesson I tried to teach you."

"What lesson," Saul growled, as though he hardly cared any more.

"Adonai expects obedience, my son. Not sacrifice. If you had obeyed, if you had waited - you would have destroyed the Philistines even if you were left with only a hundred men. You feared your own men more than you feared your God, Saul. You're finished. Adonai can no longer use you."

"What?" Saul started, and stared at him, incredulous. "What do you mean, finished?"

"Your reign is over. Your dynasty is ended before it has begun. Jonathan will never be king. Adonai will find the kind of man he wants, and make him ruler in your place."

Instinctively I took Saul by the arm, but he shook me off. He threw down his blood-drenched sword and went for Samuel, his eyes bleeding poison. He gripped him by the shoulders, and all at once the fearsome mouth-piece of Adonai was a frail old man, a withered skin stretched over brittle bones. He was trembling as any man would have trembled: Saul was frenetic.

"You hate me, don't you?" he spat at him, jerking the seer's scrawny body back and forth to reinforce each syllable. "Oh, it's all clear to me now. Deep down in that sanctimonious, self-righteous heart of yours, you're as jealous as hell, Samuel ben Elkanah, because you were never king, and I am. Well I don't need you, do you hear me? I've never needed you! Get out of my sight - you make my skin crawl! I never want to see your nauseating face again!"

He thrust the old man away from him so roughly that he stumbled and fell to his knees. Horrified, I scrambled to help him up, and flinched, for there wasn't a flicker of resentment in the seer's eyes. He just looked sad, very sad. He said nothing more, but simply walked away, the awe-struck soldiers shuffling hurriedly backwards to let him past. They continued to sit in subdued silence, presumably awaiting some order, but Saul gave none. With the flames on the altar still burning, the stench of smouldering flesh floating acrid across the field on the still air, he dashed the bowl to the ground, picked up his sword, and stormed back to his tent.

CHAPTER 13

Over the next few days I grew increasingly worried about Saul. He was sullen and listless and hardly ate. He spent long hours alone, either shut in his tent or away in the hills where no one could disturb him. But not once did I find him praying. He just sat, his chin on his hands, staring as though at some invisible spirit hovering on the air in front of him. And despite the fact that the sacrifice was done, he didn't attack the Philistines.

Several times I made serious efforts to force him to talk, but to no avail. It was as though the last half of his life had fallen away from him like a chrysalis, but instead of a butterfly, the larva still remained. I was sure that his passionate faith in Adonai hadn't just been a veneer. He *had* been reborn. But for how long had he been taking Adonai for granted? For how long had he neglected what he used to say was his constant need: to remain closer to his God than he was even to me? Had his outburst of piety in the tent the other night merely been the product of a guilty mind? I didn't know what was troubling him most - being let down by Samuel; the severing of their friendship; being humiliated in front of his men. Or despite his brave words, perhaps what the old seer had said had truly shaken him.

"I thought Adonai was a God of mercy and for-giveness?" I said to him. "Why don't you tell him you're sorry for what you did? Perhaps then he'll relent, and return the kingship to you and your family."

But all I received in return was the cutting edge of his anger.

"I haven't lost it, have I? Look, I'm still in charge here. I still have my army, my Companions - those who are still living. And I'm not sorry. I had no choice. It's that senile old bag of bones who should be sorry. He should have come when he was needed."

Abner, Eliab and Jonathan still chafed at the bit; and the troops of course had no more reason to be happy than before the sacrifice had been made. Still they could do nothing but sit and wait, at the mercy of the Philistines should they decide to mount another attack. More of them had left and gone back to their families, and now they were doing it openly, in full light of day. It was even rumoured that some had turned traitor and gone to join the ranks of the enemy. At the finish we had barely six hundred men left.

Three days after the sacrifice, I was taking my turn on guard duty at the entrance to the royal tent. It was early morning, so early that dawn had barely begun to show in the sky; away from the deep blue horizon, stars still glittered. For three nights I had hardly slept; I had tossed and sweated in my bed, and now, squatting in the doorway,

I was dozing. A sudden movement from inside the tent startled me awake. My hand went to my scabbard and I swung round, to see Jonathan crawling towards me through the gloom. His sword was buckled to his belt, his bow and quiver slung across his shoulder. I opened my mouth to say something but he raised a finger to his lips and winked at me askance; then when he was level with me he whispered, "I'm just going out for a while. Don't tell my father."

"Going where?" I muttered. "It's the middle of the night."

"I can't tell you, Eliphaz. You'll have to trust me."

I wasn't sure whether I trusted him or not. I was sure of very little any more, but I did know that my first duty was to Saul. So when his son crept outside, I took note of which way he went, and slipped silently into Abner's tent to wake him and have him take over my watch. Fully alert now, I tailed Jonathan he dodged in and out between the tents, cloaking myself in the shroud of the shadows. Having chosen a devious and indirect route, he eventually ducked into the tent which Eliab shared with Abinadab his brother. Puzzled, I crouched outside the entrance and waited. Presently he reappeared, followed by a young man who at first I took to be Abinadab himself, but then saw that the lad was little older than Jonathan himself. Peering into the darkness I recognized Shammah, Abinadab's younger brother. Undetected, I stalked them to the edge of the camp, wondering whose tent they could be making for now, but to my surprise they kept going, out westwards in the direction of the mountains. The sky was brightening: I could see my way clearer but also knew myself more vulnerable to discovery.

Steadily we began to climb, first the foothills, then over rocky ground up into the mountains themselves, when suddenly it dawned on me that I knew where we were heading. We were making a bee-line for the pass of Michmash which led directly to the Philistine camp.

I paused, racked with clashing loyalties, furiously debating whether to intercept the youths or not. Jonathan was notorious enough already for his impulsiveness - I hadn't forgotten Geba - and I was dreading what this latest escapade might be leading to. Finally I could stand the uncertainty no longer - I would have to risk the wrath of Jonathan, and perhaps of Saul himself, and break cover.

As the two youngsters halted to catch their breath, I walked out from my hiding place among the boulders. Their hands went for their swords, then Jonathan saw who I was; but I knelt with bowed head before him in a deliberate show of humility. I had no desire to belittle him in front of his companion. His eyes flared up, alarmed but savage.

"Forgive me, my prince," I said as calmly and formally as I could, "But for the sake of your father I had to follow you. I beg you to think again before you risk your life doing something foolish."

He bristled, but made no response. No doubt he resented being made to feel fifteen years old; but that's all he was. Shammah too held his peace.

"My lord Jonathan," I continued patiently, "I take it that you are not so disappointed in your father as to be deserting to the enemy."

Jonathan's indignation at this suggestion loosed his tongue. "How dare you say that!" he hissed at me, and his fingers had tightened around his sword-hilt. "How could you think such a thing!"

Maintaining my composure with some difficulty I said, "Then please be so kind as to give me some other explanation to believe."

They exchanged furtive glances, then suddenly Jonathan let go of his weapon and seized both my hands in his, scanning my face with burning eyes. "Eliphaz - I can't tolerate this inaction any longer. All this waiting, waiting... for what? Just so the Philistines can attack us again, and keep picking us off until no one is left to fight? I've had enough."

"Haven't we all," I said bitterly. "But you still haven't told me what you're doing."

"You wouldn't understand."

I rolled my eyes skywards. "Try me."

"I have to know if Adonai is with us."

He was right: I *was* shocked. Never before had I heard him so much as mention God, except during lessons or prescribed prayers. Suddenly he could have been Saul at fifteen, and it made my heart race. I said quietly, "What do you mean?"

"Eliphaz, we're wasting time!" He squeezed my hands earnestly. "Please, let me go..."

"What do you mean!" I repeated, louder.

"I mean that I have to know if my father is the man I always thought he was! I have to know if we *are* the Chosen People, if we can *really* expect help from Adonai! Or if Adonai has abandoned us because of what... I mean... if all the time my father has been..." His words fragmented, fell apart, and he broke off, unwilling to voice whatever alternatives were in his mind.

I blew the breath out between my teeth. "So what are you going to do."

"We're going to break into the Philistine camp and make an attack."

"God have mercy! Just the two of you? You can't mean it."

"Only Shammah would come, of all those I asked. And it's like the prophet said, Eliphaz. If Adonai is with us, nothing can keep victory from us. It wouldn't matter if there was only me."

I was lost for words. I doubted that the two of them would ever even reach their destination; the cliffs they would have to scale were precipitous.

"Please let us go, Eliphaz," he repeated. "I have to know. And please - please promise not to tell anyone where we've gone. If you won't promise I..." And his hand went back to his sword, hovered there and shook.

"You don't need to threaten me, Jonathan," I said crisply. "Your mind is clearly made up."

His strained features relaxed. He almost smiled, then set off walking again, motioning Shammah to follow him before I changed my mind. For some time I stood helplessly watching their retreating backs until their forms were swallowed up among the rocks ahead; then I sat down, my head thudding, thinking, Saul will go out of his mind if anything happens to his beloved son. I cursed myself for letting them go, and almost ran to catch them, but something stopped me, and still swearing under my breath, I turned round and slowly retraced my steps back to the valley below.

As I trudged on, I heard a low sound like thunder

behind me; I drew in my cloak around my shoulders and quickened my pace, fearing that a storm was gathering. By the time I came within sight of the camp, it was almost full daylight and I could see that everyone was up and moving about. The familiar sights and sounds reassured me, and I began to wonder if I could sneak back to the tent without Saul even knowing I had been gone. Then as I drew closer, I became aware that the camp buzzed with more than the normal level of noise and activity. The cool morning air sparked with excitement; men stood about in animated clusters jabbering and gesticulating. I walked in, grabbed the nearest soldier by the arm, and demanded to know what was happening.

"Our scouts have reported confusion in the Philistine camp," he told me, glad to have found someone to tell who didn't already know. "There's been some kind of earthquake up in the mountains. They say many Philistines are dead, and the whole camp is in disarray."

I had to find somewhere to sit down. I felt like a ship whose moorings have come adrift in a surging ocean. My bearings were gone, my convictions hurled to the four winds, my assumptions uprooted and thrown back down again all jumbled together. Answered prayers I had learned to cope with. Prophecies coming true I had been forced to acknowledge. Even Saul's mystical communion with his God I had grown to accept. But the Divine invading, intervening directly in the things of nature, was another thing, and I was stricken. How could I have thought a storm was coming, or that I'd heard thunder? The sky was as blue as the Salt Sea, there was no cloud to be seen anywhere. But miracles were not exactly something which my calculations regularly allowed for. Yes, I knew the stories as well as any native Israelite: Noah surviving the flood, Moses calling down the ten plagues on Egypt and parting the Red Sea, Joshua razing the walls of Jericho with a shout. And I had believed them, in my own way. I had even accepted circumcision as a sign of my willingness to embrace the Hebrew faith. But this was something only dreams are made of. In all the time that Saul had known Adonai, his God had never chosen this way of showing himself. But then, Saul would never have taken this kind of risk. Recklessness or faith on Jonathan's part, call it what you will, but I found myself thinking: maybe this is the kind of daring that Adonai can really work with.

As I huddled there awestruck, more than one person came and asked me if I was all right, but it was no use trying to explain. No one else knew where Jonathan was, nor what he had said and done, and I was sworn to secrecy. No one else had reason to view this as anything more than a random but admittedly fortunate quirk of nature.

Gradually further reports began to filter through. An earthquake might indeed have spread fear and panic among the Philistines, but it wasn't what had caused most of the casualties. They bore the marks of having died in combat - but with whom, our scouts couldn't make out. Speculation ran riot among our six hundred. Some thought that a band of our deserters must have returned, regrouped and organized their own assault. Some were convinced that our traitors had turned coat for a second time and begun to butcher those that harboured them. Others reckoned that some other mutual enemy must have arrived on the scene - perhaps an Ammonite remnant had crossed the Jordan, or the Syrians had swept down from the north. Yet others suggested that a party had gone out unauthorized from our own camp; and this possibility appeared to rankle Saul more than any of the others.

Hastily the army was ordered to muster by tribes and clans, for a systematic roll-call to be taken. Abner and Eliab began walking among the ranks checking off names and accounting for any absentees. Saul himself appeared and paced up and down with knitted brows in front of the troops, his eyes scanning the rows with increasing agitation. All I could do was sit silent and wait for him to discover the inevitable, and then for him to realize that it was I who must have been on guard duty at the hour when Jonathan presumably made his sortie. Unwilling to be summoned in public so that I would have to come forward with six hundred pairs of eyes pinned to my back, I got up unbidden and slipped unobtrusively to Saul's side. But he said nothing to me; he motioned to Eliab and ordered, "Get someone to bring the ephod. This may be the time to make our attack."

When Samuel wasn't with us, the Sacred Lots were left in the keeping of the priest Ahimelech who was marching with our army. But in all the time that Saul had been king, I had never once known him use them to divine God's will. He simply didn't need to. He had always gone apart to pray, and then he would know. I wasn't even sure if he was entitled to use them: the ephod belonged to the priests, and I recollected with a shudder that Saul was no priest.

But even while the ephod was being fetched, another message came through. Discipline in the enemy camp had utterly broken down, for there had been a further tremor and in the ensuing chaos the terrified Philistine soldiers had even begun fighting with one another.

Saul's frown vanished and his eyes flamed with sudden excitement.

"There's no need to consult Adonai now," he announced. "Abner, form up the troops for battle. It's time to launch our attack!"

A great roar of approval erupted from every quarter. Within minutes our men were pouring out of the camp and flocking up the hillsides into the Pass of Michmash, spurred on by wild enthusiasm and the promise of certain victory. Saul's melancholia had dropped from his shoulders as lightly as a discarded mantle, and he led the ascent yelling like a maniac, with the raw fury of Leviathan and the agility of a gazelle. When we fell upon our opponents he fought with frenzied aberration, cutting down all who came at him as though they were no more than grasshoppers.

Our victory was total, and the carnage beyond description. The Philistine camp was devastated, with negligible loss to Israel. In fact when you counted the deserters who returned and the traitors who retracted, our army finished the day larger than it began. Jonathan and Shammah came back intoxicated with their triumph; Saul, battle-crazed and hysterical, proclaimed them heroes, and the king and his son were once more the darlings of our fickle army. The men bore them back in jubilation, shouting, "Hail King Saul! Hail Prince Jonathan!" until the whole valley echoed with the tumult.

It was well into the night when we crawled to our beds, for the celebrations continued long and unrestrained. Hundreds of people from the nearby villages thronged into the camp bringing with them food and drink in abundance; animals were slaughtered and roasted over the roaring campfires, the wine flowed, musicians played harps and flutes and drums, and the army and peasants together sang and circled and danced, faces glowing in the firelight. Inhibitions and taboos were thrown to the winds; our woman-starved warriors argued and fought over the village girls' favours and I am sure that some who came as virgins went home guilty and frightened.

And I had never seen Saul so drunk. His face was flushed, his eyes rolling; he joined in the dancing half-paralysed with laughter, winking and pouting at the girls, clad only in his torn battle-tunic, his back naked, his sinuous body swaying snake-like to the music. His curling hair was loose and soaked with sweat, and on top of his golden circlet he wore a lopsided coronet of fig leaves which some equally drunken reveller had rammed onto his head. Grateful villagers scrabbled to present him with bulging wine-skins which he was draining one after another until he could scarcely stand.

But although in no state to think clearly myself, I was acutely aware that all was not as it should be. The revelry had deteriorated into debauchery. When I looked at Saul, the same questions kept pulsing and pounding in my head: what exactly is he trying to prove, and to whom? Perhaps to his men, who had been so ready to desert him; perhaps to his son, who had come so close to despising him; perhaps to Abner and Eliab, or to me. Or perhaps - and grimly I concluded this to be the most likely - to Samuel, though the seer was far away in Ramah, and had probably yet to be told of our victory.

When I awoke early next morning, I expected Saul to be nursing a ferocious hangover, but I was wrong. I was feeling unpleasantly groggy myself, and was stumbling round our tent looking for some water to clear my head, when I came upon Saul offensively sober and buckling on his armour. When he saw me he grinned broadly.

"What a night, eh, Eli?" he remarked, chuckling to see me looking so rough. "I haven't enjoyed myself as much as that for years."

"Hmph," I grunted, blundering into a pitcher and managing to dash some water into my mouth and over my aching head.

"Oh, Eli, what a killjoy you are sometimes! You need to let your hair down once in a while, you know."

His unexpected vivacity so early in the morning was starting to grate on my nerves so I decided to go out for some air. But he shouted after me, "Eli, go and find Abner, will you? And Eliab. I need to discuss some strategy with them."

Muttering under my breath I set off to comply with his wishes. Abner was lying flat on his back on his mattress and he groaned when I entered, screwing up his eyes against the light I'd let in under the tent-flap.

"Eliphaz, my head!" he moaned, then smiled wanly. "Did I dream last night? You know, I never did find out the name of that girl I was with. And I could have sworn I saw Saul dancing."

"You did," I said icily. "Abner, you'd better get up. He wants to see you."

"What, now? I don't believe it." He rolled over and flung one arm across his eyes in a last vain attempt to block out the day.

"And fetch Eliab," I called over my shoulder as I left. When I got back to our tent, Jonathan was up, and sitting outside in the hazy morning sunshine, his tousled head bent, engrossed in cleaning and honing his war-gear. He didn't look up. Inside, Saul was sitting cross-legged on a couch, fully armed and appearing pensive.

"Ah, Eli," he said genially. "I'm considering having a monument built to my victories, at Carmel. What do you think?"

"I'm sure I don't know." I shrugged vaguely. "You do as you please."

"Good. Then I shall have it done at once," he asserted. "I shall get Abner to see to it. Oh - and Eli, don't have any breakfast, will you."

"What?"

"I want you to have this order put all round camp immediately: I am dedicating this day as a holy fast before Adonai. Anyone who takes food before sunset this evening will be deemed a traitor and put to death. The men must prepare for battle at once. We are going to take our revenge on the Philistines."

"But...?" I protested vaguely, then broke off, shrugging again - I was beginning to wish seriously that I hadn't got up.

"Yesterday was just the beginning, Eli. We have only destroyed one stronghold. We must follow up our victory while the enemy are still reeling under the shock. We must hound them until we drive them right back to their cities on the coast - and then into the sea!"

I mumbled, "Yes, sir." His reasoning was sound

enough, but the deep sense of unease with which I had gone to bed last night had returned, and now it was stronger. I thought, in the days of Joshua they built monuments to the glory of Adonai, not to their own pride; but I carried out his instructions nonetheless, and before the sun had cleared the horizon the troops were once more lined up in battle formation. However, the atmosphere today was very different. The men were quiet and subdued as they stood awaiting Saul's orders, and today's mood was one of passive acquiescence rather than yesterday's heedless enthusiasm for the fray. They were hungry, tired and hung over, and most of them were in no fit state for a long march on empty stomachs.

But Saul's mind was made up. And exhausted as we were, he was right, in that the Philistines we dredged up that day, whether desperately struggling to cling onto their encampments and outposts, or attempting to hide from us in ones and twos, were as weak as we were, and infinitely more terrified. What was left of the main Philistine army had already fled westwards last night, and vanished; all that remained of it were the sick and the wounded who couldn't keep up with the flight and had taken refuge in caves and tombs and among the barren rock outcrops on the hillsides. Saul quickly realized that there was no need for our army to remain as one mass - if we split up into separate parties we would be able to cover more ground and ensure that every last Philistine in Israelite territory be put to the sword.

Accordingly we divided into four detachments, under the command of Saul, Abner, Eliab and Jonathan respectively, each of the latter three having instructions to meet Saul and our party back at the camp at sundown after sweeping clean as much of the hill-country as they could manage.

It wasn't a pleasant day for me. I have a strong enough stomach for battle and have probably despatched several hundred men to the pit of Sheol in my time, but I dislike butchering the defenceless and wounded when there seems to be no real reason for it. However, Saul's resolution was firm: every last man was to die, in accordance with the ban of herem, the law of holy war. When you fight for Adonai there are to be no prisoners and no spoils; everything belongs to God. But this show of piety on his part today did nothing to quell my misgivings: I was still sure he was out to prove something, and I didn't like it. Neither did the men.

Some time around noon we came upon a small Philistine station, huddled at the head of a lush green valley high up in the mountains. It had fertile fields encircling it; and some Israelite cattle which the garrison had taken from one of our settlements grazed placidly round about. When the few remaining defenders had been disposed of, three of our famished soldiers slaughtered one of the animals on the spot and began making a meal of the meat, with the blood still in it - which of course, besides defying the king's fast, would have been anathema in Adonai's eyes at any time. Saul flew into a rage, accusing the three of the vilest treachery; he strangled the ringleader where he stood, with his own bare hands, and had me execute the other two. After this, no one made any further attempt to contravene the royal decree, nor doubted that Saul meant what he said; but suitably chastened marched on meekly, their bellies cramped with hunger, content to take the cattle along with them to be butchered lawfully when we returned to the camp that night.

In spite of the strained atmosphere, the day's operations were hailed as a resounding success. By the time the sun had set, and all four parties were safely back in camp, we were confident that no live Philistine remained anywhere east of Aijalon, a town on the extreme western fringe of the mountains. Saul persisted with his display of public piety by having an altar built to Adonai, where the men joyously broke their fast by slaughtering and eating the cattle we had brought back with us; not even Saul regarded these as unlawful spoils, since they had been stolen from our people in the first place.

But still Saul wasn't satisfied. He was edgy, tense and taut like a bowstring; restless, as though something were devouring him from inside. He sat wide awake outside the tent in the twilight, staring up fretfully at the full moon, and the stars which were sparking on one by one in the clear evening sky.

"This night will be as bright as day, Eli," he murmured. "We could take a squadron of the strongest men and press on with the hunt by moonlight, beyond Aijalon, all the way down to the coast."

"Saul, don't you think we need to rest?" I pleaded, dropping wearily on the grass beside him. "And what about you? You're driving yourself too hard. You'll burn yourself out."

"I will not rest until the last Philistine is banished from our shores," he said between ground teeth. "We've never before had them on the run like this. We must make the best of it while Adonai is on our side."

I hung my head and said nothing.

"What's on your mind, Eli?" Saul's voice was quiet, but his tone like cold metal.

"Nothing," I lied, without conviction.

"Oh, come on, Eli. I can see you trembling. Why are you afraid?"

"I'm not afraid. I'm - just thinking. Wondering."

"Wondering what?"

"If Adonai still *is* on our side?" The words tumbled out unchecked; I gazed at him imploringly, desperately, wishing with all my heart that he would tell me how it truly was with him, how he really stood with Adonai.

But he just smiled, and answered evenly, "You've seen how the war has gone for us these last few days. What more proof do you need?"

"Oh, Saul, how should I know? I don't understand these things. But it just doesn't feel right to me. I think we should... consult God before we go out to fight again. I think we should find out what he really wants us to do. I think you should..."

"Very well, then," he interrupted curtly. "Fetch the ephod, Eli."

"What - now?"

"Well when else?"

I tried to think of a suitable reply, but came up with none. For several moments I hesitated and stared into his hardened features and simmering eyes, and knew that once again he had made his decision. So I sighed and got up to obey, feeling no happier; and went in search of the aged priest Ahimelech. Samuel not being with us, the ephod was in Ahimelech's charge.

Already there was something unnatural about that night. There was no breath of wind and the camp was unusually silent. No men chattered, no owl hooted, no insects droned. The moon hung large and bright as white fire in the velvet sky; the camp was washed in a ghostly waxen light and deep black shadows. I shivered involuntarily, though I wasn't cold.

Ahimelech, a thin, nervy little man with a wispy grey beard and three score years in Adonai's service to his credit, was sleeping in his tent, and not pleased to be woken up. He was even less pleased when I told him what I wanted. His pale eyes dilated and the blue veins in his scaly forehead worked furiously as he answered me in an anxious whisper, "I'm sorry, Eliphaz. I can't give you the ephod. The Urim and Thummim are to be used by priests alone. I can come with you, but you cannot take it."

I said brusquely, "Then come with me."

Mumbling to himself inaudibly, the old man eased himself to his feet and shuffled to the back of the tent. Presently he came back carrying a carved wooden case darkened by the years, inlaid with enamel and gold leaf which glinted in the flickering lamplight. Together we made our way back to the royal tent, where Saul still sat in the doorway, his head cocked backwards at the clear, moon-bathed sky, his fingers drumming on his knees. He started when he saw Ahimelech.

"Who told you to come?" he demanded. Ahimelech bowed so low that his chin almost scraped the ground and I thought his stiff old back would never be able to bring him upright again.

"I'm sorry, my lord," he apologized nervously, and

launched afresh into his explanation. "The Urim and the Thummim are to be..."

"I know, I know," Saul snapped at him. "And what is a priest if not a mediator between a god and his people? And what is a king, if he is not one and the same?"

Before Ahimelech could open his mouth to protest, Saul seized the case from him. He lifted the lid hurriedly - too hurriedly - and took out the linen mantle with its two pockets in which the sacred lots were stored. He picked up the stones, one in each hand, and stared at them as one bewitched. On the surface they were nothing but large circular pebbles, flattened like Passover bread, polished with age and use, and carved with ornate Hebrew letters which were worn, cracked and faded. But they were the holiest objects in all Israel, save for the tablets in the Ark on which Moses himself had inscribed the ten commandments of Adonai. Saul closed his eyes momentarily and murmured under his breath, then cast the stones onto the ground before him. He opened his eyes, looked - and frowned. Then he picked them up and dropped them again; and scratched his temples.

"What's the matter?" I whispered apprehensively.

Saul hunched his shoulders, threw up his hands in a gesture of confusion. "They are giving no answer at all, neither yes nor no."

"What do you mean? How do you know?"

Saul pointed to the faded letters on the upturned faces. "If both land this way, the answer is yes; if both this way, it is no. But one each way - means no answer."

He dropped them a third time, but the result was the same. He glanced at Ahimelech, who sat crouched on the ground an arm's length away, muttering. He looked up sideways, saw Saul watching him, and hissed, "Adonai is displeased. It is I who should cast the stones."

"Cast them, then." Saul stood up, strode out of the way, and waved Ahimelech forward. The old man grovelled towards him and gathered up the stones in his clawed hands.

But again the same thing happened. Ahimelech cringed.

"What can it mean?" I ventured.

King and priest exchanged glances. Saul said, "It means that someone has committed a capital crime and it has not been atoned for."

I whistled between my teeth. The three of us stood looking down at the Urim and the Thummim where they lay side by side on the sandy floor, blatantly contradicting one another. Saul said, "There is nothing else for it. We must assemble the army again and find out who has transgressed. Then he must die."

He ran his fingers through his hair and walked away distractedly, presumably in search of Abner and Eliab. Ahimelech grumbled quietly to himself and scooped up the stones, dusting the sand from them and replacing them reverently inside the ephod. Then he shambled off after Saul. I leaned back against the tent-pole, heartily wishing I had never suggested consulting God in the first place, yet helpless to understand how it could possibly have been the wrong thing to do. Why couldn't Saul just have prayed like he used to, I asked myself, why must he use the Urim and Thummim like this, when once he would simply have gone into his tent and been as intimate with Adonai as he was with Ahinoam?

Disconsolate, I trailed off to join the men, who once again were gathered in their clans, bleary with sleep, mystified as to what their king could possibly want with them at this time of night. He stood before them, moonlight slanting white on his earnest face, with his three senior officers behind him and the stooping Ahimelech at his side. I pushed forward abstractedly, not looking where I was going, feeling distant, apart, despite the crowd around me. I heard Saul's voice ringing strong and clear across the assembly, but his words washed over me as though he spoke in a foreign tongue; I barely made sense of a quarter of what he said. He spoke of victory, of the great purging of the mountains, of the banishing of the Philistine scum from our shores, of the will of Adonai. Then he spoke of the Urim and the Thummim, and the fact that someone had to die. In no doubt now that he meant this seriously, I stopped moving forward, and stood transfixed.

A heaviness had settled on the gathering. Ahimelech shuffled forward with the ephod and this time meekly allowed the king to take out the lots without complaining. Saul stretched out his arms and held the timeworn stones in his upturned palms for all to witness. His eyes glinted and grew and swam in the pallid moonlight; in his hands the lots seemed to glow, to take on the life and colour which had been sapped from all about them. Every neck craned forward, every eye lured and held by the compelling power of the ancient.

"We shall enquire first whether the fault lies with the army or its leaders," he said, not loudly, but there was no one who didn't hear. He bent down, and threw the pebbles onto the ground. Six hundred heads leaned forward by instinct, though only the first few rows had any hope of seeing what was happening.

At once an audible gasp arose, took wings, and hovered above the ocean of men, and I staggered, seeing what it meant. Alert now with morbid apprehension, I watched Abner, Eliab and Jonathan come forward and stand with Saul, the four warlords together, their arms and fortunes entwined by the verdict of the lots. A shadow walked across Saul's eyes. He cast the stones again, without speaking, and Eliab stepped back, acquitted. He threw again; Abner went free. Now the dream was becoming a nightmare. Numb with shock, I stared as Saul and Jonathan stood, their arms linked, their faces white, their heads bowed together.

I couldn't bring myself to watch him make the final casting. The next thing I was aware of was Saul's voice, broken and shaking, saying, "In God's name, Jonathan, what have you done."

I had to look. Jonathan was backing away, cheeks ashen in the moonglow.

"It wasn't my fault," he stammered. "I didn't hear the order."

"What order?" Saul's face was as grey as his son's, and his voice was weaker.

"The order for the fast. I got up early - while you must have been telling Eliphaz, I was outside cleaning my weapons. When they took the message through the camp, everyone assumed I knew. Who would think to come to our own tent? We came to a wood, there was honey, I was so hungry... but I only ate a little, I swear it! I stopped as soon as they told me." His voice dried up; his fear had made him babble, and he knew it. He gazed into his father's eyes, contrition, perplexity, and raw terror mingled in his own. Saul pulled back from his son's embrace. He looked in consternation at Abner, then at Eliab, then back at the stricken youth.

He whispered, "You have confessed your guilt with your own lips. Jonathan - you must die."

Numb with disbelief, I watched Saul beckon Abner and Eliab forward and motion them to take Jonathan captive. Jonathan hung between them quaking, his face contorted with conflicting emotions. Abner and Eliab had their heads bowed, not daring to raise their eyes. Saul had turned and now stood with his back to all of them and his fists clenched.

Then panic released me and impelled me forward. I lunged to the front, elbowing men out of my path, and grabbed Saul by the arm.

"For pity's sake!" I heard myself shouting. "You cannot kill your own son! He loves you! He loves Adonai! After you he is the finest warrior in Israel."

"We have no choice, Eli." His voice sounded strange, far away. "I made a proclamation. He has sinned. Adonai's decision is irrevocable. Unless he dies, we can pursue the Philistines no further. Atonement must be made."

"Then Saul, I beg you - take me instead! It was my fault. I was entrusted with the message about the fast. Let me die in his place." I was grovelling on my knees now in front of him, raving and clutching at his cloak.

"I'm sorry, Eliphaz, but that is not acceptable. The

guilt is Jonathan's. He must pay."

"But Saul... Adonai is with him! I know he is!" I screamed at him. "That is the only reason we were victorious at Michmash yesterday. He only went to the Philistine camp because he wanted to prove that. I know it! I know it!" Despairing, I beat the ground with my fists, my forehead pressed to the earth, my mouth biting the gagging soil. Dimly from above me I heard Saul's trembling voice nagging at me, demanding to be told how I came to know this, but my anguish only intensified as I realized that now I was trapped as well as desperate. I couldn't lie to him. And if I told the truth, I would have to admit everything, and break the oath I had sworn to his doomed son.

Then I heard Jonathan's voice, steady and clear now, saying, "It's all right, Father. I've sinned. I'm ready to die."

But before Abner and Eliab could take him away, mayhem erupted above my head. Terrified, I curled up on the ground as hundreds of men surged forward roaring and yelling, so that all I had time to do was clasp my hands over my head to protect myself from being crushed in the stampede. When I next dared look up, Jonathan was being carried off on the shoulders of the shouting mob, and the neatly ordered ranks had dissolved into anarchy. Saul was nowhere to be seen; I spluttered and choked, convinced he must have fallen victim to the rioting horde. Coughing the dust from my lungs, I tottered to my feet, hazily surprised to find I had no broken bones, and dragged my battered body back to the tent.

Saul was there. Weak with pain and relief, I fell against him, but he growled and deposited me on a couch. Blinking tears and grit from my eyes, I saw that he was seething.

"This is it," he muttered, more to himself than to me. "I've had enough. Tomorrow morning we're going home." He stripped off his armour and threw it aside angrily, so that the bronze breastplate clanged against a tent pole and jarred my shattered nerves. He tore off his battle tunic and threw himself naked on his mattress, his chest heaving, his hair fallen matted across his face. Almost at once he was asleep, as though all his nervous energy were suddenly spent and he wanted to shut out all awareness of what the night had brought with it.

It was almost daybreak when I heard footsteps, and then Jonathan's voice whispering, "Eliphaz, is that you?"

"Yes."

"Thank God." He let go the breath he had been holding, and came to sit beside me, furtively scanning his surroundings with dark troubled eyes. "Where is he?"

"Your father? Asleep inside."

"Asleep!" He sounded bitter, but then smiled ruefully. "I don't know how to thank you for what you did today. You really would have died for me, wouldn't you?"

I chuckled softly. "Jonathan, I was so miserable I would have died for anyone."

"Oh Eliphaz, I'm just so worried about him!" Jonathan seized my hand and nearly crushed it in his urgency. "He would have gone through with it and had me executed today, if they had let him."

"I know." I wanted to say more, but had no words.

"Do you think I'm safe even now?" he pressed me. "Do you think he still means to do it?"

I shook my head. "I doubt it. He has given up on the

idea of pursuing the Philistines any further. I think he has washed his hands of the whole affair."

"I just couldn't believe it was happening to me! How could he have let himself get into that position?" Jonathan ran his fingers through his hair in vexation, a gesture so reminiscent of Saul that it made me wince. "Why did he even proclaim that pathetic fast in the first place? It was insanity! Expecting men to march and kill on empty stomachs - I am sure he never got the notion from Adonai. I don't think he even hears from him any more, Eliphaz. That's what worries me the most. I mean - would *you* describe him as a Shining One, if you met him now, for the first time?"

Reluctantly I had to shake my head again. "I don't think he hears from him at the moment any more than you or I do," I admitted.

"And probably less," said Jonathan grimly.

CHAPTER 14

Our journey back to Gibeah wasn't a happy one. Saul and Jonathan looked askance at one another but didn't speak. The column of troops behind us marched in cowed silence, in the cold light of dawn seemingly shocked at their own sedition and glad enough now to toe the line. Their numbers dwindled as they scattered to their towns and villages, but even the home-comings seemed subdued. Of the Twenty Companions who had entered Saul's service, only thirteen remained. Er and Ahimaaz had died at Kiriath. Joab and Jannai lay buried at Gilgal. Simeon had survived the loss of his forearm only to contract fever and die in his own tent. Lamech and Harim hadn't been seen since disappearing from the Gilgal camp. The thirteen still with us Saul sent home and gave them leave to stay there for three Sabbaths with their families. Even Abner was grateful.

I walked apart, keeping my own counsel. When we came over the final ridge the sun was setting, bathing the walls and rooftops of Gibeah in mellow golden light, but neither the beauty nor the familiarity lifted my spirits. The news of our coming had run before us; the streets were lined with waving people, but none of us felt much like heroes, least of all Saul or Jonathan. As we entered the fortress gates, thankfully depositing our weapons and baggage in the courtyard, the children flew at us, whooping in delight, and immediately their father and brother were swamped beneath a tidal wave of flailing limbs and bouncing dark heads. Saul's expression softened; he swept up his two daughters into his arms, and ruffled his sons' hair, though as always the sight of the youngest, Malchishua, stirred the memories behind his eyes.

We'd been in the field long enough for each one of the children to have changed. The girls had already grown disconcertingly pretty. Ishvi and Abinadab had lost their puppy fat and become sturdy, healthy boys. All of them were talking and shouting at once, tugging at Saul's cloak, climbing on Jonathan's back, blithely prattling their news and not listening to a word each other said. None of them seemed to sense the atmosphere.

With Saul and Jonathan caught up in this boisterous reunion, it was I who first noticed the solitary white-haired figure seated beside the pool. He got up slowly and with difficulty; age or anxiety had taken a cruel toll on him in the little time since we had seen him. He walked forward without speaking, and Saul's smile congealed on his lips. Merab and Michal set off impulsively across the yard and each took hold of one of the prophet's hands, eagerly pulling him towards us.

"Look, Uncle Samuel! Father has come home from the war," Merab was piping.

"And Jonathan!" chirped Michal. "They're safe!"

Still Samuel held his peace. Nor was there any clear message on his face; I saw love and sadness, expectation and disappointment, esteem and disapproval, all mingled and shaken together. Saul, with his three younger sons still clinging to him in wide-eyed non-comprehension, met the prophet's gaze with mounting antagonism. Then he said, "I told you I never wanted to see you again."

The seer's features remained set and inscrutable.

"Didn't you hear me? I said I wanted nothing more to do with you! And now I find you waiting for me in my own house, ingratiating yourself with my family. Get out of here, Samuel."

"No, Saul." The voice was still firm and clear even though the body was failing. "I must speak with you alone."

"Have you taken leave of your senses?" Saul's eyes flashed the venom which it seemed only Samuel could draw from them. "If you value your shrivelled skin you'll leave now, before I have you thrown out."

"For your own sake I'm glad I fear God more than I fear you. Please ask everyone else to leave."

I decided it was time to take things into my own hands. Catching Jonathan's eye, I hastily gathered the children around me, and we led them away inside the house. In the living-quarters I came upon Boaz lying on a couch, his head propped on cushions, struggling to raise himself onto one elbow.

"Master Eliphaz! Thanks be to Adonai you're all safe. Please forgive me, I can't get up to greet you."

I went over and took his hand. "What happened?"

"I had a fall; it was some months ago now. Old

bones don't heal so quickly." He squeezed my fingers. "A man who lives to my age can't complain. I can still give orders, so the household functions well enough. And things have been easier with Samuel here to assist me."

"He's been *staying* here?" I tried not to sound shocked. "For how long?"

"He arrived unannounced several days ago. It's been a pleasure and an honour to have him as our guest, and he's been so considerate. I know he's like a father to Saul, and the little ones have taken to him like a grandfather. I told him I had no idea when the king would be returning. But Samuel said it would be soon, and that he would wait."

I sighed. "He *was* like a father. I fear there's little love between him and Saul now."

"Have I done wrongly, Master?"

I smiled and patted his frail shrunken hand. "No, Boaz. Of course not. Don't worry."

The air in the room was stale and I felt claustrophobic. I got up and went to the door. Away across the courtyard I could see Saul and Samuel seated at the pool, heads bowed together. I couldn't see Saul's face. Behind me inside the room Jonathan was keeping the children amused, telling them of battles and banquets, letting Ishvi and Abinadab handle the sword that had slain the commander of a Philistine garrison and taken countless enemy lives. Everything here felt so familiar, yet so strange - I had a sudden need to be alone. I slipped out and climbed the steps to the battlements, and leaned out between the teeth, drinking in the view I had grown up with, listening to the evening birdsong, breathing the tranquillity. It was all so gentle and fresh after the harsh sounds and smells of war, but there was no peace in my soul.

I had been there quite some time when I heard heavy footsteps mounting the stairs below me.

Saul looked dreadful. He was white and shaking, and the apple in his throat pumped up and down as though he were choking. I couldn't read his eyes; as Samuel's had done, they spoke a mixed message: hope and despair, yearning and resignation, appeal and reproach.

"What did he say to you, Saul."

He seemed about to tell me, then changed his mind. His hand went to his head and I could tell that it was aching. Eventually he muttered, "I'm sorry, Eli," and turned back downstairs.

I went after him, but he had shut himself in the study and blocked the door. I shook and rattled it and shouted his name, but he must have dragged some huge chest up behind it, for I was unable to force my way in. I went for Jonathan but when we returned, Saul was gone. I don't know where he went: probably one of our special childhood places up in the hills, where he could take stock of himself and think. But he didn't come back for three days. When he did reappear, he was moody and morose. He avoided everyone, but particularly me.

At the height of summer he fell sick. I'd watched it coming for some time, but said nothing. There were black shadows under his eyes, his cheeks were pale and sunken and he tired easily. At first he threw himself into his work and tried to ignore it, but soon he could no longer keep up the pretence and physicians were summoned. They could find nothing wrong with him, and I was worried, for like me Saul was normally healthy and fit; I had never known him spend a day in his bed other than when he'd been wounded in action or had too much to drink. He would have no one with him except the physician who came by once a day and gave him noxious-smelling potions, but lay there sweating and suffering alone. Finally, when I least expected it, he sent for me.

It was the middle of the night. I had only just got to sleep when one of the servants shook me and told me he was shouting my name. I panicked, thinking his end had come, because all that day they said he had been delirious and incoherent. I leapt out of bed like a fired arrow, and ran, but when I reached his room he was calm and in his right mind, and sitting up tensely watching the doorway, the lamplight washing in milky pools over his sallow face. Once he saw me he relaxed against his pillows. He looked exhausted, like Jacob after fighting with the angel.

"It's no good, Eli," he said. "I shall have to tell you. There's no way out."

"Tell me what?" Hesitantly I crossed the room and sat down on the edge of his bed.

"What Samuel said!" he answered impatiently, as though it were only yesterday and no water had passed beneath the bridge in between. "I didn't want to. I've kicked against it. I've tried everything. And now I've come to this."

"You don't need to tell me," I reassured him. "Not if it's so distressing for you. I know we said we'd have no secrets. But don't feel guilty if it's something I shouldn't know. I don't want you suffering because of me."

"No." He winced; a fork of pain stabbed at his face. "You don't understand. You see - I must go to war again. With Amalek."

I had imagined myself prepared for anything he might say, but I wasn't. In the pit of my stomach the anger was building, and I had to swallow hard before I trusted myself to speak.

"Saul," I implored him, "Why must you still feel obliged to do as the old meddler tells you? Will you never shake off his yoke? He cares nothing for you. You should have had him thrown out like you threatened."

"You still don't understand." Saul looked at me bleakly, defeated. "Please - let me tell you what he told me. He said he'd spent many days in prayer after what happened at Gilgal. He pleaded with Adonai, fought with him, wanting to know what it all meant, how God could have chosen me then so pitilessly cast me off. And he said - it may be that Adonai will yet relent and forgive me for what I did that day. He may even allow my sons to prosper and rule after me. Eli - Jonathan may yet sit on the throne of Israel! But only on one condition. I must become the instrument of Adonai's revenge upon Amalek."

He leaned forward; his face was less than a hand's breadth from mine, but all I could see was red. I mumbled, "He's blackmailing you. He's only said this because I am your friend, and he knows what I think of him."

Saul lay back again and pressed his palms against his eyelids. "I wish you were right. I really do. But this is no new thing, Eli. You know that. You know that Adonai resolved to destroy Amalek in the days of Moses."

Of course I knew it. There was no way I could forget it. Moses, Joshua, Deborah, Gideon, Samson... all had been great warriors in the cause of Adonai, yet none of them had accomplished what their God had sworn to do.

Now the baleful challenge confronted Saul, and I knew why he'd been avoiding me. I wanted to be sick.

"What will you do," I said faintly.

"Oh, Eli, what choice do I have? If I turn down this chance, or if I make no decision at all and lie here wasting away - then Eli, this time you really will be building my tomb. If I accept the challenge and succeed - it may be that Adonai will love me again. It may be that things will be like they used to be."

I was too upset to resist asking the question I'd been carrying around for so long it had become part of me.

"Saul - how *is* it, between you and Adonai?"

He pushed one hand up through his hair, tugging at it wretchedly. "It has never been the same since Gilgal."

"I thought not."

He didn't elaborate, and I didn't have the heart to press the matter. I said, "But you're in no state to go off fighting. Just look at you."

"There's nothing to keep me like this now. A few days, maybe, I'll be right. But we'll have to move soon. I want it all settled before the rains come."

I said, "Three days in the desert and you'll be begging for rain." Then the piece dropped into place, and I repeated, "We?"

He looked at me blankly.

"You don't seriously expect me to come with you? To take up arms against my own people? To fight hand to hand with my own kin? My own father and brother?"

"They aren't your people any more, Eli."

"No? Then why have you left it until now to break all this to me? Why didn't you tell me straight away what

Samuel said, if that's what you thought?"

"I should have done. I know I should. But you're an Israelite, Eli. A son of the Covenant. You bear the mark of Adonai."

I said nothing. Saul started coughing; he held a cloth to his mouth, and when it was over he looked more weary than ever. Then he croaked, "Say something, Eli. Don't just look at me like that."

"I bear the mark of your father's knife between my legs, Saul. That's all it is."

"You don't believe that for a second. You follow our laws, obey our Torah. You've done it for years."

"Privileges indeed! Empty rules and regulations and a red weal on my flesh!" I hadn't meant to say all this; I was sorry I was saying it now. "Oh, I used to think I belonged. When I ate that first Passover with you and your parents, and I could still feel the pain where the knife had cut me. But I don't know what I believe any more. I just don't understand Adonai's ways. I don't think I ever did."

"No man has ever lived who understands God fully." Saul closed his eyes for a moment; the pain passed off. He went on, "But this time he's made it clear what he wants me to do. I still have a chance."

There was a pause. Then I said, "You mean, you're going to buy your own peace of mind with the blood of an entire people. My people."

He looked me full in the face. His was haggard.

"Is that how you see it?"

"How else *can* I see it?"

"It's not my peace of mind that matters, Eli. It's the future of Israel. The outworking of the purposes of Adonai.

The Amalekites sinned against his Chosen Race. The curse still applies."

"But that was generations ago!" I found myself reiterating the old arguments I'd laid before Kish. "Did *my* mother and father hurt *you*, or your household? Do my brother and sister deserve to die for what was done by ancestors they never even knew?"

"Children do suffer for the folly of their parents, Eli. And by heaven I should know."

I held my head. All of a sudden I couldn't even believe we were having this conversation. From somewhere a long way distant I heard my own voice saying, "Then let me save them."

"What?"

"Let me save my own family. Give me some time. I'll go back to Amalek and get them away."

"You still don't see it, do you?"

"I don't see what?"

"No one is exempted from Adonai's curse. All must die. Every last Amalekite. Man, woman and child. Their blood must be poured out, their seed made barren."

"An entire race." I held my head, incredulous. "You mean to wipe an entire race from the face of the earth."

"It's what they tried to do to us at Rephidim. They all but succeeded. And they would do it again tomorrow, given the opportunity. The nations still mock because we never took revenge. Adonai will not be mocked, Eli. And don't look so outraged. You know all this is true."

I got up and paced to the window. The sky was still inky black, but my despair was blacker. I said, "And what about *my* blood, Saul."

"I don't know what you're talking about."

"I carry the same tainted blood, the same poisoned seed as the members of my family."

"Eli, I'm in no mood for playing games. I told you: you are an Amalekite no longer. You shared your blood with *me,* or don't you remember? Now stop trying to goad me. I haven't the energy to argue with you."

"Playing games? You think that's what I'm doing? I *don't* belong to Israel. I don't think I even want to any more! I - think I'll go home."

"You *are* at home."

"Are you telling me I can't leave?" My ear was pierced; he had every right to.

"You do whatever you like, Eli. I'm tired." He rolled over and pulled in the coverings about his head.

I stalked back to my room, my mind in turmoil. I slept, in fits and starts, and each time I woke my resolve had changed. I would go back to Saul and apologize; I would fight at his side and exorcize whatever of Amalek was left in me. Or I would go back to the desert and find my family and lead them heroically to safety, forcing them to weep for what they'd done to me as a child, and we would all be dramatically and gloriously reconciled. Or I would go further, and take up arms against Israel, exorcizing instead the stain my soul had acquired when I turned traitor to my birth and let Rachael steal my amulet.

I even went so far as to write the note to tell Saul I was going. I crept into the room where he still lay sleeping, and hung in the doorway gazing, torn and doubting. He'd thrown off the bedclothes and sprawled in a sweat, his damp curls tumbling, his cheeks florid; my courage failed me and I crawled back to bed.

In the end I did nothing. Days passed; they said Saul was mending, but I didn't go to see. He still hadn't spoken to Jonathan; now he wasn't speaking to me either. It wasn't just his relationship with Adonai that was under strain.

Within a week he was making preparations for the campaign. Within two weeks he was gone. I didn't say goodbye. When he left, Jonathan and the remaining Companions with him, I had gone to the market to get provisions, and there I stayed until I got word that the king had departed. Within three weeks, I was wishing I was with him, and within four I was missing him hopelessly.

Since the day we shared blood, we had never been apart two Sabbaths running. He had filled the gap in my life which the loss of my twin sister Timna had made; now I had neither of them, and inside a month Timna would be dead. Perhaps Saul would be dead too; until then it had never occurred to me that he might not come back.

I took to moping by the pool-side the way Saul used to, watching the tiny golden fishes flick back and forth, back and forth, as the sunlight caught them. One day Michal sat down beside me.

"Please don't look so sad, Eliphaz." She smiled at me: Saul's smile, Saul's eyes. She even had Saul's hair, so thick, and tinged with red. "He'll be home soon."

I wanted to tell her how much more there was to my sorrow than that, but she was so young, she'd seen so little of life. Still, her garments were filling, and no longer hung straight from shoulder to waist. I was suddenly confused, and tried not to look.

She asked, "Are you sad because of Amalek? You shouldn't be, you know. The Amalekites are only brutish barbarians. You're not like them."

Even in my misery I felt obliged to correct her. "They're people, just like we are, Michal. Some of them are my family."

She shrugged her slight shoulders. "They sold you into slavery at eight years old. You don't owe them anything. Look; I've drawn this picture of my father and my brother going off to fight. Do you like it?"

I had to smile; she was trying so hard to cheer me up. I took the tablet she held out to me and studied the figures engraved in the wax, shown arm in arm. They were surprisingly well executed. I chuckled grimly, and scratched "Saul" and "Jonathan" underneath.

"Eliphaz, would you teach *me* to write? Ishvi and Abinadab are learning, they have a tutor. It isn't fair that Merab and I can't do it. Oh, go on, please, will you?" She looked so eager, so like Saul, that I said yes.

This was how we came to spend so much time together, and how I came to lose my heart to her, and how she came to know that she was no longer a child.

"I wonder what my father will say when he gets back," she giggled. "Won't he be surprised if I put a banner up to celebrate, with 'Welcome home' on it, in letters I've done myself."

"He certainly will," I agreed, still more grimly, for the first time feeling guilty, and she studied me with troubled, innocent eyes.

"We're not doing anything wrong, are we?" she enquired, putting out one hand and touching my cheek.

"No," I said, but my face was burning where her fingers had brushed against it, and all my insides felt to be melting. I was over thirty years old, and had never known a woman. But I knew that what Michal truly needed was a mother.

"You don't have to spend so much time with me, you know," I said to her, many days later, as we sat side by side beneath a tree in one of Saul's olive groves, eating roasted grain and dates from a basket and drinking too much wine in the sunshine. "I'm far too old for you. You should set your sights on a nice rich lad from Gibeah, who you can get your father to betroth you to one day."

"What would I want with a silly boy?" She laughed, and impulsively popped a date into my mouth. All of a sudden I found myself wondering if she really was so innocent after all. "Anyway, you don't know that I *haven't* set my sights on someone. Merab has; I'll bet you didn't know that, now did you? She's in love with a goat-breeder called Adriel. She used to spend all her days mooning about hoping he'd notice her, before he left his goats to go off to Amalek with Father's army. Besides..." - and she pouted mischievously - "Who says I can't marry *you*, Eliphaz?"

I grimaced. "Saul will, and that's for sure. He wouldn't marry his daughter to a slave. And certainly not to an Amalekite."

"Oh, don't start *that* again!" She twisted out of my reach and lay down in the grass, her tunic slipping awry to bare her shoulder and most of one breast. She didn't pull it up. "He doesn't see you as a slave any more. And much less as an Amalekite."

"And what about how I see myself?" I retorted, too

agitated by the direction our conversation was taking to pay conscious heed to the lie of her garments.

"Eliphaz, you're getting as moody as Father. You men are all the same. You're enough to drive anyone up the wall."

I chuckled, but without mirth. "Does Saul drive you up the wall, then?"

"When he gets into one of his stews. He seems to be doing that more and more. And I don't like it when Adonai's inside him either."

I rolled onto my side and looked down into her face, my head propped on one elbow. "What do you mean?"

"You know what I mean." She went unexpectedly coy; then defensive. "When he locks himself in his room to pray, and doesn't come out for ages. And when he prophesies. I've heard him sometimes. I've stood outside his door and listened. He's talking all funny and I can't understand what he's saying. That scares me."

I said, "It scares me too, Michal. But I think it scares me more when he doesn't do it."

"What?"

"Well, how long is it since you heard him pray like that? Since he even mentioned Adonai in passing? The only prayers he says these days are the blessings before meals."

She reached up one hand and pulled my face towards hers. "I don't want to talk about him, Eliphaz. You see – I think I'm more interested in us."

Then she parted her lips and wrapped her arms around me, and I was undone. Throwing caution and all my better judgments to the wind, I swam in the scent of her red-tinged hair and the joy of her reckless love.

CHAPTER 15

Six weeks after Saul had left Gibeah, we got word. Amalek was defeated; the troops were on their way home; a celebration was to be held at Gilgal, and I was to meet Saul at Carmel on the way there.

"Carmel?" I asked the runner who came with the news.

"The victory stele is finished and His Majesty wishes to see it. He will spend a few days there with an elder from the city, a guest-friend of his father's. He expressly wants you to see it too."

So he really had got them to put up that confounded monument. I shook my head wryly. "And why Gilgal?"

The messenger smiled. "He said you would ask. He says the place holds bad memories for him. He wants to put them to rest."

Finally I couldn't risk asking, though I didn't want to know, "And the Amalekite people: are they all dead? Can Saul be sure? Every one?"

"Every one who fled for refuge to the city. It was the most foolish thing those crazy nomads could have done. Spread all over the desert, we'd never have rounded them all up. Hordes of them would have escaped. I suppose some probably did, mind you. We'd no means of checking."

I said, "They would have gone into the city for water. Saul will have had the springs and wells at the oases poisoned."

"Yes, so they told us. But so many refugees all cooped up, with their tents and animals and equipment - if our army hadn't got them, plague or fire would have done."

I asked, "And which of those things was it that got them in the end?"

He answered, "None of them," then begged leave to depart.

Two days later, I set out alone for Carmel. The rest of Saul's household were to join us at Gilgal; Ner, now too old for campaigning, would bring them. I wondered what mood Saul would be in, and there was apprehension mixed with my excitement at the prospect. He was always high for weeks after a major victory, but would there be peace now beneath the surface exuberance?

When I arrived, the celebration had already started. Although still on route to Gilgal, Saul and his entourage were being entertained in fine enough style at Carmel, where they had taken up residence that same afternoon. The common soldiers were billeted throughout the town, whilst the king and his officers were eating and drinking at the elder's table. The evening meal was well advanced when I walked in; Saul leapt from his place the worse for drink and threw his arms around me, dragging me to sit next to him and plying me with delicacies from his own plate. He was full of himself, as I knew he would be, oblivious to my mood and blatantly insensitive. At his other side sat a man I'd never seen before, smooth cheeked, smooth mannered, and dressed in desert fashion. Two brawny Israelite spearmen stood behind him. The stranger didn't so much as nod to me when I sat down, but Saul began fussing over me extravagantly and I was embarrassed. Before long I was as drunk as he was.

By the time they brought on musicians and singers, I was feeling pleasantly sleepy. Most of our comrades, well oiled too, were chattering and joking brazenly amongst themselves, but for some reason Saul was starting to get restless. At length he sprang up from his couch and motioned me to follow him.

Outside the stars were kindling, passing the light from one to the next until the whole arch of the sky sparkled. The moon was rising, the air was clear, and Saul said, "Come with me, Eli. I want to see the monument."

"What, now?" I asked muzzily. "Can't it wait till morning?"

But I saw from his face that it was useless to protest. The keen night air pretty soon sobered me up. Together we walked through the darkened streets, and he told me over and over how much he'd missed me. But I found that I didn't know what to say to him. The things that had come between us before he left were still there, and now there was more besides. Of course, he wanted to tell me all about the campaign and the siege of Amalek city, but I didn't want to hear.

We fetched up on a low hill at the edge of town, and there it stood, a single column of stone rearing black against the night, twice the height of a man. Saul's pace quickened; he walked in a circle around it, his head thrown back so he could see its apex thrusting high above him, solid and opaque in stark contrast to the translucent, star-studded sky that formed its backcloth. He ventured up closer, and ran his hands over its dressed faces as though caressing the flesh of a woman. I thought of Michal, and tasted guilt at the back of my throat.

The pillar was inscribed with Hebrew characters all down one side; however, that face was plunged in shadow, having its back to the moon, and it was too dark to read the legend. But you could feel the shapes of the words carved deep into the stonework; Saul stood and traced the lines with his finger, then grasped my hand and made me follow the letters of his own name. The surface was still warm to the touch, for the sun had soaked into it all day, but around my shoulders the night grew chill. Somewhat peevishly I asked if we might go back now, but Saul sighed, pursed his lips and said, "So even you don't see what this means to me."

I shrugged. "It's a block of stone, and you've had it put here yourself. It isn't even a tribute from your grateful subjects. What *should* it mean?" I was thinking: it's no different from the rocks you carved your name on as a child. You still haven't grown out of that.

"I don't mean the monument itself, Eli. I mean what it stands for. Winning all these victories, putting down Israel's enemies one after another... don't you realize I'm the first warlord since Joshua set foot in Canaan to see all Israel march into battle as one nation?"

"You don't need to tell me about your achievements, Saul. I know how much you've accomplished. I know what you've done for Israel better than anyone."

Only now did he tear his eyes from the pillar and meet mine. I believe it was the first time he'd really looked at me all night. "You think I'm boasting, don't you? You think that's all this is. But it's the opposite, Eli. I would never have dreamed I could do it. I doubted myself so much; I still do. And I *haven't* done it, any of it. It's Adonai who's won these victories. Every one. Even Amalek. That's what matters. It proves he's still with me."

I said pointedly, "You used not to need proof."

But he didn't seem to hear me, or pretended not to. "The way we got into their stronghold was proof enough," he went on regardless, determined to make me hear the detestable details. "You were right, it was so hot and dry down there, I thought we were done for when the bastards got themselves all walled up in the royal city. They had water and shelter, we were weak from the march in, and our supplies were running low. And then we just - walked in and fired the place, with less than a dozen casualties on our side. All those makeshift huts and tents crammed on top of each other, all that wood and skin; the whole lot went up like tinder."

I shuddered, and not from the cold.

"Go on, Eli. Ask me how it happened; how we could just have walked in like angels." I didn't, but he told me anyway. "King Agag sent word: the gates to be opened at night, in return for his life. I couldn't get over our luck. We'd never have kept up a siege long enough to starve them out. I reckon that annihilating every Amalekite except one was more faithful to Adonai's command than frying ourselves alive in the wilderness and failing to put down any of them. Wouldn't you think so?"

I couldn't answer. My blood was boiling.

"Of course, Abner said we should get rid of Agag too, once we had him in our hands. But after all, I'd given him my word, as one king to another. Besides, I rather like the man. He has a certain barbaric charm, and you can't say he isn't sharp."

I couldn't smother my rage any longer. All those weeks I had agonized over my loyalties, and the noble King of Amalek himself had bartered his people's lives for his own slimy skin, apparently without so much as a twinge of conscience. I blurted, "You should cut the wretch's head off. Where is he? I'll do it."

"Eli, steady on! What's got into you tonight? You've seen him, anyway. He was with me at dinner."

"What?" I exploded at him. "He's eaten at your table? Dipped his bread in the same bowl? I don't believe it!"

"Oh, he'll have his share of humiliation to bear. He'll be paraded with the spoils at Gilgal, and the cattle we brought back with us to sacrifice."

"Ye gods!" I was too cut up about Agag to register the significance of the rest of what he said. I knew the law of herem as well as anyone; but Saul should have known it better.

After that I couldn't stand being alone with Saul another second. I stormed off without him back into the town, but presently I heard his footsteps coming after me, and we walked back into our host's dining room together. The carousal was still in full spate. Someone had passed a harp to Eliab, and he was playing it with a surprising show of virtuosity in spite of being utterly inebriated. The others were clapping and stamping their feet with the rhythm, and praising his skill, wanting to know where he'd got his talent and how he'd kept it hidden all this time. He said it ran in his family, but that it was the runt of the litter, not he, who was the true master. Saul roared his appreciation and knocked back several more goblets of wine. I smouldered in silence, my eyes fixed on Agag.

He was still under guard, but not letting on if it bothered him. A young man, probably younger than Saul and myself, he was of handsome lean appearance, with an elegant black beard, long aquiline nose, and languid, hooded eyes. He was attired in nomadic style but with Egyptian opulence: his silken headdress flowed to his waist, his belt was worked in gold, and his spider-thin fingers he clearly used for nothing except displaying his flamboyant jewelry. In common with all the sons of the desert, he liked his riches gaudy, and he liked them portable. He wore rings in his earlobes, kohl round his eyes, his hair reeked of spice, and I had never in my life seen anyone so offensively smug. I could have strangled him on the spot.

We passed two more nights at Carmel, then the following morning struck out for Gilgal. All that day we spent on the road, and the night camping out on a lonely plain curtained with date-palms, just short of Jericho. From here it was barely a grasshopper's leap to Gilgal, so the sun was still low as we approached the meeting-place. But here too it seemed that the festivities had already commenced. We heard the music first: the distant shrilling of flutes and trumpets carrying over the misty morning meadows, the thumping of drums that made the earth pulse under our feet. We were quite a company now, for our host from Carmel and his family had joined us, along with a throng of their townsfolk and some other hangers-on whom we had picked up along the route. Now there was the smell of the campfires, the heady scent of woodsmoke mixed with meat juices, and as we got beyond the final stand of palm-trees and saw the multitude crowding like ants over the plain, the word spread that the king was here, and a roar of acclamation rose fit to burst our ears. As we passed among the people, they laid branches of palm at our feet and crowned Saul with freshly-cut garlands of blossom. They cheered when they saw Agag brought in chains between Abner and Eliab, and some coarse youths spat on him as he neared them, whilst others laughed and egged them on.

The focus of the assembly was provided by a rough-hewn limestone altar around which a clearing had been made, and as we drew closer I could see the old priest Ahimelech standing waiting, with the cattle and some sheep and goats from Amalek tethered nearby. A cluster of giggling village-girls made an arch with their arms for the king and his retinue to pass beneath, whilst others played pipes and lyres in our honour, threw flowers for Saul and Jonathan and pinned ribbons to their clothes. Children tugged at their mothers' skirts and asked which was King Saul, then broke off in mid-sentence as he came past, because they knew.

I suppose I should have expected that Samuel would

be there. But for some reason it came as a shock when I saw him. It wasn't simply the fact of his presence that made me start; it was the very look of him. He was frailer, thinner, more wizened than ever, dried up and brittle as a long-dead locust, and his blue blue eyes floated huge and fathomless in his white sunken face. The faded brown cloak, threadbare and shapeless with decay, hung in tatters about what remained of his body, a withered sack of crumbling bones and slack, sallow skin. He stood behind Ahimelech, motionless and unassuming, leaning heavily on his staff. In his hands he held a garland of myrtle, and in his eyes glistened the faintest suggestion of tears.

Ahimelech was forgotten. Saul dropped to one knee in the dust in front of the seer who had been his mentor, but this time there wasn't a trace of humility in the gesture. He looked the old man straight in the eye and said with a certain taut defiance, "Well, Samuel, I have done it. I have destroyed the power of Amalek and fulfilled Adonai's will. I have done everything you said I had to."

"Yes, you have done it, true enough." There were still tears in the old man's eyes. "But done what, Saul? Done what?" And he hadn't offered the garland.

A dark cloud passed briefly across Saul's face; he looked confused. He began again, less positively, as though he feared the aged prophet's wits might be failing. ".The will of Adonai; I have done it, as you told me..."

"Saul, my son." The voice of the seer cut him short, and it was weary with the burden of a thousand lifetimes. "Come with me."

Without awaiting a response, Samuel turned and began to plough a furrow through the milling crowds. No one could have heard his words to Saul - the people went on shouting as before, the flutes and trumpets squealed, the young men and girls danced and sang, ate and drank. But now it all came at me from a distance. A cocoon of uncanny silence had descended upon the three of us, sealing us off from the tumult, a silence that seemed to issue from the prophet's very flesh. Behind him dripped a trail of myrtle leaves, and I saw that as he walked, little by little he was stripping the foliage from the garland until it was as bare as winter.

For a timeless interval Saul had remained where he was, rendered powerless to move or speak, kneeling on the ground with the flowers and ribbons still hanging around his neck and in his hair. Perhaps that was where I should have left him. After all, he had no real obligation to do as Samuel asked. Yet the seer's quiet authority commanded obedience; even now there was something about him that made you swallow your objections and do what he wanted. Gently I took Saul's arm and raised him to his feet, and together we followed Samuel's retreating back, threading our way amongst the revellers, who still stamped and whistled, between the smouldering campfires, past the euphoric musicians and prattling children, until the crowd had thinned, the noise of the celebrations had died away behind us, and the air grew quiet and hotly oppressive. Presently we found ourselves walking through an olive grove. Gnarled trees offered patchy shade from the glare of the climbing sun; crickets rasped and a bird sang tunelessly.

Without warning, Samuel stopped in his tracks, swung round and peered at Saul. Saul said, quietly but frostily, "Why have you brought us here."

"Us?" Samuel flicked his blue eyes towards me, evidently noticing me for the first time. "Saul, send Eliphaz back to the assembly."

"No," Saul snapped, and his unwarranted aggression betrayed his unease. Grimly I recalled how differently he'd reacted when faced with a similar request that first morning at Ramah, so long ago. "Tell me why we have come here. I should be with my people. They are waiting to begin the sacrifice."

Samuel said, "There should be no sacrifice. It is unlawful."

"What?" Saul was almost laughing, but there wasn't a hint of humour in the sound, more like a fraught kind of exasperation. "I don't know what you're talking about. Just tell me why we are here."

"Then you tell me why you have disobeyed Adonai. Again."

"What?" Saul retorted a second time, and now his tone was incredulous: he really had no inkling of what the old man could be getting at. Temporarily there was neither anger nor fear in his voice, and for the moment it was the same with Samuel. "I haven't disobeyed. I have destroyed Amalek as you told me. I have made sure she will never recover enough to threaten Israel again."

"And you have spared the life of her king. And allowed your own soldiers to seize loot from the city and keep the best of the livestock." The last leaf of the myrtle garland wafted to the ground; Samuel let the shorn chaplet fall from his hand. "You know what all that means as well as I do."

Saul expelled the breath heavily from his lungs as

though too weary to want to explain. He leaned back against one of the olive trunks and studied Samuel with jaded eyes. Finally he said, "I gave King Agag my word. The cattle are to be sacrificed to Adonai. And don't you think my men deserved some reward for their pains? Because I do."

"So you suppose that this is what matters now? What I think? What you think?" A bitter savour had crept into Samuel's tone, though he seemed to be fighting to quell it. Clearly he was wanting to stay calm, to deliver his verdict with composure. "Did you ever stop to ask Adonai what *he* thinks?"

"Don't you think I have known him long enough to discern his will for myself?" Now I could hear the irritation in Saul's voice too, only he made no attempt to disguise it.

"To discern his will without asking?" Samuel rejoined. "You must have been treading dangerous ground for some time, my son. No one can presume to know the mind of God."

"No?" Saul was gripping the tree behind him to keep himself from violence. "And I suppose Adonai specifically told you to delay for so many days before coming to offer the sacrifices at Gilgal last time? I have led the army of God to victory - against Amalek, and time after time before that, and don't you forget it! And all *you* did was to linger until that army was almost destroyed!"

Momentarily I shut my eyes. I could no longer bear to watch the colour rising in Saul's face, his eyes throwing fire. I heard Samuel begin to say something, but Saul wasn't through.

"Which do you think would have been better, then,

old man? To wipe out every Amalekite but one, the way I did it? Or to lose half my army from thirst and starvation, maintaining a hopeless siege in the wilderness? Opportunities like the one I took don't arise by accident."

"Opportunities?" roared Samuel, and his composure had evaporated. "Underhand scheming, you mean! Encouraging a king to betray his own subjects, then offering the coward safe conduct! Do you think our God needs to win that kind of victory? Have you learned nothing?"

"Oh, I have learned something all right. I have learned to hate you."

Saul had let go of the tree and was advancing on Samuel with clenched fists. On impulse I ran forward and tried to restrain him, but he threw me off as though I were nothing more than an interfering child. "You ruined the effect of the last sacrifice at Gilgal, and now you're doing your best to ruin this one," he growled. "Oh yes, I could have slaughtered the cattle down there in the desert. Or I can sacrifice them today, at a holy place, in the presence of God's people..."

"... so they can gorge themselves on the meat and have you to thank for it! You still fear men more than God, Saul. It has ruined you."

"No, I won't listen to this foolishness! What kind of leader doesn't take advice from his counsellors? Abner and Eliab suggested bringing the cattle back here. They showed me the sense of it."

"So Abner and Eliab rule Israel now? Well maybe soon they will. Because *you* will not."

Now I was sure that Saul was going to go for him.

But I was wrong. Suddenly his anger seemed to melt away, as though he no longer considered the seer worth arguing with. He looked at Samuel steadily and said, apparently hardly caring, "So it has come to this again."

It seemed that Samuel too was thrown by this response. For the first time ever, I saw him off his guard and lost for words, and I watched it dawn on Saul that while this moment lasted, he had the upper hand. He took another step towards the seer, with a wry smile playing on his lips. "You never change, do you, old man?" he said, and as he spoke he was advancing steadily upon Samuel until the seer must have felt the spray from the king's breath on his cheeks. "You still think you have a monopoly on Adonai's favour and can keep me cringing in terror every time I disagree with you. And now you think you can dangle the carrot of his forgiveness just out of my reach, so that when I try to bite it, you can snatch it away and drag me along with it. Well, we've been through all this before, Methuselah. And I no longer have time to waste on you. Come along, Eli. We're going back."

He strode resolutely towards me, the ribbons streaming behind him, the scent of the flowers still wedged in his circlet hovering potent on the sultry morning air. He thrust out his arm for me to link, but I was standing bewitched, for Samuel was weeping.

He had subsided onto the ground like a heap of dried twigs. Great sobs jarred his shrunken body until I thought they would shake him to pieces. Tears ran between the bony fingers he had pressed to his face, and into his beard and down his rotting cloak. Once I'd pulled myself together, my first instinct was to go and offer him comfort.

But then I looked at Saul. Ashen-faced, he was trembling visibly from head to foot, and I was convinced he was going to pass out. Caught helpless between them I felt myself torn in two. Then the old prophet fell sideways into the dust.

I ran towards him and lifted him against me, though the feel of his wrinkled flesh and brittle bones made me shudder, and I heard him mumbling under his breath, "Saul, oh my son, my son," over and over like a bereaved mother. I could think of nothing to say, so I just held him in my arms and looked desperately for Saul to help. But he was still in no state to do anything. The sight of Samuel broken and grovelling had shocked him witless and he crouched on the ground transfixed. I thought, so much for burying his memories of Gilgal. Then slowly he gathered the remnants of his senses, crawled forward and touched the prophet's hands, drawing them away from his face, and their eyes met.

Saul murmured thickly, "I'm sorry. For speaking like that. I don't know what got into me. I'm sorry."

Samuel said, "It's too late, Saul. It's too late to be sorry."

"No," Saul entreated, squeezed Samuel's hands, pulled them towards him. "Don't say that. It can never be too late with God."

Clearing his clogged up throat, Samuel fixed Saul with brimming eyes.

"All those years, when you thought I hated you... Saul, if only you could have known! If only you could have seen how many hours I spent in prayer for you, how I've wept for you, how I've pleaded with Adonai to open your eyes, to give you courage, to make you believe in yourself! Yet you're still scared of men, underneath it all you still think you are nothing, you still use your aggression as a cover for your fear. You bow to Abner and Eliab, you pander to the desires of your army, but you don't submit to Adonai even now. He doesn't want sacrifice, Saul! He doesn't want your generosity and your good ideas. He wants a relationship - and you used to know that! That's why you were chosen, in preference to any of the chieftains or warriors or scholars in Israel. You wanted to know Adonai. And you knew what *he* wanted, too. Obedience - your obedience!

"But now you cannot give it. You never could, not for very long. You always wanted your own way, you always wanted the glory from your battles - and the praise of your people. You never got it from your father, so you wanted it from men. But it was all rebellion, Saul. And rebellion is as bad as witchcraft. Arrogance is as much a sin as idolatry."

Saul said nothing. He hung his head, and one of the flowers came loose and dropped onto the soil in front of him. I longed to reach out to him, to touch him, to reassure him, to offer him some hope. But Samuel still sagged against me, weakened and spent, and besides, I had no hope to give. All I could think of was that Saul had known all this when he was a boy, and that the kingship had ruined him.

When at last he broke the silence, his voice was barely audible, and it quivered like olive leaves do when the fruit is shaken down. "I know you're right. I know I've sinned, I can't escape it. But I can't bear this any longer, Samuel. Ask him to forgive me. Please. Then we can go back and worship him together."

Samuel drew out his hand from Saul's grasp, and gently touched the straining face that hung on his reply. His great blue eyes were wet and sad and full of love. But he shook his head. "You don't understand. If you had committed theft, or adultery, or even murder in a moment of anger... there might have been a way out. But pre-planned rebellion is another thing, Saul. Adonai cannot work with a king like that. There is only one way to follow God, and that is to listen to his voice, all the time; not your own, not other people's. You've had chance after chance. Now your time has run out."

"What chance after chance? There was only the sacrifice, when you didn't come. Samuel..."

"And the time when you attacked the people of Gibeon, who weren't even our enemies, and who had been assured of our protection since the days of Joshua. You see, you don't even remember, you didn't even see it as wrong. You still bear the bloodguilt for that" - and when Saul didn't reply - "You haven't truly listened to him for a long time, have you."

Saul held his head as though it hurt. "It's so hard, Samuel. I've had so many things to do. I have felt so much strain... it gets difficult to hear him. I get so anxious."

"Did I ever say it would be easy?" Samuel was stroking Saul's face, watching his eyes, for the tears were starting. "Oh Saul, Saul! Did you think I wanted to see you ruined? After I had anointed you, and crowned you Adonai's chosen king? Did you think I imagined your downfall could ever mean my triumph? I loved you, Saul, more than I ever loved my own sons. I love you still. But it's over."

Suddenly I felt Samuel pull away from me. He summoned all his strength and levered himself upright on his staff. I think he knew that if he stayed there any longer, the sight of Saul's anguish might weaken his resolve. The King of Israel still crouched there in the dust, pale and shaking; but as Samuel turned to leave he lunged forward in despair and clutched at the seer's cloak. The mouldering fabric came away in his hand.

"Samuel, please - at least show me some respect in front of the people. At least come back with me for today, so we can have the celebration."

"So that is what really matters to you? How you appear to the people? What about how you appear to God?"

"It isn't like that, Samuel. You know it isn't."

Samuel paused. He looked at the piece of torn cloth in Saul's hand. He said, "Adonai has torn the kingdom of Israel from you today, and he will give it to someone more worthy. God is not a man. He doesn't change his mind."

"Then what would you have me do? Abdicate? Give up my crown? Abandon Israel to her enemies?"

"You do as you please," said Samuel. "You always have."

Saul could take no more. He wrenched the garlands from his neck, and ripped the circlet from his head. Then he fell forward on the ground, with his fingers clawing the dirt beneath him. Samuel turned, and his face had softened, and I saw the pity in his eyes.

Gently he coaxed Saul onto his feet. He set the circlet in his hair and wound the garlands round his neck. Saul said nothing; he was like a man in a dream, his haunted eyes wet with unspilt tears, and unfocussed, seeing nothing. He looked as young and vulnerable as I had seen him when he stood on the road out of Ramah, so long ago, his curls still slick with the oil of his anointing. Though I knew he was acting against his own better judgment, Samuel slipped his arm through Saul's, and Saul wilted against him, and meekly let us lead him back through the olive grove, across the fields, towards the noise of the assembly which rose to greet us once more as we came into view. If anything the acclamations swelled louder than before; I could hear men shouting in praise of Saul's victories, women in praise of his beauty, but he didn't hear them, and I thought, much good has it all brought him.

At the altar Ahimelech still waited; Jonathan started forward to greet us, then thought better of it; Abner and Eliab sat resignedly on the ground with Agag still chained between them.

Samuel said, "Bring the Amalekite here."

Agag looked up. The day's shame and degradation must have sapped his spirit, for his eyes were listless and there was still spittle on his clothes which he hadn't bothered to wipe away. Abner and Eliab exchanged glances and got to their feet, and Samuel removed the chains from Agag's wrists. For a moment I saw the wretch dare to hope, then realization dawned and he shrank back towards the altar. Samuel took Abner's sword and without flinching slit the royal throat in a single stroke.

Unconsciousness was instant. His body pitched forward, the blood spilling red at our feet, his final breath gurgling at his neck. I retched, and looked at Saul, but his eyes still gave nothing; he was like a dead man standing.

Samuel stooped, hacked the corpse to pieces, flung them on the altar and watched the flames take them. I waited for him to come and do the same to me, but he ignored me. I was too miserable to grasp what that meant. Then he looked at Saul and whispered:

"You once said you never wanted to see me again. Now you shall have your wish." And dropping Abner's sword, he walked away.

CHAPTER 16

I hardly saw Saul for a week after the celebration. No one did. I'm not sure exactly where he went - his usual haunts, I suppose, out in the fields or up in the hills, anywhere he could be alone. The house was quiet, as with death; Jonathan was abnormally preoccupied, Michal looked tense, and the others crept about with long faces. After the first few days, I realized that now I was hardly seeing anyone, but it took me some while to grasp that this was because they were all avoiding me. Even Michal kept out of my way, and I was forced to admit that I wasn't making much effort to be easy to live with. I was doing a great deal of thinking, and as one does at such times, a great deal of apportioning blame; but most of it I assigned to myself, and that made me wretched. It was I who had poisoned Saul against Samuel. Now I was convinced I'd been wrong, now I was sure the seer had loved him, but it was too late.

So I went about my chores and directed the servants, and tried to keep the place together. Meanwhile, Saul tried to keep himself together. When I was tidying his room, I twice found empty wine-skins by the bedside, and with sinking heart realized that I had no choice but to confront him.

"I can't sleep, Eli," he confessed to me when I finally caught up with him, and his eyes were indeed ringed with black in his pallid face. "I can't relax except with wine. My head is in turmoil."

"And does the wine help?"

"A little. But when I sleep I only dream, and the dreams are so bad I wake up screaming. In fact - I want you to sleep in my room again, like you did when we were boys. That way you can wake me as soon as I start."

I guess to him it sounded like screaming; in reality he barely murmured, but the dreams and the fear were real enough, for whenever I woke him he was sweating and shaking and his fists were clenched so that his nails bit his flesh. I said, "Give it up, Saul. Resign the kingship. Maybe then Adonai will accept you as a man, if not as a monarch."

"Adonai?" he retorted. "Don't speak to me about Adonai. He has made a wreck of my faith; now he's set upon destroying my health. But I won't give up my crown. The people still love me, they still need me, even if he doesn't."

"Don't be a fool, Saul," I warned him. "You're not indispensable. Go to Samuel and tell him you've had enough. Leave him to sort things out."

"Don't *you* be a fool," he snapped back at me. "What do you think would happen if the Philistines heard I'd stepped down? And the remnants of Moab, and Edom, even Amalek? They would all be jostling at our borders before the week was out."

I sighed and saw his point, and gave up pressing.

But I also saw that the kingship weighed heavier on his shoulders than it ever had. Situations he once would have ridden with ease preyed on his mind for days, giving judgments made him anxious, making decisions scared him rigid. I would find him in the study late at night, poring over correspondence and tablets of figures in the lamplight, his brow furrowed and his hair greasy with the sweat of his fingers. All this, while Israel was at peace and still prospering; all this, while the people as yet knew nothing of Samuel's verdict.

Soon the agonies that plagued his nights invaded his days also. He would fret by the pool-side with harrowed face; when I disturbed him he scarcely noticed me, and I had to shake him to gain his attention. He woke up depressed in the mornings and kept his bed late. He would repeat the same fears and doubts in a hundred conversations, and sometimes his mind would wander and I couldn't follow where he led me. There were occasions when he flared up at me or ordered me to leave him alone, but they didn't last long, and he always sought me out afterwards to apologize, until I grew tireder of his remorse than I did of his temper.

Of course I tried to make him relax, to lift his mind above his troubles. I would take him hunting, or walking, and when the heat kept us inside I would read to him, or bring the harp he still kept by his bedside.

"When we were boys you would play, and it always cheered you," I coaxed him. "When your father was angry, or your lessons were hard. You used to love music so much

- and you were so talented."

But he would wave his hand, shake his head miserably, and tell me he couldn't concentrate, or he had forgotten the skill.

Once I even suggested he should marry again, or take a concubine - I suppose my ongoing guilt-spiced intimacy with Michal made me think that something like it would work for him too - but he stared at me in horror and kept talking of Ahinoam and how he loved her and would love her till he died.

I said, "Other kings have concubines. Even Abraham had his women."

But he closed his eyes and turned away, though he did say it was time Jonathan found himself a wife.

This notion disturbed me for weeks, and I wished I'd never broached the subject, for Michal wasn't so much younger than her brother. It was small comfort that Merab was a year her senior and must marry first, for I knew very well that the day couldn't be long off when I should have to stand by and watch Michal taken from me in her bridal procession while everyone else waved and cheered and threw flowers. She would go with her maidenlhead intact, at least so far as I was concerned, for I had more sense than to let my feelings run that far away with me. But whether her conscience would be so clear was another thing.

Then one day I found her in tears by the pool-side, with a heap of broken tablets at her feet. She could barely get the words out to tell me what had happened; but it emerged that Saul had discovered her practising her letters and flown into a fury, swearing that no respectable man would marry a woman who had been taught such shamelessness.

Enraged, I went to look for him with my arguments ready marshalled: how did *you* feel, I should ask him, when *your* father disapproved of your accomplishments? When he tried to stop you hunting, or training for battle? How did *you* feel when you could never do quite right? But there was no need for me to rehearse my reasoning, for when I found him, he was beside himself with guilt: it came out that he'd struck her, which he'd never done to either of his daughters in his life, and now he was in torment.

"I don't know what gets into me," he pleaded, catching my sleeve, desperate that I should hear him out. "I didn't want to do it. I don't know how I could have. But I'm not myself, Eli, and I'm frightened of what's happening to me. I lose my temper over nothing, I forget things. You've got to help me."

I looked him up and down: the dishevelled hair, the sallow face, the stricken eyes, and knew he meant every word, but I felt so helpless. You would never have guessed he had once known Adonai, you could never have imagined anyone less like a Shining One. Nothing shone from him now except despair.

At least I wasn't alone in my concern. Jonathan and Abner, and even Eliab, each of whom had loved Saul in his own way, would sit with me in the evenings when Saul had retired to bed, and over their wine they would talk to me about him and we would ask one another in hushed tones what we could do. But they didn't know what I knew; they didn't know what Samuel had said to him, and I didn't feel that I could tell them.

"He looks like he's under a curse," said Jonathan.

"He just isn't acting like himself. And I haven't seen him praying for weeks."

Eliab remarked, "I knew a man with a devil once. He was like that - one moment calm, the next moment like someone crazed. Only every now and then he used to writhe on the ground, and foam at the mouth."

"They say there is power in music," Abner observed. "Even over evil forces, I've heard it said, though I don't know if there's much truth in it myself."

I sighed heavily. "I've tried that. I've tried to get him to play his harp, but he can't settle to it."

"Perhaps we could find someone else to play for him," suggested Jonathan. "What about that brother of yours, Eliab? The master musician?"

Eliab chuckled mirthlessly. "The runt, you mean? My father dotes on him; he would never let him out of his sight. Besides, he's only a boy."

"No, that's a good idea!" I interrupted, suddenly excited. "Suppose we explained to your father what it was for? Surely he would do it for the king?"

Eliab shrugged his shoulders. "You can try, Eliphaz. But you can count me out of it. I can't say I want the little rat here with me at Gibeah."

I announced, "I shall talk to Saul about it. Then he can send a letter with his seal. That might re-order your father's priorities a little."

When I raised the matter with Saul, he scarcely shared my enthusiasm, but was willing to let me try, and gave me his seal. I don't know if it was optimism on my part, or more a clutching at straws, for I couldn't bear to stand by any longer and watch him suffer without trying something, however desperate. I set out alone for Jesse's house at Bethlehem, for Eliab refused to come, and Abner and Jonathan had other duties to attend to.

Bethlehem is a sleepy, attractive little town nestling among low hills south of Jebus, barely a morning's walk from Gibeah. The one I chose for my journey was overcast, heavy with cloud; the first rains of autumn were due any day now, and the sky was gathering its forces. I left early; after another night of nightmares Saul was at last deeply asleep and the house was silent. If the sun had been visible, it wouldn't have reached its peak by the time I arrived at my destination.

I had no difficulty in finding Jesse's home, for it transpired that all the townsfolk knew him. He was a well-respected man with eight handsome sons, two of whom were Companions of the King, and the people of Bethlehem seemed happy to bask in the reflected glory. After making a few enquiries I found the house, a sizeable white-washed residence on the edge of the town, but with patches of peeling plaster here and there hinting that Eliab's family was perhaps not as wealthy as it once had been. When I knocked on the door, Jesse answered it himself; I told him I'd come from Saul, and he looked alarmed. I suppose he assumed I must be bringing some dread news about Eliab or Abinadab, but when I reassured him that they were safe and well, his brow cleared. He invited me inside, and his wife brought me a bowl to wash my feet, and a tray of food.

They were an elderly couple, both grey and stooping, and had that rapport between them which only comes after a lifetime together. When I said it was their youngest son I'd come to see, they were taken aback, and when I said what it was for, they were astounded. I didn't say that the king was afflicted; only that he wanted a musician.

"David isn't yet fourteen years old," Jesse said, scratching his beard as he passed me more bread. "He's too young to be leaving home alone. His place is here, taking care of my flocks."

"Gibeah is hardly far away," I pointed out, "And he would be with his brothers. I'm sure His Majesty would pay you enough to hire ten shepherds in your boy's place. Besides - he would want to hear him play first, before anything was decided."

"He's out in the fields with the sheep now," Jesse told me. "And I have no one to send for him; those of his brothers who are here are all out working. You're welcome to go and look for him yourself, if you care to."

So when I'd eaten my fill I set out for the pasturelands, following Jesse's directions and equipped with a description of his youngest son. The fields around the town had all been grazed to dust, for it was many months now since the last rains, and the shepherds were no doubt searching further and further each day for sparser and sparser patches of stubble. They would be peering with mounting hope at today's leaden sky. I passed several small boys out tending their flocks, who gazed at me dark-eyed and curious from beneath their knotted headscarves, but none of them was the one I sought. Finally I met one who knew which way David had gone that morning, and who cheerfully offered to help me find him; tailed by his straggle of scrawny sheep, we struck out towards the rocky knoll at which he was pointing.

I ought to have recognized him as much from

Eliab's eulogizing about his musical talent as from Jesse's description of his appearance. The poignant echo of his flute hovered wistful on the moist air, and its soft lilting grace seemed to caress the very core of my being. All shepherd boys pipe, but this was different: like the call of a dove through the noise of battle, or the voice of a friend to one alone among strangers. My youthful guide had run on ahead, clambering lightly up the stony hillside, shouting, "David? David!" with his sheep streaming at his heels, leaving me to pick my way more slowly, with the magic of the melody growing stronger the closer I got. The gentle serenity of the music was painting its own picture in my mind of the one who played it - solemn and grave, deep and otherworldly - so I was startled when confronted with the reality. I think Jesse might have been startled too.

He sat cross-legged on a tree stump with his staff across his lap, stripped to the waist, tanned and hardened by the sun and by his work. His sparkling black eyes radiated mischief, his chin was dimpled, his mouth curved up as though it couldn't help but smile. He was slender, lithe, and probably tall, perhaps as tall for his years as Saul had been at his age, but here the similarity ended. David had none of Saul's svelte elegance; he was lean, sinewy, taut like a bow held ready to fire. His feet and legs were bare, his coarse black hair wild and uncovered, and it bristled in untamed spikes from his bowed head. His fingers flew so quickly across the holes on his pipe that my eyes couldn't follow them, but when he saw me, he broke off playing, lifted an eyebrow inquisitively, and finally uncurled like a leopard and stood up. The face that looked at me was open and attractive, and his startlingly compelling eyes danced with the sheer joy of being alive.

My guide whispered something in his ear and ran off, leaving me facing him and wondering where to start. So I said, "Don't stop playing, for me. I'm tired from the climb - I'll sit a while and listen."

But he shook his head and appeared suddenly embarrassed; I don't suppose he was used to an audience. "You play beautifully, you know," I encouraged him. "I never heard anything quite like that before."

Now he grinned and shrugged, and cocked his head at me like a bird does, so that I wondered if he had a tongue in his head at all.

"My name is Eliphaz, son of Korah," I continued awkwardly, aware that I wasn't making a very good job of putting the boy at his ease. "I am cupbearer to King Saul. He sent me here to find you."

His eyes widened, and at last he found his voice. "You're Eliphaz? My brothers have told me about you. But I can't think Saul would have sent you to find *me*. You must have got the wrong person."

"You're David, son of Jesse, aren't you? The king desires to hear you play your harp. If you play it half as well as you play the flute, there's a chance he may want to take you into his service."

David's mouth went very round and he began studying my face keenly. Then he answered, "I don't think that would be a very good idea."

His reply and his staring threw me. I demanded, "Why not?" more sharply than I'd intended, and then regretted it, for he looked startled, lapsed back into silence, and fell to toying with his flute, his eyes hidden under his spiky fringe. Around us Jesse's ewes were bleating; one of this year's lambs nuzzled David's hand and made him smile.

After a while I ventured, "I've spoken to your father. I think he'll let you come," but he shrugged his shoulders again, meaning that this wasn't the problem. I was beginning to feel even more awkward, and decided that the next attempt would be my last. "There's no need to be shy of playing in public. With a gift like yours you could charm the birds from the trees."

Still he said nothing, but now there was an odd expression on his face. He looked as though he wanted to explain something, but wasn't sure where to start. Finally I gave a sigh and turned to leave. "Well, I'm not here to force you. I know they say a true musician can't perform to order. Maybe I was wrong to come."

But as I set off to go back the way I had come, he called after me, "Perhaps it would've been better if you had."

I swung round, surprised. "If I had what?"

"If you had ordered me." Unexpectedly he put down his flute and walked towards me, as if all this time he'd been weighing me up and had just decided I'd passed the test. "You see - I've been told to be obedient to Saul in every-thing."

Now I was more perplexed than ever. I suggested we should sit down again, and he agreed, folding himself cross-legged once more on his tree stump, and I sat opposite him on the thorny ground. I leaned forward and asked, "Told by whom?"

This time he didn't hesitate. He looked straight at me and answered, "By Adonai."

Now I knew what it was about his eyes, about his face, even about his music, that was so unexpectedly compelling. Stunned, I whispered, "You know Adonai? You're a Shining One? At thirteen years old?"

He couldn't resist a giggle at my confusion, and I thought how unlike Saul he was, yet even so I could see that the same mark was on him. I said, "How? How come? How did you - meet him?"

He seemed set to reply at once; an excitement grew in his eyes, and I thought maybe he hadn't told many people; perhaps I was even the first. But then the words died on his lips, and he glanced round to check we were alone. Eventually he asked softly, and a little timidly, "Do you know King Saul well?"

"Since we were boys. We grew up together," I said; then added, "We're like brothers." Even as I spoke, I was asking myself: why am I telling him all this?

"I thought so. I don't think I'd better tell you after all. That's why I didn't want to come with you. Eliphaz - I think maybe it would be better if we forgot we'd met."

I studied his face: the boyish innocence and the sparkle; the honest freshness, the dimple that worked in and out when he smiled, yet all of it tempered with a disarming wisdom beyond its years; and I knew I had to trust him. I said urgently, "David - Saul is in desperate trouble. Everything has started to go wrong for him. He's so depressed, and he sinks lower every day. I'm at my wits' end - you were my only hope. And if you know Adonai, perhaps you really can help him. For his sake, please tell me what happened to you. Please tell me the truth."

David pulled his knees up under his chin, and sat

thinking, his eyes far away. I didn't try to hurry him, and presently he nodded and said, "Adonai's ways are strange, Eliphaz. I'm not sure where all this is leading. But perhaps your coming here was meant to be, after all. You see, all this is new to me. Listening to Adonai, hearing what he's saying inside my head. It only began for me a few weeks ago when Samuel came."

"Samuel? He came to Bethlehem?"

"He came to our house."

My heart was pounding; now I had to know, even if I had to drag it out of him. I persisted, "What did he want?"

"He said he wanted to offer a sacrifice to God. He asked to see my father and all my brothers."

"Well, go on."

It was clear he wasn't sure whether he should continue, but the expression on his face was strange again, as though it was me he was scared for, rather than himself. My eyes were glued to his, I was hanging on his words, and when at last they came, they gushed from him in a torrent, so that the pain would be over quickly.

"It happened that my brothers were all at home - Eliab, Abinadab and Shammah, too, for it was olive-harvest and all hands were needed. I was out here with the sheep - I didn't even know the seer had come, until they sent for me and said he wanted to see me. I couldn't believe it - they were all lined up and watching me, like I'd grown an extra nose: all my brothers, my father, my mother. Then he poured olive-oil over my head; he performed the sacrifice, and went away. That's when I felt it - Adonai's power."

For an age I could do nothing but stare at him. He scanned my face, watching for my reaction. I murmured,

"Did he say what it meant? When he poured the oil on your head - did he say anything?"

David looked at the ground. "No. But I knew."

"Oh, my God."

Suddenly everything was clear to me, and I felt that the earth had been swept from under me. I became light-headed. David's fresh, transparent face swam before my eyes and I thought, it's true. Saul is finished. Adonai has turned from him, he has found another, and the whole horrible cycle is going to begin again. Another young life will be ruined, another family smitten and crushed by the yoke of their God. The burden is too great for anyone to bear. And yet I looked at David, and saw that he was different. I saw the confidence, the candour, the simple warmth in him; I saw everything that Saul was not.

Then I felt his hand on mine.

"Don't be frightened, Eliphaz," he said, as though I were the boy and he the man. "Nothing is too hard if the Lord is with you. I've learnt that already. And don't fear for Saul. I told you - I am to obey him in everything." He saw the strain on my face and winked at me, then rolled his eyes heavenward in comic piety. "My time has not yet come."

I smiled weakly. So he had the inner sight too, like Saul had; like Samuel. He said with a swift grin, "You still haven't heard me play my harp, anyway. You might change your mind about the whole thing after that. Shall we go home?"

He whistled the sheep to follow him, and with my mind still racing, I threaded my way after him downhill through the stones and the thistles. David was as sure-footed as a wild goat, but he waited uncomplaining for me to catch up. As we walked, he caught hold of my sleeve and said, "Eliphaz, you mustn't tell anyone what I've told you. No one else knows. Not even my parents or my brothers - they didn't know what it meant, when Samuel..."

I ground my teeth. "Saul must not know, anyway. Not yet. It would be the death of him." I chuckled ruefully. "You know, we once took an oath we would have no secrets between us. But lately..."

"Don't blame yourself. You had no choice."

I glanced at him and smiled. He smiled back at me and ran on ahead, darting from the path to chivvy a lamb which had wandered off alone. Presently we came upon the shepherd boy who had acted as my guide; David left the sheep with him and we went on into the town.

As we entered the house, Jesse looked up in horror. He threw David a cap, and ordered him to cover himself up: had he no respect, did he not know who I was? David muttered an apology and said he hadn't thought; but he winked again sideways at me as he pulled his tunic up over his chest and tried unsuccessfully to flatten his hair with the cap.

Then he fetched his harp and played for me, and as he stroked the music from its strings I was bewitched. The storm inside my head was calmed, my tangled thoughts were combed smooth; in spite of myself I felt the laughter rise within me. And when he sang, when his voice soared clear and true and free, I was catapulted into paradise, and I knew Saul had to hear him.

.

CHAPTER 17

During our walk back to Gibeah he never stopped talking. As I struggled to match his pace, holding a pack of his belongings across my back, with the other hand labouring to control the gift-laden donkey which Jesse had forced upon us, he skipped at my side carrying his harp, his pipe and some provisions - which he ate his way through as we went along - and plied me with questions. He wanted to know all about Saul, what sort of person he was in private, whether he had other children besides the famous Jonathan, and whether they would accept him if he stayed. He wanted to know if Saul were truly as brave in battle as his brothers had told him, and was he just as handsome as people said.

When I could squeeze a question in edgeways, he told me about himself too - yes, he'd loved music for as long as he could remember; and yes, he'd taught himself to play. He liked to invent his own songs and to teach them to others, but he usually practised on his sheep, because they didn't laugh at his mistakes. I told him I was sure no one could laugh at a talent like his, but he said his brothers would laugh at anything - they thought he was their father's favourite, and frequently made him suffer for it.

He chattered about the places we passed on our way: he pointed out a tree he'd once fallen from as a child, and showed me a cave where he'd built a den last winter. When we came in sight of Jebus he told me how he thought it was the most beautiful city in Canaan, and how when he was king he would take it from the Jebusites and build his palace inside it.

"But I do think Jebus is such an unimpressive name for a capital city, don't you agree? My father says the Assyrians used to call it Urusalim - don't you think that sounds much more fitting?"

I grunted a response and he saw that he'd needled me, so he let the matter drop and presently began prattling about something else. By the time we got back to the fortress, we felt to have known each other for years; the curious feeling of warmth I'd conceived for him, in spite of what I knew he was, seemed to be mutual - he said I was just as friendly and kind as he'd imagined me from his brothers' descriptions - and the journey had passed with our scarcely noticing the lapse of time.

When we entered the courtyard Abner and Eliab were playing dice by the pool-side surrounded by an inquisitive audience of Saul's children, but there was no sign of Saul himself. Eliab acknowledged David's presence with a grudging smile, and David shrugged in response. I drew Jonathan to one side and asked if he knew where his father was, and he said yes, he was still in bed.

"In bed?" I exclaimed. "It's way past noon.."

"He says he's ill," Jonathan answered, but I didn't think much of his tone, so I told David to wait in the courtyard and went to see for myself. Behind me I heard Jonathan now welcoming David warmly and starting to introduce him to his siblings, so I worried no further about my young charge and switched my concern to Saul.

His room was in thick darkness; the lamp had long gone out and there was a blanket stuffed into the window-space. There was no sound of him stirring as I entered; the air was rancid with stale sweat and vomit, and I was shocked. I called, "Saul? Saul?" softly, because I was loath to wake him if he was sleeping, but then his voice came, weak but aggressive, asking who it was, followed by a string of words I wouldn't care to record, and had never before heard him use.

"It's me. Eli," I said, then stumbled over something left lying invisible on the floor. I went for another lamp, but when I brought it he cursed again and told me to take it away, it hurt his eyes.

"Saul, I can't see a thing in here." I set it down on a table as close to his mattress as I thought I could get away with, and asked, "What is the matter?"

He turned his face to the other side. His features were contorted, his lips white and bloodless. I put my hand on his brow to check for fever, and he recoiled wincing as if I'd struck him. I repeated, "What is it? What's wrong?" and then he exploded at me like a thunder-clap.

"My head is on fire, my eyes are on fire, and I feel sick as a pregnant woman. Now get out before…" but I never found out before what, because a sudden spasm of pain seized him, and he went rigid with his fists clenched and his eyes bulging.

I fled back to the courtyard, where the game of dice was still in progress. Abner and Eliab were arguing heatedly about the last throw, much to the amusement of Jonathan and the others. With fear fuelling my irritation I grabbed Jonathan by the shoulders and shouted, "How can you play around like this when your father is in dire straits? Why have you left him alone in there? Why hasn't someone sent for a physician?"

Jonathan grimaced until I let him go, then said, "Have you tried staying in there with him? Besides, he's been like this before, when we were in Amalek. There's nothing we can do but let him sleep it off."

I said, "He isn't going to get any sleep. He's in pain."

But Jonathan sighed and turned up his palms, then went back to the game. David had been playing too, but now he had withdrawn and sat on the pool-side wall looking pensive. In exasperation I went to the kitchen to find a cloth I could dampen to soothe Saul's forehead, but was waylaid by one of the servants asking whether David and I wanted anything to eat. I was momentarily flustered, realizing that by now I probably should be hungry, but feeling too agitated to want anything. I muttered something about David having been eating all the way here, before managing to tear myself away and finally find what I was looking for. When I got back, there was music coming from Saul's room.

I hung in the doorway, marvelling. In the low light from the lamp I could see David's shadow projected on the wall behind, and the air shivered with the rising and falling of his voice and the lilting of the harmonies his fingers drew from the harpstrings. He was squatting on the mattress, and beside him Saul lay abandoned in sleep, all the tension gone, his brow smooth and clear, his features relaxed and at peace. David sensed my presence; he didn't stop playing, but looked up at me and smiled as he sang - and I saw he was as surprised and delighted as I was. Gradually he let his voice sink softer, gradually the music ebbed away, and when he was satisfied that Saul still slept, he let the song die, and crept outside into the daylight with me.

He said, "This is where I should be, Eliphaz. It was Adonai who told you to fetch me. I know it now."

I made no reply, but became aware that the dice-game had stopped, and all eyes were on David. Eliab scowled faintly; Jonathan looked as though he'd seen a ghost; Michal's veil had fallen from her face and she stared at David, wonder-struck. I saw his eyes flick towards her, then away again as hers met them. Then David put down his harp, walked across the courtyard grinning, and took the dice from Abner's hand. He said lightly, "I'll challenge anyone at double or die. Come on, Eliab. Let's show them how it's done."

They were still engrossed in their game when Saul appeared. He had washed, oiled and scented himself, and combed his hair, he wore a fine linen robe and his royal circlet, and he looked better than I had seen him since the Celebration. There was colour in his cheeks, he was calm and composed, and he sat down next to me on the edge of the pool to watch the dicing. But as soon as he arrived, David left off playing and stood up, bowing his head and waiting for Saul to speak. There was respect in his manner, and there was humility, but there was no fear. I watched their eyes meet, and something pass between them, but I didn't know what. Then Saul caught David's hand and said, "Welcome," and I knew that David would be staying.

So the message was sent to Jesse, David was enrolled as a member of the royal staff, and as the days and weeks passed by, he began to settle in to daily life at Gibeah. Everyone warmed to him as I had done, for he was so open and light in his ways that you couldn't have resented him even if you'd wanted to. So there was no jealousy, no friction as he found his place among the rustic royal household of Saul. He put on no airs, despite his talent and what he knew about himself, but neither was he an angel. He always found something to laugh at, and if there was nothing, he would make something. He would hide and leap out at you, throw your things out of reach, pull faces behind your back; and whenever there was mischief, David would generally be at the root of it.

Jonathan found in him a kindred spirit and spent hours with him, though David was closer in age to Ishvi and Abinadab, and Jesse's son took to Jonathan with immediate and equal enthusiasm. I know they say that opposites attract one another when it comes to building friendships, and certainly that had always been true of Saul and me. But with Jonathan and David, it was their affinity. They were both reckless and headstrong, easygoing and unreserved, in love with life and with laughter, and each brought out the exuberance latent in the other. The girls too grew quickly fond of the newcomer, for he had a way with them uncommon in boys of his age. I told myself that they only saw him as another brother, yet occasionally it worried me that they felt so at ease with him, and talked to him unveiled. If Michal sensed my disquiet she didn't say so, yet it felt to me that when she kissed me these days there was distance in it, when she touched me the flame was less hot.

Saul grew closer to David by the day, for it seemed that all the time his need of the boy was growing greater. The headaches came more often, the nausea and the pain-attacks, and each time they struck with more severity than the last. Once he passed out with the agony of it all, and it was becoming difficult to keep his affliction secret from outsiders. When he sat in his state room hearing cases or discussing policy with the tribe-leaders, I made sure I was there at his side, in case I saw it coming on and had to get him away. The nightmares grew worse, and he talked in his sleep incessantly; most nights I had to wake him, until I felt the lack of sleep myself. Soon he really was screaming, and it became hard to rouse him. I had to shake him, or even slap his cheek before his eyes would blink open and focus on my face.

"What do you see, Saul?" I would prompt him, when the sweating had passed and he slumped exhausted against me. "What frightens you so much?"

At first he wouldn't tell me, just shook his head and gasped for breath, but one night he was so distressed he let me persuade him that it might ease the fear, to share it.

"It's always the same," he said, shivering. "I'm lying on the ground, and I'm bleeding, dying, and there are faces all around me, just watching me suffer. Then they all reach out their hands, and they drag the circlet from my head, only... some of my hair comes with it, and some of my scalp... and some of the people are tossing my crown around between them like a plaything, and the others..." He faltered and made a choking sound in his throat. I soothed him more earnestly and he blurted: "The others are pulling at my arm to take my wristband, and my neck to get the chain, then they just start wrenching all my limbs from their sockets, and their faces ... oh, God, their faces..."

"Who are they?" I whispered, "Whose are the faces?"

"Oh, Eli, I don't know! Men who hate me, men who are dead, men I have killed myself - Philistines, Moabites... and Agag. There is always King Agag, and he's always laughing. "

"But you didn't kill him," I reassured him. "You spared his life."

"I know, I know, but he's still laughing, exulting... and then his face changes. All the faces change. They turn hideous, inhuman, like an army of devils, and they start clawing at my chest, trying to wrench my heart from my body..." - I saw the sweat break out on his brow - "...and that's when you wake me."

Yet still David could calm him, however bad things got; he could always bring peace, or release, or confidence, or even dreamless sleep: whatever was needed. I watched Saul grow dependent on him as though under a spell, and I wished David could cure him, once and for all, and set him free. But this one thing it seemed he couldn't do. Once I even caught myself wondering if David really wanted it this way, if he were not of Adonai at all, but something else; then I remembered my misjudgment of Samuel, and fought to repress it. I thought, I must just be jealous of how close they have grown, and that is madness.

So I made myself spend time with David, especially

when the doubts came. In any case that was no hardship, for he was good company, and he would play and sing for me too if I asked him. Often he sang love-songs of his own composing, and their intensity surprised me. I would lie on my back and let the words wash over me, dreaming of Michal. Once as he finished, I rolled over and teased him, "Aren't you too young to be singing songs like that?"

He shrugged and grinned, in the way he always did, and answered, "I wish you were right, Eliphaz. But we all have our weaknesses."

"So you have felt it yourself, what you sing about?"

"I have more than felt it." He put down his harp and studied my face, testing me again. Then he said softly, "There was a girl back in Bethlehem. She was older than me, and she said she'd teach me to be a man... How could I refuse? Anyway..." He looked down suddenly and began picking at his tunic. "I don't sing my love-songs for her any more. I sing them to Adonai."

I said nothing, but I thought about Saul, and grew confused. After an interval he asked, "What's troubling you, Eliphaz?"

"I don't know. I wish I did. I guess..." I pushed myself round on my elbow and sat up. "Why do you think Adonai chose you, David? You aren't perfect. You play tricks on people, sometimes in poor taste, and you hurt them; you have violated your own chastity and you aren't yet fourteen years old. While Saul... all his life he has tried to do right, I don't once remember him setting out to hurt anyone. But now... I think Adonai must be the cruellest god in heaven. I just don't understand."

"So many questions at once, Eliphaz! And yet

301

everything is so simple, so clear. Even a child could understand it."

"Saul did understand it, when he was a child," I agreed woefully. "I even thought I understood it. But not any more. Adonai has destroyed him, David. And he's going to destroy me with him."

David grew suddenly grave. "Adonai destroys no one," he asserted levelly. "He gives us the tree of life to feed on and to enjoy, but we eat from the tree of knowledge, at our peril. I think that this is what Saul has done."

I shook my head, for it was pounding. "I don't see it, David. He's always done right, or tried to, like I said. He has never lied, or cheated, never been unfaithful, or deliberately heartless, or mean. He was a victim - of his father who on the surface always seemed to be so kind; of the kingship; of... Adonai."

"You're bitter, Eliphaz," David chided. "You'll never understand while you're bitter."

But now my tongue was unleashed, and I wanted to tell him everything, to heave the burden of the years from my chest. "If only you'd known him as a boy," I persisted. "He was so sensitive, so intelligent, so *deep* somehow. And he was always so good to me, even though I was only his slave..."

"And so proud, and so jealous."

"What?" I jerked my head up, met his eyes, and they were burning.

"He didn't always love you, did he? You had to earn his friendship, and it was hard."

I was thrown, and gaped at him. "How did you know?"

"It's written all over you. That's why he means so much to you. It isn't easy to watch yourself losing something you fought so hard to win."

I glared at his face, the boyish sparkle, the adult wisdom, and mumbled, "What do you mean."

"I mean we're losing Saul, Eliphaz. Something is taking him from us. When you say he isn't himself - you're right. He's being eaten away from the inside, and we can't do anything to stop it."

For a while I said nothing. Then I whispered hoarsely, "You mean - he's possessed? He has a demon?"

"Something like that." David sat with his dimpled chin in his hands, frowning. "I can see it in his eyes. He's like two people: himself - and this thing which is devouring him. And you know it, too."

I swallowed hard. "How is it possible? He knows Adonai. He's one of the Few, the Shining Ones."

"He was." David sighed and moistened his lips. "He did have Adonai inside him. But now there's an emptiness. A void. And empty places are quickly filled. Canaan wasn't a depopulated paradise when Moses returned with the slaves from Egypt. Something is filling Saul's emptiness, and it's something too strong for me. I can quieten it with my music, I know that now. But I can't exorcize it. It would take someone much more powerful than me. Someone who has known Adonai for longer, seen more of his spirit at work."

"But who?"

He said, "There is only one man in Israel who knows Adonai better than Saul has known him."

I knew who he meant, and so I said nothing. My

thoughts were spinning a web inside my head, until my mind was thick with them and I could see nothing clearly. From somewhere far away David was saying, "You mustn't blame Adonai, Eliphaz. He can forgive sins. He forgave mine. But he cannot let the man who rules on his behalf be his own judge. I've talked to Saul when he's been able to keep the madness at bay. He thought he could decide for himself what was good and what was evil; he took the Law into his own hands."

I murmured from my distance, "Obedience, not sacrifice."

"Samuel's words." David nodded. "That's the key, Eliphaz. But somehow along the journey, Saul lost it. He lost the way of listening to Adonai in his heart, and laid himself open. Now something else has filled the empty space."

I said uselessly, "He used to listen. Adonai would speak right into his head. It scared me. It was incredible."

"I know. That's why he's in such agony now. But the more powerful you are, the harder it is to keep your ear tuned. The pressure of the Charisma is heavy to bear. You must know that yourself."

"What?" All at once I became sharply aware of what he was implying. His smile returned and his eyes glinted with amusement. "You've experienced Adonai yourself. I can see it in you, too. I saw it the moment we met. That's why I decided to tell you the truth. I knew you'd understand."

I began shaking my head, protesting, saying he had everything wrong, that my only encounter with Adonai had left me lying flat on my face pinned to the ground while the sons of the prophets cavorted around me. But he was undeterred.

"That was only because you fought him. And you're still fighting."

"No, David," I repeated. "All that's beyond me." My mind was searching frantically for a way to change the subject, and I said hurriedly, "You still haven't told me why he would choose you."

"His choices aren't always our choices," he replied with a shrug. "I was young, unheard-of, a nobody. His favourite kind of tool."

I said, "There are thousands of young nobodies in Israel. Why you?"

"Because I was always searching for him," answered David. "Just like Saul was. And just like you are."

For a while after that I avoided him. His fourteenth birthday came and went, and I noticed that his voice was breaking. He rarely sang to Saul now, but simply played, for it seemed to work the same magic whether the words were there or not. Yet I became aware of a change in him; the edge went from his sense of humour, his expression wasn't so open or so fresh, and I decided that he must be grieving for the high notes he could no longer reach. Somehow I have seldom seen what I don't want to see, until it's too late.

It was less than a month afterwards when I went into Michal's room and found them. No one had seen her all day, and I was starting to grow anxious; when I pushed on the door, there was something rammed hard up against it on the other side and I was afraid she might be ill and not want to worry anyone. I put my shoulder to the door, heaved the chest aside; and saw them.

David was still naked but for a towel he had grabbed to hide himself. Michal lay half hidden in the cushions with her hair loose and disordered; and they gaped at me like the pair of frightened children that they were.

I was too appalled to be angry. I backed out of the room speechless, first with embarrassment, then with guilt and misery. Feeling my eyes smarting, I went up onto the battlements to be alone; I hung my head over the parapet, and gave my tears free rein. I didn't know exactly why I was weeping, though I could think of a hundred possibilities. I hadn't cried so shamelessly since I was a child. So I didn't notice anyone creep up behind me or place anything by my side. But when I came to myself and my vision cleared, there was a clay tablet lying on the wall by my elbow. I brushed my arm across my eyes and read it.

Eliphaz; I am so sorry. You cannot imagine how ashamed I feel. I told you my weakness; I honestly thought I had conquered it, but I was wrong. So I can't stay any longer. I can't face Saul; for Michal's sake, don't tell him what happened. Please see she's all right; but it wasn't all my fault. This wasn't the first time. Make sure Saul realizes I'm not coming back. Tell him it's because of my voice, or that my father needs me. Tell him anything - I'll back you up. I'm sorry, Eliphaz, please believe me. - David.

In a spasm of fury I hurled the tablet from the parapet and watched it shatter into a thousand fragments out in the street below. I thought, sorry for what you have done, or sorry you were found out? But there was nothing I could say or do; it was already too late. He couldn't have known about Michal and me. He couldn't know that he'd taken what I hadn't stooped - hadn't dared to take. Now everything was over. Michal and I were finished. I was helpless, betrayed, used. I felt the tears starting again, but this time they were for Saul as much as for myself. For I dreaded to think what would become of him, now that David was gone.

CHAPTER 18

I broke the news to Saul myself, because I knew he would take it badly. I was going to say that old Jesse was ill, until I remembered that Eliab was here, and knew it wouldn't wash. So I used the excuse about David's voice breaking; it was hardly a good one, but I could think of nothing better.

When Saul's black moods came, or the anger, or the headaches, I had to manage as best I could. I kept the others away from him, I gave him wine though it worried me to do so, I even tried to sing and play the harp to him myself. But whilst things grew no better, they didn't get worse. The melancholy and the pain and the sickness would pass, and I would sigh with relief, until the next time.

Michal, however, wouldn't speak to me. She mostly kept to her room; I knew she pined for David, and it cut me to the quick. I'd been such a fool, such a gullible fool. As the days stretched into weeks and months, I saw that at least she couldn't be carrying his child.

It was in the spring of the year after David left us

that we got wind of new growth on the stump of Philistia. At first we just caught rumours from traders or bards; then came the official statements from our garrisons in the west. Their old military outposts were slowly being re-manned, their troops had been observed drilling and exercising on the coastal plain. We didn't know if they had got wind of Saul's malady, but clearly they had grown weary of licking their wounds and were making ready once more to rise and regain the ground they had lost.

As the reports accumulated, Abner was growing increasingly restless and impatient, and I could well see why. Israel had put no army in the field since the destruction of Amalek which was well over a year ago already, and our men by now would be out of condition, out of practice, and unused to obeying orders and coping with the stress of battle. What was worse, only six of the Companions remained loyal. As for the others, when they had dedicated their lives to the service of their king, they had presumably banked on his remaining rational.

Still Saul made no response to the dispatches we were receiving; no training programmes had been set up, nor instructions given for the mustering of our forces in the event of an emergency; and it was Abner who would wind up having to pick up the pieces. Finally he drew me to one side after supper, and hissed in my ear, "Eliphaz, you have got to talk to him for me, to make him see reason! If we don't do something soon, the Philistines will certainly realize we have problems, and pounce while they know they'll be unopposed."

I asked, "Have you said anything to him?"

"Twice, and I thought he was going to take my head

off." Abner blew the breath out through his teeth as though he were still not over the shock of it. He lowered his voice still further and whispered, "I suggested he let me take overall charge of organizing the resistance, and he started yelling, claiming that I was trying to steal his crown, that I wanted to see him dead so I could be king myself. I have never heard anything like it. He must be losing his grip on reality, Eliphaz. But he still listens to you. For God's sake talk some sense into him."

So I waited for a day when the sun was shining and the birds were singing, Saul and I were walking alone in the green cornfields, and he was relatively in control; then I reiterated to him Abner's proposal.

"He only wants to take some of the burden from your shoulders," I pointed out gently. "He's your own cousin, he has always adored you, and never wanted anything but the best for you."

"I know, I know," he said tetchily, and instinctively his fingers went to his hair. "But sometimes Abner is in my dream. And Eliab. Even Jonathan. I don't feel there's anyone I can trust any more."

"What about me?" I reminded him. "Or am I in the dream too?"

We stopped walking; I turned to face him and saw with relief that he wasn't angry, his eyes were clear, and he was master of his mind. The sun shone on his fire-flecked hair, on the golden circlet; for a moment he could have been the Saul whom Samuel had anointed king.

"No," he answered. "Never you." He smiled a little and ran his hand lightly over his wrist. "I still have the scar, Eli. It helps me remember."

It was a long time since he'd spoken expressly of our friendship, and it moved me profoundly. Then I remembered Michal, and David, and swallowed the guilt. I said, "So you will let Abner take command?"

He nodded slightly. "If you think it best."

"I do."

"But I'll still fight. I'll still march at the head of my troops. You mustn't let him take that away from me."

I saw the sadness in his eyes, the reluctance, the resignation. I said, "So long as you're well enough."

He sighed and said nothing, but he knew what I meant.

And so Abner found himself on a free rein, licensed to co-ordinate our counter-preparations however he saw fit. What he lacked in flair he more than made up for in sheer hard graft, and within days had the tribe leaders and clan chiefs briefed and equipped and putting their men through their paces. Neglected weapons were brought out of storage, inspected and repaired, armour was dusted and polished, everywhere men worked on target practice and combat training. Ishvi, Abinadab, and even Malchishua were each considered old enough - albeit chiefly by themselves - to bear arms for their country, and their eyes burned with the battle-ardour you only see in the untried.

But as it had happened before, the days became weeks, the weeks dragged out into months, and still the Philistines scarcely ventured beyond the coastal regions they already controlled. There were skirmishes here, cattle raids there, but no offensive occurred to speak of, no action involving more than a score of men on either side. Yet where Saul might have panicked and grown afraid of mutiny, Abner stayed calm and kept his chiefs at the ready; Eliab and the other Companions who remained - his brother Abinadab; Barak, Nathan and Joseph - maintained order and discipline among what passed for our regular army, and staved off the curse of complacency.

Saul himself seemed to rally somewhat now he had one less responsibility weighing on him, and something definite to do. He made me go hunting with him, to recover his skill and bolster his confidence; he practised sparring with Abner, he wrestled with Jonathan, and it was good to see them at last rubbing shoulders again as father and son. Saul had armour made for his other sons - like all younger siblings, they benefited from the victory their older brother had won for them, when it came to their involvement in warfare - and he began to teach them what he should have taught them years ago. They would ask him about the battles he'd weathered and the enemies he'd sent to Sheol, and it did him good to tell them.

The next autumn's rains were almost upon us when our heralds brought the message that the Philistines were gathering for war. The news sent a ripple of shock throughout Israel: the campaigning season was almost at an end and we hadn't thought to face a serious encounter at this late stage of the year. Squadrons from each of the five Philistine cities were reported to be converging on Ephes Dammim, a village in the foothills between Socoh and Azekah where the coastal plain meets the mountains: an army running into the tens of thousands was gradually amassing, indicating that this was no petty autumn raiding expedition - this time they were planning a major invasion of our territory. It was a hazardous undertaking for their officers to contemplate, for they no longer had any footholds in the hill country; the terrain was unfamiliar to them and riddled with our settlements. Yet to win any more land for themselves they had no alternative, and to entice Israel to risk her army in the field they had to brave the uplands.

So the call to arms went out among our people. In the valley of Elah our troops began assembling, and the months of waiting were all at once a part of the past. As we organized our belongings and made ready to march, Saul's mask was grim and gave nothing away.

It is less than a day's march from Gibeah to Socoh; the weather was kind and we made good time. The valley of Elah is enclosed by low rocky hills, their lines softened intermittently by graceful stands of pine trees. The land-scape shimmered yellow and green and grey in the late summer sunshine, the heat was less intense now, the first rainclouds were gathering.

Abner deployed us on the crest of a hilltop, where we couldn't be assailed from above, and from which we should be able to see the Philistines' movements should they choose to take up a position along the ridge opposite, which it seemed most likely they would do. Our forces made an impressive display: row upon row of tight-lipped veterans and dreamy-eyed boys, leather-clad and earnest, hungry for pagan blood. But somehow I could no longer share in their excitement; perhaps because of Saul, or perhaps I was just growing older. And it didn't escape my attention that our spear-heads were still bronze, whereas the Philistines had iron, we still marched on foot, whilst the Philistines had chariots. Not that their chariots would be of much use to them here.

And Saul was still coping. Dressed in his battle-white, with his bronze armour burnished and gleaming, I don't suppose many of our men noticed the change in him. But any who studied him at closer quarters would have observed that he hadn't gone apart to pray, nor did he get up to address the troops. He just stood next to Abner surveying the horizon, aloof and unapproachable.

The Philistines made no appearance that day, nor the next. Our scouts reported that they were still camped at Ephes Dammim, almost within shouting range, but we could see or hear nothing of them, for the hillside in front that stood between us. So we camped where we were - our fires by night gleamed the length of the ridgeway - we ate the provisions we had brought, and slept wrapped in our cloaks, king, cupbearer, and commander, on the stony ground like the rest.

Then on the third morning we sighted them. One moment the horizon was clear and blue and translucent with haze; the next it had a crown of spears running along the length of it facing our own. We heard them too - brash against the still morning air, they were banging on their shields and hurling abuse the way armies do, but they were too far away for us to hear their words, which we would likely not have understood in any case. Eliab and Jonathan had us shouting in response, and from the ranks behind me trumpet calls cut through the rural tranquillity, and the din of bronze on bronze rang in my ears. I heard Abinadab, Eliab's brother, call across to Abner, "Shall I have the heralds sound the attack, sir?"

"No," Abner yelled back at him, "If we lose our height advantage we're finished. We'll wait here for them to attack us. This war is their initiative, after all."

So with the clangour of clashing shields drumming in our ears, we stood our ground and waited to see if the Philistines would risk a descent into the valley that separated our two armies; but their commanders must have been having the same thoughts as Abner, for they remained stolidly where they were, a black and gold border on the skyline. Eventually our men grew tired of taunting, and their voices hoarse with shouting; the noise subsided and we settled to wait once more.

The deadlock persisted for three further days. We lazed among the rocks gaming and chatting; we ate army rations of roasted grain and thin lentil stew, and we huddled into our cloaks for warmth at night. Every so often the Philistines would start up their chanting again, and we would jeer in return, but presently they would leave off and we would return to our dice and our gossiping.

On the third night, it rained. I woke up shivering, with water trickling down my neck and running in my eyes. I roused Saul, and between us we threw up a makeshift shelter of stones, branches and cloaks to give us some protection from the elements. There was no room along the ridge for erecting tents, and we hadn't expected to be here long enough to need them. All along our battle lines other groups of soldiers were attempting to follow our example, until the trampled earth became a quagmire, and no one got any more sleep that night. By morning the men were grumbling and some were threatening to go home; two who tried to convert their words into action were caught and brought to Abner. He had them beheaded, and their bodies hung on stakes as a warning to the rest.

The following morning we spent as usual in idle chatter and amusement, but less comfortably than before, because the soil had turned to mud, there was a chilling breeze, and we were all damp and cold. Then unexpectedly Eliab pointed at the hillside opposite, and moving down the rocky slope was a black shape which had detached itself from the battle-line above and was heading straight down into the valley. Jonathan scrambled up inquisitively to gain a better view, and with some surprise said, "It looks like a heavy-armed warrior with a shield-bearer. But the lad can't be much above eight years old, judging by the size of him."

"Eight years old, eh?" Abner sneered. "Who would send a boy that small into battle? Typical pagan barbarity."

"Perhaps it's one of their kings come to sue for peace, and he's brought his little son with him to soften our hearts," suggested Eliab.

"Soften our heads, more like," Abner rejoined. "I reckon the rain has already softened theirs. A little water has washed away their courage."

By now all of our front few ranks were on their feet and watching; the shape, now clearly recognizable as two figures, a large and a small, had almost reached the bed of the valley. The larger of the two was shouting up at us as we craned closer, but his words were lost on the moist autumn wind. Presumably, in any case, he didn't speak Hebrew; Abner began casting about for Barak, who had a few words of the Philistine language and might be able to make sense of what the fellow could be demanding. Presently Barak himself, accompanied by Nathan and Joseph, began making his way down the hillside, arms held out beside him to show he was unarmed. Saul was standing forward of our front line, his eyes glued to the two figures below, his cheeks wan, and the muscles in his neck straining.

When they returned, Barak's face was set. He looked at Jonathan and said, "His shield-bearer is sixteen."

For a significant interval no one spoke, as we digested his meaning. Then Barak continued, "The warrior is an iron-worker from Gath. He says, why pour out an ocean of young blood on the soil, why waste any more of our lives wallowing in mud on these godforsaken mountains. He wants us to find a champion to settle the outcome by single combat."

Abner made a contemptuous sound in his throat; Eliab made a gesture with his fingers that meant the same. Saul continued to gaze abstractedly into the valley, and only Jonathan looked surprised. Then Abner said, "What is he proposing as his terms?"

"Whichever champion loses, his people become slaves to the enemy."

The officers looked at one another in silence. At our backs, the ranks of men had grown quiet, and there was an oppressive stillness among us despite the wind. Then Saul said, "Get me some wine, Eli. I'm going to fight him."

The silence exploded. Protocol discarded, Abner shouted, "Don't be a fool! What do you think will become of our morale if the men see you die?" Jonathan was gripping Saul's arm, repeating, "Father? Father!" and I was yelling at him louder than any of them, but I have no idea what I said. I think in a moment of heroism or insanity I must have offered to go in his place, because suddenly they were all crowding round me, saying I should be throwing myself right into the jaws of Sheol. Now Eliab and

Jonathan, and even Nathan and Joseph, were each offering to go instead, until finally Abner shouted all of us into silence and said: no, no one was going.

So we stood and stared at one another a while longer, whilst Abner growled and muttered and demanded to know what we could be thinking of; whoever took that giant on would wind up as carrion, and then we should be no better off than before: we should have to advance and attack the enemy from below after all, for which of us was going to drop our weapons voluntarily and wait to be enslaved?

"So what answer do I take him?" Barak ventured into the awkwardness.

Abner grunted, "No answer," and he turned and walked away in search of something to eat.

Shortly after, we saw the two figures turn, and move slowly back up the far hillside.

But the next day at dawn, they were back. Only today they weren't content to wait in the valley bottom; they began ascending the slope towards us, and halted only just out of bowshot. Now I could see all too clearly why Jonathan had taken the shield-bearer for a child. The warrior was the tallest man I have ever laid eyes on, and as broad across the shoulders as a pedigree bull. He was fully armed, in bronze breastplate, helmet and greaves, and his spear would have caused me problems to carry, let alone throw. Beside him his young shield-bearer looked as slight and fragile as a sparrow, yet he would have made more than a match for Saul or Jonathan at wrestling. This time the pair were close enough for us to hear their voices clearly; though the warrior's words meant nothing to us, we scarcely

needed Barak's translation to grasp the gist of his senti-
ments. We were all cowards, wretches, slaves of Saul, none
of us deserved even to crawl upon the earth. I could see
Saul's hackles rising; I found myself praying - exactly to
what or to whom, I had no idea - please don't let him do
anything foolish. But Abner had his strong rough hands
planted firmly on his cousin's shoulders, and again we gave
no reply.

The following day the same thing happened; and the
next, and the next, until it felt like a bizarre ritual in a
recurring nightmare. Each time Saul grew angrier, each time
my prayer became more desperate. Then one night, for the
first time since we'd been here, Saul awoke screaming and I
knew that neither of us could take any more of it. His
outburst brought Jonathan and Abner running, but I told
them it was nothing and sent them away. Until then, I'd
succeeded in keeping this side of his affliction more or less
a secret from them. The night was inky black; our campfire
had gone out with the rain, and the clouds had devoured
the moon and the starlight. In the darkness of our tiny
shelter I could see nothing but the febrile glint of Saul's
eyes, and I felt his fingers grip my cloak. He whispered,
"Tomorrow, if he comes, I shall fight him."

I was too weary to go through all the same old
arguments, but awake enough to realize with a shudder that
he meant what he said. He no longer felt he had anything to
lose. When I was sure he was asleep again I got up and
found Abner, and shook him awake. For all his
responsibility, I never knew Ner's son to lose any sleep. I
hissed in his ear, "Abner, we have got to find a champion.
Saul cannot sit back and listen to that braggart's derision

any longer. If we don't find someone to fight him to-morrow, Saul will do it himself."

Abner groaned. "Go back to sleep, Eliphaz. Saul's terrified of that uncircumcised swine. It's written all over him; he won't dare go out there. Stop worrying."

"Abner, he will, whether he's terrified or not. I know it."

"Look, we'll discuss it in the morning. Go and get some rest. That's an order."

Exasperated I obeyed him, but I lay wide awake. When morning came and Saul got up, I snatched his weapons and railed at him, but he thrust me out of his way and began kitting himself out for combat. His bronze crested helmet hid the pallor of his face; his long white cloak and studded greaves disguised his shaking legs. When Abner saw him, he caught his breath and looked at me, then he motioned urgently to Eliab and barked at him, "Have the message sent back through the ranks immediately that we want a champion. It must be someone at least a head taller than you are, with a minimum of ten years' experience in battle, and full bronze armour. Move."

It's always the way of things, that you can laze about for days with nothing to do, but when things begin to happen, they all come at once. As I hunted about for my own cloak and helmet, I heard a scuffle outside the shelter, and when I ducked out to look, there was a long lanky youth in a tightly twisted turban being dragged in front of Saul and Abner. At first I thought he was another captured deserter; then I realized that the hands he was dodging were trying to pull him back rather than forward. He was handsome and fresh-faced but with the beginnings of a

320

beard, and there was something decidedly familiar about him. However, while I squatted on my haunches pondering this enigma, and wondering what the lad could possibly want with Saul - at least he appeared to be unarmed - I felt an earnest jab in my ribcage, and young Malchishua was tugging at my sleeve, begging, "Eliphaz, come quickly! Ishvi and Abinadab are fighting."

I never found out what had caused their quarrel - some brotherly nonsense no doubt - but Saul's middle two sons were lashing out at each other with enough venom to have done serious harm had their duel been allowed to go unchecked. A gaggle of youths stood around them, but they were yelling encouragement rather than breaking them apart, and it took me considerable effort to get them separated. Then, as they stood panting, and glaring daggers at one another, I saw that Ishbosheth's nose was cut and bleeding, and both Abinadab's eyes were starting to swell. By the time I had given them a severe talking-to and patched up their faces, I realized that our army was in uproar.

Anxious as always for Saul, I elbowed my way through the ranks of chanting soldiers and clanging shields, but he was still standing with the front line, and Jonathan and Abner had hold of his shoulders. For some reason he had stripped off his armour; his helmet and breastplate lay discarded behind him in the mud, and Jonathan was wearing his cloak. Breaking through to stand beside him, I saw that there was someone descending to the valley below. A closer look told me that it was the long lanky youth who had stood squirming before Saul only moments earlier, struggling to gain a hearing. He wore no armour of any kind, and carried nothing in the way of weapons but a leather sling which he twirled around one wrist, whilst with the other hand he juggled deftly with four or five pebbles.

Now I could see that Saul was in an advanced state of agitation. He was striving to free his arms, and shouting at Abner, "Who is that boy? I don't even know what his name is."

Abner said, "I have no idea who he is. But you should never have let him go down there equipped like that. He'll be cut to pieces."

"I offered him my own armour, you heard me!" Saul berated him. "But for God's sake find out who he is, will you?"

Jonathan said, with a curious expression on his face, "He told me his name. He said it was Elhanan, and he's a shepherd from Bethlehem."

"Elhanan?" growled Abner, "Never heard of him. I asked for a warrior, not a shepherd."

Then suddenly I felt another tug at my sleeve, and someone pulled me backwards so roughly that I almost fell. Swinging round, I half expected to see Malchishua again, but saw with surprise that it was Eliab. His eyes were round with terror: he looked the way Saul did when I roused him from a nightmare. I had never before seen Eliab lose his nerve.

"Eliphaz!" he gasped at me, "What is Saul thinking of? Don't you realize who that is?"

I stared, not understanding. "Who what is?"

"Down there; that boy. It's David, Eliphaz. My brother, David."

I blinked at him in confusion. I was sure he couldn't

be right. But I hadn't seen David for over two years. I had never seen him in a turban. And the youth's quiet confidence, the rakish tilt of his head, the lightness in his step, the pert defiance as he tossed the stones in the palm of his hand... I had opened my mouth to tell Eliab he must be mistaken, but when my words came out, they were, "Yes. I know."

Eliab said faintly, "He's only here because Mother sent him with a parcel of food from home. Now the little fool is going to get himself killed, and I shall finish up being blamed for it. Come with me, Eliphaz. I can't bear to watch."

Without waiting for me to voice my agreement, he dragged me back from the crest of the ridge; we found a dry boulder to sit on, and Eliab crouched with his arms coiled over his neck, his fingers locked around clumps of his hair. We must have been the only two men in the Israelite army who weren't scrabbling and shoving, desperate to win a place from which to view what was happening. As the noise increased, Eliab rammed his fingers in his ears, so when the chant of encouragement erupted into the psalm of victory, he didn't notice. I had to force his hands away from his head so that he could hear it for himself.

It was only now that the colour left his face, he started shaking, and his voice died in his throat; his lips mouthed the words: Adonai be praised.

And I thought: so it's true. Adonai yet lives, and in spite of everything, he still loves David.

CHAPTER 19

I don't think that Saul had any notion of who the young hero was until, sprinting back up the hillside with the Philistine's blood-soaked head in one hand, he tore off his turban with the other, hurling it into the air with a whoop of self-congratulation, and his black spiky hair blew free. Saul had been too agitated either to see or to think clearly; but when the realization came, he was ecstatic. Buckling on his breastplate and replacing his helmet, he yelled out the war-cry, and as he ran to embrace David our men with one mind streamed down the hill after him.

At the same instant, we saw the black and gold crown on the opposite hillcrest break apart and begin flowing downwards to meet us - whether under orders, or following a breakdown of discipline, we couldn't tell. Not that this was exactly clear in our own case: certainly Abner had issued no command, but he was running with the pack none the less. Someone threw David a spear and a shield, and he wielded his victim's own sword, which he'd used to sever the head from the felled body. With the clash of metal on metal, howling and screaming, our two armies met head on and we were in the thick of battle; so much for David's single combat with the giant eliminating the need for any further bloodshed. As for Saul, fighting his way forward at the head of his troops, he drifted in and out of my field of vision, but I quickly gave up worrying about him, as he was exultant and battle-crazed, cutting down all who blocked his path. Unnerved by the demise of their champion the Philistines were soon on the run, and before noon had passed, their dead lay in heaps and the muddy plain swam with the blood of the fallen. I escaped this time with no more than cuts and grazes; Jonathan earned a gash in the arm which I bound with cloth torn from my tunic; Saul and David were unscathed.

As we marched back in triumph to Gibeah, the two of them walked with arms linked and fire in their eyes. The villagers poured from their homes and tossed garlands and flowers; it was like old times once more. We threw open the gates of the fortress, and far into the night the wine flowed and the flutes shrilled, peasants danced in the streets and sang psalms for the king and his young champion. When David wasn't with Saul he was with Jonathan. The months of separation seemed to have welded their closeness, and they talked and laughed and drank like brothers.

But I noticed that despite his high spirits, David had drunk more water than wine; his eyes were undimmed and his movements controlled. Saul, by contrast, had drunk freely of everything. He swayed on his feet and was slurring his speech. He was toasting David with a great show of solemnity, banging his fist on the table for silence, and making David sit down while the rest of us stood to do him honour.

"To David the Giantslayer!" Saul proclaimed muzzily, waving his goblet above his head so the wine sloshed out of it, and tottering so I had to hold him steady as he stood. "Old Jesse will not cheat me of your company again, my fearless little friend. You shall carry my shield into battle, like that boy did for the blacksmith of Gath. No - you shall be an officer in my army and butcher Philistines by their hundreds!"

Everyone around him was cheering and clapping; David grinned like a crocodile and Jonathan was pounding him on the back with his uninjured arm. A chain of dancing women with tabors and tambourines filed in, and began weaving and plaiting between the tables, chanting, "Saul has killed his thousands, David ten times more!" and I saw Saul frown a little, but he was too drunk to make an issue of it. I tried to prize his cup from his hands and make him go to bed, but he pushed me away, muttering. In the morning he was slumped snoring in the courtyard, having slept where he dropped, and Jonathan slumbered beside him, but David was gone.

I sighed and began clearing up around them. The yard looked like the aftermath of a riot: there was spilled wine everywhere, and the flagstones were littered with smashed bowls and plates. Then David appeared - washed, dressed and sober - and started to help. I said, "You needn't be doing this," but he shrugged and said, "Nonsense," and we worked side by side, mopping up the wine-dregs and throwing the broken pottery into sacks. After a while I remarked, "So you're staying this time?"

He said, "It's what His Majesty wishes. And probably needs."

"And Michal?" I tried to keep the acrimony out of my tone.

He exhaled heavily. "I don't know, Eliphaz. She was looking at me again last night. I shall have to be strong. But - I think I've grown up since I was last here."

Just then Saul stirred; he moaned and half opened his eyes. David and I exchanged charged glances and worked on in silence. There was so much I wanted to say to him, yet so much I knew I couldn't, and I was sorry.

And so things returned to what passed for normal: David played and sang when Saul's depression flared, though now he had the voice of a man, not a boy, and when Saul was well, David went off hunting with Jonathan, or taught him his songs, or they wrestled and fenced. As the days flew by I watched the two youths grow closer, and pondered the irony in the heir to the throne befriending the one who was destined one day to snatch it from his grasp. And also I felt the sting of envy, for it seemed to me that they had what Saul and I had once had, yet somehow rarely knew any more.

I'm not sure when or why I first sensed that all was not well between David and Saul. There was nothing I could put my finger on; just something in the air I became aware of when I saw them together. I think I discerned it before David himself, though he learned of it soon enough, but I still knew Saul better than he did, and I knew when he was fighting something. When I asked him what bothered him, he feigned surprise, but not many days had passed before he admitted that David had been in his dream too.

We were sitting by the table after supper, just the two of us; everyone else had retired to bed. Saul had had enough wine to loosen his tongue, and I was in the mood for drawing him out.

He said, "There's just something about him. Something that troubles me, but I can't spell out what. He's always polite to me, he always shows me respect, but in his eyes..."

I made no reply, waiting for him to go on, but he leaned forward suddenly and said, "Haven't *you* noticed it? Don't *you* think there's something unusual? In his face? His expression? His whole manner?"

Fearing that he might have learnt somehow about the anointing, I tried to divert him a little from the scent, I said, "He knows Adonai. Perhaps that's it."

"What?" His head jerked up; he looked straight at me.

"Have you never realized it before?" I asked. "I could tell as soon as I met him, two years back. He sweats Adonai from his pores."

"You could tell? You?" Saul groaned and held his head, and I was taken aback at his reaction. "I should have seen it. I should have realized," he muttered, and he kept repeating the words, over and over, and I could see the thoughts running behind his eyes.

But once I'd told him this, things seemed to get worse instead of better. He stiffened every time he found David praying, even if he were only saying the blessing before he ate. He bristled visibly when David read from the Torah scrolls, or sat in meditation by the pool-side. Then one day he sent for me and said he no longer wanted David to sing or play his harp for him, as it made him feel worse than he had felt before, and that scared him.

"But his songs used to bring you such peace, and calm your temper," I pleaded with him. "What's happened? What has gone wrong?"

He answered, "I don't know, Eli. I wish I did. But now it just churns me up inside; I see black in front of my eyes, and I can't think straight. Please speak to him for me. I don't want to hurt him, or his father. I can't send him home. But part of me can't even talk to him any more without wanting to wring his neck."

Now I was seriously worried, and had to find David at once. He was sitting cross-legged in the courtyard, tuning his harp, with his tousled black head bent and listening. I glimpsed Michal watching him from the shadows; she saw me and melted away. I sat by his side, and said, "David, I need to talk to you about Saul. We have to talk now."

"Yes, I know." He looked up at me, and his face was troubled. "He's getting worse. The evil spirit in him is growing stronger."

"But how can it be happening?" I implored him. "Your music used to soothe him, but now he says it just makes him angry. What can have changed?"

"He's fighting me now." David sighed, and twisted the peg he was holding, putting his ear to the string and smiling a little as the note came true. "He's fighting Adonai. When God's spirit is present, the demon is exposed in him. At the moment he can contain it, but he won't do for long."

"What do you mean?" I said, shaken.

"I mean, we've seen nothing yet. The evil is taking him over, and sooner or later it will tear him to pieces. It's feeding on his jealousy."

I shook my head, wretched. "So you've seen it too."

"There's no way he can hide it. He's as jealous as hell, because I have what he once had. Oh, he scorns Adonai with his lips, but in his heart he knows the truth."

I said, "He's seen you in the dream he has, the dream where men try to steal his crown."

He knitted his brow. "Does he know about me and Samuel?"

"I don't think so. But you have to convince him of your loyalty to him somehow, David. For your own good." I meant: for your own survival.

"Eliphaz, it's impossible. When he's himself, he's convinced already. But the demon in him can never be persuaded."

Nevertheless, I tried. I spent hours with Saul, talking it all through, explaining, reasoning, reassuring, swearing to him that David's only desire was to serve him faithfully. But the more we discussed it, the more fraught he got; he would grip me by the shoulders and shout, "I know all this, Eli, I know! But it doesn't alter how I feel when I see him! It doesn't make the dreams go away. It doesn't stop the song going round and round in my head."

"What song?"

"Saul has killed his thousands, David ten times more, Saul has killed his thousands, David ten times more... I don't even know where I heard it. But I can't get it out of my mind."

I knew, but didn't say. And it was undoubtedly true that David was attracting a good deal of attention from the outside world. Anonymous admirers sent him gifts, invited him to parties, even named their children for him, and each new honour he received served to fuel Saul's rancour.

I was polishing the silver goblets in the kitchen one day when I heard the yell. I dropped everything and ran. In the dining room Saul sagged trembling on his couch, with David backed against the wall opposite, his harp lying twisted on the floor, and Saul's grandfather's spear vibrating from a crossbeam less than a hand's breadth away from his head. David's eyes were wide with horror and disbelief, and Saul looked as though he'd just awoken from one of his nightmares. While I hovered aghast in the doorway, David slowly sank down the wall until he was slumped in a heap on the ground, then hesitantly he reached out for the broken harp and held it like a baby to his breast.

I demanded to know what had happened, but neither of them could speak. David suddenly scrambled to his feet and fled; Saul crumpled and mauled at his temples. Nervously I crossed the room towards him, but there was no need for me to fear him now. His fury was used up, and he was devastated. I tried to comfort him, but he went rigid when I touched him, and mumbled, "He's trying to bewitch me. His music is enchanted. He's a magician; he's trying to kill me with spells. He wants to see me dead, I know it."

I saw it was futile to attempt to reason with him. I waited until he'd stopped raving, then I brought him some wine and he calmed down. I found David huddled in the courtyard with Jonathan, staring at the wreckage of his harp and wondering miserably if he could mend it. I thought, you should thank your God it was only the harp.

When I learned the next day that David had left Gibeah in charge of a raid on a Philistine garrison, I thought at first that this was Abner's doing, to get him out of Saul's way. It was much later that I realized the order had been Saul's own, and later still that I understood why, though at first I refused to accept it.

"Come on, don't be naive, Eliphaz," said Jonathan, as we sat late at table, feeling the loss of him. "Father knows he can't finish him himself and get away with it. So he'll put him in the front line and let the Philistines do it for him."

I shook my head stubbornly. "He wouldn't do that, Jonathan. Not in cold blood. He wasn't himself when he threw that spear, it was a moment of madness. He wouldn't *plan* to harm David. Not when he's in his right mind."

"Is he ever, these days?" objected Jonathan bitterly. "He's not the father I once looked up to, Eliphaz. Nor the friend you once loved, if you'd only admit it."

But I didn't want to listen. I went off to do some chores, and tried to get the whole business out of my head.

However, if Jonathan was right, Saul's plan had miscarried. Each new day brought fresh news of David's heroism; the initial raid being successful, he had gone on to attack one Philistine outpost after another, and each time he emerged the victor. His fame and popularity increased; Saul seethed and simmered, and I was forced to acknowledge that Jonathan wasn't overreacting.

I was still more confused about Saul's motives when he told me that he intended giving Merab to David in marriage. He said it was in recognition of David's valour, and to please the people, who had made him their darling, but it was Jonathan again who opened my eyes.

"He wants her to spy on him," he sneered in disgust. "He wants someone close to David who he can trust, so he can find out what David is plotting."

I said, "And what *is* he plotting?"

"Nothing; he wouldn't be so stupid. What could he hope to gain by it? He has everything he could want already."

Nevertheless, this plan miscarried too. Merab refused to comply with Saul's wishes, and said that if he forced her, she would swallow poison. I think she would have done it, too, for she'd loved her goat-breeder Adriel from being twelve years old, and lately he'd started to notice her, too. I think it was Merab who told her father about Michal; that Michal had been attracted to David ever since she'd laid eyes on him. Of course this suited Saul's purposes equally well, so all was arranged, and with embarrassing speed. Merab must marry first, for she was the older, then Michal straight after, as soon as was practicable.

Not that the girls had any reason to complain. Merab was overjoyed; Adriel, her unassuming sweetheart from the backwoods, couldn't believe his good fortune. And Michal was in ecstasy. She drifted about the fortress dazed and dreamy-eyed while the necessary preparations were made round about her and she waited distractedly for David to come home from his campaigning. Of course, when it came to it, I knew that I would play my part nobly. I pretended to be glad for her. I helped organize the celebrations, I smiled at the women who came to take the measurements for her robe and discuss how she should wear her hair and paint her face. But inside I was falling to pieces, for I'd never stopped loving her. I only wished that David would come back quickly so we could get the thing over with; I couldn't imagine what kept him in the field.

"He hasn't saved the bride-price," Jonathan disclosed to me. "The cost is high, you know, to marry a king's daughter."

"How high?" I enquired, detecting his cynicism.

"A hundred Philistine foreskins; that's what my father says he will accept for her. *Now* do you see what he's up to?"

I couldn't credit that Saul would mean this literally; but David delivered the goods twice over, in an upturned helmet, and according to Jonathan, counted them out to the king one by one on the table. Knowing David, I can quite believe it. I'm not sure why David, for his part, agreed to the marriage, for he must have suspected Saul's intentions. Perhaps he thought it might atone for his sin; or prevent him from repeating it. Or perhaps he simply loved Michal.

I think it was David who conceived the notion of a double wedding. Jonathan was his senior by some few years, and still not married. Though Saul had mentioned it before, he'd had too much on his mind to pursue the matter. It was certainly David who introduced his friend to Sarah, a cousin of his from Bethlehem as comely as Dinah and beguiling as Eve - I caught myself wondering just how well David knew her. I was happy enough to arrange things for Jonathan - in the absence of his mother, negotiations fell to me - but I dreaded the wedding as a coward dreads battle.

Saul wasn't a happy man either. He drank a great deal, yet couldn't forget himself; he pined for Ahinoam and felt her loss keenly. I found myself suggesting once more that he should remarry, or at least take a concubine to satisfy his longing, but once more he shook his head and told me not to speak of it again. There was music and dancing, laughter and joy, but for Saul and me it was all away in the distance. Our gloom drew us temporarily close, though neither of us could fully appreciate what the other truly grieved for. While the revellers caroused in the courtyard below us, we sat on the ramparts with the stars overhead and the breeze in our hair, and Saul said, "Show me your wrist, Eli. I need to know you still have your scar too."

David had a house built for himself and Michal not far from our own, in the centre of Gibeah; Jonathan brought Sarah to live at the fortress, and I soon grew to think of her as a younger sister. She was a thoughtful girl as well as an attractive one, impossible not to like, but I missed Michal with a fervency that frightened me. In less time than it takes the olives to ripen, we heard that Sarah was with child, and it amused me to think that Saul would be a grandfather before he had a grey hair. But there was no news of that kind about Michal, and in a strange and selfish way, I was glad.

It was nearing the time of Sarah's confinement when Saul first admitted frankly, and not merely to himself or to me, that he wanted David dead. We were in the grip of the hardest winter I had ever known: the frost nipped our fingers, many ancient olive-trees died, and there had been snow at Jebus. The nights fell early, and we would sit around late after supper, warming ourselves by the glowing brazier, staving off the moment when we would have to leave the comforting heat of the fire and go to our beds. That night there were six of us huddled round the smoking embers - Abner, Eliab, Barak, Jonathan, Saul and myself - and as it so often did, the conversation turned upon David and his continuing Philistine campaign.

"I can't think why they persist in coming out to fight him," Abner was saying. "They haven't beaten him in a single encounter to date. He has pushed them back almost as far as the walls of their five cities again."

"I think they still can't believe they won't win, so long as Israel's army is commanded by someone other than its king," remarked Eliab. "To them David is a nobody, just a temporarily lucky nobody. They are convinced he must crumble before long."

"David *is* a nobody," growled Saul, his eyes dark and smouldering in the firelight. "And he is not in command of Israel's army. He captains a band of landless ruffians who have nothing better to do than volunteer for certain death at the hands of godless heathen who lie sharpening their claws ready for tearing their prey to pieces."

"You gave him the commission, Father," Jonathan objected. "And yet now you talk as though he's set himself up as some kind of outlaw. Just remember - we owe it to him more than to anyone else that we're still free men."

"Because he has toppled a few paltry fortlets and scattered half a dozen raiding parties?" I saw that Saul's colour was rising, and not only from the deepening orange glow of the brazier. I bit my tongue, and noticed Abner and Eliab exchange knowing glances, as they so often did.

"Because he killed Goliath," Jonathan snarled.

"The uncircumcised blacksmith? You think that is what saved us? Do you seriously imagine that the Philistines would have sat on their backsides and waited for us to pierce their earlobes just because one of them had been knocked out of action by a slingstone?" Saul was leaning forward with his lips drawn taut, the knuckles around his wine-cup standing out white. "Was it David who led our troops in the charge that put them to flight? Was it? The victory was *mine* that day, Jonathan ben Saul, but everyone has conveniently chosen to forget it - even you. Well, you won't be allowed to forget it for long, you can be sure of that."

Jonathan drew back a little, sniffing his father's anger and not caring to provoke it further. There was a short silence; the fire crackled, awkwardness hung in the air. To revive the conversation Barak commented, "He must surely return home soon for the winter. He cannot hope to mount an attack on any of their cities before next season. It's too wet down there on the plains. His men will grow demoralized."

"They will grow mushrooms, more like - behind their ears," Abner sniggered disdainfully.

"David will not live to see the next season," said Saul.

Five pairs of eyes fixed him. He looked from each to the next, glowering. "He is undermining the unity of Israel," he continued stiffly. "He has even been the cause of friction here tonight, among my own Companions. He scatters seeds of dissension wherever he goes, whatever he does. Now it is time to pull the weed by its root."

I said, "Come on, Saul, it's late. Let's discuss this in the morning."

"No," he retorted, "We'll discuss it now. It's time we decided who is king in this land. I wear the coronet and

337

carry the mace, I enforce the laws, I make the decisions. I am sick and tired of hearing of nothing but David's victories, David's initiatives, David's charisma. He is subverting my authority, and I will not have it. If he wants to sit on my throne, let him fight me for it."

"Don't be ridiculous," Jonathan muttered. "He doesn't want to be king."

"No. Saul is right."

The interjection came from Eliab; and it drew a fresh thread across the thickening web of tension that was spanning the atmosphere between us.

"He should never have come here. He shouldn't even have been at Elah to hear Goliath's challenge. He has done nothing all his life but interfere and meddle in affairs which are none of his business. I suggest we relieve him of his command and send him back to his sheep."

I thought, you are as jealous as Saul is; but I held my tongue.

Saul said, "At least there is one man still prepared to stand by me."

"Two," grunted Abner.

I said, "I'm tired. I'm going to bed."

The following day, Sarah's labour came early, and thankfully, for the present, David was forgotten. She gave birth to twins, who were scrawny and small but not sickly: both boys, and they were given the names Mephibosheth and Mebunnai. Merab and Michal both came home to help out with them, and Jonathan was as besotted as Saul had been all those years ago, when he who was now the father had been the son. When the eighth day came, the day of circumcision, the fortress was once again crowded with well-wishers; and into the midst of the festivities walked David.

Jonathan ran to embrace him, but even in the flush of his pride I saw his face cloud over, and when he drew David quietly to one side, I knew what he must be saying. Later that evening they came to me together, and asked me to walk with them alone; and I went.

We strolled in the fields, our feet wrapped in sheepskin, our cloaks drawn tight.

Jonathan said, "Eliphaz, do you think he was serious? Do you think it's even safe for David to spend the night here?"

I shrugged my shoulders vaguely. "I only wish I could say yes and be sure of it. But I just don't know any more. I don't even know if Saul still trusts me."

"He wouldn't if he knew you were here with us," David observed grimly. His hair still sprang in boyish spikes from his head, but his face was older; there was experience there, and there was caution tempering the zeal of youth. You could see that he had fought and killed, and that he had learnt what it is to lead men.

"Do you think he would listen, if you and I went to him and pleaded David's case together, Eliphaz?" asked Jonathan. "Surely, out of all the love he once had for us, something must be left." Then he smacked his hand against his thigh. "We have to try. David - take Michal and sleep at your own house tonight. But be on your guard; don't trust anyone."

Fate temporarily decided to favour us. The following day, Saul was calm and receptive and agreed to see Jonathan and me without hesitation. Jonathan drew up a stool and sat at Saul's feet, talking him gently through David's record of service towards him, stressing his devotion, reminding him of how at only thirteen years of age David had willingly left his home and family to bring Saul comfort, of how he had risked his life against Goliath so that Saul might cheat death. David had never once asked for the honours he received from the people. Even after Saul had tried to kill him, he hadn't turned against him. He was the truest and most loyal officer Saul had.

"Father," he concluded, "If you love me at all, please spare David's life. He's like a brother to me - if you kill him, you'll be killing me too."

I could see the struggle that raged in Saul's mind, I could see the emotions fighting for supremacy in his eyes. Jonathan had pushed aside the stool, and was kneeling on the floor beside his father. I watched Saul's resolve crumble. He reached out and took Jonathan's hand in his own, and said, "I do love you."

That night he awoke screaming so hideously that I heard the new babies start howling. I thought he was ill: his body twisted and convulsed, and though his eyes were open, they stared right through me. After a time, his muscles relaxed and he seemed to sleep again, but I sat up beside him until morning. When it was barely light, his eyes flicked open, and he said, "Fetch Abner and Eliab."

He spoke quietly, but with such force that I obeyed without thinking; when we returned he was up and pacing the room, and he said, "Thank you, Eli. You may go."

I don't know what made me defy him - maybe just the way he was being so oddly formal with me. I didn't disobey overtly, but made as if to leave, then crouched outside the doorway and heard the order given. A few months before, I wouldn't have believed what I was hearing. Now, I had no choice. And I knew what I had to do.

Abner and Eliab went for David as they had been instructed, but they went openly and asked to see him, naturally assuming that Michal suspected nothing. She told them he was ill and wouldn't see anyone; when they forced their way in, they found an idol in the bed in David's place, and he was gone. Saul exploded in fury on being informed of what had happened; he had Michal dragged before him, and I thought he would strike her, as he had done once before. But she told him David had threatened to kill her if she didn't help him escape, so he calmed down and let her go.

I should have realized that Saul would find out sooner or later how she had learned of his intentions. I think he accused Jonathan at first, but somehow he discovered the truth. He didn't denounce me directly; he simply left a clay tablet on my mattress, saying that I was no longer to eat with him and his Companions, nor to act as his cupbearer, nor to sleep in his room. I was to share quarters with the other servants, and take my orders from Boaz.

I was devastated. I stood with the tablet in my hand and the chagrin in my throat, and knew I had to have it out with him. He was in the study, writing something; he didn't look up when I entered, but he knew well enough who it was, for he said, "Go away, Eliphaz. I'm busy."

So, I was Eliphaz now, even in private. My lips went dry, but I stood my ground.

"I said, go away." There was some other emotion mixed with the anger in his voice, but I wasn't sure what it was.

I was determined to make him face me. "What is the meaning of this message?" I demanded. "Am I to be given no explanation?"

He still didn't look at me. "You betrayed me, Eliphaz. You should be thankful I haven't turned you out into the street."

"Betrayed you? Because I stopped you destroying yourself by murdering the most gifted man in your kingdom, and the husband of your own daughter? You have a strange concept of loyalty, Saul."

"I don't wish to discuss it," he said. "Now leave before I have you thrown out."

So for the next two days I worked with the servants. Old Boaz was kind to me; Jonathan treated me as though nothing had changed. But Abner and Eliab would cross the courtyard if they saw me coming.

On the third day, Jonathan told me that David was at Ramah with Samuel.

On the fourth day, Saul found out.

He was incensed: to him this could be nothing other than a conclusive confirmation of his worst suspicions. We were all hauled up before him, one by one - Jonathan, Michal, myself, even Abner and Eliab, but Saul was so consumed with rage that we could barely make sense of what he said to us. His face was purple, the veins in his forehead bulged and writhed, he spluttered and gasped until I feared he was going to break down utterly. Finally he grabbed me round the neck and shook me so violently that

I was choking; and demanded out of the blue to know if David had been anointed.

Coughing, I shook my head dumbly, but he didn't believe me. He pinned me back against the wall and I smelt the wine on his breath as he asked me again; a second time I lied to him, but I felt my cheeks burning. Then he struck me across the face so hard that my head hit the wall; and with blood streaming from my nostrils, I told him the truth.

If Abner and Eliab hadn't heard my shouting and got him away from me, I might well not have lived to begin this chronicle, let alone complete it. Somehow they dragged him off me; I crawled into a corner and lay coughing blood. I don't have much recollection of what happened next, but I wound up lying on my pallet in the servants' quarters, with Jonathan patching me up and smoothing wine and oil into my torn flesh. I mouthed, "Where's Saul?" but Jonathan shrugged his shoulders and told me not to fret. Then he said that Abner and Eliab had been sent in search of David, but hadn't returned.

By sunset they still hadn't come back. The following morning, Abinadab and Barak were sent after them, but they didn't return either. The third day, Nathan and Joseph went in pursuit also, and by that evening Saul was alone at the fortress with two men he no longer trusted, and a handful of servants who wouldn't go anywhere near him..

It was almost dark when he came in with Jonathan in tow and asked if I was fit to travel. There was no concern in his voice. He didn't refer to what had passed between us, but his tone was dry as tinder. I nodded absently, and he said, "Then get up. We're going to Ramah."

There was no sign of life at Samuel's house. The

door wasn't barred; Saul swung it open and walked in, but the place was empty and chill - no fire had burned in the grate today.

"The sanctuary," said Saul between clenched teeth, and drawing us after him with a sweeping glance, he headed off up the track leading to the summit of the hill.

Again, we heard them before we saw them; and we felt them before we heard them. I grabbed Jonathan's arm and hissed at him, "Stay back!" It had been half a lifetime ago, but it felt like yesterday.

The circling and twisting of the bodies in the light of the fire that leapt on the altar... the flying of the faded brown cloaks in the moon-glow... the transported, bearded faces plunging and rising, plunging and rising... and in the centre of everything, David playing his harp, his eyes gleaming with the fire of ecstasy. His face wore the expression of a man on the brink of a startling discovery; he was exploring the gift he had known for years was within him and yet without until now having realized the half of its true power. He was grinning absurdly at Samuel, who leaned heavily on his staff, his hooded eyes nodding, his wizened face softened by a wavering smile.

Abinadab, Barak, Nathan and Joseph were dancing. Caught up in the holy rapture, helpless to resist the wild energy that swept through them, their limbs writhed and coiled of their own volition; their faces were altered, so that at first I didn't even know them. Abner and Eliab lay face down on the ice-bound earth, their hands pressed to their ears, their bodies contorted in raw agony.

In abject dismay I watched Saul drawn forward inexorably into the ferment. His face was flushed in the soaring firelight, his eyes flaring and his hair streaming in the ice-fingered wind. His expression was unfathomable - not ecstasy, not dread, yet certainly not neutral. As the worshippers revolved around him, I saw them holding out their hands to draw him in; whether or not they knew who he was, I had no means to tell. As he was gathered among them I saw his mouth moving - perhaps he was prophesying, but I couldn't hear his voice above the driving music. His limbs were moving as though he danced, yet not of himself; then I lost sight of him among the whirling figures. The drums beat harder, the flutes wailed higher, the dance swept faster. Then I glimpsed Saul again.

He was naked; how or why he had stripped off his clothes, I had no idea. He no longer danced; he staggered like a drunkard, and appeared to be in pain. He clutched at his stomach and shook himself, seemingly trying to hurl something from his shoulders, but however hard he tried, it wouldn't come free. He bent double, sagged to his knees, pitched forward onto the ground amid the thrashing limbs and swirling cloaks. Now he was screaming, loud enough for the sound to rise and carry above the screeching pipes, the throbbing tabors - and the sound was not human. The furore continued around him unabated; but between the weaving bodies I saw that David had flung down his harp. Saul was tearing at the frost-hardened earth with trembling fingers; his body jerked and convulsed and there was saliva issuing between his teeth. David was pointing at him with one hand and gripping Samuel's cloak with the other, shouting at him and imploring him, though his words were lost in the chaos. But the seer merely shook his head, his eyes leaden as clouds in a storm.

Eventually I could stand it no longer. I hauled Jonathan to his feet, and ran. We stumbled and lurched down the hillside until the music and the voices were drowned in the biting wind above us, then breathless and shaken we dropped to the ground again and collapsed exhausted among the boulders. We said nothing to one another, for there was nothing we dared say, but we knew we couldn't go home without him. We huddled together for warmth and consolation, and resisted the desire to drift into sleep, for in that cold I knew we would never wake again. I could only hope we would know when it was safe to go back for Saul, and that this wouldn't come too late. I watched the stars float across the sky, and not long after midnight the cloaked figures began to pass us in twos and threes on their way back to the town. I waited until the stream of them had thinned and gone, then nudged Jonathan, and numb and stiff with cold we made our way slowly back up the hillside.

The sanctuary was silent. The altar smouldered, a faint twist of smoke rising from it in a dying red glow. Saul lay prone, wrapped only in a mound of cloaks. He didn't move; whether he was dead, swooning or sleeping, we couldn't tell. David had been weeping. His face was still streaked with tears and he sat slumped on the ground with the seer beside him. Samuel, frail and shrivelled as a dried fig, sat motionless, neither shivering nor shuffling, his arm round David's shoulders, his eyes watching Saul without expression.

We went as near as we dared, then David looked up and his countenance brightened. He beckoned us closer, and I gestured towards Saul. At first neither of them spoke, but then David said evenly, "Samuel calmed him. He says he will be all right."

I whispered hoarsely, "What happened?"

David made as if to speak again, but then no words came. He frowned slightly, as if even he were unsure about what exactly had taken place here. It was Samuel who said, "Evil cannot remain concealed when the spirit of Adonai is present in power."

"What do you mean?" I felt weakened, drained; the seer's dry, cracked voice grated on my shattered nerves and I was in no mood for a sermon.

"What is in him came out," he replied, as though that were an answer.

"Came out?" I repeated. "It's gone?"

"No." Samuel sighed heavily. David was staring at the earth - I think he wished it would devour him. "It manifested itself, but will never leave him, Eliphaz. Not while he wants it to stay."

CHAPTER 20

For hours Saul lay insensible on his mattress, with Sarah to watch him. At daybreak we had got him back to Gibeah strapped to a donkey of Samuel's, and now David, Jonathan and I crouched about the hearth in the dining room, awaiting and dreading him waking. We'd seen nothing of Abner and Eliab, nor the other Companions, though we knew they'd been home. Clearly they had no desire to discuss with us the events of last night. Of course, this came as no surprise, but the wedge being driven between us and them was worrying me deeply. David and Jonathan were sharing a cup of warmed wine to cheer their spirits and thaw their limbs, and David still looked more shaken than I'd ever seen him. Though quiet enough, his shoulders sagged and his face was pale. Jonathan stared into the wine-cup, lacing his fingers nervously round the rim, and brooded with Saul's eyes.

David said flatly, "He came up to the sanctuary to kill me" - and when neither of us saw fit to answer - "Didn't

348

he? That's why he went to Ramah. That's why he'd sent the others. He won't rest until I'm dead."

"Things may be different when he wakes," murmured Jonathan.

"I doubt it." David passed one hand across his half-closed eyes. "Oh, I know I'm being foolish, I know he's not himself. But sometimes I'd just like to know what I've done to deserve all this from him. Sometimes I can't believe it's all happening to me."

I said, "I'm sorry, David. I'm sorry it had to come to this. I just wish I'd never brought you to Gibeah in the first place. It's all my fault."

He raised his head to look at me; it seemed to take all the strength he could muster. "Don't apologize, Eliphaz. It wasn't your fault I came here." He smiled a little, ruefully, rousing himself from his unwonted self-pity enough to see that I was looking as wretched as he felt. "It was what Adonai planned for me. I'm as sure of that as I ever was."

"What Adonai planned?" I was startled to hear how bitter I sounded - I hadn't meant to. It was so unfair, with David in this state. But I couldn't stop myself going on. "How could Adonai plan a nightmare like this? It just doesn't make any sense."

"Shut up, Eliphaz." It was Jonathan who silenced me. He must have guessed what effect my heresy would be having on his friend.

"No. It's all right." David sank lower on his haunches, until he was sitting on the ground, his head propped on his knees, gazing into the firelight. "I don't mind talking about it. It might even help." Unexpectedly he smiled at me. "Sometimes it's so hard to see what Adonai is doing. But it's always for the best. In all the time I've known him, it's only ever been for the best."

Jonathan choked back a laugh that was more like a sob. "How can you say that, David? How can you possibly think Adonai always does what's best? My father nearly had me killed because of what Adonai told him. The sacred stones... and I hadn't even heard my father's order! You think that was for the best? You think that was fair?"

He was hardly making himself clear, but David knew what he meant well enough; I wondered how often they had talked of this before. Momentarily David looked so sad, I cursed myself again for stirring all this up, thinking: it's so wrong of us, to be testing his faith at a time like this. But this was David, not Saul. He just said, "Jonathan, Jonathan," in a patient, weary voice, "You can't blame Adonai for that. Saul's spirit was in the wilderness when he announced the fast in the first place, and you knew it perfectly well at the time. The sacred lots only showed him what he asked them to reveal." I knew he wasn't just defending his God out of duty. He was shattered, confused, depressed even, but he still believed. He added, "No one can manipulate Adonai and get away with it. Not even a king."

I too was staring at the fire, but suddenly it wasn't what I was seeing. I was seeing Saul, laid out on the ground up at the high place, struck senseless by the power of the one he'd supposedly tried to control, and I blurted, "Saul, manipulate Adonai? You can't mean that, David. Adonai has manipulated *him*, all along. Forcing him to accept the kingship against his will, when he *knew* it was beyond him. Don't you realize he was nearly sick, the day they crowned him? He wanted nothing more than to run away. I nearly went with him. Perhaps I should have."

"You're talking like a fool, Eliphaz." David bowed his head again, so the words came out muted. "Saul wanted nothing more than to be *king*. That's what you *should* have said. I've talked to him too, you know. To do something great, to be remembered by future generations... *those* are the things he wanted. And more than anything else he wanted to know God. All three of his prayers were answered."

"And look what good it's done him." Then all at once the guilt-pangs came back, and I mumbled, "I'm sorry, David. I shouldn't be talking like this. It's just... that if Adonai is the kind of God you say he is - all-knowing, always loving, always wanting what's best for us - then surely he would never have answered those prayers. If Adonai is that kind of friend to those who know him... well it's like they say: who needs enemies?"

"Saul has only ever had one real enemy." David looked back at me, watching for my reaction. "He's his own worst enemy, Eliphaz. To crave success whilst being terrified of failing, to brood and hide your feelings when they're strong enough to break you, to fear men more than you fear God..."

He broke off, because he knew I was no longer listening. The misery was welling up inside me until everything else was engulfed in it. I said, "So this is it, then, David. There can be no hope for Saul. He will wake up, and everything will be as bad as ever. We must just sit back and watch, while he gradually falls apart. Well I can't do it, David. I just can't."

I don't remember consciously taking the little

jewelled knife out of its pocket, but somehow I found that I was holding it against my wrist. My fingers trembled and I couldn't have seen well enough through my tears to do myself serious damage even if David hadn't wrested it from my grasp and sent it spinning onto the floor. I pressed my hands to my face, and the tears ran between them.

"It's never too late with Adonai," whispered David. "He loves Saul more than any of us do, Eliphaz." And when I made no response he said it again, and a third time, until he saw me nodding. "Perhaps Saul has gone too far to get back everything he's lost. But he needn't be in this torment. If only he could repent, if he could renounce the sins that ruined him..."

I sobbed, "Of course he's sorry. Of course he regrets what he did."

"I didn't say regret. I said repent. And he will not."

There was nothing I could say. Taking my hands from my face, I stared once more into the fire. It was dying, but I didn't care. I was already cold inside.

Presently Jonathan whispered, "So what are you going to do, David."

"I shall have to leave Gibeah again, at least for now. I don't have a choice. He won't rest until I'm dead."

"Leave?" Jonathan sounded bewildered, as though he didn't understand what his own tongue was saying. "He can't make you leave. I won't let him."

"He's already done it. If I don't leave on my feet, I'll be leaving on my shield. I'm not ready for that."

Jonathan was incredulous. "But this is madness! David, you can't let him get away with it! Eliphaz, talk to him! Tell him he can't leave. Tell him we need him here."

Still wrapped in my own desolation, I thought, *you need him*; David said softly, "You aren't thinking, Jonathan. Do you want me dead too?"

"Don't even say such a thing!" Jonathan was so wound up now that I roused myself at last to look at him. His eyes sparked; Saul had planted his seed in all his children, and it grew in them as they grew. "At least wait until he comes round. What happened to him up there must surely change something."

"You're clutching at straws, Jonathan. I've made up my mind."

For a moment they regarded one another, Jonathan seething, David smiling faintly. Then the fire in Jonathan ebbed; he sat down again, pressed his palms against his closed eyes, and said, "Where will you go."

"To the hills. Somewhere he will never find me."

I started, the implications of what he was saying freeing my thickened tongue. "Alone? In this weather? There are bandits and God knows what wild beasts up there - you won't last the week out."

"I grew up in those mountains, Eliphaz. Sleeping rough will come as nothing new to me. Besides - I shan't be alone."

"You wouldn't subject Michal to that?"

David sighed heavily. "Of course Michal must stay here. But I have friends, men who will follow me. Don't forget - I haven't been fighting the Philistines on my own."

I exclaimed, "You mean to raise your own army? To set up in opposition to Saul?"

"No, Eliphaz." David kept his voice down, but his patience sounded laboured. I bristled, piqued at being patronized by a youth with little more than down on his cheeks. "Only a fool sets himself against the Lord's Anointed. You know I would never harm him, any more than you would. And underneath it all, he knows it too. But the Philistines won't go away simply because Israel has troubles of her own. The land still needs defending, and someone must do it."

"Then I'm coming with you." Jonathan stood up suddenly, and crossed to the table, behind which the larger part of his great-grandfather's panoply still hung dusty and unused on the wall. He took down a wide bronze sword, felt it for weight, made as if to put it through his belt. David shook his head, laid one hand on Jonathan's shoulder, and prized the sword from his fingers. "Don't be foolish, Jonathan. You are the king's son. Your place is here."

"But he will send more men, to hunt you down and kill you," Jonathan persisted, and his voice was choked with emotion. "What if he sends me?"

David sighed. "Let's cross that bridge when we come to it. And I don't think we will, somehow."

Saul's son drooped on to one of the couches; his life seemed to be draining from some invisible wound which wouldn't be stemmed. David's face softened.

"Listen, Jonathan. You wait until your father wakes, if that will make you feel better. I will hide out in the fields and wait for you to come and tell me how it is with him. Then we shall decide together."

"And if I come, and you haven't waited?"

"Trust me, Jonathan. You have my word."

Jonathan said, "I will talk to him as soon as he comes to. I will ask him straight out what he intends for you."

"And if he lies to you?"

"My father may be many things, but he is no liar. He will tell me what he's minded to do, if I ask him. He always does."

Again David shook his head. "He knows how close we are. He isn't going to tell you outright that he means to kill me. No; tomorrow is the first day of the New Moon Festival and I am supposed to eat with you all here at the fortress, but I won't be there. When Saul asks where I am, you must tell him I have gone home to Bethlehem for family sacrifices. If he accepts what you say without reacting, maybe I'll believe he has relented. If he gets angry - then we shall know the truth."

Jonathan sat a while and thought, and said nothing. Then he whispered, "Tell me where you'll be hiding."

"No."

"No?" Jonathan ran his fingers through his coarse black hair. "Then how..?"

"Suppose he asks you where I am, and you actually know? He'll get the truth out of you, however he has to do it. No one must know where I am. We shall arrange a signal - you will come out into the fields and fire an arrow in a place where I'll be able to see you: I'll show you where to stand. We shall have one token for safety, one for danger. When it's safe, I'll come out to you."

"You promise?"

"Of course I promise."

It was late in the afternoon when Saul revived. Sarah came through into the dining room and said he was asking for me.

I was surprised, after all that had happened between us. His room was in darkness; I fetched a lamp and he screwed up his eyes against it but didn't tell me to take it away. He looked dreadful. His cheeks were ashen and his hair matted. He asked muzzily, "What happened to me, Eli? All I can remember is the mountain, music, David chanting spells... then just pain, an awful pain..."

I answered, "David wasn't chanting spells, Saul. He was worshipping Adonai."

But Saul pulled the cushions close around his head. "They were spells, they must have been. They brought the pain. He tried to kill me, Eli, with evil magic. He's a sorcerer - he knows the black ways of the Canaanites. We have to destroy him."

He was struggling to raise himself on one elbow; I pushed him back gently and said to humour him, "Yes, Saul," and gave him more wine. Inside, my heart was sinking. I knew what David and Jonathan would have to face.

Saul didn't get up that day. He drifted in and out of consciousness, and rambled, both when he was asleep and when he was awake, but nothing he said made much sense. Without awaiting a change of orders, I slept in his room that night, and when he awoke next morning he didn't scold me for it.

He seemed better; he got up and went about his business, though he was withdrawn and subdued, and said little. At the evening meal I didn't risk taking my old place at table, for I knew that Abner or Eliab would challenge me. But I made sure I was there serving food and clearing away dishes.

Abner, Eliab and Abinadab, Barak, Nathan and Joseph had all reappeared, in ones and twos, but no one spoke of Ramah. They sat round the table to eat, and David's place was empty, but Saul made no comment. He pronounced the blessings over the meal, but apart from this, he didn't speak. I watched Jonathan's anxiety mounting - unless Saul asked, there was nothing he could say. Saul ate nothing, and Jonathan only picked at his food. When the meal was over, he left the room without giving excuse, and I followed him into the darkened courtyard. He swung round and gripped me by my cloak-pins, the whites of his eyes large and glittering.

"What shall I do?" he hissed at me. "What signal can I give to David?"

I said, "You can't give him any signal, it's too dangerous. Tomorrow is the second day of the Festival. Saul is bound to say something."

Jonathan was beside himself. He stalked the courtyard, paced the ramparts, wouldn't sleep. The following evening saw Saul's household gathered round the table as yesterday, and again there was the empty place. This time, Saul asked.

He must have known Jonathan was lying; the apple in his neck tensed and twisted and made him hoarse as he stumbled through the false explanation. For a harrowing and timeless interval Saul said nothing, merely staring at his son and simmering in silence. The Companions shuffled and sought to smother their embarrassment.

Then Saul lost control. His features locked into a mask of malevolence, he clenched his fists until the knuckles stood white, then started shouting. He shrieked like a wild thing, cursing Jonathan as a bastard, a traitor, and countless other names I couldn't bring myself to repeat. He accused him of conspiring with David to overthrow his sovereignty, of being David's lover, of being the son of his mother's whoring, of having no blood of Saul's line in his body.

"Don't you realize?" Saul was ranting at him. "You'll never be king while David lives. He wants your throne, and he'll get it, even if he has to kill you first. He has no love for you, you wretched fool! He's deceiving you so he can steal what is yours without your so much as complaining. He's an impostor and a sorcerer. He's using you!"

Jonathan had had enough. He picked up his goblet and dashed its contents in Saul's face to put an end to his tirade, then he yelled, "I don't want to be king! I never want to be king, are you listening to me? I've seen what it's done to you!"

He flung round and made for the door, but his great-grandfather's spear got there before he did. It quivered from the splintered doorframe, and Saul stood heaving and panting and sweating like a bull. For a moment Jonathan couldn't move. Then he turned and ran.

No one followed him. No one breathed. Everyone tried to avoid Saul's gaze. He looked from one to the next with blood-red eyes, then he fled too.

I pursued him without hesitation, mostly because I thought he might have gone after Jonathan. I ran into the courtyard, but Jonathan was gone. Saul lay face down on the pool-side wall and wept. He was talking, but his voice was muffled and broken, and I could only make out the words, "My son, my own son, for God's sake!" endlessly repeated as the remorse devoured him. His fingers clutched at my garments, and the scent in his hair made me nauseous. He said, "Eli, I could have killed him." There was no sense in disagreeing with him, for it was true and we both knew it.

It was at noon the following day when Saul's son, hero of a dozen battles, slunk in, red-eyed and stricken, and sagged wrung out against the doorpost.

I bided my time while Sarah embraced him; while he smiled feebly at his sons but lacked the strength to hold them. She put them down and went to get food. I said, "Jonathan, thank God. Your father has been worried sick."

His eyes flicked towards me and he made a faintly contemptuous sound in his throat, that said: you expect me to believe that? Aloud he said, "My father doesn't want to see either me or David ever again. Well, he won't have to see David. He's gone."

"What happened."

His shoulders went up; I didn't know if it was a shudder or a shrug. "Oh, God, Eliphaz! We wept, we swore friendship. What else could we do?"

I sighed; he was exhausted and grieving and in no mood to respond civilly to a barrage of questions. But I couldn't resist asking one more. "What about Michal?"

"He gave me a note for her. It says he'll come back for her when all this is over." He dropped his head onto his arms. "But it cannot end till either my friend or my father is dead.."

CHAPTER 21

Saul's resolve to take David's life hardened into pre-occupation, then into obsession. As the days unfolded, I watched the thing consume him, until he could speak or think of nothing else. I could only be thankful that he was too distracted for the present to think clearly about how to convert his purpose into action. We began to hear of men flocking to join David up in the mountains; the promise of Philistine blood still drew the rabble like a charm, and there was always someone who could tell them where to find David the Giantslayer. But no one would tell Saul.

Not two Sabbaths had passed before Abinadab and Nathan left us to join the horde in the hills. Abinadab was David's own brother after all, and Nathan was apparently kin in some way. None of us dared tell Saul where they had gone, but he found out soon enough and was confounded. Blind terror and rage engulfed him, and the rest of us were hauled up before him and forced to swear fresh oaths of allegiance to him on pain of death. It wouldn't have surprised me if he'd made us sign with our own blood. The whole performance was as futile as it was pathetic. Abner I know would have died by his own hand sooner than betray his beloved cousin. Eliab hated David so intensely by now that he would have followed anyone who was sworn to kill him. Barak and Joseph, solid and dependable like Abner, had given their lives for a cause and would never break their word. As for me, I showed Saul my scar and he seemed content. Jonathan would promise nothing, and defied his father to lay a finger on him; Saul simmered in silence but didn't press the matter further.

The third Sabbath was scarcely past when Michal was told that her marriage to David was over. Saul reckoned David's desertion as being tantamount to divorce, and found his daughter another husband. The man's name was Paltiel, a wealthy merchant from Kiriath Jearim, whose business ventures had derived considerable benefit from Saul's military successes and the peace and prosperity he had brought to Israel. He was as loyal to Saul, in his own way, as either Abner or Eliab. I suppose he was a good enough man, too - kind and courteous, fastidious and urbane - but he was a stranger, and Kiriath Jearim seemed a long way from home.

The hunt began in earnest in the spring. All I can recall of the months that followed is an endless chain of exhausting days wasted chasing false trails, and wearisome nights spent in tents or under the stars. We collected clues, we followed up hunches, we investigated rumours: David was in the desert; he was home in Bethlehem; he had gone way up north into the mountains of Ephraim.

At first Saul himself came with us - he was resolute

and rabid with single-minded energy, and the rest of us had no choice but to strive to keep up with him. But it was only the obsession that kept him going; he was still scarcely eating, and he was having to drink more and more before he could find enough peace to sleep. For a time none of us noticed the further deterioration in him, for it crept upon us imperceptibly. But later I would catch an unexpected glimpse of him from the corner of my eye and be shocked, for he looked like someone else. He grew gaunt and wasted, with face always pinched and eyes too large, and there were shadows beneath them which he couldn't disguise. Eventually I persuaded him to go back home or there would be no battle to fight; reluctantly he had to agree, provided we promised to continue the search unabated.

Fruitlessly we trailed our dejected company up and down the length of Canaan, and from time to time I would call at Gibeah to see how Saul was, and always he was worse. Sometimes I found him drunk, sometimes asleep way after noon; more than once I resolved to abandon everything and stay there with him after all, but always he made me go back, saying that the only way to restore him was to bring him David, dead or alive. And so the miserable search went on, and I both longed for and dreaded its end.

The second time I returned home, Michal was gone; the third, Saul had taken a concubine.

I suppose I should have long since ceased being shocked by his unpredictable behaviour, but after he had so vehemently resisted the suggestion when it came from me, I had hardly expected he would ever change his mind. Her name was Rizpah, and she was quite the unlikeliest companion for him I could ever have imagined. She was small, pale, fragile, with a plain, pinched little face and faded blue eyes. Her hair seemed faded too - it was fine and wispy and the shade of bleached corn. I had never seen a girl with such odd colouring nor such an unfeminine figure, and I was taken aback, for Saul could still have had the pick of any maiden in Israel. Boaz said that Saul had bought her from a travelling trader at the city gates; she was a slave from some country far to the north which none of us had ever heard of, and her real name wasn't Rizpah at all but something outlandish and unpronounceable. She'd been a slave for as long as she could remember, and had spent her life being handed on from one cruel master to another, all of whom had abused her in every imaginable way: despite her frail appearance, she had developed some remarkably effective strategies for survival, and could bite and scratch like a tigress.

For some time I couldn't fathom why on earth Saul had acquired her. In the end I concluded that it was her very fragility. It seemed to bring out what remained of his better nature - Boaz said that in all the time Rizpah had been here, Saul had never once lifted a finger or even his voice against her. She was silent and withdrawn and would talk to no one; but she talked to Saul, for hours. The irony of the whole arrangement intrigued me, but there was no denying that they were good for one another. He gave her security, status and respect; fine-spun clothes and jewels fit for the queen she almost was. She gave him the love she had nurtured deep inside herself since childhood, hidden beneath her cold hard shell, and it seemed to be important to him that he could still bring someone happiness. I don't even think he slept with her until she herself desired it, then on my visits to Gibeah I was once more banished from his bedroom.

As well as rumours of his whereabouts, we also received endless reports of David's victories. A skirmish here, a raid there - he continued to harass the Philistines whenever an opportunity presented itself. His unruly following had grown to a sizeable army; a constant stream of debtors, landless beggars, criminals and outcasts - Israel's misfits of every kind, only too keen to run from their responsibilities - gathered to his standard in their hundreds. We heard that he was in Judah, in Moab, even in Philistia; then one night Abner came to me in camp near Bethlehem and announced that there was a man outside who wanted to see me, alone and urgently - he would give his information to no one else, but said it concerned David.

I was puzzled. I recognized the name of the man, Doeg, but had never met him, and couldn't see why he should want to speak to me. I had Abner show him in.

He was a big, rawboned man with huge hands, and skin leathered and rough from a life of heavy manual work and exposure to wind and sun. Apparently he'd been appointed as king's chief herdsman, though he hadn't had the job long; he'd worked his way up from a labourer, and sheer sweat and industry had earned him the respect of Yezanel, who still managed the royal estates. I invited him to sit down, for his height and decidedly boorish manner made me nervous, but he continued to stoop in the doorway, and asked me again if I really were Eliphaz, cupbearer to Saul, and if we were alone.

I assured him that I was, and that we were. His eyes searched the tent - deep-set, restless eyes that flicked and probed and never stayed long in one place - then warily he lowered himself among the floor cushions, saying without further formalities, "I have seen David. And I can take you to a man who knows where he's gone."

I regarded him steadily. "Why have you chosen me to approach with this story?"

He answered, "Because David has done an unspeakable thing. I thought I might not be believed. But I have it from Yezanel that His Majesty speaks highly of you, and he says you can be trusted."

Inside I felt the guilt come again, but it wasn't so strong these days. Aloud I asked, "So, what has he done?"

"He has corrupted Ahimelech, the priest of Adonai."

Now I was genuinely startled. Ahimelech, the aged holy man, guardian of the Urim and Thummim, who had dared defy Saul himself - corrupted? And by David? Doeg must have sensed my disbelief; he grunted and began muttering that he shouldn't have come. I motioned him to be at ease, and said, "How?"

He looked round again, then in lowered voice answered, "He gave him and his men food, and weapons. He - violated the sanctuary of Adonai for them."

I drew in a sharp breath. "Violated the sanctuary? What do you mean? Are you sure?"

He opened his mouth to respond, but clamped it shut again. Then unexpectedly he leaned forward and grasped me by the wrist. His hand was heavy, coarse, his grip like iron, and I had to struggle not to show pain. He said, "I want you to get me permission to speak with His Majesty myself. I don't think I should tell anyone but him. But I saw it. With my own eyes."

For a while neither of us spoke further. I studied his face intently, and he returned my gaze without flinching; I was certain he wasn't lying. But there was something about his eyes that made me distinctly uneasy. For some reason I wished he'd never come. Finally I said, "So where is David now?"

"That I don't know," Doeg replied. "But Ahimelech knows."

"Saul will want to question Ahimelech himself if he finds out about this," I said. "He will be very angry. I'm not sure it's wise."

Doeg was patently growing tired of my stalling. He growled, "You don't intend to keep information of such critical significance secret from him?"

"I don't know..." My words came slowly but I was trying desperately to think fast. At length I squared my shoulders and demanded, as crisply as I could, "Why do you hate David, Doeg?"

He seemed put out by this question, which was the reaction I had hoped for. He shifted his bulk uncomfortably among the cushions, and muttered, "He is betraying the king. Isn't that sufficient reason?"

I thought, perhaps it would be, in other circumstances; but not when you know Saul, and you know David, and when you trust your informant as little as I trust you. So I said, "I don't know. Is it?"

I watched him wrestling with himself. As I did so it came to me with the swiftness and the certainty of a well-aimed arrow, that I knew what it was about him that was making me so suspicious and edgy.

Bitterness.

Once the word had formed in my mind, I seemed to see it inscribed all over his face, running through his veins, knotted round his heart. Doeg was bitter, against David and against David's family. Somehow their histories were linked, and now this man was dangerous.

In the end I said I would think over what he'd said, and let him know presently what I intended to do about it; but that I would repeat what he'd told me to no one, since he'd spoken in confidence. And he must repeat it to no one, either.

I kept my word - indeed, I was determined that no one should find out the substance of what Doeg had said to me until I'd had chance to think about it seriously. But the more I pondered it, the worse I felt, and I became more and more convinced that I shouldn't let Doeg get anywhere near Saul. I knew my instinct made no sense, yet it was too strong for me to ignore. Later Eliab accosted me and demanded to know why we were harbouring a sworn enemy of his family.

I enquired, a little too keenly, "Doeg? You know him?"

"Of course I know him. He's plagued my father for years, ever since we did him a favour by buying his land. That's the gratitude we got. Don't trust him, Eliphaz."

"I don't." I smiled at him without much warmth. "But why shouldn't I?"

He was none too keen to elaborate upon his warning, but did so. He had first set eyes on Doeg about three or four years earlier, when his father Jesse had taken pity on the fellow and bought his land from him, despite the fact that it had been burned and salted rendered barren by parties of raiders from the south. Doeg, himself of Edomite ancestry, had needed desperately to clinch the sale, to give him the means to buy food for his wife and son. So Jesse bought the land, but then Doeg begged him to take him on as a hired labourer, and this Jesse couldn't afford to do. He already had eight sons of his own to work his farm, and scarcely enough food to feed even them, when times were thin.

Eventually, unable to find work, Doeg had been forced to sell his only son into slavery, thinking he could buy him back later, or that he would reclaim him rightfully in any case, in the seventh year. However, the Israelite he sold him to had sold him on to some foreign traders, to whom the seventh-year law meant nothing, and now he was gone for good. But Doeg was a man who needed someone to blame, and he'd never let Jesse forget it. He held him personally responsible for the loss of his child, against all sense of justice, and had sworn vengeance upon him, and upon all eight of the fine healthy sons the old miser still had.

I didn't tell Eliab that it was David who was under threat, not him, though I would have liked to reassure him. I said, "He's Saul's chief herdsman. He wanted to see me."

"Yes," he said, "That's what worries me. I suppose he's loyal enough - after all, he and his wife were very nearly starving when Yezanel took them on, from what I've heard, so he owes Saul his life, indirectly. But I don't like him, Eliphaz. He's up to something. I wish you'd send him away."

I thanked Eliab for his advice, but although it helped me to understand, it didn't help me decide what to do. Then as events turned out, the choice was snatched from my hand, for Abner found out what Doeg had told me.

He came to me in a state of high dudgeon, and virtually accused me of treachery. I had information about David and had not passed it on immediately; I was entertaining as my guest a man who could lead us straight to the most notorious outlaw in Israel, and I had done nothing about it. He didn't know what I could be thinking of; but if I wished to allay suspicion, I'd better put matters to rights straight away.

It was all so simple for Abner. He saw things black and white, for or against. To him, Saul was king and kinsman and could do no wrong, so David must be hunted down and made to face him; and that was the whole of it. Abner cared little for the things that make life complex - good and evil, moods and feelings, gods and God. Loyalty he understood, and betrayal, and he hadn't trusted me for months, but like a fool, I let him persuade me. At dawn next day, our men struck camp, and we set out to escort Doeg to the king.

It isn't far from Bethlehem to Gibeah, less than half a day's march, even taken at leisurely pace. But by now we were well into summer, the heat was overpowering, and all of us were weary and dispirited, so progress was slow. Abner insisted on walking beside me and talking at me most of the way, only leaving me in peace when we made stops, and then he went off to cheer and exhort the men.

I suppose he wanted to reassure himself about me, and to justify himself and his confidence in Doeg. He spoke of him incessantly, until the very name irked me; of how the two of them had drunk and diced together last night, and how Doeg owed his life and everything he had to Saul, and how he was devoted to him utterly, although they'd never met. Saul had brought back peace and prosperity to Israel, driven off and punished the raiders who had stolen Doeg's inheritance, as well as offering him hope and status and a future when he'd thought that all was lost.

I did my best to tell him that Doeg hated David much more than he loved Saul; that his affection for the latter was rooted in his irrational loathing for the father of the former; that seeing Jesse extract profit from the land which had once been his must be driving him to distraction - yet I could tell he wasn't listening, he could not or would not see my meaning, so I lapsed into silence and let him talk on, while I drank in the beauty of the hills and fields around us, watched the sheep grazing, and envied them.

Doeg marched alone, conversing only with his thoughts, his sly furtive eyes drawn inexorably towards Gibeah. Eliab fetched up the rear, but I could feel his mistrust across the distance; neither he nor Abner had faith in me any more, but now for opposite reasons, and for the first time in almost twenty years, they no longer had faith in each other.

We reached Gibeah around sunset. Reluctantly I took Doeg to the fortress, and Abner and Joseph came with me, for I don't think they trusted me to toe the line without supervision.

Saul wasn't at home. We came upon Jonathan and Sarah, playing with their twin sons by the pool-side; Jonathan started when he saw us, supposing that our unexpected return could mean only one thing. His arched brow asked the question; I shook my head slightly, and he relaxed. He confessed that he didn't actually know where Saul was, but he sent Sarah to ask of Rizpah. She said he'd woken with a headache, and had gone out walking, somewhere north of the town; he'd been away all day.

I suggested to Doeg that we wait until morning and see the king then, but his anger flared in silence and I feared a confrontation. Abner too was muttering, so grudgingly I agreed that we should set out and look for Saul now. I led the search-party myself, heading for our childhood haunts in the hills. It was months since I'd seen him and I was ill-prepared for what I saw.

The place he had chosen for his retreat was lovely. Delicate scale-leaved tamarisk trees laced their slender branches across the reddening sky. Among the motionless grasses, the unblinking faces of the summer flowers, Saul lay sprawled and senseless, the wine flagon spilled and empty beside him, his cloak thrown up over his head, as if he'd tried to pray. I went forward with cold round my heart.

He was breathing. Relief washed over me, but it was short-lived. Gently I raised his head from the ground; he had vomited, and his lips were yellow with crust. There was no weight in his body, and I could feel the bones through his clothing. The flesh on them had shrunk and withered, his face was cold and white as marble. Nauseous myself, I patted his cheeks, and shook his emaciated shoulders, put water to his lips from the pack I still had with me from the journey. There was no response, so I spoke his name, then poured water over his brow, so it trickled through the mane of untrimmed, unkempt hair, and at length his eyes drifted open, swam, focussed dimly on my face, and a dark fire sparked behind them. He croaked, "David?"

I said, "Saul, it's Eli. Don't worry, you're all right now. Everything is going to be all right."

But he repeated, "David!" louder and more urgently, his eyes rolled wildly, and he grasped my cloak with twisted, skeletal fingers. "Is he dead? Have you killed him?"

My heart sank. "No, Saul, he..."

"Then is he here? Have you brought him to me?"

"Saul, we haven't even seen him. But - there is some-one..."

He pulled himself up by the fabric of my cloak, so it cut into my neck. "Where is Abner?" He hissed at me, "And Eliab? Where are they?"

I prized his fingers from my clothes, tried to hold him in my arms, but he tore away, then staggered drunkenly onto his feet. Abner came forward uncertainly; Joseph and Doeg kept to the shadows, and I was glad I couldn't see Doeg's face. Saul's dazed eyes lighted on Abner and he stumbled forward until he stood between the two of us, swaying and reaching out for the trees to steady himself.

"Why haven't you found him?" he demanded, and as soon as he raised his voice it became apparent that he was still slurring his speech. "What have you been doing all this time, for God's sake? Don't you even care that he's trying to kill me? Is there no one I can rely on to perform a simple task any more? Don't you..?"

"Saul," I said patiently. "Please, Saul. Calm yourself. You're not thinking."

"Not thinking?" he shrieked, and his eyes were like burning cinders floating on milk. "I'm thinking all too hard, Eliphaz. And you know what I'm thinking? I'm thinking you're *all* plotting against me, every one of you! You're conspiring with him behind my back. You're laughing at me, aren't you? Laughing at how blind and stupid I've been. What do you think David will give you for your pains - gold? Jewels? Fields, and vineyards - and make you all officers in his army? Is that what you want? To see me dead, and David king in my place?"

Suddenly he lurched helplessly to one side, fell against the tree he was gripping, his mouth choked with lather, his whole body shuddering. For a dozen heart-beats he was silent, hanging his head, accumulating what feeble strength he still possessed; when he looked up again, his eyes were as fuddled as if someone had punched him in the face, and saliva glistened in his hair where his hand had smeared it. He whispered, "None of you even told me that my own son was David's lover. None of you care that the product of my own flesh and blood is trying to take my life. None of you care about me at all. You all wish I was dead."

He slumped against the trunk of the tree, grasping at it uselessly, then sagged and slid until he was on the ground, his energy sapped. Then a gruff voice from behind me said, "I have seen David. And I know someone who helped him."

Doeg walked forward in the dying light, his head erect, his heavy shoulders drawn square with the cool aplomb of a man who holds the only key to your cell, and knows it. He bowed low before Saul, without a trace of revulsion, as though the King of Israel were enthroned in splendour and decked with jewels, not grovelling and soiled with filth. Saul blinked his eyes into focus, and stared puzzled at Doeg's face. The stranger saluted and said smoothly, "Doeg, son of Esau the Edomite, your herdsman and your servant. May the king live for ever."

A weird light played in Saul's eyes, and reflected in Doeg's. I saw something spark between them, almost physically. The mutual hatred of David that burned in their guts had brought them together, created instant understanding.

Saul said quietly, "Welcome. Tell me what you know."

Doeg answered without hesitation. "Ahimelech the priest has harboured him. He gave him shelter and weapons, and knows where he has gone. And he gave him the consecrated bread from Adonai's own table, and used the holy ephod to give him counsel."

I felt my heart lurch within my breast. Saul went on staring at Doeg like someone bewitched, and breathed, "Are you sure of this?"

"I witnessed all of it myself."

Saul said, "Abner," and waved one hand listlessly.

Abner came forward, hovered, looked askance at Doeg.

"Have Ahimelech the priest brought here. And all in his family who share his calling. I will demonstrate the fate of those who betray me."

No one moved. Abner asked nervously, "Now, Your Majesty? It's nearly dark."

"Do it!" screamed Saul, lashing out violently with one scrawny arm, so that Abner jumped and almost knocked me to the ground. With undignified haste he scrambled to obey; Joseph sprang to his side and they turned and went. Saul let Doeg sponge the grime from his face and hair and clothing.

It's no distance from Gibeah to Nob, the stronghold of the priestly families - a child could run it without tiring. I had no doubt that Ahimelech would come, with a handful of his kinsmen perhaps, but when Abner returned with what looked like close on a hundred men, I was stunned. It occurred to me that maybe the priests had anticipated trouble, and intended to make a fight of it; then I saw that Abner had them under heavily armed guard. As well as Joseph, he had Eliab and Barak with him, and a sizeable force from the camp, and even as I watched, they paced up and down among their bewildered prisoners and disarmed any who still concealed weapons in their clothing. The captives stood speechless and mystified, and Saul stalked round them like a lion worrying its prey. Doeg watched approvingly from the shadows. Abner stepped forward with a bent and wizened man at his side. Ahimelech.

I listened with growing alarm as Saul questioned, probed, interrogated, his voice escalating higher and wilder, while Ahimelech whispered, placated, soothed. The old man seemed genuinely surprised to be under arrest; all this business had taken place months ago, he said, when David had only just left Gibeah - neither he nor anyone else in Nob had even known of the rift between the king and his young officer at the time. David had said he was on His Majesty's business, that he and his men were ritually pure, and that there was no reason for them not to be given the sacred bread to eat, nor to be denied access to guidance from the Lord. It was true that he had sent David on with his blessing, and that David had gone on to King Achish of Gath. (Gath? I thought; Gath, in *Philistia?*) And at least, said Ahimelech, when I consult God for someone, I can still get an answer, which is much more than you can.

He must have known he had grazed Saul's sorest spot; he must have known he had opened an infected wound that was scored right through Saul's heart. But he showed no emotion; he studied Saul's face steadily and watched the rage simmering, boiling, erupting. Even when Saul began screaming about sacrilege and treachery, I don't think Ahimelech saw what was coming. None of them did. I was the only one who didn't gasp aloud when Saul said to Abner, "Kill him."

Abner gaped at him, nonplussed, incredulous.

"You heard me!" Saul screeched. "Kill him! Kill all of them!"

Abner backed away, shaking his head, his eyes fixed stupidly on the king's face. Never in his life had he disobeyed an order from his idol, or even failed to indulge a single one of his whims. But now things had gone too far even for him. Saul swung round, half crazed with wrath, and went for Eliab. "You! You kill him!" he yelled at him, then at Barak, at Joseph, at me. None of us moved. Saul drew his sword and swung it haphazardly in the air; we cowered, not knowing if he meant to use it on us, on Ahimelech, or on himself. Then again came Doeg's voice, quiet, calm, self-assured.

"I will kill him, my lord."

He drew his butcher's knife from his belt and strolled with apparent nonchalance towards Ahimelech. I had seen the aged priest cringe and scrape once before, when Saul had first confronted him over the ephod so long ago. But this time he didn't flinch. He looked Doeg full in the face, and as the blade opened his throat he died without a murmur, his blinded eyes still riveted on his murderer's face. Saul stared vacantly at the crumpled body fallen at his feet, the slow stream of blood fanning out across the parched earth, seeping into the cracks, turning the ground into a wrinkled brown skin threaded with scarlet veins. Then he said hoarsely, "Kill them all."

I don't know how Saul wasn't sick. He stood and watched, while the crisis evolved into a massacre, and the wooded glade became a reeking bloodbath; he watched every man fall and die, he watched their blood mingling and gurgling and congealing, without expression, while I watched him. Doeg was a trained slaughterer, and must have seen them as so many sheep; I don't suppose they felt much pain - at least, those who didn't struggle. Some tried to resist him, but they were careless in their fear, and didn't act together. Doeg was ruthless and he made no mistakes. Those who struggled died in agony; for the rest, the end was swift. The twisted bodies fell entangled, limbs contorted, entrails spilled, bulging eyes and lacerated throats crying out to God for justice, for revenge. Somewhere close behind me, one of Abner's men was weeping; somewhere else another was heaving up his guts. I was in shock, and I did nothing. I felt the blood drain from my head, I was seeing double and longed to faint, but oblivion wouldn't come. The world had become an altar, the priests the sacrifice. But Saul was laughing. Circling the corpses, revelling in the carnage, his eyes bright in his white wasted face, he was Death incarnate, Destruction in human form. The old order had passed away, and no one could know what would rise from its ashes.

CHAPTER 22

If Saul imagined that making an example of the priest and
his kin in this way would somehow strengthen the loyalty of
the rest of Israel, he was of course tragically mistaken. A
wave of disbelief, then of outrage, swept the nation; every
home went into mourning, every heart reeled in shock. That
Saul their beloved, Saul their hero, Saul the Lord's
Anointed, could perpetrate such an appalling atrocity, few
could credit - and against Adonai's own priests; it was
unthinkable. But Saul suffered no remorse this time, no
crisis of conscience; in fact he proceeded to issue the order
that every person left in Nob should die, in the wake of
their ill-fated kinsfolk - men, women, children, babies: the
entire, wretched population.

The name of Doeg became a byword for terror, and
to make matters still worse, if that were possible, Saul went
on to appoint him as his personal armour-bearer, something
he had never previously had, and patently didn't need. I
think it was at this time that I first became aware of the

ground-swell of general discontent among the people against the person of the king himself; murmurings that Samuel had been right after all, that Israel never should have had a human king in the first place, that he would inspire within his subjects nothing but fear and restlessness and a romantic nostalgia for the past. Saul was creating the fulfillment of his own forebodings. No one had been plotting his downfall when he began to fear it. But now that he no longer seemed capable of responding, it was happening in pockets all over the country.

However, the steady stream of warriors gravitating towards David soon dried up. Saul had it put about that he had gone over to the Philistines, and blasphemed against Adonai himself. There were many who believed it, too, because they chose to. They had idolized Saul for too long to reject him out of hand. Besides, there was just enough truth in the rumour to convince them: David had indeed entered into negotiations with the enemy, including the forging of links with none other than Achish himself, King of Gath; though at any one time he was just as likely to be harassing these pagans as consorting with them. I had long since given up trying to make sense of his motives, but the strongest of them was probably survival, and to that end, he needed places to run.

In the weeks that followed, I came close once again to packing my bags, and would probably have left, had I had anywhere to go. Saul and Doeg became thicker than thieves, and I watched Saul sink further into the abyss by the day. He neglected his duties, he disregarded obligations, he ignored mounting evidence that the Philistines were spreading their wings once again. Much of his day to day business devolved onto me, and somehow I found myself hearing cases, giving judgments, entertaining embassies. I don't know if Saul either knew or cared, but I couldn't bring myself to sit back and watch while things crumbled.

As the summer was approaching its height, we received the first up-to-date and reliably corroborated reports about David's whereabouts which had come through to us in all this time. He was alleged by several reputable sources to be in Keilah, a small city a day's march through the hills to the south west, being wined and dined with his men in sumptuous style, for he'd succeeded in repulsing a Philistine attack and thus saved the city from capture. No doubt the assault had only been a petty one, an unimaginative attempt to plunder the newly-harvested corn, but David was cast in the role of redeemer none the less.

Saul went into ecstasy. David had walked like a blind man into a net, trapping himself within the walls of a fortified stronghold. We had only to march there and surround him, and he would be in our hands before his hangover had cleared. The order was given, and we set out at daybreak with Abner's standing forces; a gruelling trek through daunting terrain and blistering heat ahead of us. This time Saul was with us; an army of demons couldn't have kept him at home.

We were at Keilah before sunset - Abner had pushed us to our limits - but David and his men were already gone. We were confounded. It was impossible that David could have got wind of our coming in time to shift his entire army out of the way so comprehensively that once again no one could tell us where he was. The elders of Keilah welcomed us with deference but claimed to know nothing; it was many months later we found out that David had learned of our march before we'd begun it, in fact before we'd conceived it. A shrewd relative of Ahimelech, who'd fled from Nob in the nick of time, had found refuge with David - and taken the ephod with him.

It was some time during the week that followed that I first weighed seriously in my mind the notion of going to join David myself. After all, I had nothing left to keep me in Gibeah - Saul had Doeg to confide in and Rizpah to love, and had scarcely spoken to me for weeks; Michal was gone to Kiriath Jearim; Jonathan had Sarah and his sons. David was Israel's future, and I knew it; I became willing prey to a compelling desire to be for once on the winning side. And yet I didn't go. Something still held me back, though I wasn't quite sure what. It was certainly not that I didn't know where to find David. I had no doubt that once I detached myself from Saul, there would be no shortage of guides to direct me.

Then one night soon after, as I lay awake sweating in the heat back in Gibeah, Jonathan came in and sat down beside me. He told me he'd had a message from David.

I sat up at once and looked about me. Because of Rizpah I was still condemned to sleeping in the servants' quarters, and we weren't alone. Motioning him to be silent, I swung my legs to the floor and we slipped out into the night.

The courtyard was deserted and awash with moon-light, the air sweet with the scent of flowers. Jonathan's eyes glowed with excitement, and in his hand he held a clay tablet wrapped in cloth and embossed with a curious six-pointed star, two interlocked triangles stamped in red. I had never seen anything like it; it meant nothing to me.

I whispered, "What is that? Where did you get it?"

He said, "Abinadab! David's brother Abinadab came here! He gave it to me after dark... Eliphaz, this is David's cipher. He wants to see me."

I stared. "You know where he is?"

Jonathan shook his head, his thick black hair rippling back over his neck, the face that could have been the young Saul's earnest and grave. "He wants me to go to the place where I shot those arrows and he came to me. There will be someone there waiting to take me."

I said dubiously, "Are you sure this isn't a trick?"

"Would Abinadab trick me?" Jonathan retorted, and I had to caution him again to keep his voice down. I whispered, "When?"

"Tonight! I must leave before dawn."

"I needn't ask if you intend to go."

"Eliphaz..." He looked suddenly nervous. "I want you to come with me."

I stared again. He thrust the tablet under my nose, curled my fingers round it and held them in his own, beseeching, like a child begging for a gift. My head swam; his face was Saul's, then Michal's, then his own once more. I mouthed, "Why?"

He answered promptly, "So that I will come back."

I said, "Sarah and your sons are here. Won't they be enough to draw you?"

He looked ashamed, a little. "I don't know." Then, excited again, "Eliphaz, will you come?" He did not need to ask a third time.

We didn't take much with us; we wanted to attract

no attention. I buckled my sword to my belt, felt guiltily for the jewelled knife inside my tunic, threw my cloak around my shoulders though I doubted I should need it, and we were gone.

I half expected our guide to be Abinadab himself, but I was wrong. Evidently he had considered it too dangerous to linger, being who he was. The man waiting for us was a stranger to me, though clearly he knew very well who we were; but he drew from his clothing another tablet bearing David's emblem, so I swallowed my reservations.

Day wasn't yet a hint on the horizon, but the moon was full and unveiled - David had chosen his timing well. We were heading south to begin with, through upland country cloaked with pine trees. Our guide seemed confident of his route, though I was lost within hours; if he'd chosen to abandon us among those forested hills we might well have ended our days there. He didn't utter a word to us all the way, so that I wondered if he possessed the means of speech at all. He was a middle-aged man with a hard-bitten face, and he was swathed in the costume of the desert - flowing robes and headdress - so it took no genius to work out where we were going. When the sun rose, we were travelling south-east, the trees were thinning, and the red peaks of the wilderness shimmered ahead.

We had brought no provisions, but our guide knew well what he was about. We journeyed all that day, but whenever we were hungry, thirsty or tired, he took us into some dwelling where the people seemed to know who he was, and whose business he was on, and supplied us liberally with whatever we had need of. David must have eyes, ears, fingers everywhere; I was impressed, and uneasy.

We had to rest fairly frequently, for the heat rose and became crushing, and Jonathan was flagging. I was glad I'd come with him: the months spent inactive at home, fretting for his friend and struggling to prevent himself being torn in two, had sapped his strength.

Once or twice I asked our silent chaperon whether we were nearing our destination, but he only shook his head grimly. All the following day we walked, surrounded on all sides now by bare red crags and swirling dust, and I became convinced that we were being led in circles, and not by accident. Surly as he was, our guide was not without compassion; he kept a wary eye on Jonathan, and made sure we rested when it was wise to. Eventually as the second day's sun began to swell and redden, he pointed up at the mountain ahead of us, and I understood that this was our goal.

The ascent was gruelling after two days' continuous exertion. There was no beaten pathway up the hillside; I got the impression it was always climbed by different routes so no track would evolve and arouse suspicion. Much of the rock was loose; we tripped and stumbled, and our clothes were tinged red, and stiffly sticky with sand and sweat.

Had we been left to ourselves to locate the cave-mouth we might well still have been searching. We found ourselves squeezing through a narrow fissure in the rock; crudely scratched in the uneven surface of a boulder, at elbow height, was the six-pointed star, but you would have to have known where to look. The opening gave onto a confined, low-roofed passageway, pitch black at first, but once round the first corner, lit dimly with flickering oil-lamps set into crannies in the walls. The unseasonal cold of the cave-world chilled my face and fingered my flesh, and I was glad of my cloak after all. Then we rounded another corner, the channel erupted into a gaping cavern, and I found myself face to face with the man Saul would have given half his kingdom to get his hands on.

If I hadn't expected him to be there, for a second time I wouldn't have known him. Dressed desert-fashion, with a rakish checkered cloth tossed carelessly about his head and shoulders, ankle-length robes and a camel-hair belt, I might easily have taken him for a survivor from Amalek. He wasn't alone. A handful of laid-back, rough-looking attendants sat on guard or relaxed among the cushions strewn on the floor, but as their chief saw us and sprang forward, they melted into the background, and left us to grope for appropriate words of greeting. For a few moments the three of us stood and regarded one another, and Jonathan and I tried to smile our way out of our awkwardness - David looked wild and hardened, whilst we were both conspicuously out of condition. Then his tanned face creased into a grin, the dimple in his chin puckered, and spreading his hands wide, he gathered us both in his arms. With the warmth of our bodies pressed together and, the sound of our laughter echoing through the cavern, my uneasiness shattered; he was the David we knew.

"Fetch us wine and some food," he ordered one attendant, with the air of a man used to being obeyed. "This calls for a celebration." He seemed all at once so much older than his twenty or so years, until you looked at him, and saw the boyish light dancing in his eyes. He was a Shining One still, with no shred of a doubt: you couldn't look at him and not be moved.

At first we talked lightly, of Sarah, and the children, of Gibeah, and if the old place looked the same. A feast of bread and fruit was set before us, and a silver jug of wine; David and his men appeared to be short of nothing, and I wondered where the wealth came from, but deemed it prudent not to ask. However, the unrisked questions hung poised in the air; and presently David asked after Michal.

Jonathan would say nothing. While we'd been eating he had withdrawn into an awkward silence. I heard myself telling David the whole sordid truth, as though the words were another's; I wasn't conscious of choosing them. I couldn't tell how he was taking it, for he made no response, just stared into the dregs of his wine. Jonathan appeared increasingly distressed; he seemed altogether unable to cope with the whole situation. There was a long, frigid pause. Then David said heavily, "How is Saul?"

I said, "Bad. And getting worse. Ever since Doeg..."

"Ah yes. Doeg." David nodded, still gazing into his cup. "I know about him."

"I haven't been able to get near Saul since he arrived," I continued, "Let alone get through to him. I don't know what to do. I even thought I might..."

"Come here to join me?" David looked up at last, swiftly, as he finished my sentence for me; our eyes met and I bit my tongue. He said simply, "It wouldn't be right," then he rose to his feet, paced the cavern a little, thinking, and went to stand behind Jonathan. Saul's son sat hunched up with his arms hugging his knees; gently David laid his hands on his old friend's shoulders. "It wouldn't be right for either of you."

For a while none of us spoke. Then unexpectedly

Jonathan sighed into the silence, "He tried to kill me."

"I know," said David. "You told me."

"He tried to kill me!" Jonathan said again, but this time he shouted it, so that the cavern caught his voice and threw it from wall to wall. "He wants me to hate you, David. He wants me to turn against you and swear allegiance to him. But I can't. I can't, do you hear me? He says I will never be king while you live, he says you're using me, you've never really cared for me. He says you want his throne, my throne, but I don't care about that! I don't care! I..."

He couldn't continue. He choked on his words and started shaking. He must have been chewing every bitter word Saul had spoken, every callous thing he had done, over and over in his mind until it was he who was being devoured. Then David said softly, "He's right, Jonathan."

"What?"

David let go of his shoulders, squatted down beside him, and tilted Jonathan's chin with one cupped hand until their eyes met. "Oh, I care about you. God knows I care! But there's something you have to know. That's why I wanted to see you. I should have told you long ago. I have the Anointing."

Jonathan's eyes went wide, vacant. But he knew what David meant. In a broken whisper he asked, "How? When?"

"Since before I even met you. Samuel came to our house, but even my father didn't understand what was happening. I was scarcely more than a child. But - he anointed me, Jonathan. Saul knows it. Eliphaz here knows it; but no one else. Not until now. You see - that's how I know Adonai."

"Why didn't you tell me?" Jonathan's voice was barely audible, and he asked the question as though he cared little about the answer.

"I was afraid."

David dropped his gaze; it was the only time I ever knew him deliberately render himself vulnerable. "I thought - you might turn against me if you knew. You might no longer want me as a friend."

Jonathan murmured, "You have all this. Servants to wait on you, guards to protect you, a whole army to worship you and kiss the hem of your garments. I wouldn't have mattered. It wouldn't matter to you if I were dead."

David caught his breath; went pale. Jonathan looked shocked. In a feeble voice he asked, "Would it?"

David said hoarsely, "More than anything."

Suddenly both of them were weeping; all of us were weeping. Somewhere far away David was asking Jonathan if he could still love him now that he knew the truth; and then they were both laughing and crying together, vowing eternal friendship all over again.

David said, "We should pray. The three of us, while there's still time. Before you have to go back." He drew up the hem of his headdress and doubled it forward, shrouding his face. Jonathan and I began gathering the folds of our cloaks to cover our hair. Then there was a scuffling close by, and a voice barked into the cave, "Saul is here. We are betrayed."

I felt the sweat break out on my brow, and I seized Jonathan's wrist.

David leapt to his feet. "Here?" he demanded.

"Alone?"

The messenger said, "With his army, my lord. On the other side of the mountain. He knows our hideout is up here. It can only be hours at most before he finds us."

"Assemble the men, Abishai."

His subordinate nodded crisply and saluted his way out. A plague of possibilities was breaking out in my mind: we'd been followed; we'd been tricked; we'd been set up from the moment we left Gibeah. I dreaded to imagine what David might be thinking. All at once the cavern came alive with activity. Figures darted in every direction, appearing from nowhere, grabbing armour and weapons and bawling commands. Someone brought David his equipment; he was already buckling on his breastplate when suddenly he seemed to remember us. He put his hands briefly on our shoulders, his expression now grim and calculating.

"Jonathan, Eliphaz," he ordered, "You have to leave. At once. Please - just go."

"Go?" I stammered. "Go where? To Saul?"

"Go anywhere! Go back to Gibeah. The guide who brought you will be waiting outside. Please... we don't have much time."

We travelled all night, for we couldn't risk stopping. Behind us, the battle might already be raging, for the sky was still clear, and the moon bright and full. We moved fast, for Jonathan had discovered a new reserve of strength buried within him. He had seen his friend, and embraced him, and talked with him, and in spite of everything else he seemed content.

389

CHAPTER 23

By some miracle, we made it back to Gibeah without encountering either Saul and his army, or any of his scouts or couriers. The following day, news reached us that Saul had been victorious.

Against the Philistines.

"The Philistines?" I exclaimed to one of my fellow-servants, who had gleaned the information from merchants in the market-place. "But..." Then I clamped my mouth shut in mid-sentence, suddenly remembering, and not wanting to say more. I went to find Jonathan, who'd had the same story from a travelling musician: Saul was on his way home, having stemmed an invasion.

I was thrown into perplexity; nothing made sense. There had been no mention of David; presumably, then, he must still be alive. I said so to Jonathan, but he had no need any longer of my reassurance. Now he shared David's unshakeable confidence that Adonai would protect his own.

The wave of euphoria reached Gibeah before Saul

did. Children came running, women dancing; the accounts of what had passed leapt like torch-fire from one person to the next. Saul had never seen David at all, for before he could find him, or the place he was hiding, he'd learned of a Philistine offensive to the west. In a way I was mildly surprised that he'd responded, so obsessed had he grown with the crushing of Jesse's son. But the Philistine force had been too strong to ignore, and presumably Abner had made him see reason.

Saul entered the fortress astride Doeg's shoulders, drinking from a wine-filled helmet being passed around among his officers and men. Outside in the streets, the people were chanting, fickle as ever. Saul was once more their darling. But underneath the exhilaration, his face still looked ghastly, and he was so horribly thin and fragile. Doeg was pitching him from side to side, laughing. Was I really the only one who could see the king wincing?

As festivities ensued, I became increasingly convinced that Saul was on the verge of collapse. I cursed Doeg, who neither noticed nor cared, but wouldn't let me get near. He said nothing to me, but his eyes warned me off; I seethed in silence. After eating barely enough to sustain life for months, Saul was now feasting with the best of them, and it was doing him no good. He was rubbing his stomach absently, too drunk to do anything about it, even to stop eating, so I wasn't surprised when he staggered from the table with his hand plastered to his mouth.

I found him in the courtyard, hanging his head over the pool. I grasped him under the armpits, and it still shocked me to feel the fleshless bones between my fingers. I said, "Saul, you're ill. You should be in bed."

He raised his head, fixing me with bright sunken eyes. "We won, Eli!" he croaked at me, "We defeated the Philistines! I fought a battle, after all this time, I killed men, I saw them fall... and we beat them. We drove them off. We slaughtered hundreds, maybe thousands, I don't know..."

I demanded, more sharply than I meant to, "So now are you trying to kill yourself? Come on." I hauled him to his feet, and we stumbled through the heaving crowds to his room. Before I could fetch anything, he was sick on the floor; then I found myself retching too, for he'd soiled his loincloth. I had no choice but to stay with him and try to clean up, though he scarcely acknowledged my presence. Around midnight there was a bang on the door, and Doeg's gruff voice shouting, but I told him to go away and he obeyed. Perhaps the smell put him off.

Shortly before dawn he came back. Saul was no better, but had slept a little. This time Doeg was persistent. When I refused for the third time to open the door, he lunged at it with his bull-broad shoulders so that in the end I had to give in, before the door did.

Saul was huddled on his mattress wrapped in a blanket, his back propped against the wall. Doeg merely saluted briskly and announced, "David is in En Gedi."

Saul pushed back his tousled hair and peered at him, apparently not understanding.

"When we left to fight the Philistines, I had two spies stay behind. So when David and his men broke cover to find a new hiding place, they tailed him. We know exactly where he is."

I said, "Get out, Doeg. Forget David for once. Think about Saul."

Doeg bristled. He was a big man; I was nervous and no doubt showed it. He sauntered towards me with a faint sideways scowl on his lips, and retorted, "No, you get out, you accursed Amalekite. You have no place here. We don't want your odious breath spreading its infection among us; it's no wonder the king is sick. I am His Majesty's personal servant now. You go back to your camels."

I chewed my lip, wishing desperately I had the courage and the sheer physical strength to resist him, to wipe the scorn from his leering face and make him eat his words. I was certain that he cared nothing for Saul; he cared only for himself and for his own advancement. Then with sinking heart I heard Saul's voice, thin and faint from behind me.

"David? You've found David?"

"Yes, Your Majesty. In the wilderness at En Gedi. He's taken over the oasis there. There's no time to waste, or he may move on again."

"Have Abner reassemble the men. As many as are still in Gibeah and can get themselves ready to march. I'll be there by sunrise."

Doeg bowed and left. I was speechless. I gawped at Saul inanely as he dragged himself out of bed and lurched against the wall, swallowing and grimacing. He found some clean clothes and began to get dressed.

En Gedi is a long, weary haul from Gibeah, and lies in the heart of the Salt Sea desert. It was already hot, up here in the hill-country; down there it would be unbearable, even for a healthy man. Saul was fiercely determined to show no weakness, and made a passably successful job of it to begin with, at least as far as the others could discern. But after we'd been marching for some hours, and Abner called a halt for rest and refreshment, Saul tried to eat to keep his strength up and was promptly sick all over again. Eliab, Barak and Joseph exchanged glances, but were either too mortified or too in awe of him to say anything. Abner cleared his throat, then thought better of it and made himself scarce. Doeg shoved a cup of wine at Saul, and he managed to keep it down, but of course it did little to improve his condition. After that we had to stop continually for him to go behind a rock or a clump of bushes for one reason or the other, and the gross absurdity of the whole scenario was becoming embarrassing. Only Doeg maintained his composure. The rest of us either groused and grumbled or joked to relieve our awkwardness. We were three thousand strong, yet we felt foolish as children playing blind man's buff, and there was no one who didn't want to crawl home and hide.

The following day Saul seemed a little stronger. He was no longer being sick, but because he'd eaten and his body wasn't used to it, his guts weren't coping and we still had to keep stopping. It was almost the hottest part of the day when we neared En Gedi, and Abner insisted that we rest. He despatched some scouts to make a preliminary search for clues as to David's passing; the rest of us settled to await their findings, quenching our thirst from the spring-water, and concentrating on keeping out of the sun.

En Gedi is a verdant, vibrant stripe of life flung into the midst of the death that is the desert. The gash of green against the harsh red backcloth is like the gleam of a perfect emerald set in clay. A fresh-water stream cascades from the mountains and brings the dust alive with luxuriant foliage and iridescent flowers, before becoming choked with giant reeds and plunging to its own suicide in the stale salt lake below. There are caves and grottos, palm trees, shrubs, grasses, the mingled scents of blossom. Majestic fissured cliffs tower above the enchanted glen on either side; gazelle and ibex leap among the rocks and vanish when they see you coming. It would be hard to imagine a more beautiful place for an outlaw to choose to make his secret lair.

Our men were now strung out along each of the stream-banks, filling up empty water-skins, stretching themselves out for their siestas wherever there was shade. I sat dangling my feet in the gentle current, dreamily watching the ripples flow between my toes and over my ankles, breathing deeply, absorbing the beauty, thankful for a whisper of peace in my troubled existence and forcing myself to make the most of it.

Through the haze of my reverie I heard Saul tell Doeg he was going to relieve himself again, and I raised my head enough to watch him ploughing his way rapidly up the far bank - it seemed that the business was urgent. I sighed with strained forbearance. There was little privacy anywhere but in the caves, most of which were situated either a fair way up the loose, steep cliffs, or some distance upstream. Presently he disappeared from view behind a dense clump of the giant reeds that infested a large portion of the river-course; I lowered my head once more, resting it on my elbows, and sank back into my abstraction, allowing myself the luxury of dozing. Around me the men were chatting and laughing, but their voices seemed distant and unreal, time grew and shrank and grew again until I drifted on a soft ocean of drowsiness. I have no idea how long I sat there, but when I surfaced, most of the others were sleeping, Doeg included, and Saul hadn't returned. Dormant memories stirred inside me, and it was hard to swallow them.

My shield was heavy, so I left it behind, along with my spear and helmet. Taking my sword in my hand, I started to pick my way along the bank in the direction I'd seen Saul heading. I had to clamber over inert bodies, and tangle with the mass of undergrowth that clung to the sides of the stream for dear life, and I finished up hacking through reeds and rushes with my sword-blade. The going was tough, but it was hard to feel panic, with the peaceful gurgling of the water below me, the muted trilling of the birds among the trees and bushes, the droning of the flies and the crickets; everywhere the heady vitality of summer.

I called his name hesitantly as I threaded my way through the jungle, for by now I'd left the others behind and I was alone with my apprehensions and with the crashing of my feet through the undergrowth. I was fairly sure that I was heading the right way, for I could see where the grass had been trampled, and the reeds and branches bent back, but I was surprised he should have gone so far - I'd judged his errand to be more pressing. The vegetation grew densely right up the sides of the gorge now, for there were other springs oozing out from the cliffs above me, and I could see the raw, naked gullies where the floodwaters deluge down when the heavy rains come. Startled birds shrieked and flapped among the greenery as I disturbed them, but there was no answer from Saul.

Eventually I chanced upon a low cave-entrance right beside the river-bank. It was totally invisible until you were almost on top of it, so thick was the encroaching vegetation. Here all evidence of further penetration through the brush abruptly ceased, and I concluded that there was only one place he could be.

With my sword still unsheathed, I ducked into the blackness, sneezing as a curtain of cobwebs brushed my face. Edging further into the cavern, feeling the cold and the dark fingering my crawling flesh, unexpectedly I heard the swish of metal and saw a blade glint barely a cubit from my face. I held my breath. Then a voice hailed me in a loud whisper from the gloom not far ahead.

"Doeg? Doeg, is that you?"

Relief.

"No, it's me; Eli. Are you all right?"

"Eli..." He repeated the name vaguely, and, I thought, with disappointment. He so rarely used it any more. Then he seemed to recover himself. "Eli, thank God. Listen - there's someone in here. Someone or something."

"Are you sure?" I asked pointlessly, and wished at once that I hadn't. I was casting doubt upon his sanity almost constantly now, and it couldn't be helping him.

"I heard noises, in the back of the cave. I - think I must have fallen asleep, I don't know. I wasn't feeling so good. Then I came round and - there were voices. I'm sure they were voices."

I was still doubting; I still thought the voices might be in his head. But then I heard something too, a peculiar scratching, back in the creeping black depths, then what sounded like a shuffling of feet. Of course, it could be rats, but it could just as likely be bandits. Or anything. Then there was something moving towards us.

It was too dark to make out the shape of it, whether

animal or human. It was just a solid black presence, solider and blacker than the gloom surrounding it.

"Who's there?" Saul barked into the shadows. "Who is it? Identify yourself, or I'll slice you to ribbons."

There was a silence, and I could hear my own heartbeat. Then a muffled scrabbling, a stifled giggle, and a familiar voice said, "I wouldn't. Not if I were you."

He strolled out from his hiding place relaxed and smiling. His teeth showed white against the darkness around him, then a shaft of light from the cave-mouth fell on his face, and I could see the rakish dimple. He wore the plain, coarse tunic of a wilderness brigand, caught up carelessly into his belt, and a narrow leather thong twisted in his spiky hair. In one hand he held his sword, and the other was hidden behind his back. For a moment Saul stood stupefied, then before I could restrain him, he pitched forward and plunged his sword into the space where his victim was standing.

David stepped neatly to one side. "I'm afraid that wouldn't be wise," he remarked casually. "Not when you're surrounded. Welcome to my humble abode - Your Majesty."

I backed up in alarm. All at once it seemed that the cave walls were stippled with eyes, a hundred pairs of eyes gleaming bright from the shadows like cats' eyes in the night, looming larger, closer, acquiring faces and bodies, arms and legs. A web of criss-crossing swords wove around us, and David said smoothly, "Drop your weapons."

I obeyed at once; Saul hesitated, and the blades pressed closer. At length he complied. His sword clattered on the rocky floor and sent a jarring metallic echo bouncing from the walls. David came nearer; his eyes flicked from Saul to me, and back again. There was a significance in them, but I couldn't read it.

Saul said, "Just kill us, David. Don't waste time. Get it over with."

He didn't flinch as David studied his face, and his voice hadn't wavered as he spoke the words. Momentarily I was impressed by this unforeseen show of courage on Saul's part, then recognized dully that perhaps this was what he wanted. To die honourably, defending his crown.

David smiled again, an open, guileless smile, with no hint of relish. "Strange," he observed. "That's just what Abishai said I should do. But if I'd really wanted to kill you, I'd have done it before."

He brought out the hand he was holding behind him, and uncurled the fingers. A deftly cut corner of Saul's white cloak fluttered to the ground.

Saul stared at it, bewildered. My eyes were fixed on David; I couldn't tear them away. Saul stammered, "Why didn't you? Why didn't you kill me, you little fool? You know I would have killed *you*."

"It is hardly a noble act, to kill a man who's already lying all but unconscious at your feet." David crouched and picked up the piece of cloth, then held it out for Saul to take. "You're a sick man, Saul. You should be convalescing at Gibeah, not running around in the desert."

I could see Saul's anger boiling; he thought the saucy youth was playing games with him, though for once I don't think he meant to. Still on his knees on the floor, David on an impulse threw down his sword and seized Saul's hand. "When are you going to believe me?" he pleaded. "I don't *want* to kill you. I don't mean you any harm at all. I want to help you."

"Then you're more of a fool than I thought," answered Saul, but his voice was starting to crack. He stared at his hand, held clasped between both of David's, yet he didn't pull it free. When he spoke again, his words were barely audible. "You must want to kill me, after all I've done to you. Anyone would. You ought to hate me, David. I - *want* you to hate me."

"Then I'm sorry, Saul. In anything else I would obey you. In this, I can't." Calmly David got to his feet, and I saw the deliberation creep into his eyes as he pondered the risk he was wanting to take. He moved closer to Saul; he was almost as tall now. He pinned his gaze to Saul's, then gradually wound his arms around Saul's wasted body. Saul just gaped at him, blank, disbelieving. David said simply, "You're the king of all Israel, Saul. You're my king. You're anointed by Adonai. How can I hate you?"

Saul's legs were shaking, and there were tears dewing his lashes. My mind was running away with itself: could David truly break through to him? He'd matured so much in the time he'd been away; no doubt his faith had matured too. Could his forgiveness shatter the evil that pervaded Saul's spirit after all? I caught David's eye, and thought, he is wondering the same. He pulled Saul closer; suddenly Saul put his arms around David's neck and buried his head in his shoulder. He was mumbling through his tears; I couldn't make out what he said, except for, My God, and, My son, helplessly echoed, and, What have I done, Why can't I stop it. David was holding him, stroking his hair; around us David's men sat muttering and cursing, for none of them either understood or approved.

I wondered if David himself would look back and regret what he'd done, but for the moment he was smiling. He placed a hand on Saul's head, and I saw that he was praying, though Saul hadn't even grasped what was happening. An eternity passed; I began to hope frantically. Then Saul drew back. He said, "You're a good man, David ben Jesse. You'll make a fine king."

David took his hand from Saul's head. With the other arm he still embraced him. For a while he stood looking into Saul's face; then he said, "You felt something, didn't you."

Saul repeated feebly, "Felt something?"

"When I prayed for you. What happened?"

I watched the horror break out on Saul's face. "You..? Then..? You mustn't! David - you must never try that again."

David mouthed, "Why?" with both his hands now on Saul's shoulders, but Saul shrank back, the whites of his eyes showing all round the irises.

"Up at the sanctuary... Samuel... David, it hurt so much. I couldn't go through that again."

"But you needn't! If you stopped fighting... I could help you now, Saul. I'm sure of it."

"It's too late, David."

"It's never too late."

"Samuel thought so."

David opened his mouth to respond, but his tongue wouldn't obey him. For one harrowing moment they gazed at each other. Then Saul said stiffly, "If you aren't going to kill us, David, let us go. Now, please. I can't stand any more of this. Remember my sons, when you are king."

David made one last attempt. "You can still know Adonai's peace, Saul. It isn't my time yet. I'm not ready to be king."

Saul sighed, from somewhere a long way down inside him. "Nor was I."

"Yes, you were." Impulsively David leapt forward, caught Saul by the cloak-pins, made him look him in the face. "Adonai's timing is always perfect. His will is always within our reach. You made it hard, Saul. You made it hard for yourself."

But Saul shook his head without speaking. He picked up his sword from where it had fallen, ran the fingers of one hand reflectively along the blade. "We have spared each other's lives, David." He stood up, stepped backwards towards the vivid slash of daylight, so that his form was a black silhouette against the dazzling sky. "Let that be enough. And - please promise me you'll remember my sons, when your time comes. Spare their lives; don't let my name be forgotten."

CHAPTER 24

On the day the first rains of autumn fell, they told us that Samuel was dead.

A bedraggled company of his disciples brought the news, rain-sodden and grey-faced, their brown cloaks plastered to their bodies, and torn as a witness to their grief. I received them myself, but they wouldn't give me their message, though I knew what it was at once by the sight of them, and by the way my blood ran thin. They wanted Saul.

I didn't know where he'd gone. These days it was more unusual if I did know. He'd disappeared from the fortress early that morning, with Rizpah, and a day's supply of provisions; they were probably wandering the hills somewhere, or in the forests taking shelter from the deluge. Since making his uneasy peace with David, Saul had seemed better, at least on the surface. His temper was less ferocious, and I thought he was beginning to put flesh on.

In this fatuous optimism I wasn't alone. Jonathan was buoyant, and he imagined it could only be a matter of time before David came home. Abner and Eliab had let themselves unwind; though Eliab, as ever, had little time for David, he'd grown to loathe Saul's obsession still more. Only Doeg seemed to be aggrieved; his plans were being thwarted, but he was generally content to bide his time. He must have known as well as I should have done that the respite could only be temporary.

I brought our guests food and wine, and dry clothes, but even thus refreshed they looked little less forlorn. They were young men, five of them, black-bearded and unkempt; their presence made me uneasy. I fussed about them, and tried feebly to make conversation, but they made no effort to humour me. By the time I heard voices in the courtyard, my nerves were in tatters.

I heard Rizpah first. She was laughing, a fluting, high-pitched laughter that sounded like birdsong and cut through the heavy atmosphere like crystal. We were sitting in the state-room, where all official guests were entertained, and I was sure the couple wouldn't come in here; I would have to go out and fetch him in. But Rizpah's giggles were drawing closer, and I heard her chirping voice say, "Make me queen, Saul. Sit me on your throne," so I knew they were coming.

They appeared on the threshold, and he was carrying her in his arms. He wasn't sharing her laughter, but he was smiling faintly. She reached up to touch his face, to brush the raindrops from his nose and cheeks, but then he saw us.

Without speaking he slipped Rizpah to the ground. The smile died on his lips, for he too knew what was coming. He walked across the room and sat down on the great carved chair. Without waiting for introductions, he said, "Tell me how it happened."

One of the five opened his mouth to reply, but another put his hand to his comrade's lips. Recollecting himself, the first stated brusquely, "Our message is for the king's ears alone."

I hovered, uncertain if Saul would bid me go or stay; then suddenly I couldn't bear to be in the same room with Samuel's miserable followers any longer. I mumbled something and bowed my way out into the courtyard. The rain still heaved from a turbulent sky, gushing over the pavement like a river in spate, cascading in sheets from the ramparts into the yard below. Rizpah stood pressed against the wall for shelter, shivering still, yet unwilling to venture far from Saul in order to get dry.

When he emerged his face was devoid of all life and colour, his eyes wandered and his expression was distracted. Then unsteadily he lurched across the courtyard, making for the gates. I shouted his name but he didn't answer, so I started after him. He got the gates open, and went running down the hill, kicking up the puddles, the mud splashing his legs, and in my panic I ran after him, my sandalled feet slipping and sliding in the sodden dust. Twice I tripped and fell; my clothes were spattered with dirt, and Saul was outstripping me. I didn't know where he had found this sudden reserve of stamina. Behind me I could still hear Rizpah striving to catch up.

We had reached the bottom of the hill, and up ahead I could see the city walls rising to meet us. I tripped and went sprawling in the churned-up soil; Rizpah managed to haul me up and we stumbled on side by side. Through the city gates, out into the rain battered fields, and still Saul showed no signs of stopping. I don't think he was even aware that we were pursuing him. He seemed crazed and frantic, oblivious to everything around him. The road we were taking had started to climb, the cultivated fields giving way to common scrub, then to bushes and fir trees. Forested slopes rose up on either side of us, and the moist air was sweet and sickly with the scent of wet pine.

Then it came to me that I knew where we were going.

It was all still there, just as I remembered it. The sudden clearing on the summit of the hill, the derelict weed-choked precinct, the ruined shrine with its toppled wooden pole, and the solitary standing-stone glaring fierce and defiant at the elements that beat upon it.

Saul sank to his knees in the centre of the pavement, hugging himself and coughing, his energy burnt out, and gazing about him as though he'd no idea of how he came to be there. Not stopping to think, I crossed the yard to reach him with Rizpah trailing after me, and we tried to drag him out of the rain beneath the shelter of the trees. But he shook us away, staring through us as though we were phantoms, his chest still heaving with the exertion, his mouth open and gaping for air. I seized him by the shoulders, but he either wouldn't or couldn't meet my gaze. He appeared entranced, his eyes drifted vacantly and he didn't respond even when I screamed his name. Then Rizpah bent down and slapped his face so hard that her hand left a mark on his cheek, and he came round.

Startled, he peered at Rizpah, then at me, his eyes shot through with manic fear, his lips mouthing: where are we, why have we come here, can we go home. Then something must have made him remember. He shrieked, "Samuel is dead! Samuel is dead!" until the whole glade echoed it back at him.

I said, "Don't take it so hard, Saul. He was an old man; his time had run out." But he looked right at me and said, "You don't understand, do you, Eli. You never do. I'm finished."

"Saul, don't be ridiculous. You haven't seen anything of Samuel for ages. How can what's happened make any difference to you now? He's been as good as dead to you since Gilgal."

At the mention of Gilgal he howled like a wounded animal, and crumpled visibly, clinging to Rizpah and whimpering. He seemed to be vacillating between this world and some other; one moment with us, the next lost, wandering, helpless.

"They want me to perform the funeral rites for him," he said absently. "They say it's what Samuel wanted. Can you believe that? But I can't do it. I don't think I even want to be there."

"Saul, you must go. You are king; he was the greatest prophet since Moses. What would people think if you stayed away?"

"What would people think?" he railed at me. "What about what *I* think, for a change? If I go there, I'll be watching my *own* funeral. I can't go through with that."

His eyes clouded again; he was drifting off. I shook him frantically.

"Can't you see it yet, Eli?" He sounded so weary, so oppressed. "While he was alive there was still hope for me. To be reconciled, forgiven..."

407

"Perhaps that's what this means," I suggested gently. "Why else should Samuel want you to conduct his funeral? Perhaps it's his way of forgiving you."

"Or of rubbing salt in my wounds." He flung back his head, letting the rain cool his face. "Oh, Eli, I don't know. I don't just mean Samuel's forgiveness. That isn't what really matters, not in the end."

I murmured cynically, "What does matter." I wasn't expecting an answer.

"*Adonai*, Eli! *Adonai's* forgiveness! Samuel was the only link with him I had left. You must at least understand that. Now the wall between us is complete. It's all over."

He went limp against me; I started, and shook him again. His eyes swam open. I whispered, "What about David? He still believes he can help you."

Saul shuddered and looked away from me. "He hasn't the power. I know it. He thinks he can do anything because he's anointed, but he's wrong. Of all people, I should know that. He can't exorcize what is killing me."

Rizpah made a faint strangled sound in her throat. I said, "Don't talk like that Saul. It's - unlucky."

"Why not, if it's the truth?" The pitch of his voice was rising; he was losing control. "Why will nobody speak the truth to me? Why do you all try to stop me from seeing what I ought to see? Damn you all, I'm dying. I can't think about anything else. And I'm not ready to go. I don't want to die, Eli!"

"You aren't going to die," I said, and was alarmed when I realized how much my own voice was trembling. "This is superstitious foolishness. You're still young, with years ahead of you."

He sighed, a long, enervated sigh, and felt for my hand with his own. "You still don't see. I don't know how you can be so blind... it's not because I'm clinging to life that I'm not ready. I don't want life any more. I hate it. If I thought death meant release from it, I would have fallen on my sword long ago. I ache for oblivion. But I don't know if that's what would be waiting for me."

I groaned. "How can anyone be ready to die."

"I don't know, I don't know!" He took in a great juddering gasp of air; his whole body jarred, but his voice came steadier. "But what's on the other side, Eli? Do we just grope around in Sheol, all the same, all grey, lifeless shades for the rest of eternity, all together, the wise, the foolish, the merciful, the cruel? Or is there to be a judgment after all - with rewards, punishments? And if there is - what happens to me, Eli? What happens to me?"

There was no answer I could give him. He winced, loosened his hold on my hand and I pulled it free.

He said, "Now Samuel is gone, we never will know. Never. And I'll never know why nothing I've done could ever be good enough, ever be... Eli, don't you remember?"

His question, coming so abruptly, shook me alert. I mumbled, "Remember what?"

"This place. When I brought you here, when we were children... don't you remember what we talked about?"

"Of course I remember. I couldn't face any of it then, Saul, and I can't face it now. Please - let's go home."

"Lately I've been coming here more and more, Eli. I think that's why I came today. I *need* this place. There's something here that draws me, I can't keep away..."

I shook my head, helpless, exasperated. "You're sick,

Saul. You aren't going to find answers here. It's a pagan place, it's evil. It makes my skin crawl."

"But you can still *feel* something here." Suddenly he sat up, pushed the tangled hair from his eyes, stared around at the weeping grey trees, the overgrown courtyard mirror-bright with rain, the blackened stone standing guard, grim and sightless. "I need to feel something. Something greater than myself, something outside, beyond... it's been so long..."

Again I whispered, "Let's go home, please. We could send for David, he would understand..." I was out of my depth and I knew it. There were voices in my head and all around me. Forgotten gods and formless spirits laughed at me in hideous silence from the forest.

"You're naive, Eli, so naive. He will never come. He knows there can be no end to our feud, as well as I do. He knows what would happen."

I pressed my hands to my temples.

"I - don't know what you mean."

"I can never be part of what he stands for. Something new is starting with him, Eli. A new kind of Israel. A new kind of world. We can never go back; it's all dead where we came from. The ways we grew up with, the tribes we belonged to, the customs we treasured, the simple farmers banding together to fight a holy war... it's all dead, and I killed it. I killed it when I let them put a mace in my hand and a crown on my head and call me king. But I can't cross over, Eli. I can't be part of what is coming. Israel will become like the nations, David will have a fine palace and grovelling courtiers, a harem of women, an army like the Egyptians have, horses and chariots like the Philistines...

and Adonai will love him all the same."

Something inside me shattered; the voices vanished, the laughter died. I hung my head. "I still don't know what you're talking about."

"Perhaps I don't either. But I do know this: I can't make it work, Eli. Not any more; not in the kind of world this is becoming. Listening to Adonai's voice inside me, trusting him to reveal his will, moment by moment. I know now I can't take the strain of it; I never could. But David will. I've accomplished nothing, Eli. I've failed."

"No!" Something within me refused to let him say it, to let him even think it; I suppose because it had to mean that I had failed too. I said, "You *have* accomplished something. Whatever David achieves when - if - he becomes king; he could never have done any of it without you."

For a moment he stared at me and didn't speak. Then he said, "So that is what you think, Eli. You think my entire purpose has been to waste more than half my life building a throne so that another man can sit on it."

I protested feebly, "I didn't say that."

"But it's what you meant." He closed his eyes, shut me out of his world. "You're as bad as the rest of them, Eliphaz of Amalek. You all want me dead. You all want to see David on the throne of Israel, then you think everything will be all right. Well, he won't get it without a struggle. At least I can die fighting."

And I thought: oh God, oh God, it is all starting again.

Saul didn't attend Samuel's funeral. Doeg had me go out to Ramah and explain that the king was ill and couldn't make the journey. I seethed with indignation at taking his orders, but as he took pleasure in pointing out to me, he was a free man and I was still legally a slave. I don't know who performed the rites, except that I made it my business to check it hadn't been David. I didn't go myself, for I was reluctant to let Saul or Doeg out of my sight, even though my influence there seemed to have withered to nothing. Saul cut his hair, and smeared his head with ashes, he tore his clothes as a token of sorrow, but he stayed at the fortress and spoke to no one, and I wondered exactly whose death he was mourning.

Although we remained aloof from the rituals, we couldn't protect ourselves from the gloom that swamped Israel. Ever since Saul had come to the throne, Israel had known stability; but with Samuel gone, it was as though we all awoke as one from a dream, to know in an instant where our security had come from.

Saul himself sought refuge in isolation; he withdrew from everyone, and even Doeg and Rizpah I think found him trying. At first I feared he was going to stop eating again; then I realized almost at once that I was wrong, and that I knew why. For as soon as the official time of mourning for Samuel was ended, the loathsome hunt for David began again. Saul pursued it with grim determination and renewed vigour, as though he had concluded this time that there would be no need to maintain the pressure for long. Doeg acquired an aspect of sleek satisfaction, meticulously apportioning his valuable time between collating reports of sightings of his quarry, and poisoning Saul's mind further against David himself, and also, I was convinced, against me.

I don't honestly know where Saul imagined things were heading. Perhaps he saw his own ultimate defeat as inescapable; but clearly Doeg didn't share this view. He was working single-mindedly for the downfall and destruction of the man upon whom he had chosen to focus all the venom of his hate, the overwhelming passion for whose annihilation was the driving force of his life. Saul seemed totally unaware that he was being used.

We had with us a sizeable armed force - perhaps amounting to a few thousand men under Abner's command. He was solid and strong enough to ensure that Doeg wasn't allowed to forget his place. The ex-herdsman he saw as Saul's armour-bearer and nothing more, and he took pains to ensure that as such, he gained no in-appropriate authority over the troops. I found myself watching Abner increasingly closely, without at first being aware that I was doing it, still less, why. Then I realized that he too was growing progressively withdrawn and unlike himself. No longer permitted to share Saul's tent, I took to sharing Abner's; to my initial surprise, he raised no ob-jections and seemed glad enough of my company. In the long cold evenings we would sit and drink together and I would try to encourage him to talk, but it was a frustrating occupation, for he was a man of few words at the best of times, and that scarcely described our current circum-stances.

But one evening he arrived back looking still more harassed than usual, and I resolved that I would draw him tonight whether he fought me or not.

He came in shivering, and blowing on his hands; I had a small fire going in the makeshift stone hearth, and the tent was pleasantly muggy with warm smoke. He grunted me a greeting and lowered himself painfully onto his mattress, uncoiling the strips of cloth he had bound around his legs to keep out the frost. I grinned at him and handed him a cup of wine, which he accepted without speaking, then I made several attempts to engage him in trivial conversation about this and that, which he deflected with little effort. Finally I said:

"Come out with it, Abner. Something is vexing you. Get it off your chest before the suspense kills me."

He grunted again, blew into his wine, and answered laconically, "Philistines."

"Philistines? Is that all?" I'd expected him to say nothing, or to make some reference to Saul and David.

"Is that all? It will be more than enough before the next campaigning season's out." He stamped his feet on the floor to bring back the feeling, and took a large draught of wine.

I asked, "Are they rumbling again?"

"Rumbling, eh? I wish that was all they were doing."

"What do you mean?"

He glowered at me with some irritation; it appeared that he regarded discussing this kind of issue with me as pointless, and would rather I left him alone to get some rest. Eventually, seeing that I wasn't about to give in, he smacked his lips and said, "Very well, Eliphaz. If my sources are correct - and I have every reason to believe they are - the Philistines are in the process of amassing the largest army they have ever fielded, with the intention of mounting another all-out invasion. Lack of planning thwarted them last time, but they won't make the same

414

mistake again. And can I get Saul to listen to me? Not a chance. Not a chance in hell, Eliphaz, because Doeg censors everything he hears. So we waste valuable time and squander precious energy in this fruitless mockery of a civil war, while our real enemy prepares to snatch the ground from under our feet. This whole business makes me sick."

I stared in bewilderment. "I've heard nothing of this. Are their preparations far advanced?"

"Far enough for them to be able to make a move as soon as the spring rains are past," he said glumly. "But that isn't the whole of it, I'm afraid. Some of my informants are concerned that David may be intending to join them."

Now I was indignant. "David, fight against the people of Adonai? I don't think that's even worth worrying about."

"He has made overtures to the King of Gath before now," Abner reminded me, and I couldn't deny the truth of it. "He's well thought of in those circles. And the Philistines can't fail to have noticed by now that all is not well between him and his king. Surely he will only tolerate Saul's treatment of him for so long. He's a brilliant tactician, as well as a brave fighter in his own right. If he turns against us, instead of being content to keep avoiding us, and he has the whole might of Philistia behind him..."

I shuddered, and gazed into the fire; the warm flicker of the flames made me feel better. So did Abner's decision to confide in me, even though it had been reluctantly made. Presumably his distrust of both Doeg and David was at least sufficient to outweigh his old misgivings about me. Abner lapsed back into a meditative silence, tapping one foot restively on the ground, his heavy features drawn into a frown. On an impulse I said, "Abner, why do you stay with him?"

He made a contemptuous sound at the back of his throat. "With Saul? I wonder myself, sometimes."

"No, I mean it. You're a fine soldier, a respected commander of men, and here you are wasting your talents on this pathetic vendetta. You must know you can never gain anything from it."

He shrugged his shoulders with a dry smile and began scribbling absently in the dust with his finger. "He's my cousin, and I've sworn allegiance to him." Then he shrugged again. "I don't suppose I've thought about it in a long time. It doesn't pay to think too deeply." He sighed, his brow darkened once more, and he looked away from me again into his wine. "I do my duty by him, Eliphaz. What else could I do?"

"Join David."

"Never!" But his eyes flicked briefly away from me, and it struck me, with some surprise, that he had considered it after all. Then unexpectedly he looked back at me and retaliated, "What about you, then? Why do *you* stay? He loved you once, now he treats you like dirt. You have more reason to complain of him than I have."

I had no idea what to say to him.

"I suppose I keep hoping he'll..."

"Get better?" He made the rough sound in his throat again, and swilled a draught of wine around his mouth. "There's no cure for insanity."

Then he stood up and began clumping about the tent, sorting through his things and preparing for sleep. I thought I wouldn't sleep, yet I must have drifted off quite soon and slept unusually heavily, for the next thing I knew, it was pitch dark, the fire had gone out, and there was a cacophony of voices shouting outside the tent.

I sat bolt upright peering into the blackness, groggily trying to make sense of what I was hearing. I decided it must be a gang of our men who had been drinking and got themselves into an argument. Then gradually I realized that they were shouting for Abner. Puzzled, I listened for some moments without moving, then I crawled out of bed and felt my way over to his mattress to rouse him. But he was already awake. Just as I reached him, he called out, making me start, "Who's there? Who is it, creating all that noise at this time of night, for God's sake? You'll wake the king."

But the disturbance continued, louder. Cursing, Abner got up and groped blindly for the door. I ducked under the flap after him, feeling the wall of cold hit my face, unexpectedly dazed by the brilliance of the crystal-clear sky, peppered with stars, that arched above us, mocking the stunted black silhouettes of the tents huddled beneath its grandeur. The air was still, breathless, and it dawned on me slowly that the voices were carrying some distance. They weren't coming from our camp.

Abner was muttering to himself, stomping up and down and fuming. I could hear men stirring in the sur-rounding tents; here and there torches appeared, and a hum of speculation rose like a pall of smoke above the camp. Then abruptly the commotion ceased. Abner and I hovered uncertainly, exchanging glances and wondering whether to ignore it all and go back to bed. Then a familiar voice shattered the silence.

"Abner, I thought you were the king's trustiest

protector! The greatest warrior in Israel after Saul himself! Why aren't you doing your duty, Abner? And what about you, Eliphaz and Doeg? Where were you when the king needed you?" Then the chorus of shouting erupted again, and drowned him out; "Abner! Doeg! Eliphaz! Abner! Abner!" echoed in our ears until I thought it was never going to stop.

"David!" hissed Abner, his muscles taut with indignation. "Where the hell is he? He sounds so close!"

I said, "It's very still tonight. He could be a fair way from here."

"But what does he want? What does he want with *me,* damn him?" Not waiting for my response, Abner pulled his cloak impatiently around his neck and set off walking in the direction the voices had come from. Stumbling over a tent-peg, he swore loudly, and presumably realizing the futility of pursuit, yelled into the void, "This is Abner. Now clear off, do you hear me? Get moving, before I sound the attack."

A howl of laughter answered him. Then David's voice again.

"You couldn't catch me when I came to visit your delightful little camp this evening. So I don't see what chance you have now."

I stood transfixed, unable to comprehend what I was hearing. Abner's fists were clenched and his eyes spat fire. There was more stifled sniggering, then David called, with obvious enjoyment, "You deserve to die, Abner ben Ner. And you, Eliphaz. And Doeg. You're all supposed to be protecting your king, aren't you? Why don't you ask him where his spear is? Or his water jar?"

This time the laughter rained down on us uninhibited, barbed as a volley of arrows. Lights flared throughout the camp; Eliab, Barak and Joseph had appeared at my shoulder, and everyone was talking at once, demanding to be told what was happening. Abner grabbed my arm and said, "Eliphaz, where *is* Saul? Surely he can't have slept through all this."

I threw up my hands, we exchanged glances again, communicating courage to one another, then together we made for the royal tent, and Abner flung back the flap. Suddenly he was lunging forward in front of me; there was a scuffle and I saw the glint of metal against the darkness. Abner yanked the knife away from Doeg's throat then knocked it clean out of his hand, and it scudded across the floor, clattering to a standstill against the tent pole. "Don't be a fool," Abner growled. "No one is dead."

"They've taken the king," quavered Doeg's voice from the shadows. "I don't understand it. I was here all the time... I don't know how they could have got away with it." I'd never before known him show fear, and his pathetic whining disgusted me.

"Nonsense." Abner hauled Doeg to his feet and we dragged him outside into the night. "If David had Saul, he would have taken great pleasure in telling us so. What about the spear and the water jar - are they gone?"

Doeg took an involuntary gulp of the bitter-cold air and spluttered, "I think so. I can't find them."

"And you slept through it? David - or someone - broke into your tent; and you slept through it?"

"I told you, Abner. I don't understand! They would have had to get past the camp guards first. Then past all the tents without waking everyone. His Majesty is right - the man must be a sorcerer."

Abner grunted derisively, shaking Doeg by the scruff of his neck like a dog. My mind was racing, striving to sort through what must have taken place. The uncannily still cold air, my oddly deep sleep - it was true that no feat seemed beyond David's reach, but he was no wizard. A different kind of magic was at work here, a spirit of an altogether different origin from the powers of darkness that the magicians call upon. I said, "Saul must have gone to try to speak with him. I'll go after him, if someone will come with me."

But Abner wouldn't allow it. There was no hope of finding either of them in the darkness, and I should probably wind up lost too. No, we would sit it out and await Saul's return, and if he didn't come by daybreak, then a party would be despatched to find him.

There was already a mellow light on the horizon when the tent-flap was drawn back and Saul's gaunt figure appeared, black against the birth of the dawn. He must have found his own tent empty, but if he wanted company it wasn't for conversation, because he sat down by the hearth without speaking. Abner passed him the wine-cup, which he drained in one gulp, and wiped his sleeve across his mouth. He looked weary, grim and old. But he would give nothing, even when we plucked up the courage to question him. He slumped staring into the dying embers of our fire, his eyes dark and distant, and there were lines around them which I'd no recollection of seeing there before.

I never did find out for sure what had passed between Saul and David that night, though for some reason

I was never in any doubt that they had met. For what it's worth, my guess is that Saul will have broken down in remorse all over again, just like last time, blessing David for sparing his life once more, probably begging his forgiveness and swearing never to harm a hair of his anointed head from that moment on.

But David must have known it would all turn out to be empty words, and I think in his heart Saul must have known it too. At all events, the next we heard of David was that he was in Philistia with Achish of Gath, and all reports of sightings of him on Israelite soil abruptly ceased.

CHAPTER 25

After this, Saul lost all will to live. He stopped eating again, and barely slept. He went about with his hair untrimmed and his body unwashed; there were bags beneath his eyes the size of pomegranates, and his skin was dull and sallow and flaking. He haunted the fortress like his own ghost, drinking heavily, and fluctuating randomly between total withdrawal and raw violence. He behaved in ways calculated to alienate all who came near him: Jonathan and myself, Doeg and even Rizpah. I have no idea why he should have wanted to hurt her - no doubt he was too drunk to care - but he threw her bodily against a wall because of some trifling misdemeanour and punched her face until it bled, her cheeks swelled and she could barely see. I don't know why she didn't run away; except that, like me, she had nowhere to run, and there are few places where a woman can safely live alone for a single week. Or perhaps it was because she already knew something I only found out much later: she was carrying Saul's child.

When the sharp cold of winter melted into the warm rains of spring, there could be no doubt that the Philistines were mobilizing for war. Abner's concern had been no groundless fancy. The first reports of serious activity began to trickle in with leaders of tribes and elders of cities who came urgently seeking audience with the king, along with a constant stream of ordinary peasant folk who had observed the great Philistine host assembling and were desperate to preserve what little they possessed from destruction. Eventually Abner got Saul to agree once more to his assuming responsibility for planning our response, and so yet again we polished our armour and tested our weapons and prepared ourselves to defend our lands.

At first the Philistines' movements confused us, and even Abner was perplexed as to their exact intentions. The greater portion of their army had allegedly detached itself from the rest, and appeared to be marching steadily north along our western seaboard, presumably because the going was relatively flat over there, and they had a considerable number of horses and chariots. They seemed to be making for the Plain of Megiddo, way to the north of most of our major cities and settlements, though they would no doubt cause untold mayhem and slaughter as they went, plundering the coastal towns and wiping out any who dared oppose them. Though it grieved him to admit it, Abner was forced to acknowledge that we could do little to stay their advance in that direction; no matter how large a force we could muster, we should never be a match for them in a pitched battle on the plain. We still had no soldiers but infantry, and no weapons but bronze - and that, at best: many of our warriors even now had no more than staves and clubs to fight with. Our only hope against the enemy forces was to catch them off guard from positions in the mountains, where their chariots would be useless and their superior numbers of little relevance; and they could never truly crush Israelite resistance until they were prepared to risk an engagement in the hill-country which we controlled.

But for what conceivable purpose could they be heading so far north? At the fortress, each man had his different view, and in the lengthening evenings as we sat up in informal council we must have argued them through a hundred times.

Jonathan suggested that they had no long-term strategy, but as they had failed to defeat us by pressing east before, they had simply decided to try something original. Barak thought that they were basically out to demoralize us, by picking off our most indefensible communities, provocatively, one by one. Joseph agreed with him, as he generally did, and both of them feared that this plan was succeeding, in that morale among our people could hardly have been lower. It was Eliab's opinion that all of us were missing the point: they had no interest in enticing us to fight them at all, but were aiming to annex territory from our northern tribes who were too weak to offer any real opposition. I suppose by this he meant Asher and Naphtali, whose lands were green and fertile, but whose influence was indeed small because of their geographical isolation. We were compelled to admit that these tactics stood a fair chance of working, for there was a real possibility that we might have to abandon the northerners to their fate rather than risk maintaining an army so far from home.

But Abner's theory seemed likeliest to me, as was

usually the case in matters of war. He became firmly convinced that the Philistines were planning to veer east at the Vale of Jezreel, and then, having obtained fresh supplies and rested up for a while at their stronghold of Beth Shan, to mount a brisk sweep down the Jordan Valley with their horses and chariots still intact. Then the second division of their host, which had remained near Ashdod, would squeeze us from the west while the first menaced us from the east, and we would be trapped in the hills between them and then gradually crushed into submission.

None of these alternatives gave us much to look forward to, but while the heralds were still out calling Israel to arms, we heard of a fresh danger flaring to the south. A number of villages had been looted and burned, by what appeared to be loosely co-ordinated raiding parties who at first were feared to be in league with Philistia. Then it emerged that they operated independently - and that they called themselves Amalekites.

No one at Gibeah could work out what to make of this, me least of all. So far as we were concerned, the power of Amalek lay trampled beneath Saul's feet, never to rear its baleful head again. It seemed inconceivable that a remnant of survivors could have re-grouped, re-armed and wrought so much havoc in so short a time. I did hear it suggested that these weren't true Amalekites at all, but a hybrid assortment of nomads using the label as a banner to unite them. As for me, I didn't know whether to weep or to rejoice that the name of my own people was again on so many lips.

Abner of course faced an agonizing decision. Our forces were poised in readiness to march north, and now suddenly we were facing a fresh crisis in the south. While he was still weighing up what to do, reports filtered through that the so-called Amalekites were already under attack, and had retreated for the present deep into the wilderness. No one seemed to know who was responsible for their repulse, but then left behind after one of the skirmishes was a dinted shield embossed with a six-pointed star.

And so it was decided that we should march north at once, before any more of our neighbours thought to follow the Amalekite example. It appeared already that Abner was right: the Philistine horde had turned to go east, crossing the hills at their lowest point, and passed through the Plain of Megiddo to camp at Shunem on the edge of the Vale of Jezreel. For the moment they seemed in no hurry to move on, which was certainly good news for us.

But now Abner faced a second decision, and one no less crucial than the first. It was essential to settle as quickly as possible what should be the role of Saul himself in the conflict that was inevitably coming. For myself I would rather have left him at Gibeah, because he seemed altogether too unpredictable a quantity to risk taking with us. But Abner was under no illusions about his own limitations, and was grimly aware that he lacked both the authority and the charisma to unite Israel behind him on his own account. To raise the nation's morale from the pit, her king had to march with her, and to march at her head. Unless we could bring this about, everything was lost.

Luckily Doeg was in full agreement; at the back of his mind no doubt was the notion that if David were truly in league with Philistia, we might find him marching with their army and thus be able to kill him as a traitor with impunity. Against all odds, he somehow contrived to pull

Saul together enough for him to be able to travel; drugged with wine so he barely knew what was happening to him, and weak from lack of food and sleep, he was installed in an ox-cart, on the pretext that this was a more regal way for a king to proceed than on foot.

It was a fine morning in early summer when we set out from Gibeah. I had to admit it felt good to be striding out once more with an expanding army falling in behind us, knowing that we marched against a foreign power instead of turning our energies inward upon one of our own kind. And it was good to have Jonathan beside me, for now that the object of our aggression had changed, he'd returned to the ranks, and I could see something of his old fire quickening. Striking out in the van, Abner himself cut an impressively hefty and resplendent figure, his jaw locked in determination, his cloak swirling in the breeze behind him.

I tried not to look at Saul.

We'd been marching for four days when we came to the end of our road. The mountains fell away at our backs, and beneath our feet the Jezreel Valley lay spread like an open green scroll whose spindles were lost in the haze of distance. We stood on the crest of Mount Gilboa, up to our knees in waving grasses, and the stunning purple irises which some say grow nowhere else. I had never seen anywhere on earth more lovely.

At first it was too hazy, and then it was too dark, to ascertain the exact location of the Philistine host; but we knew they must be there, waiting at Shunem, in the foothills on the opposite side of the valley. Inside our tent I kindled a hearth-fire to cook our provisions, and Abner, Jonathan and the other Companions gathered around it to debate our next move. Saul and Doeg had remained in their own tent, for which I think that Abner was profoundly grateful; he shouldered the yoke of command less awkwardly when Saul himself was out of the way.

I held myself apart from their debating, occupying myself with preparing a meal, for as I saw it, I had neither military office nor a head for strategy. I listened to the arguments they proposed and parried, glimpsing their earnest faces bathed red in the firelight: Abner grave and calculating, Jonathan eager and aglow now with something of his father's old charisma, Eliab frowning, deep in thought, Barak and Joseph struggling to gain a hearing.

They considered attacking, they contemplated waiting, they examined every conceivable configuration of our troops, and it seemed to me that the balance of opinion was tipping progressively in favour of charging the Philistines before our men lost their nerve, and before our food supplies started to give out. The whole business seemed risky to me. Whatever we did, we should inevitably be outnumbered, and be forced to fight a pitched battle on the open plain, which we were no more likely to win than we ever had been. Nevertheless, it was true that we had little alternative, for on no account must the enemy be permitted to break through to Beth Shan and down into the Jordan Valley.

The meal was devoured greedily; the marching and the fresh spring air had whetted our hunger and my simple vegetable broth tasted like some exotic delicacy. As we dipped our bread into the bubbling pot and the wine-goblet was passed around, Abner drew together the threads of the discussion, and proposed that we launch an all-out attack at the earliest possible opportunity.

He'd barely finished speaking when there was a shuffling outside, the tent-flap jerked backwards and Saul stood in the doorway. He was clad only in his undertunic, with his feet bare, eyes feral, and cheeks florid with drink. He tottered unsteadily, looking from one face to the next in search of whoever it was he wanted. Instinctively we all got to our feet, but no one spoke. Finally Saul fixed his gaze with some difficulty on Abner. Then he said in a slurred stammer, "You - will do no such thing. I - absolutely - forbid it."

Abner's eyes widened; he could find no words to reply. Saul moved closer, staggering erratically, steadying himself against Jonathan's shoulder as he came within our stunned circle. Jonathan flinched, recoiled almost imperceptibly, then must have felt guilty, for he put his hand on his father's belt and looked at the ground. Saul was still staring muzzily at Abner. He spluttered, "Did you hear me? I said - I won't - allow you - to attack."

Abner cleared his throat. He began, rather fatuously I thought, "With respect, Your Majesty, you gave me permission..."

"Well I take it back!" Suddenly Saul was shouting, and his eyes sparked like flint from their hollows, gouged hideously black against the flickering orange fireglow that danced over his features. He raked his fingers savagely through his unkempt hair. "This is the army of Israel, the army of Adonai! You haven't consulted Adonai! You dare to presume to go into battle without the blessing of Adonai..." He staggered again, brushed saliva from his lips, heaved himself upright once more against his son's tensed body. I glanced mortified at Jonathan's face, then at Eliab's; each of them grimaced with embarrassment. Abner was shocked speechless. I could sense that the methodical side of him was desperately wanting to argue rationally with his cousin, yet he could see that it was useless. There was simply no point in reminding Saul that he hadn't made contact with his God in years.

"Very well," said Abner a good while later. "What do you suggest."

His answer, though slow in coming, impressed me. It was quite the wisest thing he could have said under the circumstances. Saul had clearly been expecting a confrontation, and Abner's response threw him totally. Stricken, he stared once more at each of our faces in turn, then pushed Jonathan aside and bolted from the tent.

Again no one spoke, and the air between us bristled and crackled like stormclouds. Jonathan shook his bowed head from one side to the other, several times, and his fists were clenched behind his back. Then Barak could stand the dreadful silence no longer. He whispered hoarsely, "So what the hell do we do now."

Another short awkwardness, then in a remarkably smooth voice Eliab stated, "I say we attack anyway."

"What?" Abner rounded on him with such acrimony that Eliab almost choked on his own breath.

More uncertainly, and backing out of Abner's range, he repeated, "I - think we should go ahead with our attack. We decided it was the best policy, and nothing has changed. What can Saul do about consulting Adonai in his condition? What can he do about anything?"

Abner answered gruffly, "Eliab, he is the king. We

must do as he says." He swung round, and cursing under his breath, began making for the door. None of us dared say anything to deter him, but our bewildered faces must have asked our question for us, because he roared, "To find a priest with enough sense to hear what God ought to be saying!" Then he thrust back the tent-flap and strode out into the night.

Eliab blew out his cheeks. The hissing of the fire echoed loud as thunder in my ears; the pot of stew still simmered, but no one could face food any longer. Jonathan leaned against the tent-pole, crippled with shame.

We sat in prickling silence, willing Abner to return, but he didn't. I found myself obsessively counting my own heartbeats and couldn't make myself stop. I had reached several thousands when the flap was torn aside and Abner stormed in, angrier even than he'd been when he left. Again none of us ventured to question him; again he answered us anyway.

"Saul, confound him! He's been all through the camp threatening every priest, prophet and dreamer in sight to bring him a true word from Adonai. He's terrified half the army out of its wits. Now no one knows where he is - I tell you, we've got to find him before we have a riot on our hands."

We didn't need telling twice. As one, we went for our weapons and issued from the tent, fanning out and separating, each to comb a different quarter of the camp. By instinct I went to Saul's tent before trying anywhere else, bursting in with my sword drawn, thus betraying my dread of what I might find.

What I did find was Doeg, cowering in one corner

with his eyes crossed dumbly on the point of my blade. The smell of his fear aroused me, and I did what I'd longed to do for months: I seized him around the neck and held my sword at his throat.

"Where is he?" I demanded, and I think I was as shocked by my forcefulness as he was. "Why aren't you out looking for him? Anything could have happened! Which way did he go? Speak, you worm, before I slice your gullet."

I must confess I wasn't making speech easy for him: I'd pulled the fabric of his tunic so tight at his neck that he was having problems enough breathing. He shook his head frantically, waving his arms to indicate that he knew nothing. Cursing, I dragged him up onto his knees – suddenly he was hardly any heavier than I was - and growled in his ear, "Then you can come with me and look for him now. On your feet." I pushed him outside in front of me, with my swordtip at the small of his back, and in that fashion we proceeded to scour my portion of the camp.

There was an unmistakeable odour of unease in the air: men stood huddled in anxious groups outside their tents, whispering amongst themselves. Some of them glanced at us askance as we passed, but asked no questions. I was cautious about whom I chose to approach - I had no wish to raise the general level of tension any higher - but any men I knew to be priests or prophets I stopped and questioned, and most of them had seen him. Some still bore the marks of his fingers on their flesh, but none knew where he'd gone. After a while we ran into Abner, and then Barak and Joseph, but none of them had had any success either. Reluctantly I escorted Doeg back to the royal tent, and there we found him.

It seemed only moments since I had discovered Doeg here alone, but enough time had elapsed for almost every object in the place to have been overturned. Plates and goblets littered the floor, wine leaked like a blood flow across the hard-packed dust, clothes and weapons were strewn among the scattered cushions. A water jar lay smashed and shattered into a thousand jagged fragments, and one of the tent-poles leaned drunkenly where someone or something had collided with it. One small lamp remained unspilled; by its guttering light I saw Saul's eyes, rabid and glistening black, and his hand holding a dagger at the chest of the terror-stricken priest who writhed white-faced in his arms. Clutched in the frightened holy man's hands were the sacred stones, and he cried out in pain as Saul's knee thrust into his back, and Saul screamed at him, "Throw again!"

I took in at a glance what must have happened, but for what seemed like forever I stood awe-struck, at a loss for what to do next. I hadn't even been aware that the ephod had found its way back into Saul's control; the last I'd heard, it had still been in the possession of David. Presumably after Saul's last resounding victory over the Philistines, the movement between the two rival Israelite camps hadn't been entirely in one direction.

Saul must have seen us come in, but he gave no indication of it, and I was terrified that any sudden move on my part might mean the end for the poor wretch squirming in his grasp. The stones tumbled forward onto the earthy floor; tightening his hold, Saul jerked his head towards them to look for their response. Even from where I stood, with Doeg still cringing at the point of my sword, I could see that they were giving no answer. One lay this way, one that;

I wondered how many times this had already happened before we'd broken in. Saul screamed again, and sent his victim scrabbling on the ground to retrieve them ready for another throw, but he pushed him so hard that the priest fell heavily onto his forehead and split his nose. As he struggled to right himself, with one hand clasped against his face in pain, the blood gushed between his trembling fingers, and I'd had enough.

Not knowing where my authority came from, I shouted, "Let him go, Saul, or Doeg dies." As I spoke, I reached forward and grabbed Doeg by the hair, bringing my sword up so that the length of my blade ran across his throat. He must have felt the cold of the metal keen against his skin.

Thankfully, Saul was sober enough to grasp what was happening, and I must have been angry enough to look as though I meant what I said. Glancing at me in sudden panic, he let his arms spring apart, and the frightened holy man backed away as far from him as he could get, holding his cloak to his nose to stem the stream of blood, and gazing fearfully at the sacred stones which now lay out of his reach. Then Saul went to pieces.

Whimpering and moaning, he shrank into a heap on the ground, his head pressed to his knees, his fingers tearing into the sand. He was trying to speak, repeating the same syllable obsessively, but I couldn't make out what it was. The more I bade him relax and be quiet, the more he struggled to be understood, and at last I caught his meaning. He was calling for Samuel.

All the life was ebbing out of me; I knew I'd come to the end of myself. Saul was living in a dreamworld, where

Adonai still spoke to him, where Samuel still lived. Finally I could take no more of it; I yelled back at him, "Samuel is dead!" as many times as it took to stop him whining, then I seized his arms and forced him to look me in the face. He was silent now, even if only because his strength was gone, so I stressed again softly, "Samuel is dead," because now I was sure he could hear me.

His head lolled onto his chest. He whispered, "I don't care. I have to speak to him."

"Saul, the man is dead, for God's sake! Pull yourself together."

"I said, I have to speak to him, Eli! I've sought the voice of Adonai in dreams, from priests, from seers, from the sacred lots... Samuel is our only hope, Eli, our only link. If he is dead - we must find someone who can reach him."

I said feebly, "Saul, you're sick. This is sheer madness. Why don't you just leave the decisions and the war-craft to Abner? I don't even know what you're talking about." At least, I hoped I didn't.

"Abner knows nothing of Adonai! He sows in the fields of his own conceit, and he will reap destruction on us all! Eli, find me a medium. Someone who can call up the spirits of the dead. I must speak to Samuel. I have to."

So he did mean it. I said, "Witchcraft is an abomination to Adonai. There are no mediums left in Israel." What was the point of reminding him that he'd banished them himself?

Doeg said quietly, "Yes, there are."

I'd almost forgotten he was there. He stood pressed against the tent-pole behind me, watching Saul and trembling, but when I looked at him he flicked his gaze towards me, and must have read enough disgust and despair there for him to overcome his new-found fear of me. He came forward hesitantly and knelt beside Saul. He took Saul's hands in his own, and with a weird light playing about his face, said, "I have heard that there is a woman up in the hills at Endor, less than half a day's walk from here. She speaks with the dead."

Saul said nothing. He peered deep into Doeg's eyes, as though searching for something he longed yet feared to find. From the far corner of the tent I heard muttering and fidgeting, and the priest crawled out of the shadows, scooping up the Urim and Thummim in his bloodstained cloak, growling abuse and calling down upon Saul every foul curse under the sun for even daring to contemplate such a dreadful sin. No one paid him any attention. Doeg said to Saul, "We could go there at daybreak. I know a man who knows the way."

Saul answered, "Take me now."

"Now?" Even Doeg was shocked. "It's the middle of the night, Your Majesty. You need to get some rest. You'll never make it."

"Take me now!" Saul hauled himself up by the tent-pole. "Both of you. I need you both."

CHAPTER 26

The night was clear but moonless as we crept out of the royal tent. We carried torches with us, but feared to light them until we were well out of sight of the camp, for Saul was adamant that no one should learn of our absence. Threading our way between the tents by the dim red glow of dying campfires, with cloaks thrown over our heads to conceal our identity, we padded after the guide Doeg had found for us, a surly peasant farmer from the humblest ranks of our army, whose sliver of land was nearby and who knew the landscape as he knew the palms of his own hands.

For once it was as well that our guards were lax in their duties. We headed off in silence down the darkened hillside, following gullies and streambeds towards the Vale of Jezreel. Once hidden from view by the rising ground behind us, we lit our torches and began to move faster, but the going was rough, snarled with thorny undergrowth, and often sharply downhill. It worried me that Saul had eaten so little for weeks, and drunk so much, but to begin with sheer

437

desperation kept him going, and the flame in his eyes burned as fiercely as his torch.

The ground had levelled out now; to our rear the slopes of Gilboa rose black and opaque against the starry sky, and ahead the valley stretched wide and flat but invisible. Somewhere in front of us and to our left, the Philistine monster must be lying shrouded in the darkness.

We must have been about half way there when the inevitable caught up with us, and Saul began to falter. He was too stubborn to ask to rest, but I could hear him heaving for breath and he was slowing our pace. I hailed our guide, and we sat down to let him recover. Doeg pulled a flagon of wine from the folds of his tunic and held it to his master's dry lips. He took a large draught, and I wished Doeg had brought water instead. Presently he was breathing normally once more, though his face was haggard and his eyelids drooped, and I motioned to our guide that we ought to carry on, before His Majesty fell asleep.

As we approached Endor the ground began to rise, and along with the hills came forest. Now that we were climbing, Saul was struggling more and more. Twice he dropped his torch, and we had to stamp out the stray sparks that flared in the creeping underbrush. Then he singed his cloak, and I decided to take the torch away from him. He didn't even have the energy to fight me, and I started to have serious doubts about us ever reaching our destination.

The trees jostled closer on either side, unseen shoots scratching our faces and catching in our clothing. Here and there a shaft of moonlight penetrated, causing a pool of white radiance to shimmer where it kissed the sleeping earth. Our torches were sputtering, and I dreaded being left in darkness at the mercy of whatever spirits might dwell here. Then abruptly the trees thinned out, the moon hung full and silver above us, we emerged breathless into an ocean of eerie light, and our guide stopped walking.

He grunted, and waved his staff towards the far side of the clearing. I could see nothing but the empty space spreading out from our feet, and the trunks of the trees crowding together around the edge of it, as though some magical barrier kept them at bay. Our guide brandished his staff again, motioning us forward, but his gesture made it clear that he wouldn't be coming with us. Saul pushed his cloak down from his head, but Doeg at once pulled it back up for him, grimacing: there was no way that we would be entertained for a second by any spirit-raiser if Saul revealed who he was. All Israel knew that the practice of wizardry was outlawed, by command of the king; a visit from His Majesty in person could be viewed as nothing but a trap.

For what seemed like an age, the three of us stood transfixed at the centre of the glowing white circle, our shadows stretched black and attenuated behind us like silken trains looped at our ankles. The peasant had disappeared, lost among the trees; Saul stared at the point which he'd indicated, his face expressionless, his eyes unblinking. Then with measured steps he began to walk forward, and we followed him. Never in my life have I been more petrified. The very air we were breathing was poisoned with evil, the boughs and the leaves of the trees were impregnated with its odourless stench. I could hardly put down one foot in front of the other to go after Saul, yet I couldn't let him go on without me. We passed out of the clearing, walked between the massing trunks, and then suddenly there wasn't wood on either side of us, but rock, and no branches above our heads, but roof; and it was coming lower.

I couldn't make out what manner of place we'd come to, whether it was a cave or a man-made structure of some kind. The roof was solid, but whether it was hewn from living rock or built of bricks or mud, there was no means of telling. I took Saul by the elbow, as much to reassure myself as to offer him support.

The silence enveloping was thicker than butter; it crushed into my ears until they hurt. Then instantaneously it shattered into a million tiny fragments. A woman's voice called from the blackness up ahead, "Who's there? Who is it? What do you want?"

Saul jumped, betraying his raw nerves. I stood frozen to the spot, and Doeg must have done the same. When none of us could find it within us to reply, the challenge came again, this time accompanied by a spinning stone that skimmed past us not a hand's breadth from my nose, and tore the air apart like rotted cloth. As one we backed against the wall. Saul's face had set into a mask of horror in the failing torchlight, and Doeg was as pale as wax. Another stone followed the first, then a third; before I could manage to stop my teeth chattering, Doeg got a grip on himself, and called back in an impressively steady voice, "We are the sons of Jonah, prophets from Ramah. We want to see the holy-woman."

There was no reply, but the bombardment ceased, which we took to be a good sign. I glanced briefly at Saul, then at Doeg, wondering if the three of us could possibly pass for prophets, let alone brothers, but it was too late to think up an alternative now. Gingerly we groped forward along the passageway, and presently became aware that there was someone walking towards us.

She carried a small clay lamp which was alight and glimmering softly, but she wore a hooded cloak so we couldn't see her face. I saw that she moved with a young woman's grace, and for some reason I was surprised. She stopped a short distance away from us, and instinctively we halted in our turn. She spoke again, and her voice was young too. She repeated, "What do you want."

I was starting to feel not quite so debilitated; my curiosity about the mysterious figure in front of me was beginning to temper my fear. I decided she must be an acolyte, or the necromancer's pupil. Nevertheless, I resolved to leave the talking to Doeg. I'd accounted him a coward when confronted by my blade; in the presence of evil it seemed he was more at ease than I was.

He answered, in a suitably grave tone, "We have heard that there is a medium here who can speak with the dead. We wish to contact one who means much to us."

The young woman paused, and raised her lamp to study our faces. As she did so, it illumined her own, and I thought: heaven preserve us, she's little more than a girl. Her expression appeared so innocent, so unsullied; I wondered who she was, and what had brought her to a place like this. I couldn't imagine what kind of parent would sell such a comely daughter to a witch.

She explained, "There are no mediums here. They are banished, by order of His Majesty King Saul."

I sensed Saul stiffen beside me, but he held his tongue. Doeg pulled something from the folds of his clothing and said, "We can pay."

She moved forward and inspected what he held in his hand. It was a small cloth pouch, and there was a glint of gold as she ventured to open it. She looked at our faces again, her eyes half hidden by the thick woollen hood, but other than that she wore no veil. She nodded slightly and said, "Come with me."

She turned and began walking ahead of us along the tunnel, the heavy cloak swinging as she moved, swamping her slight body so that its form was lost among the layers of fabric. I kept expecting the passage to widen into a chamber, where there would be a coven of other mysterious, hooded maidens such as this one, sitting at the feet of an aged crone engaged in teaching them spells. At this point, my torch flared up in its death throes - Doeg's had already gone out - and now the only light came from the tiny clay lamp cradled in the girl's palm. Then without any warning she stopped and turned to face us, and I saw that the passageway ended in a solid blank wall, again either of rock, mud or brick, I couldn't tell. She said, "Sit down. I will light a fire."

I scarcely felt at ease enough to sit, but my legs were weary, I was breaking out in gooseflesh, I should have been in bed; and I did as she asked. Saul sat next to me, and I realized that he was shivering, from cold or from fear; it could well have been either. Doeg remained on his feet, watching the girl as she worked, kindling fire with the wick of her lamp, blowing on the dry grass and moss already arranged upon a pile of sticks on the ground. A thin wisp of smoke spiralled upward, then the spark took hold and sprang into life. The homely crackling of the flames began to hearten me, but as the light from them spread and disclosed our surroundings, my fear intensified. Hanging from the walls and arranged on rough shelves were the sinister tools of the sorcerer's trade: assorted bundles of drying vegetation, dubiously murky liquids festering in dishes and jars, bronze and clay vessels of indeterminate contents, implements whose uses I didn't dare contemplate. Scratched into the walls were symbols and ciphers, writing I could make no sense of, and various fertility images best left undescribed. And squatting in the gloom with her back against the wall was a grossly fat figure swathed in a cloak just like her servant's.

I clutched at Saul's arm in blind panic, all at once unable to discern anything but the red of the fire, the black of the ominously impending roof, the white of my own naked terror. When my vision cleared, I noticed that the girl was looking at me strangely, and then I saw.

The figure by the wall was made of stone. Its eyes were hollow sightless sockets in a grotesquely grinning face; I couldn't imagine how I could have taken it for human. Its breasts were pendulous, its belly distended, and the cloak around its shoulders was carved from solid rock. Ashtoreth, the Earth Mother of the Canaanites, fecundity personified, bestower of life and of the fruits of nature; mother, or was it sister, or was it consort, of Baal. And if there was any witch here at all, it was the young girl herself who knelt in the ashes by the glowing fire, tossing fresh sticks onto the charred remnants of the spent ones, looking at me and smiling at my credulity.

I forced myself to relax, for I knew that my fear was feeding on itself now. Breathing deeply, closing my eyes, I thought: God Almighty, all this is still going on. The primeval rituals, the invoking of spirits, no doubt the sacred prostitution, the coupling with the powers of darkness - we may have forced it underground with our enlightened reforms, but our land is still riddled with it, it eats at the roots of Israel's being like a canker. I found myself grieving for this strange young girl with the innocent face, entangled in the cruel web of evil.

Then I became aware of a pungent odour in my nostrils; I opened my eyes and realized that the girl had thrown some substance into the fire, for the colour of the flames had changed. She had begun chanting, in a language I didn't know, and she was rocking backwards and forwards on her haunches, chewing something in her sagging mouth. Her face had changed too; her eyes were open but unfocussed, and in a hoarse voice, sounding not remotely like the one she had used to us before, she asked who we wanted to see.

"Our master," answered Doeg urgently, and there was an undisguised excitement animating his features that appalled me. "Our master, the seer from Ramah." He crouched forward, watching her face with his bird-sharp eyes, as hints of dark emotion flicked across it which were gone before they could be read. I turned away, for now I couldn't bear to look at her, to accept the change that had come over her; I feared for the fate of a world where evil can pose as innocence and fool a man so easily. Pressing against my side, I could feel Saul's body tensed up, cold and quivering. Unexpectedly, he started forward also, and spoke for the first time, demanding in a tremulous voice to know what she saw.

At first she gave no indication of having heard him. She continued to sway back and forth, and her hood fell from her head, releasing a tangled, unwashed mane of dull brown hair, and unmasking a brow flushed and monstrously contorted. Suddenly her lips flared back and she screamed; her body arched rigid, and she looked straight at him. "Samuel!" she wailed. "I see Samuel... and you are King Saul!"

I stared in dismay as she vaulted across the leaping flames and tore the cloak from Saul's head. He cowered against me, wincing as she shrieked at him, "This is a trick! You've come here to kill me! May the gods strike you dead for this. You betrayed my trust."

He swallowed hard, shook his head vehemently, reached out both hands and caught her by the wrists. "This is no trick, I swear it! You won't be harmed. Please... please, call him back."

Her eyes bore into his, blinking rapidly; she was hovering between Earth and Sheol, immobilized by his desperation. Saul's unkempt curls tumbled across his forehead, his features were racked with mental pain. Perhaps she glimpsed the ghost of his beauty along with the spectre of the departed prophet; perhaps she merely pitied him. But I saw something within her soften, her suspicion of us melted away, and she even smiled a little. Then she drew her wrists effortlessly from Saul's grasp, backed away from him across the fire, and her eyes hazed over once more. She fell against the wall, intoning the same string of meaningless syllables, and we saw the seer.

There was no cloud of mist, no shimmering light, no rushing wind, or whatever else I might have expected.

There was just Samuel, standing quietly by the fireside, wrapped in his cloak and leaning on his staff the way he always did, solid enough to touch, I was sure, yet thankfully just too far out of reach for me to try. Later, a plague of questions would beset me: could this really have been Samuel himself? Was it a demon? Was it a creation of my own expectant imagination? But at the time, my mind went blank. I could see and think of nothing else but him. The girl, Doeg, even Saul, had no further existence for me, still less the fire and the objects around the walls. If my vision of the seer wasn't real, then neither was anything else that the world contained.

He was gazing fixedly at a point somewhere close to my shoulder, where I realized Saul must still be crouching, and then he spoke. His voice came slow, heavy, weary, but unexpectedly substantial, and undeniably Samuel's. He said, "So even now I'm not free of your arrogant meddling. Why have you disturbed me? Why did you make me come back? Why even now am I to be granted no peace?"

There was no malice in his tone, no edge to inspire fear, and there were real wet tears in his blue blue eyes. But Saul's voice cracked and shook, and seemed to come from far away; he croaked, "Because I'm desperate," and then he was weeping all over again. Between his sobs he was struggling to explain, but the words came out disjointed and confused. He poured out his fear and his grief and his pain all together. The Philistines were on his back, his God had abandoned him, he wouldn't answer him by any of the means that he'd tried. He had prayed, he had begged, he had screamed in frustration; and he *had* to know what to do, he *had* to know, somehow. And death was overshadowing him, there was utter darkness in his soul, he was falling apart. Samuel let him rave on unchecked until the well of his words ran dry; his voice crumbled and he finished lamely, "You're my only hope."

Still I couldn't see Saul with my eyes. But some other sense told me he was on his knees before Samuel fawning and grovelling, all pride reduced to nothing. The seer didn't move, his expression didn't change, the tears still dewed his eyes but not one of them fell. He said, "You really think so? You really think I can help you when Adonai himself has become your enemy? I have already told you what your future holds, my son. God will take away your kingdom and give it to one more worthy. The Philistines will tear your army to pieces. By this time tomorrow, you will have no need of a necromancer to contact the dead."

The outline of the prophet's form was blurring. I blinked and pressed my eyelids, and it was fainter still, then he was gone. At once I became aware again of the sights and sounds around me; acutely aware. The crackling of the fire pounded in my ears like claps of thunder, the flames were so bright I was dazzled half blind. The objects that hung on the walls spun in dizzy spirals before my eyes, and I thought momentarily that I was going to pass out. Doeg stared about him as though unsure of what had happened, the girl squatted heaving and wasted beside the fire, and Saul lay prone at my feet.

No one moved or made a sound, and I hardly dared breathe. I had known holy silence, but this was a silence from the pit. It seemed to crush my ribcage and wrap fingers around my throat. I could still hear the fire crackling, the girl panting, but they didn't touch that infernal stillness; nothing could break the spell until she who had cast it cut off its power. Gradually I sensed her breathing grow calmer, her eyes cleared over and she sat back against the wall to regain her bearings. Then she got up, poured water from a large clay amphora into a silver cup, and sipped at it slowly. Peeping out over the rim, she seemed to see Saul for the first time, still lying motionless beside me, and I watched the concern being born in her eyes. She crawled towards him across the floor and stroked his forehead with one hand. It incensed me that a creature so evil could harbour this kindness and pity in her nature. I suppose it confused me; it blurred the assumptions I still clung to.

Gently she pushed back the hair from his face and saw that he was conscious, for his eyes rolled in terror at the sight of her, and his whole body twitched and twisted when she touched him. She held the cup of water to his mouth, but he spat it away as though she were trying to make him drink poison. Then she reached for one of the jars on her shelves, and shook out some oatmeal biscuits and small barley cakes. She put her arm around Saul's back and tried to make him sit up, saying - and her voice was so horribly normal, so sickeningly gentle - "You have to eat, Your Majesty. Just look at you, you're half starved," but he shrank back quaking, his eyes black islands in the ravaged ocean of his face. "Please," she whispered. "I risked my life by doing what you asked. Please - now do what I ask."

But still he refused, turning his head away from her and curling his knees up to his chin like a frightened animal. She looked at me with something disturbingly like help-lessness, then got to her feet again and began pottering about among the containers and bunches of herbs. She said, "I'll make some stew. It'll be hot and more nourishing, easier for him to swallow."

Dazed, I sat and watched her, as I struggled to re-order the chaos in my head. I had just seen Samuel, a man who was dead, apparently breathing and moving and talking, with real tears lodged in his eyes. Now here was the girl who had brought it all about, chopping salted meat and vegetables as though nothing out of the ordinary had happened, while the King of Israel sprawled insensible by her fireside, out of his wits with hunger and fright. I crouched down beside him and draped my cloak around his shoulders, for he was still shaking convulsively; when I glanced up, Doeg was squatting opposite me, peering at me curiously, and mouthing: What happened?

I frowned at him, uncertain what he meant; then like a thunderbolt the realization hit me. I said, "You didn't see a thing, did you? And you didn't hear anything, either. I can't believe it."

"See what? Hear what?" He gaped at me, baffled, then I noticed that the girl had left off from her chores and come to kneel once more beside me. I flicked my eyes towards her, and away again quickly, for she was studying me intently.

"Did you see Samuel too?" she murmured, wiping flour from her fingers down the front of her robe, and reaching to take my hand. A wave of revulsion swept through me, but I was too slow to pull away.

I growled, "Of course. Is there some reason why I shouldn't have?"

"It's unusual." She looked down at Saul again,

smiling sadly as though he were a dying child. "It was the king who wanted the contact." So Doeg's ruses hadn't deceived her. Then she turned her smile on me. "You must be very close."

I couldn't speak.

"Come," she invited me gently. "Let's make him more comfortable."

There was a straw bed in one corner, next to the image of the goddess. Between us we got him lying on it, wrapped in our cloaks and some blankets, and the girl went back to her domestic preparations. The stew when it came was too good to refuse, and we forced Saul to have some. His fingers trembled too much to hold the bowl, but he let me feed him with bread soaked in the juices, and he revived slightly. Presently he began mumbling again, repeating distractedly that we had to get back, we must be in camp before sunrise, but I don't think he even knew what he was saying. I shook my head forcefully, knowing there was no way he was fit to travel, but the girl touched my wrist and said, "His Majesty is right. If you're found here, they must put all of you to death."

I thought, And you too. Yet I knew she spoke the truth.

It was when we got back that the misery hit me. Collapsed on my bed, listening to the sounds of the waking camp drifting on the morning like meaningless echoes from another world, I was drowning in an ocean of over-whelming desolation. My eyelids ached and my ears rang, the spectre of Samuel haunted me, and I couldn't cast it from my mind whether I forced my eyes open or screwed them shut. But it was laughing not weeping, as it chanted at me cruelly: *Adonai has rejected Saul as a man; by tomorrow he will need no medium to contact the dead.* Only now did his meaning break through to me, and then the tears poured down my face unrestrained.

That was the moment when I found I was praying. I didn't decide to, I didn't even want to. But all at once I was pouring out my heart as I'd never done before, and I knew I was praying to Adonai. I hadn't stopped to think, to reassess what I believed. I no longer even knew what was real any more. But suddenly, unaccountably, I knew there was nowhere else I could run. I had reached rock bottom and found myself still falling, my resources had run out and I had nothing else.

Aloud I flung at him all my doubts and accusations, aloud I released all my wretchedness and fright. The despair, the loneliness, the confusion, the bitterness, the guilt and the agony of all my thirty eight years spilled from me, and I gave him the lot, until I wound up begging and bawling for forgiveness, and pleading for Saul with every shred that remained of my tattered emotions: Oh God, please don't let him die in this torment, oh God, please don't turn from him, please don't let him go...

And as the rest of the camp ate breakfast, and made final preparations for the conflict that was coming, I slept, exhausted, stretched out on my mattress, with tears on my cheeks and a peace in my soul which I hadn't known in a lifetime.

CHAPTER 27

I awoke feeling refreshed.

No - that is far too weak a word for it. I awoke feeling elated. The moment my eyes opened I was alert, eager; I felt no fear of what I knew must lie ahead, no anxiety, none of that fluttering dread griping at my stomach. Nor did I feel numb, as though nothing were real - no, that wasn't the cause of my strange sense of well-being. On the contrary, every nerve in my body prickled with vitality. I was keenly aware of every facet of my being and every detail of my surroundings. Suddenly, absurdly, life was good.

I lay for a while on my back, looking up at the fabric of the tent rippling gently in the morning breeze, stretching vigour into my muscles, cautiously analysing why today should feel so different. One by one I combed through the concerns that were normally guaranteed to fuel my fretfulness: the Philistine threat, the mysterious Amalekite revival, the machinations of David - but none of them seemed to wield its usual power over me. Finally I risked turning my attention upon Saul, realizing in that instant that for months I'd had to banish his image from my mind a thousand times a day merely in order to preserve my own sanity. Now, for some inexplicable reason, I was no longer worried even about him.

Baffled, I twisted myself upright, and sat on the edge of my mattress to think. I told myself I was dreaming. I told myself I must at last have gone out of my senses. I ought to be more concerned about Saul now than ever before. When we'd got him into his tent at dawn that very morning he'd been like a dead man walking. He'd been conscious yet insensible: he didn't know where he was, who I was, who Doeg was. He hadn't uttered one word all the way back, just stared unblinking at everything as though his wits were elsewhere.

Just then Abner came in, and seemed about to re-buke me, either for lying so late or for last night's escapade, then for some reason as soon as he saw my face he thought better of it and stood gaping at me as though he'd walked into the wrong tent. It was only when I grinned and asked him what hour it was, that he recovered himself and launched into his tirade after all.

Presently, when he ran out of accusations to level at me, and abuse to hurl, I asked him what was the matter. He grunted, and bade me follow him outside.

It wasn't so late after all. The sun was still low in the sky, the air still cool and mild, and here and there men sat about in subdued cliques, finishing breakfast or attending to equipment. Abner led me to the edge of the camp which overlooked the valley, and pointed.

For the first time, I was confronted with the true

magnitude of the Philistine host. I'd never seen anything like it. This was no mere forest of heads and spears, no mere carpet of leather and iron spread out to air in the pale morning light. This was a spectacle of an altogether different order. It was awesome. It extended like a vast black ant-swarm out across the valley, stretching eastwards, it seemed, almost to the Jordan, westwards towards the mountains and the Plain of Megiddo.

Har-Mageddon. Momentarily my blood ran cold.

Abner said, "You see? I sit up half the night trying to decide what to do. Saul is missing. My officers are giving me earache. I know the Philistines are down there. Do I attack? Wait? Call their bluff? I listen to Jonathan and Eliab and the rest of them, arguing in circles and berating each other until I want to strangle somebody. I find priests and prophets to pronounce a dozen interpretations of the will of Adonai, prepared to sanction any confounded plan that anyone can come up with. But then the sun rises, and I see this. This is the end, Eliphaz. Any strategy we adopt is just so much futility. Either we die fighting or we die lying down. Whatever happens, we die."

"I know which I'd rather do," I muttered, more to myself than to him. He growled at me, wanting to know what I'd said; I repeated it, then raised one eyebrow, inviting a response. He shook his head gloomily.

"Me too, Eliphaz. But I don't know. I don't think we'll get the men to go along with it. I'm afraid we may finish up with a mutiny to quell."

I shrugged. "Can that be any worse than finishing up trampled to death beneath the feet of enemy horses? I reckon we should form up for battle."

"*You* reckon?" sneered Abner, and I could see him thinking: what right have you to reckon anything. "What about Saul? What about the will of Adonai?" But I could see him looking at me strangely again, as though there were something about my face that he was finding increasingly disconcerting. Despite everything, I had to smile.

"Why don't you sound the trumpets, Abner? Marshal the troops. Let's worry about that later."

Even as I spoke, I could scarcely believe that the words came from me. Certainly Abner couldn't. I don't suppose he'd ever known me have a decisive or original idea before. He stared at me a little longer, then backed off, looking perplexed; I shrugged again and went back to the tent.

So I was more than mildly surprised when soon after, I heard the trumpets calling us to muster. But still I felt no fear. Normally just hearing the first note of that fanfare is enough to cause a cold sweat to break out upon the brow of any soldier; yet as I fastened my greaves and breastplate and buckled my sword to my belt, I was calm, composed, even confident. It was uncanny.

I have never heard an army assemble so silently. Of course, Abner and I weren't the only ones to have stood on the crest of Mount Gilboa and seen what we'd seen that morning. It was sobering to read the expressions on the faces of the men milling around me: some fearful, some disbelieving, some angrily resentful, some past caring, resigned to their fate. But no one spoke. They filed to their places, tribe by tribe, clan by clan, family by family; the officers stalked up and down counting heads and checking weapons, but they did so without a murmur. The atmosphere was heavy, pregnant with apprehension. I saw fathers standing with their arms around their sons, brothers standing together side by side, friends stealing glances, hungry for reassurance. But I heard nothing.

I found myself searching among the mass of heads for some sign of Saul, but there was none. I suppose it was foolish of me to have looked for any, yet thankfully it is only human to hope, even after a lifetime of dashed expectations. But what was more, I'd seen nothing of Doeg, either. Abner paced up and down restlessly at the front of the assembly; close by, Eliab, Barak and Joseph clustered in a knot with their heads bowed together, communicating in silence, if indeed they communicated at all. Jonathan stood some distance away from them, shading his eyes with his hand, scanning the valley for signs of movement. Tall, lithe, aloof, resplendent in bronze helmet and full armour, he was again every inch his father's son. Or at least, the son of what his father had once been. I couldn't see Ishvi or Abinadab - no doubt they had taken their places with the other men of our clan. But young Malchishua lingered at his brother's side, and I felt a stab of nostalgia; I thought: Malchishua will always be a baby to me, yet already tested in battle, he marches to war with the men. It scarcely seems possible, even now. I saw Jonathan turn, and smile at him briefly, sadly. I wondered if he thought of Sarah and the twins waiting at home; or was it someone else that he was missing.

Just then, a commotion broke out among the front lines. Jonathan swung round again to look into the valley, and froze. The silence erupted and shattered all about me; suddenly everyone was shouting and gesticulating at once.

Instinctively I started forward, elbowing my way through to see what was happening, then straight away wishing I hadn't, because all at once the whole multitude was straining towards the lip of the ridge, and the neatly-edged ranks began to fray and then to fragment in disorder. But there was no mistaking the cause. The Philistine host was on the move.

To face a crisis alone is alarming. To face a crisis surrounded by thousands of panicking men is a nightmare. Discipline crumbled instantaneously. Without Saul at its head, the courage of the body disintegrated. Against the tide of soldiers pushing forward, came a counter-flow thrusting back; slowly - because to begin with I couldn't bring myself to believe it - it dawned on me that a significant proportion of our army was seriously intending to desert. Above the turbulent sea of heads and helmets I could see Abner waving and signalling to the heralds, and I could see his mouth open, shouting, but his words were lost in the swelling tumult. The heralds began blaring trumpets, urgently sounding the call to attention, but even their strident voices were ignored and soon drowned in the uproar. Bodies, propelled by other bodies, blundered into me, buffeting me until I gasped for air. On every side, men were yelling and cursing as others crushed against them. Somewhere near me a youth screamed, as a seasoned warrior who should have known better knocked him to the ground in his panic, and I barely managed to drag the lad to his feet before he was trampled. Yet even now, crowded by the surging multitude, I felt relaxed, competent, unafraid.

Then without warning the storm abated. Every head was turned in the same direction, and it wasn't towards the

Philistines in the valley bottom.

It had to be Saul. Even now he could still quell a riot by sheer force of his presence when he wanted to. Spontaneously a gangway cleared between the ranks, and he stood statuesque at the head of a widening avenue of conscience-stricken warriors, at the other end of which Abner, mortified and seething, wrung his hands and stared. You could hardly blame him for staring. There was nothing else which any man present could have done.

Saul looked horrific. His eyes burned like two blazing coals, in a face at once as white as death and black as thunder. His hair, uncut and uncombed, streamed to his shoulders in a frenzy of fire-blasted curls, rampaging like a barbarian's over the royal circlet which glittered dazzling-bright in the glaring sunshine. For months he hadn't even worn it, nor his chain of office, nor the golden wristband engraved with the symbols of the twelve tribes of Israel. But he wore them all now; and a spotless white tunic of the kind he kept for fighting, and a pure white cloak that swept in a glorious torrent from his shoulders to the studded leather greaves around his calves. His bronze breastplate, and the helmet slung at his belt, were burnished so they shone like Egyptian glass, and in his shadow hovered Doeg, who bore a great round shield, polished and gleaming like a second sun.

Before I had chance to grasp what was happening, Saul had torn his sword from its sheath with both hands, and begun swinging it savagely in circles above his head. Suddenly he was no longer Saul the ruined, lifeweary monarch, Saul the tormented, the God-forsaken, the insane. He was Saul the boy king, with the ghosts of the envoys

458

from Jabesh cowering before him, the decapitated oxen soaked in their own blood at his feet, Saul galvanized with rage, the hunger for revenge and for glory red before his eyes. Again his whirling blade sang and wailed like the keening of a thousand mourners. Again his eyes were rolling and unfocussed. But this rage was not divine. Screaming a war-cry loud enough to raise the dead, he ran headlong down the gangway, past Abner, past Jonathan, past Eliab, Barak and Joseph, and leapt shrieking over the crest of the ridge to meet the oncoming foe.

Organization and strategy were hurled to the four winds; a spirit of reckless abandon seized possession of every pounding heart, and now I was being swept forward by a charging mass of warriors, all brandishing their spears and chanting obscene jibes and taunts at the enemy.

The exhilaration was infectious; I felt my own spirit leap within me, and rise to meet the rolling wave of fervour as it reached me. Suddenly my own spear was flailing above my head and I was yelling and roaring with the best of them. Like a deluge of flood-water we poured down the slopes, and before we reached the valley-floor, battle had been joined. All at once there were screams mingled with the shouting; in front of me I could hear the clash of iron on bronze and see the shifting shapes of men grappling and falling. Unrelenting barrages of spears and arrows blackened the sky above and rained down on us, barbed and deadly; clouds of dust rose from the tramping feet of men and horses, and chariots became embedded in the soil-turned-to-mud, sending others crashing to the ground. I could no longer see anything of Saul, or of anyone else I recognized. My world was teeming with anonymous swordsmen fighting and dying, and my eyes smarted with grit. Then the man in front of me fell, and I was fighting for my life.

Alongside me I sensed my comrades gaining, pushing onward with me as the enemy gave way before us. I was walking on air, and every Israelite was my brother. Suddenly the man to my left was the youth I had pulled from the stampede; he saw me and let out a high-pitched whoop of excitement. I wondered if this were his first battle, and concluded from his face that it probably was. I clambered over a toppled chariot that was blocking my path and blundered into mortal combat with a young Philistine no older than Malchishua. He fought like a hero, and I can still see the defiance and the surprise welded together on his face, frozen into his death mask when my blade ran through his belly. I swallowed the twinge of sorrow that rose in my breast, wiped the sweat from my face, and paused for a second to catch my breath.

Then the youth I had rescued went down with a Philistine spear through his neck. He lay at my feet squirming and choking, tugging uselessly at the shaft, his eyes wide as the blood gurgled in his throat and gushed in a red lather between his teeth. I couldn't bear to look at him when I yanked the weapon free, knowing as I did that his life must come with it. As the battle raged about us, I felt the tears pricking the backs of my eyes, and when I blinked them away, the tide had turned. Those fighting next to me had perished or retreated, and now it was the Philistines who were driving forward and the Israelites falling back. No quantity of battle-madness is enough to withstand an army that outnumbers you five to one. But all at once I was out on a limb, fighting alone.

Stumbling backwards, doggedly refusing to turn and run and suffer the posthumous ignominy of being found with a weapon in my spine, I struggled to fend off sword and dagger blades whilst avoiding becoming entangled in the mutilated bodies that littered the ground. I saw Israelites and Philistines embracing in death, their blood mingled on their clothing and armour, and in the thickening sludge; contorted limbs, broken faces, mangled weapons... backing further and further up the hillside, I witnessed the carnage mounting all around me as in a landscape from the foulest nightmare. Never had I seen so much death and destruction dealt in one place, never had I smelt the stench of slaughter so putrid in my nostrils. Friend and foe lay dead in equal numbers; but there were so many more Philistines to die. Then above the din of conflict, I heard the screech of our trumpets sounding the withdrawal.

On every side our men were scattering, without sense or direction, all running for their lives. They fell with spears in their backs, or fronts, or sides, indiscriminately, any vestige of honour discarded, together with the last-minute bravado inspired by the sudden appearance of Saul. And all at once I was running with the rest, for there was nothing else to be done; I didn't know where I was going, or why, or even whether I ran east or west, up or down. I only knew that I still lived and breathed, that somehow, by some miracle, I wasn't even wounded. I ran until I tasted blood in my mouth, until I gulped for air, until I could hear my own pulse like thunder in my brain - until I knew I could run no more.

Finally I slipped in a puddle of blood and collapsed spread-eagled across some fallen veteran whose spirit still lingered, for he groaned as I came down hard on his chest. Heaving and spluttering, coughing phlegm and dust from my mouth, listening to the pounding at my temples and the ringing in my ears, I lay without moving, for I lacked the strength to stand, let alone to run. With my eyes screwed shut, I waited for the inevitable boot in my back, or corpse crashing down on me, but somehow yet again I was spared. Eventually my heart-rate slowed, it no longer hurt my lungs when I breathed, and I started to feel like myself once more. I raised my head, opened my eyes, and saw Saul.

He must only have been a stone's throw away from me, standing pressed back to back with a terrified Doeg, the focus of a ring of hefty Philistine warriors. Doeg was barely holding his own, but Saul hacked and sliced and stabbed like a wild thing, fighting them off with the kind of ruthless ferocity which only sheer desperation can provoke. For there could be no doubt but that his opponents knew exactly who he was and would persist until they finished him. Staggering upright, I took hold of my sword, and coercing my protesting limbs to respond, I ran to draw the fellows off, despatching two of them before they knew what was happening, and thus distracting the others for as long as it took Saul to fell two more, and Doeg a fifth.

Then with relief I found that we were no longer fighting alone. A dozen or so Israelites had seen and come running, and fallen upon those Philistines who still remained standing. Once again I was engulfed in the thick of the fray, locked in hand-to-hand combat, seeing red before my eyes. If anything, the battle raged fiercer than before, at least here, around Saul, where all at once we had everything to fight for and everything to lose. No longer were we playing for the mere stakes of our lives - now our king, our country, Israel's survival hung poised on the tips of our javelins and the blades of our brands. I fought and struggled with everything I had in me, until the only things that existed in my universe were Philistine armour, Philistine weapons, and the whites of Philistine eyes.

So I never saw Saul go down. I never saw the volley of arrows that poured on the tangle of warriors around him, scattering and smiting Israelite and Philistine alike, and bringing down four or five men in an instant. I only saw the soldier I was grappling with crumple to the ground at my feet, when I knew it was none of my doing, and the backs of the men who'd been pressuring me, as they threw down their shields and fled from the death-shower. No one thinks to look for arrows at this stage in a battle, not unless fresh reinforcements have arrived. Perhaps that's what everyone thought must have happened. Perhaps all of them assumed that these mysterious auxiliaries had to belong to the opposing side. But for whatever reason, unexpectedly there was empty silence all around me; I dropped to my knees, then twisted over to try to weigh up what had happened, and saw Saul writhing in the dirt.

He'd been hit at least twice. A glancing stroke down the side of his face had opened a jagged red gash in his cheek, and the blood oozed thickly over one ear and into his tangled hair - with a jolt I realized that his helmet still hung vainly at his belt. But probably he wasn't even aware of this wound, for both his hands clutched at his groin, where the arrow that had struck him down still protruded, its head sunken deep into his punctured flesh. A spreading patch of crimson marred the white of his tunic, and as he floundered and wallowed, straining to pull himself free, the leg dragged paralysed and useless behind him, and I knew that for him the battle was over.

He was screaming for Doeg, and muzzily I watched the wretch drop to his knees by his broken lord's side, shaking his head in futile denial. Saul reached for Doeg's wrist and made him clasp the shaft of the arrow, moaning and imploring him to wrench it out. But Doeg merely shook his head harder, afraid that the doing of it would hasten the end, knowing he was nothing if Saul were to die. Then Saul seized Doeg's sword, which he'd flung down beside him, and I heard him shriek, "Kill me!" as though the very earth roared it. He forced the weapon into Doeg's trembling hands, babbling, "Kill me for God's sake, or they'll take me alive! Doeg, don't let them torture me, Doeg..." But Doeg was hysterical, more frantic than Saul was.

Then suddenly Saul snatched back the sword from his grasp. His face all contorted and ghastly with pain, he heaved up onto the knee of his good leg, and shaking all over like a lily in the wind, he held the point of the blade under his breastplate. While Doeg watched in abject horror, he closed his eyes and let himself fall so that the tip pierced his belly, and he lay quivering and jerking with his face in the mud. Doeg was beside himself; he tore the sword from Saul's slackening fingers and threw himself onto it, howling his last as he collapsed weltering in gore. I thought I was fainting. Huge black patches swam before my eyes and I could hardly stand. Then I saw that Saul was still moving.

Weak and afraid, he had done the job clumsily and the blade had veered wide of the organs that mattered.

Somehow my quaking legs got me to him; I knelt in the
filth and took him in my arms. His face was still warped
grotesquely, the blood on his cheek was congealing, and his
hair was matted with sweat and grime. Even as I lifted him,
I thought his eyes were glazing; they searched my face
feebly, with no hint of recognition. He opened his mouth
but the pain was too much for him and he couldn't speak.

I said, "Saul, it's me. Eli. Please - lie still. Don't try to
talk."

He took no notice, and tried again, managing, "Eli,
Eli..." but he was repeating it inanely, as though the name
meant nothing. Then his body went rigid as a horrendous
spasm gripped him. I was distraught; all at once it counted
more than anything that he shouldn't die without knowing
who I was.

I shouted, "Eliphaz! Eliphaz Rabshakeh! Eliphaz of
Amalek."

"Am-a-lek..." Somehow the baleful syllables must
have broken through the rising wall of his suffering, and
struck some harsh chord in his brain. Suddenly he was
thrashing and convulsing in my arms, raving and moaning
that Amalek had destroyed him; he should have killed Agag,
he should have killed me. He ranted and swore until the air
was thick with his blasphemies, though mostly I couldn't
make out what he said, and perhaps that was for the best.
But I know he cursed Doeg, he cursed Abner, he cursed
David, and Samuel, and Kish - all those he had trusted, who
he believed had failed him and brought him to this. Then at
the last he cursed Adonai, and he howled and bayed and
slavered like a demon.

Stricken and appalled, I squeezed one hand against

the wound in his stomach, hopelessly striving to restrain him with the other. Then, without warning, his voice died on his lips and his body went limp. I panicked, but through the film across my eyes saw he still breathed, and there were tears seeping through the crust on his cheeks. I cradled him as he sagged against me, his breath coming shallow, rapid and grating. It hurt me so much to look at him that I made myself watch what was going on around me, but the focus of the fighting had moved on, and close by, there was no one but the dead and the dying. I stared at them listlessly: fresh-faced youths, white-bearded grandfathers, powerful warriors in the prime of life, all maimed and bloody and twisted together. I thought: this isn't real. None of it is real. Soon I'll wake up, and the nightmare will be over.

Then with a start I was dragged back to reality. Saul was pulling on the fabric of my tunic, gulping and gargling to clear his throat. He said, "None of that's true, Eli. I know it's not true. It's all been my own fault. Please - help me."

I opened my mouth, but now it was I who couldn't speak. He was still clutching at my clothing, and reaching for my face; I thought: oh God, this is worse, I wish he were dead after all. Somehow I forced the lump from my throat, but even when I found my voice, there were no words to say. I closed my eyes, hardly aware that I was praying, silently mouthing what must have sounded like nonsense, which not even I understood. And then I heard myself softly reciting the Shema, the first and last prayer that a worshipper of Adonai should hear.

"Shema Israel, Hear O Israel, the Lord your God, the Lord is One..."

But he wouldn't let me finish. Heaving in my arms,

he spluttered, "No, Eli, no, not that. Not Adonai. I can't bear to hear you..." He broke off, gasping, as another spasm racked him; when he spoke again, his voice was weaker - I didn't have long. He whispered, "Adonai hates me. He's always hated me. That isn't what I meant, Eli. Please - let me go. Set me free."

He closed his eyes and slumped against my chest. I had all his weight in my arms, yet it seemed there was no weight there. I knew what Saul wanted me to do, and I knew I couldn't do it. We'd sworn an oath, we were brothers, I could never harm him; it wasn't fair of him to expect it. Again I had reached my limit and found myself wanting. I had come to the end of myself, and it wasn't far enough. There had to be more, some source I could draw on, something outside of me, beyond me, to reach for.

That was when I understood.

Like a bolt from the heavens, the truth exploded on me, seared through my mind like sheet lightning in summer, and at last, it all came together. I knew what my prayer last night had been for. I knew where my courage this morning had come from, and now I knew what that was for too. I knew what it meant when I'd uttered those meaningless syllables in prayer over Saul.

In the same instant, I knew that for years I'd known the truth and run away from it. Saul himself had seen me running, long ago before his own faith crumbled to ruins, and in his way he'd tried to tell me. David had seen Adonai's hand upon me from the very day I met him, and striven hard to make me face it, yet from being a child I'd denied it and feared it, turning away from the one thing that could give me the security I'd always yearned for.

I knew Adonai.

I knew that he loved me. I knew I'd felt his spirit upon me years ago when Saul had prayed for me, and refused to accept it for what it was. More than once I'd known inside me things which Adonai himself had told me, and which could have come from nowhere else, but I hadn't realized. When Ahinoam died, I'd even watched Adonai answer my own prayer, yet I'd refused to see. Now I saw everything, clearer than crystal. God accepted me as one of his own. My circumcision had been so much more than a mark on my flesh.

Simultaneously, and with equal assurance, I knew he loved Saul. He'd given me the key to the door of Saul's soul, and the desire and strength to unlock it, to set him free in a way far beyond what he was asking of me.

Slowly, uncertainly at first, I put out my hand and laid it on his brow. My mind was alert in a whole new dimension, listening, absorbing; my heart was on fire, as I felt the power start to flow through me. I said, "He doesn't hate you, Saul. He longs to forgive you, even now. I'm sure of it. He told me."

"He told… you?" Saul faltered, and we opened our eyes at the same moment; his were shadowed, torpid, bewildered. But only for a second. I didn't have to explain anything. I knew my face was shining. I was in no doubt that he would see it and understand, however far gone he was. And I was right.

I didn't have to tell him to let go of his anger, to release all his bitterness, to repent of his rebellion. The tears that poured down his face were enough. For so long his tears had meant nothing except that he was falling apart inside. But these were tears of repentance, tears of wholeness, wrested from the very depths of his spirit. He sobbed, he wailed, he cried out for mercy to Adonai, to Samuel, to me, to David, to his Companions, his parents, his children. I felt my hand shaking as Adonai filled me; unknown words spilled from my mouth, as my body became a transparent channel of love, of absolution, of the sheer might of the Divine. I could almost watch the evil in him shrivelling. The lines went from Saul's face, the glaze from his eyes, and his tears washed the blood from the gash on his cheek. Miraculously there was beauty, and stillness, and peace.

And pain. In spite of all that I'd done, there was pain. As I looked at him, I felt it, as though it were my own, and I knew that here was something I still lacked the power to fight. I still wasn't able to draw the arrow from his groin, nor to stem the flow of blood from his belly. Even as I lifted my hand from his brow, I saw his face was whiter and I felt his pulse weaker. A third spasm of agony tore at his frame, yet still the life clung to him, and I knew that neither of us could take any more. I would have to do what he'd wanted after all, however abhorrent, and whatever the consequences.

I felt for the little jewelled knife inside my tunic. It was so long since I'd thought of it, yet still, by force of habit, I never went without it. I turned it over once in my hand, hesitating; he looked right into my face, and his eyes implored me to hurry.

I did it the way he'd taught me. Neatly, with one stroke, without shaking. Unconsciousness was instant, and his head hung backwards as what blood he had left gushed from the slit.

Suddenly I was starkly and cruelly aware of everything that was going on around me. There were men running towards me, bearing down on me - Israelite men, fleeing and scattering before the pursuing foe, but the realization simply didn't interest me. I didn't care if I were trampled to death. I didn't care if I got a spear through my skull. I knelt, clutching Saul's lifeless body to my breast, out of my senses with grief and ecstasy, and fought to ignore the fact that someone was tugging at my cloak-pins and shouting something in my ear. Then someone else was shaking me and sliding rough hands under my armpits. A voice said, "Come on, man, or you'll be dead too," and all at once there were pounding feet all around me. Dazed and spent, I heard myself protesting, moaning that I wanted to stay with Saul; then someone slapped my face, and it was Jonathan.

He said, "For God's sake, Eliphaz, think of the future," and for some reason his urgency got through my stupor. In my madness I thought: perhaps Jonathan is the future, and I gulped and nodded and let him persuade me. Gently I laid Saul's body on the ground, and without really thinking why I was doing it, I slipped the circlet from his head, and the band from his wrist, and the great gold chain from his blood-drenched neck. Then before I could change my mind, I was running: blindly, madly, stumbling and staggering, my fogged eyes pinned unblinking on the back of the man who fled in front of me.

We hadn't gone ten spearlengths when Jonathan fell, with an arrow in his back. For a moment I faltered, but the man right behind me dug me in the ribs, and I kept on running.

Still, I knew I couldn't keep going much longer. My energy was exhausted, and my world finished, and I wasn't even looking where I was going any more. Men were passing me, leaving me standing, and I hadn't the slightest desire to catch them.

Presently my legs simply gave way under me and I sank into the dirt, panting like a sick dog. Then clutching the royal regalia beneath me, I stretched out on the ground, and waited to die.

EPILOGUE

I am to be executed at dawn tomorrow.

Now, it is late afternoon; outside my cell, the sky is still blue and the sun is still shining, there are birds singing, and I can hear crickets rasping in the trees. I can no longer remember how many days it is since I began this work, but probably not as many as it feels. I've lost all track of time; it's not important any more. Saul now knows the answer to the question we first asked as boys, then many times as men: what lies in wait for our souls after death. Soon I too shall know, and I'm ready.

I thought I was ready when I lay down to die in the mud of the battlefield, shattered, inconsolable, insensible. When I came to myself and found I still lived, I got up cursing - desolate, angry and cheated, I believed that there was nothing left for me to do, that Adonai should have taken pity on me, and allowed me to die. I stared about me at the dismembered corpses, the broken chariots, the trampled flowers, at death flung discordant into the midst

472

of life, and realized I was utterly alone.

I set off heading south, merely because this was territory I felt to know a little; northwards all was alien and unfamiliar. Doggedly but aimlessly, I trudged on, for a while wondering vaguely if I should return to Gibeah, but knowing I couldn't bring myself to go there.

The sun was setting when at last I saw evidence that someone in the world was still living besides me. Bright against the darkening sky I glimpsed the orange glow of a campfire in the middle distance, and desperate for human contact, I made my way towards it, not much caring now whether I found friend or foe.

What I did find was half a dozen Israelite deserters, still wearing what passed for their armour. They'd seen less of the battle than I had, because they'd fled from it almost before it began, realizing at once that the odds were hopeless. But they'd met up with others since then who'd seen more, and with some clumsy attempts at sympathy, they acquainted me with a number of facts I hadn't known. Not that these were facts which I wanted to hear. They told me that both Abinadab and Malchishua were dead. Barak and Joseph hadn't been seen alive since our troops were routed; concerning Eliab, no one seemed to know anything. Alone of Saul's sons, Ishbosheth was reputed to have escaped, and Abner with him, but no one knew where they'd gone. Nor did they know anything about the movements of the of the Philistine army since its triumph. But they appeared to take it for granted that the days of Israel's autonomy were numbered. I asked them if they'd heard what had become of the bodies of Saul and his sons; but they would tell me nothing.

It was only when they asked me where I meant to go next, that I became aware of the need to make a decision. After all, I couldn't wander haphazardly for ever. I had neither food nor shelter, and would require both urgently now I'd grasped that I wasn't about to die. While I sat there in grim contemplation, they fell to talking of David, and whether he might call off his war against the raiders from the south, to march against the victorious foe from the north; and that was when I knew what I must do.

David might not even know yet that Saul was dead. Almost certainly he wouldn't know that Jonathan was dead. Someone must break it to him, someone who had understood their friendship; and it was undoubtedly for me to tell him what had happened to Saul.

That night, the fugitives let me share their fire and their food. The next morning, I set my face towards Ziklag, where they said David and his men were based. The town had been granted to them by Achish, King of Gath.

It's a good five days' walk to Ziklag from Gilboa - and that's if you know where you're going. It must have taken me eight. I can't remember much about it. I slept rough, and lived off the land; some of the fields and orchards I passed through had been abandoned, as people fled for refuge inside the walled cities from the invader who must surely be coming. I arrived here exhausted and expiring, and was challenged at the gates by a whole squadron of David's men. The town was guarded heavily, though exactly who from, I couldn't be sure. Too drained to think up an alternative, I told the sentries the truth: that I was Eliphaz of Amalek, and that King Saul was dead at my hand. There was nothing they could do but lock me up.

And so I found myself cast into this prison, with bars at the window and cold stone to sit on. Still I shouldn't be ungrateful. When I requested writing materials to set down this account, the guard obliged me. I asked him when he thought David would send for me, but he told me his lord was away fighting, and that I must remain here until he returned. I asked who he fought against; the man peered at me curiously, and answered, Amalekites.

Taken up with my writing, the days have passed; not quickly, not slowly, but timelessly - it's strange. Then at sunset last night, they came to fetch me to appear before David. I presumed that he'd just returned. In fact he'd been in Ziklag for two days, but no one had troubled to tell him about me. In all likelihood they thought he had more pressing matters to attend to, but he didn't agree. As soon as he was told, he'd sent for me; and again, I was ready.

Enthroned splendidly in a spacious hall, attended by warriors fully armed and at attention, he looked every inch a king already. But he still managed a smile when he saw me, and when he got up from his chair and came to embrace me, there was love mingled with the perplexity in his eyes. It was clear that they'd told him why I was imprisoned.

He said, " You've taken the life of the Lord's Anointed. You know I shall have to put you to death."

"I know." I nodded, and shrugged my shoulders.

David kept me with him almost until morning. I think he felt guilty about what he must do with me; he wanted to comfort me, to reassure me that he didn't hate me as a man, nor even because of my origins. To be honest, I think it was I who was the comforter. He wept for Saul, and he wept for Jonathan, and I think he wept as he thought of the future he must face. He was inheriting a kingdom whose people didn't even know of his anointing. He would have to fight for it, not only against the might of Philistia - from whose uneasy embrace he would first have to disentangle himself - and against the remnant of Amalek, but perhaps also against men of his own blood. And yet I had no doubt in my mind that he would succeed where Saul had failed.

At dawn he dried his eyes, and summoned the guards. He asked if there was anything I wanted before my execution. I said, yes, I needed one last day, to complete my account. He said that he would grant it, and asked about my purpose, and now I'm relieved, for it means that what I'm writing will survive. David himself will see to that.

I don't blame David for what he must do to me. I did what was anathema to him. And a man must not be allowed to roam at large, who has slain the Chosen One of Adonai. If David is nothing else, he's a survivor. What better way to survive than to have one's own body deemed sacrosanct?

He has proclaimed a national fast in honour of Saul and Jonathan and the thousands of our men who died glorious deaths on the slopes of Gilboa. But I'm glad that he'll have no time to brood. As soon as I'm gone, he must march north, before the Philistines steal all that is his inheritance. If he treated with them before, he has no reason to now. I know I need have no fear on that score.

As for me, I shared blood with Saul, so now I shall share his fate. It's only right.

Saul, son of Kish, first King of Israel, died on Mt. Gilboa one thousand years before the birth of Christ. According to 1 Samuel 31:4 he fell on his own sword; in 2 Samuel 1:10 he was killed at his own request by an Amalekite resident among the people of Israel. The Philistines then decapitated him and nailed his body, alongside those of three of his sons, to the walls of the city of Beth Shan. His armour was placed in the temple of Ashtoreth. Later the men of Jabesh Gilead, Saul's first beneficiaries, out of love and loyalty to their saviour, took down the bodies and gave them decent burial.

The Philistines never followed up their victory, a mystery which continues to baffle biblical scholars today. After Gilboa, there was in theory very little to prevent them from annexing the whole of Saul's kingdom, yet they patently failed to do so.

Ishbosheth (Ishvi) survived his father and brothers, and was proclaimed king by Abner at Mahanaim, east of the Jordan. His short reign came to an end when he was murdered by two of his own officers who vainly hoped to be rewarded by his rival David. He had them put to death.

Abner, fiercely loyal to his beloved cousin's family even after Saul's death, was largely responsible for the bloody civil war between the two rivals for the throne of Israel. Ishbosheth later accused him of seducing Saul's concubine Rizpah, and in his outrage at being thought capable of betraying Saul's memory in this way, Abner abandoned Ishbosheth for David. He was finally murdered by one of David's men, victim of a personal vendetta.

Rizpah, pregnant at the time of the Battle of Gilboa, was taken in by Ishbosheth and Abner when Saul died and what was left of his household dispersed. She bore Saul two sons; they were eventually hanged by the people of Gibeon, whose ancestors Saul had perfidiously put to death. Rizpah lived under a shelter of sackcloth on the rock *where the corpses were left unburied, from the beginning of harvest until the autumn rains. It is not known what became of her after this.*

Michal was sent for by David soon after Saul's death. He took her away from her second husband Paltiel, and reinstated her as his wife. Michal never got over her fear of the supernatural; she died childless, having mocked David for dancing ecstatically, almost naked, in public, when the Ark of the Covenant was brought in triumph to Jerusalem.

Jonathan was survived by one of his infant sons, Mephibosheth. But when the news of Saul and Jonathan's deaths reached Gibeah, the servants fled in panic, and in her haste his mother's nurse dropped the child, whose injuries left him permanently disabled. David restored to him all of Saul's estates and treated him as one of his own sons, because of the sacred vow of friendship he had made with Jonathan.

David overcame all rivals, defeated the Philistines decisively, and ended their stranglehold on Israel's development. He captured the city of Jebus from its Canaanite inhabitants and made it his capital, Jerusalem. He became the greatest king in the history of his people, respected for his outstanding qualities as both warlord and statesman, and beloved for his devotion to Adonai. His weakness for women remained a thorn in his flesh; one of the most memorable crises in his reign stemmed from his adultery with Bathsheba and subsequent disposal of her husband.

"Eliphaz" is a fictional character created principally from the anonymous Amalekite referred to in 2 Samuel 1, but also by amalgamating with this individual the other references to attendants of Saul found at 1 Samuel 9:3ff, 1 Samuel 16:15ff, 1 Samuel 19: 19ff, 1 Samuel 22:16ff, and 1 Samuel 28:8ff. The Amalekite in 2 Samuel 1 is particularly interesting. What was a member of this despised people doing, living in Israel? What was he doing on the battlefield at Gilboa? Why should he bother to walk almost a hundred miles to tell

David that he had killed King Saul - and especially when David had just returned from slaughtering Amalekites?

It is from some possible answers to these enigmas that this history of Eliphaz has been born and has grown.

The Amalekite in question was put to death by David, for taking the life of the Lord's Anointed.

BY THE SAME AUTHOR

FICTION

Zoheleth, Lion Publishing 1994
David's kingdom and family are torn apart by the rebellion
of his wayward son.

Hadassah, Lion Publishing 1996
The fate of the entire Jewish nation rests on the shoulders
of one young girl.

*A Fortress Among My People, Lighthouse Christian
Publishing 2012*
A lonely and timid boy is chosen as God's mouthpiece in
one of the most turbulent period's of Israel's history.

The Last Queen of Sheba, Lion Hudson 2014
The daughter of an African chieftain becomes ruler of the
Shebans, but her relationship with King Solomon of Israel
threatens both their kingdoms.

NON-FICTION

Esther: For Such a Time as This, Kingsway 2000
A character study of Esther and her significance in the
history of the Jewish and Christian peoples.